Old Goriot

Old Goriot

by Honoré de Balzac

Published for the Classics Club by

WALTER J. BLACK · ROSLYN, N. Y.

Old Goriot

Preface

HONORÉ DE BALZAC was born at Tours, France, in May 1799. When about twenty he gave up the study of law for literature, and labored for many years in poverty before recognition and success came to him. A man of prodigious energy and vast projects, he literally killed himself by overwork, dying at the age of fifty-one, with more than forty books as his gift to posterity. Shortly before his death he was married to a Russian noblewoman, Madame Evalina Hanska, to whom he had long been devoted.

Old Goriot was written in 1834, when Balzac was thirty-five and at the height of his powers. It appeared first as a serial in the *Revue de Paris* and was published as a book in 1835. It belongs in that grand procession of Balzac's works known as the *Human Comedy—La Comédie Humaine*. In this he tried to present the whole panorama of early nineteenth-century French life, as another French writer, Jules Romains, in his series of novels, *Men of Good Will*, has been attempting to do for the twentieth century.

The reader's interest is by no means monopolized by the character of the title, *Old Goriot*, and his pathetic and all-consuming passion for his daughters. It is caught, too, by the story of Eugène de Rastignac, the young provincial who comes to Paris to make a career for himself. The early struggles of talented, confused, and ambitious youth are always appealing, and in this case they possess the added interest of autobiography, for Balzac himself—during the period the novel covers—had been like Rastignac a law student from the country, making his way in

3

Paris against odds. The third important character in *Old Goriot*, the escaped convict Vautrin, though less completely realized than the other two, gives the author a chance to mount the rostrum and vent his ideas on the iniquities of the social structure.

The backdrops against which these and the other fascinating players act out their roles show Balzac's predilection for dramatic contrast. Scenes in the squalid Pension Vauquer, where penny-pinching and gossip are the chief pleasures of life, are followed by glimpses into the boudoirs of titled ladies and the dazzling ballrooms of aristocratic society. And while it may be truthfully said that Balzac was more familiar with the atmosphere of poverty than with that of high society, yet his picture of the crisis in the life of the noble Vicomtesse de Beauséant, a great lady of the old regime not wholly at home in the post-Revolutionary world, is altogether moving and real. Here, as elsewhere, Balzac displays what Victor Hugo, in his funeral discourse on his friend, declared to be his great gifts: observation *and* imagination, always inextricably blended.

The society presented in *Old Goriot* and the other novels of this magnificent series is that of France during the troubled transitional period following the upheavals of the Revolution and the Napoleonic Wars. As the power and prestige of the hereditary nobility waned, the power of money, in the hands of the rising new middle class, was becoming of paramount importance. The change is exemplified in Goriot himself, who grew rich out of the Revolution, though he neither understood nor cared for what it represented. Students of psychology may find that his very love for his daughters, so unhealthy in its intensity and ultimately so ruinous, was but another aspect of his possessive greed. No novelist has dealt more effectively with the theme of money than Balzac; and here he wrote out of full experience, for he was continually involved in business schemes of one sort or another—most of them disastrous—to better his own fortunes.

This novel has been compared to Shakespeare's *King Lear* and to Turgenev's novelette, *A Lear of the Steppes*. All three tell the story of a sacrificing father and ungrateful daughters. If Balzac and Turgenev borrowed their ideas, their borrowing was from the common pool of human experience into which great artists must always dip.

Old Goriot was chosen for the Classics Club for its qualities as a story and as a famous example of the many-sided genius of one of the greatest novelists of all time. The translation is based on that made by Ellen Marriage for the complete edition of Balzac's work edited by Professor George Saintsbury. It has been considerably revised and modernized.

F. M.

Chapter I

MME VAUQUER, *née* de Conflans, is an old lady, who for the past forty years has kept a lodginghouse in the Rue Neuve-Sainte-Geneviève, between the Latin Quarter and the Faubourg Saint-Marcel. Her house, known in the neighborhood as the Maison Vauquer, receives men and women, old and young, and no word has ever been breathed against her respectable establishment; but, at the same time, it must be admitted that as a matter of fact no young woman has been under her roof for thirty years, and that if a young man stays there for any length of time it is a sure sign that his allowance must be of the slenderest. In 1819, however, the time when this drama opens, there was an almost penniless young girl among Mme Vauquer's boarders.

That word drama has been somewhat discredited of late; it has been overworked and twisted to strange uses in these days of dolorous literature; but it must do service again here, not because this story is dramatic in the true sense of the word, but because some tears may perhaps be shed *intra et extra muros* before it is over.

Will anyone beyond the walls of Paris understand it? I doubt it. The only audience that could appreciate the results of close observation, the careful reproduction of minute detail and local color, are dwellers between the heights of Montrouge and Montmartre, a vale of crumbling stucco watered by streams of black mud, a vale of sorrows which are real and of joys too often hollow—where trouble is ever-present and only some unimaginable woe could produce any deep impression. Now and again there

7

are tragedies so awful and so grand by reason of the complication of virtues and vices that bring them about, that egoism and selfishness are forced to pause and are moved to pity; but the impression that they receive is like a luscious fruit, soon consumed. Civilization, like the car of Juggernaut, is scarcely stayed in its progress by a heart less easy to break than the others that lie in its course; this too is soon broken, and Civilization continues on her course triumphant. And you, too, will do the like; you who with this book in your white hand will sink back in your soft armchair and say to yourself, "Perhaps this may amuse me." You will read the story of Old Goriot's secret sorrows, and, dining thereafter with an unspoiled appetite, will lay the blame of your callousness upon the writer, and accuse him of romantic exaggeration. Ah! once for all, this drama is neither fiction nor romance! *All is true*—so true that everyone can discern the elements of the tragedy in his own house, perhaps in his own heart.

The lodginghouse is Mme Vauquer's own property. It is still standing at the lower end of the Rue Neuve-Sainte-Geneviève, just where the stony road slopes so sharply down to the Rue de l'Arbalète that wheeled traffic seldom passes that way. This position is sufficient to account for the silence prevalent in the streets shut in between the dome of the Panthéon and the dome of the Val-de-Grâce, two conspicuous public buildings which give a yellowish tone to the landscape and darken the whole district that lies beneath the shadow of their leaden-hued cupolas.

In this district the pavements are clean and dry; there is neither mud nor water in the gutters; grass grows in the chinks of the walls. The most heedless passer-by feels the depressing influences of a place where the sound of wheels creates a sensation. There is a grim look about the houses, a suggestion of a jail about the high garden walls. A Parisian straying into a suburb apparently composed of lodginghouses and public institutions would see poverty and dullness, old age lying down to die, and joyous youth condemned to drudgery. It is the ugliest quarter of Paris, and, it may be added, the least known. The Rue Neuve-Sainte-Gene-viève, especially, is like a bronze frame for a picture for which the mind must be well prepared by the contemplation of sad hues and sober images; just as, when the traveler descends step by step into the catacombs, the daylight decreases, and the cicerone's droning voice is hushed. A true comparison! And who shall say which is more awful, the sight of the bleached skulls or of withered human hearts?

The front of the lodginghouse is at right angles to the road, and looks out upon a little garden, so that you see the side of the house in section, as it were, from the Rue Neuve-Sainte-Gene-viève. Beneath the front wall there lies a channel, six feet wide, paved with cobblestones, and beside it runs a graveled walk bordered by geraniums, oleanders, and pomegranates growing in great blue and white glazed earthenware pots. Access into the graveled walk is afforded by a door, above which the words "MAISON VAUQUER" may be read, and beneath, in rather smaller letters, "Lodgings for both sexes; meals."

During the day a glimpse into the garden is easily obtained through a wicket to which a bell is attached. On the opposite wall, at the end of the graveled walk, a green marble arch was painted once upon a time by a local artist, and in this semblance of a shrine a statue representing Cupid is installed; a Parisian Cupid, so blistered and disfigured that he looks like a candidate for one of the adjacent hospitals, and might suggest an allegory to lovers of symbolism. The half-effaced inscription on the pedestal beneath determines the date of this work of art, for it bears witness to the widespread enthusiasm felt for Voltaire on his return to Paris in 1777:

> Whoe'er thou art, thy master see;
> He is, or was, or ought to be.

At night the wicket gate is replaced by a solid door. The little garden is no wider than the front of the house; it is shut in be-

tween the wall of the street and the partition wall of the neigh-
boring house. A mantle of ivy conceals the bricks and attracts
the eyes of passers-by to an effect which is picturesque in Paris,
for each of the walls is covered with trellised grapevines that
yield a scanty dusty crop of fruit, and furnish besides a subject
of conversation for Mme Vauquer and her lodgers; every year
the widow trembles for her vintage.

A straight path beneath the walls on either side of the garden
leads to a clump of lime trees at the further end of it—*line* trees,
as Mme Vauquer persists in calling them, in spite of the fact that
she was a de Conflans, and regardless of repeated corrections
from her lodgers.

The space between the walks is filled with artichokes and rows
of pyramid fruit trees, and surrounded by a border of lettuce,
pot-herbs, and parsley. Under the lime trees there are a few
green-painted garden seats and a wooden table, and here, during
the dog-days, such of the lodgers as are rich enough to indulge in
a cup of coffee come to take their pleasure, though it is hot
enough to cook eggs even in the shade.

The house itself is three stories high, without counting the
attic. It is built of rough stone, and covered with the yellowish
stucco that gives a mean appearance to almost every house in
Paris. There are five windows in each story in the front of the
house; all the blinds visible through the small square panes are
drawn up awry, so that the lines are all at cross purposes. At the
side of the house there are but two windows on each floor, and
the lowest of all are protected by heavy iron gratings.

Behind the house a yard extends for some twenty feet, an area
inhabited by a happy family of pigs, poultry, and rabbits; the
woodshed is situated on the further side, and on the wall between
the woodshed and the kitchen window hangs the meat-safe, just
above the place where the sink discharges its greasy streams. The
cook sweeps all the refuse out through a little door into the Rue

Neuve-Sainte-Geneviève, and frequently cleanses the yard with copious supplies of water, as a precaution against pestilence.

The house might have been built on purpose for its present uses. Access is given by a French window to the first room on the ground floor, a sitting room which looks out upon the street through the two barred windows already mentioned. Another door opens out of it into the dining room, which is separated from the kitchen by the well of the staircase, the steps being constructed partly of wood, partly of tiles, which are colored and beeswaxed. Nothing can be more depressing than the sight of that sitting room. The furniture is covered with horsehair woven in alternate dull and glossy stripes. There is a round table in the middle, with a purplish-red marble top, on which there stands, by way of ornament, the inevitable white china tea-service, covered with a half-effaced gilt network. The floor is sufficiently uneven, the wainscot rises to elbow height, and the rest of the wall space is decorated with a varnished paper, on which the principal adventures of Telemachus are depicted, the various classical figures being tinted. The subject between the two windows is the feast given by Calypso for the son of Ulysses, displayed thereon for the admiration of the boarders, and has furnished jokes these forty years to the young men who show themselves superior to their position by making fun of the dinners to which poverty condemns them. The hearth is always so clean and neat that it is evident that a fire is only kindled there on great occasions; the mantelshelf is adorned by a couple of vases filled with faded artificial flowers imprisoned under glass shades, on either side of a bluish marble clock in the very worst taste.

The first room exhales an odor for which there is no name in the language, and which should be called the *odeur de pension*, or *odeur de renfermé*—the odor of the shut-in. The damp atmosphere sends a chill through you as you breathe it; it has a stuffy, musty, and rancid quality; it permeates your clothing; after-dinner scents seem to be mingled in it with smells from the kitchen and scullery and the reek of a hospital. It might be possible to describe it if someone should discover a process by which to distil from the atmosphere all the nauseating elements with which it is charged by the catarrhal exhalations of every individual lodger, young and old. Yet, in spite of these stale horrors, the sitting room is as charming and as delicately perfumed as a boudoir, when compared with the adjoining dining room.

The paneled walls of that apartment were once painted some color, now a matter of conjecture, for the surface is encrusted with accumulated layers of grimy deposit, which cover it with curious patterns. A collection of dim-ribbed glass decanters, metal discs with a satin sheen on them, and piles of blue-edged earthenware plates of Tournai ware cover the sticky surfaces of the sideboards that line the room. In a corner stands a box with numbered pigeon-holes, in which the lodgers' table napkins, more or less greasy and stained with wine, are kept. Here you see that indestructible furniture never met with elsewhere, which finds its way into lodginghouses much as the wrecks of our civilization drift into hospitals for incurables; the barometer from which a Capuchin hops out on wet days; the execrable engravings which spoil your appetite, each framed in a black varnished frame with a gilt beading round it; the tortoise-shell clock-case, inlaid with brass; the green stove, the Argand lamps, covered with oil and dust—all have met your eyes before. The oilcloth which covers the long table is so greasy that a waggish guest will write his name on the surface with his thumb-nail. The chairs are broken-down invalids; the wretched little hempen mats slip away from under your feet without slipping away for good; and finally, the foot-warmers are miserable wrecks, hingeless, charred, broken away about the holes. To describe in detail the shaky, worm-eaten, halt, maimed, rickety, and ramshackle condition of the furniture would delay the progress of the story to an extent that impatient people would not pardon. The red tiles of the floor are full of depressions brought about by scouring and periodical renewings of color. In short, there is no illusory grace left to the poverty that reigns here; it is dire, parsimonious, concentrated, threadbare poverty; as yet it has not sunk into the mire, it is only splashed by it, and though not in rags as yet, its clothing is ready to drop to pieces.

The room appears in all its glory at seven o'clock in the morning, when Mme Vauquer's cat appears, announcing the near approach of his mistress, and jumps upon the sideboards to sniff at the milk in the bowls, each protected by a plate, while he purrs his morning greeting to the world. A moment later the widow shows her face; she is tricked out in a net cap attached to a false front set on awry, and shuffles into the room in her slipshod fashion. She is an oldish woman, with a bloated countenance and a nose like a parrot's beak set in the middle of it; her fat little hands (she is as sleek as a church rat) and her shapeless, slouching figure are in keeping with the room that reeks of misfortune, where hope is reduced to speculating for the meanest stakes. Mme Vauquer alone can breathe that tainted air without being disheartened by it. Her face is as fresh as a frosty morning in autumn; there are wrinkles about the eyes that vary in their expression from the set smile of a ballet-dancer to the dark, suspicious scowl of a money-lender; in short, everything expresses the character of the *pension*, just as the *pension* implies the existence of its mistress. You can no more imagine the one without the other than you can think of a jail without a turnkey. The unwholesome corpulence of the little woman is produced by the life she leads, just as typhus fever is bred in the tainted air of a hospital. The very knitted woolen petticoat that she wears beneath a skirt made of an old gown, with the wadding protruding through the rents in the material, is a sort of epitome of the sitting room, the dining room, and the little garden; it reveals the cook and foreshadows the lodgers; the picture of the house is completed by the portrait of its mistress.

Mme Vauquer at the age of fifty is like all women who "have seen better days." She has the glassy eyes and innocent air of a trafficker in flesh and blood, who will wax virtuously indignant to obtain a higher price for her services, but who is quite ready to betray a Georges or a Pichegru, if a Georges or a Pichegru were in hiding and still to be betrayed, or for any other expedient that may alleviate her lot. Still, "she is a good woman at bottom," said the lodgers, who believed that the widow was wholly dependent upon the money that they paid her, and sympathized when they heard her cough and groan like one of themselves.

What had M. Vauquer been? The lady was never very explicit concerning her late husband. How had she lost her money? "Through reverses," was her answer. He had treated her badly, had left her nothing but her eyes to cry over his cruelty, the house she lived in, and the privilege of pitying nobody, because, so she was wont to say, she herself had been through every possible misfortune.

Sylvie, the stout cook, hearing her mistress' shuffling footsteps, hastened to serve the lodgers' breakfasts. Besides those who lived in the house, Mme Vauquer took boarders who came for their meals; but these *externes* usually only came to dinner, for which they paid thirty francs a month.

At the time when this story begins, the lodginghouse contained seven inmates. The best rooms in the house were on the first story, Mme Vauquer herself occupying the least important, while the rest were let to a Mme Couture, the widow of an army paymaster under the Republic. With her lived Victorine Taillefer, a schoolgirl, whom she regarded as a daughter. These two ladies paid eighteen hundred francs a year.

The two sets of rooms on the second floor were respectively occupied by an old man named Poiret and a man of forty or thereabouts, the wearer of a black wig and dyed whiskers, who gave out that he was a retired merchant, and was addressed as M. Vautrin. Two of the four rooms on the third floor were also let—one to an elderly spinster, a Mlle Michonneau, and the other to a retired manufacturer of vermicelli, Italian paste, and starch, who allowed the others to address him as "Old Goriot." The remaining rooms were allotted to various birds of passage, to impecunious students, who, like Old Goriot and Mlle Michonneau, could only muster forty-five francs a month to pay for their board and lodging. Mme Vauquer had little desire for lodgers of this sort; they ate too much bread, and she only took them in default of better.

At that time one of the rooms was tenanted by a law student, a young man from the neighborhood of Angoulême, one of a large family who pinched and starved themselves to spare twelve hundred francs a year for him. Misfortune had accustomed Eugène de Rastignac, for that was his name, to work. He belonged to the number of young men who realize as children that their parents' hopes are centered on them, and deliberately prepare themselves for a great career, subordinating their studies from the first to this end, carefully watching the course of affairs, calculating the probable turn that events will take, that they may be the first to profit by them. But for his observant curiosity and the skill with which he managed to introduce himself into the salons of Paris, this story would not have been colored by the tones of truth which it certainly owes to him, for they are entirely due to his penetrating sagacity and desire to fathom the mysteries of an appalling condition of things, which was concealed as carefully by the victim as by those who had brought it to pass.

Above the third story there was a garret where the linen was hung to dry, and a couple of attics. Christophe, the man-of-all-work, slept in one, and Sylvie, the fat cook, in the other. Besides the seven inmates enumerated, some eight law or medical students dined in the house, as well as two or three regular comers who lived in the neighborhood. There were usually eighteen people at dinner, and there was room, if need be, for twenty at

Mme Vauquer's table; at breakfast, however, only the seven lodgers appeared. It was almost like a family party. Everyone came down in dressing-gown and slippers, and the conversation usually turned on anything that had happened the evening before; comments on the dress or appearance of the dinner contingent were exchanged in friendly intimacy.

These seven lodgers were Mme Vauquer's spoiled children. Among them she distributed, with astronomical precision, the exact proportion of respect and attention due to the varying amounts they paid for their board. One single consideration influenced all these human beings thrown together by chance. The two second-floor lodgers only paid seventy-two francs a month. Such prices as these are confined to the Faubourg Saint-Marcel and the district between La Bourbe and the Salpêtrière; and, as might be expected, poverty, more or less apparent, weighed upon them all, Mme Couture being the sole exception to the rule.

The dreary surroundings were reflected in the costumes of the inmates of the house; all were shabby. The color of the men's coats was problematical; their shoes, in more fashionable quarters, are such as you see lying in the gutter; the cuffs and collars were worn and frayed at the edges; every limp article of clothing looked like the ghost of its former self. The women's dresses were faded, old-fashioned, dyed and re-dyed; they wore gloves that were shiny with hard wear, much-mended lace, dingy ruffles, crumpled muslin fichus. So much for their clothing; but, for the most part, their frames were solid enough; their constitutions had weathered the storms of life; their cold, hard faces were worn like coins that have been withdrawn from circulation, but there were greedy teeth behind the withered lips. Dramas brought to a close or still in progress are foreshadowed by the sight of such actors as these, not the dramas that are played before the footlights and against a background of painted canvas, but dumb dramas of life, frost-bound dramas that sear hearts like fire, dramas that do not end with the actors' lives.

The elderly spinster, Mlle Michonneau, screened her weak
eyes from the daylight by a soiled green silk shade with a rim
of brass, an object fit to scare away the Angel of Pity himself.
Her shawl, with its scanty, draggled fringe, might have covered
a skeleton, so meager and angular was the form beneath it. Yet
she must have been pretty and shapely once. What corrosive
had destroyed the feminine outlines? Was it trouble, or vice, or
greed? Had she loved too well? Had she been a second-hand
clothes dealer, a frequenter of the backstairs of great houses, or
had she been merely a courtesan? Was she expiating the flaunting
triumphs of a youth overcrowded with pleasures by a despised
old age? Her vacant gaze sent a chill through you; her shriveled
face made you shudder. Her voice was like the shrill, thin note
of the grasshopper sounding from the thicket when winter is at
hand. She said that she had nursed an old gentleman, ill of catarrh
of the bladder, and left to die by his children, who thought that
he had nothing left. His bequest to her, a life annuity of a thousand francs, was periodically disputed by his heirs, who mingled
slander with their persecutions. In spite of the ravages of con-
flicting passions, her face retained some traces of its former fair-
ness and fineness of tissue, and vestiges of the charms of youth
might be supposed to survive in her form as well.

M. Poiret was a sort of automaton. He might be seen any day
sailing like a gray shadow along the walks of the Jardin des
Plantes, on his head a shabby cap, a cane with an old yellow
ivory handle in the tips of his thin fingers. The outspread skirts
of his threadbare overcoat failed to conceal his meager figure;
his breeches hung loosely on his shrunken limbs; the thin, blue-
stockinged legs trembled like those of a drunken man; there was
a notable breach of continuity between the dingy white waistcoat and crumpled shirt frills and the cravat twisted about a
throat like a turkey gobbler's. Altogether, his appearance set
people wondering whether this outlandish ghost belonged to the
audacious race of the sons of Japhet who flutter about on the

Boulevard Italien. What kind of toil could have so shriveled him? What devouring passions had darkened that bulbous countenance, which would have seemed outrageous as a caricature? What had he been? Perhaps he had been part of the machinery of justice, a clerk in the office to which the executioner sends in his accounts,—so much for providing black veils for parricides, so much for sawdust, so much for pulleys and cord for the knife. Or he might have been a receiver at the door of a public slaughter-house, or a sub-inspector of nuisances. Indeed, the man appeared to have been one of the beasts of burden in our great social mill; one of those Parisian Ratons whom their Bertrands do not even know by sight; a pivot in the obscure machinery that disposes of misery and things unclean; one of those men, in short, at sight of whom we are prompted to remark that, "After all, we cannot get along without them."

Stately Paris ignores the existence of these faces bleached by moral or physical suffering. But Paris is in truth an ocean that no line can plumb. You may survey its surface and describe it, but no matter what pains you take with your investigations and explorations, no matter how numerous and painstaking the toilers in this sea, there will always be lonely and unsuspected regions in its depths, caverns unknown, where flowers and pearls and monsters of the deep still lie safe, overlooked by literary divers. The Maison Vauquer is one of these curious monstrosities.

Two, however, of Mme Vauquer's boarders formed a striking contrast to the rest. There was a sickly pallor, such as is often seen in anemic girls, in Mlle Victorine Taillefer's face; and her unvarying expression of sadness, like her embarrassed manner and pinched look, was in keeping with the general wretchedness of the establishment in the Rue Neuve-Sainte-Geneviève, which forms a background to this picture; but her face was young, there was youthfulness in her voice and elasticity in her movements. She seemed like a sickly shrub newly planted in an uncongenial soil, where its leaves have already begun to wither. The outlines of her figure, revealed by her cheap and simple dress, were also youthful. There was the same kind of charm about her too slender form, her faintly colored face and light-brown hair, that modern poets find in medieval statuettes; and a sweet expression, a look of Christian resignation in the dark gray eyes. She was pretty by force of contrast; if she had been happy, she would have been charming. Happiness is the poetry of woman, as the toilette is her tinsel. If the delightful excitement of a ball had made the pale face glow; if the delights of a luxurious life had brought color to the wan cheeks that were slightly hollowed already; if love had put light into the sad eyes, then Victorine might have ranked among the fairest; but she lacked the two things which create woman a second time—pretty dresses and love-letters.

A book might have been made of her story. Her father felt that he had sufficient reason for declining to acknowledge her, and allowed her a bare six hundred francs a year; he had further taken measures to disinherit his daughter, and had converted all his real estate into personalty, that he might leave it undivided to his son. Victorine's mother had died brokenhearted in Mme Couture's house; and the latter, who was a near relation, had taken charge of the little orphan. Unluckily, the widow of the paymaster to the armies of the Republic had nothing in the world but her jointure and her widow's pension, and some day she might be obliged to leave the helpless, inexperienced girl to the mercy of the world. The good soul, therefore, took Victorine to mass every Sunday, and to confession once a fortnight, so that her ward at least should have a strict, religious upbringing. She was right; religion promised to offer a solution of the problem of the young girl's future. The poor child loved the father who refused to acknowledge her. Once every year she tried to see him to deliver her mother's message of forgiveness, but every year hitherto she had knocked at that door in vain; her father was inexorable. Her brother, who could have interceded in her behalf, had not come to see her for four years, and had sent her no assistance; yet she prayed to God to unseal her father's eyes and to soften her brother's heart; no accusations mingled with her prayers. Mme Couture and Mme Vauquer exhausted the vocabulary of abuse, and failed to find words that did justice to the banker's iniquitous conduct; but while they heaped execrations on the millionaire, Victorine's words were as gentle as the moan of the wounded dove, whose note of suffering is still the note of love.

Eugène de Rastignac was a thoroughly southern type; he had a fair complexion, blue eyes, black hair. In his figure, manner, and his whole bearing it was easy to see that he either came of a noble family, or that, from his earliest childhood, he had been gently bred. If he was careful of his wardrobe, only using last year's clothes for daily wear, upon occasion he could issue forth as a young man of fashion. Ordinarily he wore a shabby coat and waistcoat, the limp black cravat, untidily knotted, that students affect, trousers that were in keeping with the rest of his costume, and boots that had been re-soled.

Vautrin, the man of forty with the dyed whiskers, marked a transition stage between these two young people and the others. He was the kind of man that people call a "jolly fellow." He had broad shoulders, a well-developed chest, muscular arms, and strong, square hands; the joints of his fingers were covered with tufts of fiery red hair. His face was furrowed by premature wrinkles; there was a certain hardness about it, in spite of his bland and insinuating manner. His bass voice was by no means unpleasant, and was in keeping with his boisterous laughter. He was always obliging, always in good spirits; if anything went wrong with one of the locks, he would unscrew it, take it to pieces, file it, oil and clean and set it in order, and put it back in its place again. "I am an old hand at it," he used to say. He knew about ships, the sea, France, foreign countries, men, business, law, great palaces, and prisons—there was nothing, in fact, that he did not know. If anyone complained rather more than usual, he would offer his services at once. He had several times lent money to Mme Vauquer, or to the boarders; but, somehow, those whom he obliged felt that they would sooner face death than fail to repay him. A certain resolute look, sometimes seen on his face, inspired fear, for all his appearance of easy good nature. In the way he spat there was an imperturbable coolness which seemed to indicate that this was a man who would not stick at a crime to extricate himself from danger or difficulty. His eyes, like those of a pitiless judge, seemed to go to the very bottom of all questions, to read all natures, all feelings and thoughts. His habit of life was very regular; he usually went out after breakfast, returning in time for dinner, and disappeared for the rest of the evening, letting himself in about midnight with a latchkey, a privilege that Mme Vauquer accorded to no other boarder. But then he was on very good terms with the widow; he used to call her "mamma," and put his arm around her waist, a piece of flattery perhaps not appreciated to the full! The worthy woman might imagine this to be an easy feat, but, as a matter of fact, no arm but Vautrin's was long enough to encircle her.

Characteristic of Vautrin was his habit of lavishly expending fifteen francs a month for the cup of coffee with a dash of brandy in it, which he took after dinner. Less superficial observers than young men engulfed by the whirlpool of Parisian life, or old men, who took no interest in anything that did not directly concern them, would have looked beyond the vaguely unsatisfactory impression that he made upon them. He knew or guessed the concerns of everyone about him, but none of them had been able to penetrate his thoughts, or to discover his occupation. He had deliberately made his apparent good nature, his unfailing readiness to oblige, and his high spirits into a barrier between himself and the rest of them, but from time to time he gave glimpses of appalling depths of character. He seemed to delight in scourging the upper classes with the lash of his tongue, to take pleasure in convicting them of inconsistency, in mocking at law and order with a grim jest worthy of Juvenal, as if some grudge against the social system rankled in him, as if there were some mystery carefully hidden away in his life.

Mlle Taillefer was attracted, perhaps unconsciously, by the strength of the one man and the good looks of the other. Her stolen glances and secret thoughts were divided between them. Neither of them seemed to take any notice of her, although some day a chance might alter her position, and she would be a wealthy heiress. For that matter, there was not a soul in the house who took any trouble to investigate the various chronicles of misfortunes, real or imaginary, related by the rest. Indifference tempered by suspicion marked the attitude of each of them toward the others; it was a natural result of their situation in life. Practical assistance not one of them could give, this they all knew, and they had long since exhausted their stock of sympathy in previous discussions of their grievances. They were in something the same position as an elderly couple who have nothing left to say to each other. The routine of existence kept them in contact, but they were parts of a mechanism which wanted oil. There was not one of them but would have passed a blind man begging in the street, not one who felt moved to pity by a tale of misfortune, not one who did not see in death the solution of the all-absorbing problem of misery which left them cold to the most terrible anguish in others.

The happiest of these hapless beings was certainly Mme Vauquer, who reigned supreme over this hospital supported by voluntary contributions. For her, the little garden, which silence, and cold, and rain, and drought combined to make as dreary as an Asiatic steppe, was a pleasant shaded nook; the gaunt yellow house, the musty odors of a back shop had charms for her, and for her alone. Those cells belonged to her. She fed those convicts condemned to penal servitude for life, and her authority was recognized among them. Where else in Paris would they have found wholesome food in sufficient quantity at the prices she charged them, and rooms which they were at liberty to make, if not exactly elegant or comfortable, at any rate clean and healthy? If she had committed some flagrant act of injustice, the victim would have borne it in silence.

Such a gathering contained, as might have been expected, the elements out of which a complete society might be constructed. And, as in a school, as in the world itself, there was among the eighteen men and women who met round the dinner table a poor creature, despised by all the others, condemned to be the butt of all their jokes. At the beginning of Eugène de Rastignac's second year, this figure suddenly started out into bold relief against the background of human forms and faces among which the law student was to live for another two years. This laughing-stock was the retired vermicelli-merchant, old Goriot, upon whose face a painter, like the historian, would have concentrated all the light in his picture.

How had it come about that the boarders regarded him with a half-malignant contempt? Why did they subject the oldest among their number to a kind of persecution, in which there was mingled some pity but no respect for his misfortunes? Had he brought it upon himself by some eccentricity or absurdity, which is less easily forgiven or forgotten than more serious defects? The question strikes at the root of many a social injustice. Perhaps it is only human nature to inflict suffering on anything that will endure suffering, whether by reason of its genuine humility, or indifference, or sheer helplessness. Do we not, one and all, like to feel our strength even at the expense of someone or of something? The poorest sample of humanity, the street archin, will pull the bell handle at every street door in bitter weather, and scramble up to write his name on the unsullied marble of a monument.

Chapter 2

IN THE year 1813, at the age of sixty-nine or thereabouts, old Goriot had sold his business and retired—to Mme Vauquer's boardinghouse. When he first came there he had taken the rooms now occupied by Mme Couture; he had paid twelve hundred francs a year like a man to whom five louis more or less was a mere trifle. For him Mme Vauquer had made various improvements in the three rooms destined for his use, in consideration of a certain sum paid in advance, so it was said, for the miserable furniture, the yellow cotton curtains, a few chairs of stained wood covered with Utrecht velvet, several wretched colored prints in frames, and wallpaper that a little suburban tavern would have disdained. Possibly it was the careless generosity which old Goriot displayed at this period (they called him Monsieur Goriot very respectfully then) that gave Mme Vauquer the meanest opinion of his business abilities. She looked on him as an imbecile where money was concerned.

Goriot had brought with him a considerable wardrobe, the outfit of a retired tradesman who denies himself nothing. Mme Vauquer's astonished eyes beheld no less than eighteen cambric-fronted shirts, the splendor of their fineness being enhanced by a pair of pins each bearing a large diamond, and connected by a short chain, an ornament which adorned the vermicelli-maker's shirt-front. He usually wore a coat of cornflower blue; his rotund and portly person was still further set off by a clean white waistcoat, and a gold chain and seals which dangled over that broad expanse. When his hostess accused him of being "a bit of a beau," he smiled with the vanity of a citizen whose foible is gratified. His cupboards (*ormoires*, as he called them in the popular dialect) were filled with a quantity of plate that he brought with him. The widow's eyes gleamed as she obligingly helped him to unpack the soup ladles, tablespoons, forks, cruet-stands, tureens, dishes, and breakfast services—all of silver, which were duly arranged upon the shelves, besides a few more or less handsome pieces of plate, all weighing no inconsiderable number of ounces; he could not bring himself to part with these gifts that reminded him of past domestic celebrations.

"This was my wife's present to me on the first anniversary of our wedding day," he said to Mme Vauquer, as he put away a little silver porringer, with two turtle-doves billing on the cover. "Poor dear! she spent on it all the money she had saved before we married. Do you know, I would sooner scratch the earth with my nails for a living, madame, than part with that. But I shall be able to take my coffee out of it every morning for the rest of my days, thank the Lord! I am not to be pitied. There's not much fear of my starving for some time to come."

Finally, Mme Vauquer's magpie's eye had discovered and read certain entries in the list of shareholders in the state funds, and, after a rough calculation, was disposed to credit the worthy Goriot with something like ten thousand francs a year. From that day forward Mme Vauquer (*née* de Conflans), who, as a matter of fact, had seen forty-eight summers, though she would only own to thirty-nine of them—Mme Vauquer had her own ideas. Though Goriot's eyes seemed to have shrunk in their sockets, though they were weak and watery, owing to some glandular affection which compelled him to wipe them continually, she considered him to be a very gentlemanly and pleasant-looking man. Moreover, the widow saw favorable indications of character in the well-developed calves of his legs and in his square-shaped nose, indications still further borne out by the worthy man's full-moon countenance and look of stupid good nature. This, in all probability, was a strongly-built animal, whose brains consisted largely in a capacity for affection. His hair, worn in *ailes de pigeon,* and duly powdered every morning by the barber from the École Polytechnique, described five points on his low forehead, and made an elegant setting for his face. Though his manners were somewhat boorish, he was always as neat as a new pin, and he took his snuff in a lordly way, like a man who knows that his snuffbox is always likely to be filled with maccaboy; so that when Mme Vauquer lay down to rest on the day of M. Goriot's installation, her heart, like a larded partridge, sweltered before the fire of a burning desire to shake off the shroud of Vauquer and rise again as Goriot. She would marry again, sell her boardinghouse, give her hand to this fine flower of citizenship, become a lady of consequence in the quarter, and ask for subscriptions for charitable purposes; she would make little Sunday excursions to Choisy, Soisy, Gentilly; she would have a box at the theater when she liked, instead of waiting for the author's tickets that one of her boarders sometimes gave her, in July. The whole Eldorado of a little Parisian household rose up before Mme Vauquer in her dreams. Nobody knew that she herself possessed forty thousand francs, accumulated *sou* by *sou*—that was her secret. Surely, as far as money was concerned, she was a very tolerable match. "And in other respects, I am quite his equal," she said to herself, turning over in her bed, as if to assure herself of the charms of a form that the portly Sylvie found molded in down feathers every morning.

For three months from that day the Widow Vauquer availed herself of the services of M. Goriot's coiffeur, and went to some expense over her toilette, expense justifiable on the ground that she owed it to herself and her establishment to pay some attention to appearances when such highly respectable persons honored her house with their presence. She expended no small amount of ingenuity in a sort of weeding process of her lodgers, announcing her intention of receiving henceforward none but people who were in every way select. If a stranger presented himself, she let him know that M. Goriot, one of the best-known and most highly respected merchants in Paris, had singled out her boardinghouse for a residence. She drew up a prospectus headed MAISON VAUQUER, in which it was asserted that hers was "one of the oldest and most highly recommended boarding-houses in the Latin Quarter. From the windows of the house," thus ran the prospectus, "there is a charming view of the Vallée des Gobelins [so there is—from the third floor], and a *beautiful* garden, *extending* down to *an avenue of lindens* at the further end." Mention was made of the bracing air of the place and its quiet situation.

It was this prospectus that attracted Mme la Comtesse de l'Ambermesnil, a widow of thirty-six, who was awaiting the final settlement of her husband's affairs, and the pension due to her as the wife of a general who had died "on the field of battle." Mme Vauquer now began to take pains with her table, lighted a fire daily in the sitting room for nearly six months, and kept the promise of her prospectus, even going to some expense to do so. And the countess, on her side, addressed Mme Vauquer as "my dear," and promised her two more boarders, the Baronne de Vaumerland and the widow of a colonel, the late Comte de Picquoisie, who were about to leave a boardinghouse in the Marais, where the terms were higher than at the Maison Vau-quer. Both these ladies, moreover, would be very well-to-do when the people at the War Office had come to an end of their formalities. "But government departments are always so dila-tory," the lady added.

After dinner the two widows went together up to Mme Vau-quer's room, and had a snug little chat over some cordial and various delicacies reserved for the mistress of the house. Mme Vauquer's ideas as to Goriot were cordially approved by Mme de l'Ambermesnil; it was a capital notion, which for that matter she had guessed from the very first; in her opinion the vermicelli-maker was an excellent man.

"Ah, my dear lady, such a well-preserved man of his age, a man who might make a woman happy!" said the widow.

The good-natured Countess turned to the subject of Mme

Vauquer's dress, which was not in harmony with her projects. "You must put yourself on a war footing," said she.

After much serious consideration the two widows went shopping together. They purchased a hat adorned with ostrich feathers and a cap at the Palais Royal, and the countess took her friend to the Magasin de la Petite Jeannette, where they chose a dress and a scarf. Thus equipped for the campaign, the widow looked exactly like the prize animal hung out for a sign above an à-la-mode beef shop; but she herself was so much pleased with the improvement, as she considered it, in her appearance, that she felt she lay under some obligation to the countess; and, though by no means open-handed, she begged that lady to accept a hat which cost twenty francs. The fact was that she needed the countess' services on the delicate mission of sounding Goriot; the countess must sing her praises in his ears. Mme de l'Ambermesnil lent herself very good-naturedly to this maneuver, began her operations, and succeeded in obtaining a private interview. But the overtures that she made, with a view to securing him for herself, were received with embarrassment, not to say a repulse. She left him, revolted by his coarseness.

"My angel," said she to her dear friend, "you will make nothing of that man yonder. He is absurdly suspicious, a miser, an idiot, a fool; you would never be happy with him."

After what had passed between M. Goriot and Mme de l'Ambermesnil, the countess would no longer live under the same roof. She left the next day, forgot to pay for six months' board, and left behind her her wardrobe, cast-off clothing to the value of five francs. Eagerly and persistently as Mme Vauquer sought her quondam lodger, the Comtesse de l'Ambermesnil was never heard of again in Paris. The widow often talked of this deplorable business, and regretted her own too-confiding disposition. As a matter of fact, she was as suspicious as a cat; but she was like many other people, who cannot trust their own kin and put themselves at the mercy of the first chance comer—an odd but common phenomenon, whose causes may readily be traced to the depths of the human heart.

Perhaps there are people who know that they have nothing more to look for from those with whom they live; they have shown the emptiness of their hearts to their housemates, and in their secret selves they are conscious that they are severely judged, and that they deserve to be judged severely; but still they feel an unconquerable craving for praises that they do not hear, or they are consumed by a desire to appear to possess, in the eyes of a new audience, the qualities which they have not, hoping to win the admiration or affection of strangers at the risk of forfeiting it again some day. Or, again, there are other mercenary persons who never do a kindness to a friend or a relation simply because these have a claim upon them, while a service done to a stranger brings its reward to self-love. Such natures feel but little affection for those who are nearest to them; they keep their kindness for remoter circles of acquaintance and show most to those who dwell on its utmost limits. Mme Vauquer belonged to both these essentially mean, false, and execrable classes.

"If I had been here at the time," Vautrin would say at the end of the story, "I would have shown her up, and that misfortune would not have befallen you. I know that kind of woman!"

Like all narrow natures, Mme Vauquer was wont to confine her attention to events, and did not go very deeply into the causes that brought them about; she likewise preferred to throw the blame of her own mistakes on others, so she chose to consider that the honest vermicelli-maker was responsible for her misfortune. It had opened her eyes, so she said, with regard to him. As soon as she saw that her blandishments were in vain, and that the outlay on her new clothing was money thrown away, she was not slow to discover the reason of his indifference. It became plain to her at once that there was *some other attraction*, to use her own expression. In short, it was evident that the hope she had so fondly cherished was a baseless delusion, and that she would "never make anything out of that man," in the countess' forcible phrase. The countess seemed to have been a judge of character. Mme Vauquer's aversion was naturally more energetic than her friendship, for her hatred was not in proportion to her love, but to her disappointed expectations. The human heart may find here and there a resting-place short of the highest height of affection, but we seldom stop in the steep, downward slope of hatred. Still, M. Goriot was a lodger, and the widow's wounded self-love could not vent itself in an explosion of wrath; like a monk harassed by the prior of his convent, she was forced to stifle her sighs of disappointment, and to gulp down her craving for revenge. Little minds find gratification for their feelings, benevolent or otherwise, by a constant exercise of petty ingenuity. The widow employed her woman's malice to devise subtle persecutions. She began by a course of retrenchment—various luxuries which had found their way to the table appeared there no more.

"No more pickles, no more anchovies! They have made a fool of me!" she said to Sylvie one morning, and they returned to the old bill of fare.

The thrifty frugality necessary to those who mean to make their way in the world had become an inveterate habit of life with M. Goriot. Soup, boiled beef, and a dish of vegetables had been, and always would be, the dinner he liked best, so Mme Vauquer found it very difficult to annoy a boarder whose tastes were so simple. He was proof against her malice, and in desperation she spoke to him and of him slightingly before the other lodgers, who began to amuse themselves at his expense, and so gratified her desire for revenge.

Towards the end of the first year the widow's suspicions had reached such a pitch that she began to wonder how it was that a retired merchant with a secure income of seven or eight thousand livres, the owner of such magnificent plate and jewelry handsome enough for a kept mistress, should be living in her house. Why should he devote so small a proportion of his money to his expenses? Until the first year was nearly at an end, Goriot had dined out once or twice every week, but these occasions came less frequently, and at last he was scarcely absent from the dinner table twice a month. It was hardly to be expected that Mme Vauquer should regard the increased regularity of her boarder's habits with complacency, when those little excursions of his had been so much to her interest. She attributed the change not so much to a gradual diminution of fortune as to a spiteful wish to annoy his hostess. It is one of the most detestable habits of a Lilliputian mind to credit other people with its own malignant pettiness.

Unluckily, towards the end of the second year, M. Goriot's conduct gave some color to the idle talk about him. He asked Mme Vauquer to give him a room on the second floor, and to make a corresponding reduction in her charges. Apparently such strict economy was called for that he did without a fire all through the winter. Mme Vauquer asked to be paid in advance, an arrangement to which M. Goriot consented, and thenceforward she spoke of him as "old Goriot."

What had brought about this decline and fall? Conjecture was keen, but investigation was difficult. Old Goriot was not communicative; in the sham countess' phrase, he was "a sly wretch." Empty-headed people who babble about their own affairs because they have nothing else to occupy them, naturally conclude that if people say nothing of their doings it is because their doings will not bear being talked about; so the highly respectable merchant became a scoundrel, and the late beau was an old rogue. Opinion fluctuated. Sometimes, according to Vautrin, who came about this time to live in the Maison Vauquer, old Goriot was a man who *dabbled*—to use the sufficiently expressive language of the Stock Exchange—in stocks and shares, after he had ruined himself by heavy speculation. Sometimes it was held that he was one of those petty gamblers who nightly play for small stakes until they win a few francs. A theory that he was a detective in the employ of the secret service found favor at one time, but Vautrin maintained that "Goriot was not sharp enough for that." There were yet other solutions; old Goriot was a skinflint, a shark of a money lender, a man who lived by selling lottery tickets. He was by turns all the most mysterious brood of vice and shame and misery; yet, however vile his life might be, the feeling of repulsion which he aroused in others was not so strong that he must be banished from their society—he paid his way. Besides, Goriot had his uses, everyone vented his spleen or sharpened his wit on him; he was pelted with jokes and be-labored with hard words. The general consensus of opinion was in favor of a theory which seemed the most likely; this was Mme Vauquer's view. According to her, the man so well preserved at his time of life, with whom a woman might be very happy, was a libertine who had strange tastes. These are the facts upon which Mme Vauquer's slanders were based.

Early one morning, some few months after the departure of the unlucky countess who had managed to live for six months at the widow's expense, Mme Vauquer (not yet dressed) heard the rustle of a silk dress and a young woman's light footstep on the stair; someone was going to Goriot's room. He seemed to expect the visit, for his door stood ajar. The portly Sylvie presently came up to tell her mistress that a girl too pretty to be honest, "dressed like a goddess," and not a speck of mud on her laced cashmere boots, had glided in from the street like a snake, had found the kitchen, and asked for M. Goriot's room. Mme Vauquer and the cook, listening, overheard several words affectionately spoken during the visit, which lasted for some time. When M. Goriot went downstairs with the lady, the stout Sylvie forthwith took her basket and followed the lover-like couple, under pretext of going to do her marketing.

"Monsieur Goriot must be awfully rich, all the same, madame," she reported on her return, "to keep her in such style. Just imagine it! There was a splendid carriage waiting at the corner of the Place de l'Estrapade, and *she* got into it."

While they were at dinner that evening, Mme Vauquer went to the window and drew the curtain, as the sun was shining into Goriot's eyes.

"You are beloved of fair ladies, Monsieur Goriot—the sun seeks you out," she said, alluding to his visitor. "Well, you have good taste—she was very pretty."

"That was my daughter," he said, with a kind of pride in his voice, and the rest chose to consider this as the fatuity of an old man who wishes to save appearances.

A month after this visit M. Goriot received another. The same daughter who had come to see him that morning came again after dinner, this time in evening dress. The boarders, in deep discussion in the dining room, caught a glimpse of a lovely, fairhaired woman, slender, graceful, and much too distinguished-looking to be a daughter of old Goriot's.

"Two of them!" cried the fat Sylvie, who did not recognize the lady of the first visit.

A few days later, and another young lady—a tall, well-molded brunette, with dark hair and bright eyes—came to ask for M. Goriot.

"Three of them!" said Sylvie.

Then the second daughter, who had first come in the morning to see her father, came shortly afterwards in the evening. She wore a ball dress, and came in a carriage.

"Four of them!" commented Mme Vauquer and her plump handmaid. Sylvie saw not a trace of resemblance between this great lady and the girl in her simple morning dress who had entered her kitchen on the occasion of her first visit.

At that time Goriot was paying twelve hundred francs a year to his landlady, and Mme Vauquer saw nothing out of the common in the fact that a rich man had four or five mistresses; nay, she thought it very knowing of him to pass them off as his daughters. She was not at all inclined to draw a hard-and-fast line, or to take umbrage at his sending for them to the Maison Vauquer; yet, inasmuch as these visits explained her boarder's indifference to her, she went so far (at the end of the second year) as to speak of him as an "ugly old wretch." When at length her boarder was paying only nine hundred francs a year, she asked him very insolently what he took her house to be, after meeting one of these ladies on the stairs. Old Goriot answered that the lady was his eldest daughter.

"So you have two or three dozen daughters, have you?" said Mme Vauquer sharply.

"I have only two," her boarder answered meekly, like a ruined man who is broken in to all the cruel usage of misfortune.

Towards the end of the third year old Goriot reduced his expenses still further; he went up to the third story, and now paid forty-five francs a month. He did without snuff, told his hairdresser that he no longer required his services, and gave up wearing powder. When Goriot appeared for the first time in this condition, an exclamation of astonishment broke from his hostess at the color of his hair—a dingy olive gray. He had grown sadder day by day under the influence of some hidden trouble; among all the faces round the table, his was the most woebegone. There was no longer any doubt. Goriot was an elderly libertine, whose eyes had only been preserved by the skill of the physician from the malign influence of the remedies necessitated by the state of his health. The disgusting color of his hair was a result of his excesses and of the drugs which he had taken that he might continue his career. The poor old man's mental and physical condition afforded some grounds for the absurd rubbish talked about him. When his stock of fine linen was worn out, he replaced it by calico at fourteen *sous* a yard. His diamonds, his gold snuff-box, watch chain and trinkets, disappeared one by one. He had left off wearing the cornflower-blue coat, and was sumptuously arrayed, summer as winter, in a coarse chestnut-brown coat, a plush waistcoat, and doeskin breeches. He grew thinner and thinner; his legs were shrunken, his cheeks, once so puffed out by contented bourgeois prosperity, were covered with wrinkles, and the outlines of the jawbones were distinctly visible; there were deep furrows in his forehead. In the fourth year of his residence in the Rue Neuve-Sainte-Geneviève he was no longer like his former self. The hale vermicelli-manufacturer who had looked scarce forty, the stout, comfortable, prosperous trades-man, with an almost bucolic air and such a brisk demeanor that it did you good to look at him, the man with something boyish in his smile, had suddenly sunk into his dotage, and had become a feeble, vacillating septuagenarian.

The keen, bright blue eyes had grown dull, and faded to a steel-gray color; the red inflamed rims looked as though they had shed tears of blood. He excited feelings of repulsion in some, and of pity in others. The young medical students who came to the house noticed the drooping of his lower lip and the conforma-tion of the facial angle; and, after teasing him without getting any reply, they declared that cretinism was setting in.

One evening after dinner Mme Vauquer said half-banteringly to him, "So those daughters of yours don't come to see you any more, eh?" meaning to imply her doubts as to his paternity. Old Goriot shrank as if his hostess had touched him with a sword point.

"They come sometimes," he said in a tremulous voice.

"Aha, you still see them sometimes?" cried the students. "Bravo, Father Goriot!"

The old man scarcely seemed to hear the witticisms at his expense that followed on the words; he had relapsed into the dreamy state of mind that these superficial observers took for senile torpor, due to his failing intelligence. If they had only

known, they might have been deeply interested by the problem
of his condition, but few problems were more obscure. It was
easy, of course, to find out whether Goriot had really been a
vermicelli-manufacturer; the amount of his fortune was readily
discoverable; but the old people, who were most inquisitive as to
his concerns, never went beyond the limits of the Quarter, and
lived in the lodginghouse much as oysters cling to a rock. As for
the rest, the current of life in Paris daily awaited them, and
swept them away with it. So soon as they left the Rue Neuve-
Sainte-Geneviève, they forgot the existence of the old man, their
butt at dinner. For those narrow souls, or for careless youth, the
misery in old Goriot's withered face and its dull apathy were
quite incompatible with wealth or any sort of intelligence. As
for the creatures whom he called his daughters, all Mme Vauquer's boarders were of her opinion. With the severity of logic
developed in elderly women during long evenings of gossip to
a point where they can always find an hypothesis to fit all circumstances, she was wont to reason thus:

"If old Goriot had daughters of his own as rich as those ladies
who came here seemed to be, he would not be lodging in my
house, on the third floor, at forty-five francs a month, and he
would not go about dressed like a poor man."

No objection could be raised to these inferences. So by the
end of the month of November 1819, at the time when the curtain rises on this drama, everyone in the house had come to have
a very decided opinion as to the poor old man. He had never had
either wife or daughter; excesses had reduced him to this slug-
gish condition; he was a sort of human mollusc who should be
classed among the *capulidæ*, so said one of the dinner contingent,
an employee at the Museum, who had a pretty wit. Poiret was
an eagle, a gentleman, compared with Goriot. Poiret would join
the talk, argue, answer when he was spoken to; as a matter of
fact, his talk, arguments, and responses contributed nothing to
the conversation, for Poiret had a habit of repeating what the

others said in different words; still, he did join in the talk; he was alive, and seemed capable of feeling; while old Goriot—to quote the Museum official again—was invariably at zero.

Chapter 3

EUGÈNE DE RASTIGNAC had just returned to Paris in a state of mind not uncommon in young men who are conscious of unusual powers, and in those whose faculties are so stimulated by difficulties that for the time being they rise above the ordinary level.

During Rastignac's first year of study for the preliminary examinations in law he had had leisure to see the sights of Paris and to enjoy some of its amusements. A student finds his time well filled if he sets himself to learn the repertory of every theater, and to study the ins and outs of the labyrinth of Paris. To know its customs, to learn the language, and become familiar with the amusements of the capital, he must explore its recesses, good and bad, follow the studies that please him best, and form some idea of the treasures contained in galleries and museums.

At this stage of his career a student grows eager and excited about all sorts of follies that seem to him to be of immense importance. He has his hero, his great man, a professor at the Collège de France, paid to talk down to the level of his audience. He adjusts his cravat, and strikes various attitudes for the benefit of the women in the first galleries at the Opéra-Comique. As he passes through all these successive initiations, and breaks out of his sheath, the horizons of life widen around him, and at length he grasps the structure of society with the different human strata of which it is composed. If he begins by admiring the procession of carriages on sunny afternoons in the Champs-Élysées, he soon reaches the further

stage of envying their owners. Unconsciously, Eugène had
served his apprenticeship before he went back to Angoulême
for the long vacation, after taking his degrees as bachelor of
arts and bachelor of law. The illusions of childhood had vanished; so also had the ideas he brought with him from the
provinces. With intelligence developed, with loftier ambitions,
he saw things as they were at home in the old manor house. His
father and mother, his two brothers and two sisters, with an
aged aunt, whose whole fortune consisted in annuities, lived on
the little estate of Rastignac. The property brought in about
three thousand francs, and though the amount varied with the
season (as must always be the case in a vine-growing district),
they were obliged to spare an unvarying twelve hundred francs
out of their income for him. He saw how constantly the poverty,
which they had generously hidden from him, weighed upon
them. He could not help comparing the sisters, who had seemed
so beautiful to his boyish eyes, with women in Paris, who had
realized the beauty of his dreams. The uncertain future of the
whole family depended upon him. It did not escape his eyes
that not a crumb was wasted in the house, nor that the wine
they drank was made from the second pressing. A multitude of
small things, which it is useless to speak of in detail here, made
him burn to distinguish himself, and his ambition to succeed increased tenfold.

He meant, like all great souls, that his success should be due
entirely to his merits, but his was pre-eminently a southern temperament; the execution of his plans was sure to be marred by
the vertigo that seizes on men in mid-ocean when they have
lost their reckoning and know not how to steer their course,
how to set their sails. At first he determined to fling himself
heart and soul into his work, but he was diverted from this purpose by the need of society and connections; then he saw how
great an influence women exert in social life, and suddenly made
up his mind to go out into this world to seek a protectress there.

Surely a clever and high-spirited young man, whose wit and courage were set off to advantage by a graceful figure and the manly kind of beauty that readily strikes a woman's imagination, need not despair of finding a protectress. These ideas occurred to him in his country walks with his sisters, whom he had once joined so gaily. The girls thought him very much changed.

His aunt, Mme de Marcillac, had been presented at court in the days before the Revolution, and had moved among the notables of that lofty region. Suddenly the young man's ambition discerned in those recollections of hers, which had been like nursery fairy tales to her nephews and nieces, the elements of a social success at least as important as the success which he had achieved at the law school. He began to ask his aunt about her connections; some of the old ties might still hold good. After much shaking of the branches of the family tree, the old lady came to the conclusion that of all persons who could be useful to her nephew among the selfish genus of rich relations, the Vicomtesse de Beauséant was the least likely to refuse. To this lady, therefore, she wrote in the old-fashioned style, recommending Eugène to her, pointing out to her nephew that if he succeeded in pleasing Mme de Beauséant, the vicomtesse would introduce him to other relations. A few days after his return to Paris, therefore, Rastignac sent his aunt's letter to Mme de Beauséant. The vicomtesse replied by an invitation to a ball for the following evening. This was the position of affairs at the Maison Vauquer at the end of November 1819.

A few days later, after Mme de Beauséant's ball, Eugène came in at two o'clock in the morning. The persevering student meant to make up for the lost time by working until daylight. It was the first time that he had attempted to spend the night in this way in that silent quarter. The spell of a factitious energy was upon him; he had beheld the pomp and splendor of the world. He had not dined at the Maison Vauquer; the boarders probably would think that he would walk home at daybreak from the dance, as he had done sometimes on former occasions, after a fête at the Prado or a ball at the Odéon, splashing his silk stockings thereby, and ruining his pumps.

It so happened that Christophe took a look into the street before drawing the bolts of the door; and Rastignac, coming in at that moment, was able to go up to his room without making any noise, followed by Christophe, who made a great deal. Eugène exchanged his dress suit for a shabby overcoat and slippers, kindled a fire with some blocks of patent fuel, and sat down to his work so quickly that the faint sounds he made were drowned by Christophe's heavy tramp on the stairs.

Eugène sat absorbed in thought for a few moments before plunging into his law books. He had just become aware of the fact that the Vicomtesse de Beauséant was one of the queens of fashion, that her house was thought to be the pleasantest in the Faubourg Saint-Germain. And not only so, she was, by right of her fortune and the name she bore, one of the most conspicuous figures in that aristocratic world. Thanks to his aunt, thanks to Mme de Marcillac's letter of introduction, the poor student had been kindly received in that house before he knew the extent of the favor thus shown to him. It was almost like a patent of nobility to be admitted to those gilded salons; he had appeared in the most exclusive circle in Paris, and now all doors were open for him. Eugène had been dazzled at first by the brilliant assembly, and after exchanging a few words with the vicomtesse, he had been content to single out a goddess from among this throng of Parisian divinities, one of those women who are sure to attract a young man's fancy.

The Comtesse Anastasie de Restaud was tall and gracefully made; she had one of the prettiest figures in Paris. Imagine a pair of great dark eyes, a magnificently molded hand, a shapely foot. There was a fiery energy in her movements; the Marquis de Ronquerolles had called her a "thoroughbred," but this

fineness of nervous organization had brought no accompanying defect; the outlines of her form were full and rounded,
without any tendency to stoutness. "A thoroughbred," "a pure
pedigree,"—these figures of speech have replaced the "heavenly
angel" and Ossianic hyperbole; the old mythology of love is
extinct, doomed to perish by modern dandyism. But for Rastignac, Mme Anastasie de Restaud was the woman for whom
he had sighed. He had contrived to write his name twice upon
the list of partners upon her fan, and had snatched a few words
with her during the first quadrille.

"Where shall I meet you again, madame?" he asked abruptly,
and the tones of his voice were full of the vehement energy that
women like so well.

"Oh, everywhere!" said she, "in the Bois, at the Bouffons, in
my own house."

With the impetuosity of his adventurous southern temper,
he did all he could to cultivate an acquaintance with this lovely
countess, making the best of his opportunities in the quadrille
and during a waltz that she gave him. When he had told her
that he was a cousin of Mme de Beauséant's, the countess, whom
he took for a great lady, asked him to call at her house, and after
her parting smile, Rastignac felt convinced that he must make
this visit. He was so lucky as to light upon someone who did
not laugh at his ignorance, a fatal defect among the gilded and
insolent youth of that period; the coterie of Maulincourts,
Maximes de Trailles, de Marsays, Ronquerolles, Ajuda-Pintos,
and Vandenesses, who shone there in all the glory of vanity
among the best-dressed women of fashion in Paris—Lady Brandon, the Duchesse de Langeais, the Comtesse de Kergarouët,
Mme de Sérizy, the Duchesse de Carigliano, the Comtesse Fer-
raud, Mme de Lanty, the Marquise d'Aiglemont, Mme Firmiani,
the Marquise de Listomère and the Marquise d'Espard, the
Duchesse de Maufrigneuse and the Grandlieus. Luckily, therefore, for him, the novice happened upon the Marquis de Mont-

riveau, the lover of the Duchesse de Langeais, a general as simple as a child; from him Rastignac learned that the countess lived
in the Rue du Helder.

Ah, what it is to be young, eager to see the world, greedily
on the watch for any chance that brings you nearer the woman
of your dreams, and behold two houses open their doors to you!
To set foot in the Vicomtesse de Beauséant's house in the Faubourg Saint-Germain; to fall on your knees before a Comtesse
de Restaud in the Chaussée d'Antin; to be able to glance across
a vista of Paris drawing-rooms, conscious that, possessing sufficient good looks, you may hope to find aid and protection there
in a feminine heart! To feel ambitious enough to spurn the
tight-rope on which you must walk with the steady head of
an acrobat for whom a fall is impossible, and to find in a charming woman the best of all balancing poles.

He sat there with his thoughts for a while, Law on the one
hand, and Poverty on the other, beholding a radiant vision of a
woman rise above the dull, smoldering fire. Who would not have
paused and questioned the future as Eugène was doing? Who
would not have pictured it full of success? His wandering
thoughts took wings; he was transported out of the present into
that blissful future; he was sitting by Mme de Restaud's side,
when a sort of sigh, like the grunt of an overburdened St. Joseph,
broke the silence of the night. It vibrated through the student,
who took the sound for a death-groan. He opened his door noiselessly, went out upon the landing, and saw a thin streak of light
under old Goriot's door. Eugène feared that his neighbor had
been taken ill; he went over and looked through the keyhole.
The old man was busily engaged in an occupation so singular
and so suspicious that Rastignac thought the interests of society
required him to watch the vermicelli-maker's nocturnal activi-
ties.

The table was upturned, and Goriot had doubtless in some
way secured a silver plate and cup to the bar before knotting

a thick rope round them; he was pulling at this rope with such enormous force that they were being crushed and twisted out of shape. To all appearance he meant to convert the richly wrought metal into ingots.

"The devil! What a man!" said Rastignac, as he watched Goriot's muscular arms. There was not a sound in the room while the old man, with the aid of the rope, was kneading the silver like dough. Was he then, indeed, a thief, or a receiver of stolen goods, who affected imbecility and decrepitude, and lived like a beggar that he might carry on his pursuits the more securely? Eugène stood for a moment revolving these questions, then he looked again through the keyhole.

Old Goriot had unwound his coil of rope; he had covered the table with a blanket, and was now employed in rolling the flattened mass of silver into a bar, an operation which he performed with marvelous dexterity.

"Why, he must be as strong as Augustus, King of Poland!" said Eugène to himself when the bar was nearly finished.

Old Goriot looked sadly at his handiwork, tears fell from his eyes, he blew out the dip which had served him for a light while he manipulated the silver, and Eugène heard him sigh as he lay down again.

"He is mad," thought the student.

"*Poor child!*" old Goriot said aloud. Rastignac, hearing those words, concluded to keep silence; he would not hastily condemn his neighbor. He was back in the doorway of his room when a strange sound from the staircase below reached his ears. It might have been made by two men coming up in felt slippers. Eugène listened; two men there certainly were, he could hear their breathing. Yet there had been no sound of opening the street door, no footsteps in the passage. Suddenly, too, he saw a faint gleam of light on the second story; it came from M. Vautrin's room.

"There are a good many mysteries here for a lodginghouse!" he said to himself.

He went part of the way downstairs and listened again. The rattle of gold reached his ears. In another moment the light was put out, and again he distinctly heard the breathing of two men, but no sound of a door being opened or shut. The two men went downstairs, the faint sounds growing fainter as they went.

"Who is there?" cried Mme Vauquer, opening a window in her bedroom which looked on the stairs.

"I, Madame Vauquer," answered Vautrin's deep bass voice. "I am coming in."

"That is odd! Christophe drew the bolts," said Eugène, going back to his room. "You have to sit up at night, it seems, if you really mean to know all that is going on about you in Paris."

These incidents turned his thought from his ambitious dreams; he returned to his work, but his thought wandered back to old Goriot's suspicious occupation; Mme de Restaud's face swam again and again before his eyes like a vision of a brilliant future, and at last he lay down and slept with clenched fists. When a young man makes up his mind that he will work all night, the chances are that seven times out of ten he will sleep till morning. We must be more than twenty to work all night.

Chapter 4

THE NEXT morning Paris was wrapped in one of the dense fogs that throw the most punctual people out in their calculations as to the time. Even the most businesslike folk fail to keep their appointments in such weather, and ordinary mortals wake up at noon and fancy it is eight o'clock. On this morning it was half-past nine, and Mme Vauquer still lay abed. Christophe was late, Sylvie was late, but the two sat comfortably taking their coffee as usual. It was Sylvie's custom to take the cream off the milk destined for the boarders' breakfast for her own, and to boil the remainder for some time, so that Madame should not discover this illegal exaction.

"Sylvie," said Christophe, as he dipped a piece of toast into the coffee, "Monsieur Vautrin, who is not such a bad fellow, all the same, had two people come to see him again last night. If Madame says anything, mind you say nothing about it."

"Has he given you something?"

"He gave me a five-franc piece this month, which is as good as saying, 'Hold your tongue.'"

"Except him and Madame Couture, who aren't stingy, there's no one in the house that doesn't try to get back with the left hand all that they give with the right at New Year," said Sylvie.

"And, after all," said Christophe, "what do they give you? A miserable five-franc piece. There is old Goriot, who has cleaned his shoes himself these two years past. There is that old beggar Poiret, who goes without blacking altogether; he would sooner drink it than put it on his boots. Then there is that whippersnapper of a student, who gives me a couple of francs. Two francs will not pay for my brushes. And he sells his old clothes, and gets more for them than they are worth. Oh, they're a shabby lot!"

"Pooh!" said Sylvie, sipping her coffee, "our places are the best in the Quarter, that I know. But about that great big chap Vautrin, Christophe—has anyone told you anything about him?"

"Yes. I met a gentleman in the street a few days ago. He said to me, 'There's a gentleman at your place, isn't there? a tall man that dyes his whiskers?' I told him, 'No, sir; they aren't dyed. A gay fellow like him hasn't the time to do it.' And when I told Monsieur Vautrin about it afterwards, he said, 'Quite right, my boy. That is the way to answer them. There is nothing more unpleasant than to have your little weaknesses known; it might spoil many a match.'"

"Well, for my part," said Sylvie, "a man tried to tease me at the market, wanting to know if I had ever seen him put on his shirt. Such bosh! There," she cried, interrupting herself, "that's a quarter to ten striking at the Val-de-Grâce, and not a soul stirring!"

"Pooh! they are all gone out. Madame Couture and the girl went out at eight o'clock to take the wafer at Saint-Étienne. Old Goriot started off somewhere with a parcel, and the student won't be back from his lecture till ten o'clock. I saw them go while I was sweeping the stairs; old Goriot knocked up against me, and his parcel was as hard as iron. What is the old fellow up to, I wonder? He is as good as a plaything for the rest of them; they can never let him alone; but he is a good man, all the same, and worth more than all of them put together. He doesn't give you much himself, but he sometimes sends you with a message to ladies who fork out famous tips; they are finely dressed, too."

"His daughters, as he calls them, eh? There are a dozen of them."

"I have never been to more than two—the two who came here."

"There is Madame moving overhead. I must go, or she will make an uproar. Just keep an eye on the milk, Christophe—don't let the cat get at it."

Sylvie went up to her mistress' room.

"Sylvie! How is this? It's nearly ten o'clock, and you let me sleep on like a dormouse! Such a thing has never happened before."

"It's the fog; it is so thick you could cut it with a knife."

"But how about breakfast?"

"Bah! the boarders are possessed, I'm sure. They all cleared out before there was a wink of daylight."

"Do speak properly, Sylvie," Mme Vauquer retorted; "say a blink of daylight."

"Ah, well, madame, whichever you please. Anyhow, you can have breakfast at ten o'clock. La Michonnette and Poireau have neither of them stirred. There are only those two upstairs, and they are sleeping like the logs they are."

"But, Sylvie, you put their names together as if——"

"As if what?" said Sylvie, bursting into a guffaw. "The two of them make a pair."

"It is a strange thing, isn't it, Sylvie, how Monsieur Vautrin got in last night after Christophe had bolted the door?"

"Not at all, madame. Christophe heard Monsieur Vautrin, and went down and undid the door for him. And here are you imagining that——"

"Give me my wrapper, and be quick and get breakfast ready. Hash up the rest of the mutton with the potatoes, and you can put the stewed pears on the table, those at five a penny."

A few moments later Mme Vauquer came down, just in time to see the cat knock down a plate that covered a bowl of milk, and begin to lap up its contents.

"Mistigris!" she cried.

The cat fled, but promptly returned to rub against her ankles.

"Oh, yes, you can wheedle, you old hypocrite!" she said. "Sylvie! Sylvie!"

"Yes, madame, what is it?"

"Just see what the cat has done!"

"It is all that stupid Christophe's fault. I told him to stop and lay the table. What has become of him? Don't you worry, madame; old Goriot shall have it. I will fill it up with water, and he won't know the difference. He never notices anything, not even what he eats."

"I wonder where the old heathen can have gone?" said Mme Vauquer, setting the plates round the table.

"Who knows? He is up to all sorts of tricks."

"I believe I slept too long," said Mme Vauquer.

"But Madame looks as fresh as a rose, all the same."

The doorbell rang at that moment, and Vautrin came through the sitting room, singing loudly:

> " 'Tis the same old story everywhere,
>   A roving heart and a roving glance . . .

"Oh, Mamma Vauquer! good morning!" he cried at the sight of his hostess, and he put his arm gaily round her waist.

"There, there—don't!"

" 'Impertinence!' Say it!" he answered. "Come, say it! Isn't that what you really mean? Now I'll help you to set the table. Ah! I am a nice man, am I not?

> "For the locks of brown and the golden hair
>   A sighing lover . . .

"Oh! I have just seen something so funny——

>   . . . led by chance."

"What?" asked the widow.

"Old Goriot in the goldsmith's shop in the Rue Dauphine at half-past eight this morning. They buy old spoons and forks and gold lace there, and Goriot sold a piece of silver plate for a good round sum. It had been twisted out of shape very neatly for a man that's not used to the trade."

"Really? You don't say so!"

"Yes. One of my friends is expatriating himself; I had been to see him off on board the Royal Mail steamer, and was coming back here. I waited after that to see what old Goriot would do—it is a comical affair. He came back to this quarter of the world, to the Rue des Grès, and went into a money lender's house; everybody knows him, Gobseck, a complete rascal, who would make dominoes out of his father's bones; a Turk, a heathen, an old Jew, a Greek. It would be a difficult matter to rob *him*, for he puts all his coin into the bank."

"Then what was old Goriot doing there?"

"Doing?" said Vautrin. "Nothing; he was bent on his own undoing. He is a simpleton, stupid enough to ruin himself by running after——"

"There he is!" said Sylvie.

"Christophe," cried old Goriot's voice, "come upstairs with me."

Christophe went up, and shortly afterwards came down again.

"Where are you going?" Mme Vauquer asked of her servant.

"Out on an errand for Monsieur Goriot."

"What may that be?" said Vautrin, pouncing on a letter in Christophe's hand. "Mme la Comtesse Anastasie de Restaud," he read. "Where are you going with it?" he added, as he gave the letter back to Christophe.

"To the Rue du Helder. I have orders to give it into her hands myself."

"What is there inside it?" said Vautrin, holding the letter up to the light. "A bank-note? No." He peered into the envelope. "A receipted account!" he cried. "My word! What a gallant old dotard! Off with you, old fellow," he said, bringing down a hand on Christophe's head, and spinning the man round like a thimble; "you will get a good tip."

By this time the table was set. Sylvie was boiling the milk, Mme Vauquer was lighting a fire in the stove with some assistance from Vautrin, who kept on humming to himself:

"The same old story everywhere,
  A roving heart and a roving glance."

When everything was ready, Mme Couture and Mlle Taillefer came in.

"Where have you been this morning, dear lady?" said Mme Vauquer, turning to Mme Couture.

"We have just been to say our prayers at Saint-Étienne du Mont. Today is the day when we must go to see Monsieur Taillefer. Poor little thing! She is trembling like a leaf," Mme Couture went on, as she seated herself before the fire and held the steaming soles of her boots to the blaze.

"Warm yourself, Victorine," said Mme Vauquer.

"It is quite right and proper, mademoiselle, to pray to Heaven to soften your father's heart," said Vautrin, as he drew a chair nearer to the orphan girl. "But that is not enough. What you want is a friend who will give the monster a piece of his mind; a barbarian who has three millions—so they say—and will not give you a dowry. A pretty girl needs a dowry nowadays."

"Poor child!" said Mme Vauquer. "Never mind, my pet, your wretch of a father is going just the way to bring trouble upon himself."

Victorine's eyes filled with tears at the words, and the widow checked herself at a sign from Mme Couture.

"If we could only see him!" said the paymaster's widow; "if I could speak to him myself and give him his wife's last letter! I have never dared to run the risk of sending it by post; he knew my handwriting——"

" 'Oh woman, persecuted and injured innocent!' " exclaimed Vautrin, breaking in upon her. "So that's how things are. In a few days' time I'll look into your affairs, and everything will be all right, you'll see."

"Oh, sir!" said Victorine, with a tearful but eager glance at Vautrin, who showed no sign of being touched by it, "if you know of any way of communicating with my father, please be sure and tell him that his affection and my mother's honor are more to me than all the money in the world. If you can induce him to relent a little towards me, I will pray to God for you. You may be sure of my gratitude——"

"The same old story everywhere,"

sang Vautrin, with a satirical intonation. At this juncture, Goriot, Mlle Michonneau, and Poiret came downstairs together; possibly the scent of the gravy which Sylvie was making to serve with the mutton had announced breakfast. The seven people thus assembled bade each other good morning, and took their places at the table; the clock struck ten, and the student's foot-step was heard outside.

"Ah, here you are, Monsieur Eugène," said Sylvie; "everyone is breakfasting at home today."

The student exchanged greetings with the lodgers and sat down beside Goriot.

"I have just met with a queer adventure," he said, as he helped himself abundantly to the mutton, and cut a slice of bread, which Mme Vauquer's eyes gauged as usual.

"An adventure?" queried Poiret.

"Well, and what is there to astonish you in that, old boy?" Vautrin asked of Poiret. "Monsieur Eugène is cut out for that kind of thing."

Mlle Taillefer stole a timid glance at the young student.

"Tell us about your adventure," demanded Mme Vauquer.

"Yesterday evening I went to a ball given by a cousin of mine, the Vicomtesse de Beauséant. She has a magnificent house; the rooms were hung with silk—in short, it was a splendid affair, and I was as happy as a king——"

"Fisher," put in Vautrin, interrupting.

"What do you mean, sir?" said Eugène sharply.

"I said 'fisher,' because kingfishers see a good deal more fun than kings."

"Quite true. I would much rather be the little careless bird than a king," said Poiret the ditto-ist, "because——"

"Well, anyway"—the law-student cut him short—"I danced with one of the handsomest women in the room, a charming countess, the most exquisite creature I have ever seen. There were peach blossoms in her hair, and she had the loveliest bou-quet of flowers—real flowers, that scented the air—but it's no use trying to describe a woman glowing with the dance. You ought to have seen her! Well, this morning I met this divine countess about nine o'clock, on foot in the Rue des Grès. Oh! how my heart beat! I began to think——"

"That she was coming here," said Vautrin, with a keen look at the student. "I expect that she was going to call on old Gobseck, a money lender. If ever you explore a Parisian woman's heart, you will find the money lender first, and the lover afterwards. Your countess is called Anastasie de Restaud, and she lives in the Rue du Helder."

At this the student stared hard at Vautrin. Old Goriot raised his head, and gave the two speakers a glance so keen and anxious that the lodgers beheld him with astonishment.

"Then Christophe was too late, and she must have gone to him!" cried Goriot, with anguish in his voice.

"It is just as I guessed," said Vautrin, leaning over to whisper in Mme Vauquer's ear.

Goriot went on with his breakfast, but seemed unconscious of what he was doing. He had never looked more stupid or self-absorbed than he did at that moment.

"Who the devil could have told you her name, Monsieur Vautrin?" asked Eugène.

"Ha, ha!" answered Vautrin. "Old Father Goriot there knew it quite well! Why should not I know it too?"

"Monsieur Goriot?" the student cried.

"What is it?" said the old man. "So she was very beautiful, was she, yesterday night?"

"Who?"

"Madame de Restaud."

"Look at the old wretch," said Mme Vauquer, speaking to Vautrin; "how his eyes light up!"

"Then does he really keep her?" said Mlle Michonneau, in a whisper to the student.

"Oh, yes, she was tremendously pretty," Rastignac began. Old Goriot watched him with eager eyes. "If Madame de Beauséant had not been there, my divine countess would have been the queen of the ball; none of the younger men had eyes for anyone else. I was the twelfth on her list, and she danced every quadrille. The other women were furious. She must have enjoyed herself, if ever creature did! It is a true saying that there is no more beautiful sight than a frigate in full sail, a galloping horse, or a woman dancing."

"So the wheel turns," said Vautrin; "yesterday night at a duchess' ball, this morning in a money lender's office, on the lowest rung of the ladder—just like a Parisienne! If their husbands cannot afford to pay for their reckless extravagance, they will sell themselves. Or if they cannot do that, they will tear out their mothers' hearts to find something to pay for their splendor. They will turn the world upside down. Just a Parisienne through and through!"

Old Goriot's face, which had shone at the student's words like the sun on a bright day, clouded over all at once at this cruel speech of Vautrin's.

"Well," said Mme Vauquer, "but where is your adventure? Did you speak to her? Did you ask her if she wanted to study law?"

"She did not see me," said Eugène. "But think of meeting one of the prettiest women in Paris in the Rue des Grès at nine o'clock! She could not have reached home after the ball till two o'clock this morning. Wasn't it queer? There is no place like Paris for such adventures."

"Pshaw! Much funnier things than *that* happen here!" exclaimed Vautrin.

Mlle Taillefer had scarcely heeded the talk, she was so absorbed by the thought of the new attempt that she was about to make. Mme Couture made a sign that it was time to go upstairs and dress. The two ladies went out, and old Goriot followed their example.

"Well, did you see?" said Mme Vauquer, addressing Vautrin

and the rest of the circle. "He is ruining himself for those women, that is plain."

"Nothing will ever make me believe that that beautiful Comtesse de Restaud is anything to old Goriot," cried the student.

"Well, and if you don't," broke in Vautrin, "we are not set on convincing you. You are too young to know Paris thoroughly yet; later on you will find out that there are what we call men with a passion——"

Mlle Michonneau gave Vautrin a quick glance at these words. They seemed to be like the sound of a trumpet to a trooper's horse. "Aha!" said Vautrin, stopping in his speech to give her a searching glance, "so we have had our little experiences, have we?"

The old maid lowered her eyes like a nun who sees a statue.

"Yes," he went on, "when men of that kind get a notion into their heads, they cannot drop it. They must drink the water from some particular spring—it is stagnant as often as not; but they will sell their wives and families, they will sell their own souls to the devil to get it. For some this spring is gambling, or the Stock Exchange, or music, or a collection of pictures or insects; for others it is some woman who can give them the dainties they like. You might offer these last all the women on earth—they would turn up their noses; they will have the only one who can gratify their passion. It often happens that the woman does not care for them at all, and treats them cruelly; they buy their morsels of satisfaction very dear, but no matter, the fools are never tired of it. They will take their last blanket to the pawnbroker's to give their last five-franc piece to her. Old Goriot here is one of that sort. He is discreet, so the countess exploits him—just the way of the gay world. The poor old fellow thinks of her and of nothing else. In all other respects you see he is a stupid animal, but get him on that subject, and his eyes sparkle like diamonds. That secret is not difficult to guess. He took some plate himself this morning to the melting-pot, and

I saw him at Daddy Gobseck's in the Rue des Grès. And now, mark what follows—he came back here, and gave a letter for the Comtesse de Restaud to that simpleton of a Christophe, who showed us the address; there was a receipted bill inside it. It is clear that it was an urgent matter if the countess also went herself to the old money lender. Old Goriot has financed her handsomely. There is no need to piece the story together; the thing is self-evident. So that shows you, sir student, that all the time your countess was smiling, dancing, flirting, swaying her peach-flower-crowned head, with her gown gathered into her hand, her slippers were pinching her, as they say; she was thinking of her protested bills, or her lover's protested bills."

"You have made me wild to know the truth," cried Eugène; "I will go to call on Madame de Restaud tomorrow."

"Yes," echoed Poiret; "you must go and call on Madame de Restaud."

"And perhaps you will find old Goriot there, who will take payment for the assistance he politely rendered."

Eugène looked disgusted. "Why, then, this Paris of yours must be a sink of iniquity."

"And an uncommonly queer sink, too," replied Vautrin. "The mud splashes you as you drive through it in your carriage—you are a respectable person; you go afoot and are splashed—you are a scoundrel. You are so unlucky as to walk off with something or other belonging to somebody else, and they exhibit you as a curiosity in the Place du Palais-de-Justice; you steal a million, and you are pointed out in every salon as a model of virtue. And you pay thirty millions for the police and the courts of justice, for the maintenance of law and order! A pretty state of things it is!"

"What," cried Mme Vauquer, "has old Goriot really melted down his silver porringer?"

"There were two turtle-doves on the lid, were there not?" asked Eugène.

"Yes, there were."

"Then, was he fond of it?" said Eugène. "He cried while he was breaking up the cup and plate. I happened to see him by accident."

"It was dear to him as his own life," answered the widow.

"There! you see how infatuated the old fellow is!" cried Vautrin. "That woman can coax the soul out of him."

The student went up to his room. Vautrin went out, and a few minutes later Mme Couture and Victorine drove away in a cab which Sylvie had called for them. Poiret gave his arm to Mlle Michonneau, and they went together to spend the two sunniest hours of the day in the Jardin des Plantes.

"Well, those two are as good as married," was the portly Sylvie's comment. "They are going out together today for the first time. They are such a couple of dry sticks that if they happen to strike against each other they will draw sparks like flint and steel."

"Keep clear of Mademoiselle Michonneau's shawl, then," said Mme Vauquer, laughing; "it would flare up like tinder."

Chapter 5

AT FOUR o'clock that evening, when Goriot came in, he saw, by the light of two smoky lamps, that Victorine's eyes were red. Mme Vauquer was listening to the history of the visit made that morning to M. Taillefer; it had been made in vain. Taillefer was tired of the annual application made by his daughter and her elderly friend; he gave them a personal interview in order to arrive at an understanding with them.

"My dear lady," said Mme Couture, addressing Mme Vauquer, "just imagine it; he did not even ask Victorine to sit down, she was standing the whole time. He said to me quite coolly, without putting himself in a passion, that we might spare ourselves the trouble of going there; that the young lady—he would not call her his daughter—was injuring her cause by importuning him. *Importuning*! once a year, the wretch! That as Victorine's mother had nothing when he married her, Victorine ought not to expect anything from him; in fact, he said the most cruel things, that made the poor child burst out crying. The little thing threw herself at her father's feet and spoke up bravely; she said that she only persevered in her visits for her mother's sake, that she would obey him without a murmur, but that she begged him to read her poor dead mother's farewell letter. She took it up and gave it to him, saying the most beautiful things in the world, most beautifully expressed. I do not know where she learned them; God must have put them into her head, for the poor child was inspired to speak so nicely that it made me cry like a fool to hear her talk. And what do you think the monster was doing all the time? Cutting his nails! He took the letter that poor Madame Taillefer had soaked with tears, and flung it on to the chimneypiece. 'That is all right,' he said. He held out his hands to raise his daughter, but she covered them with kisses, and he drew them away again. Scandalous, isn't it? And his great booby of a son came in and took no notice of his sister."

"What inhuman wretches they must be!" said old Goriot.

"And then they both went out of the room," Mme Couture went on, without heeding the worthy vermicelli-maker's exclamation; "father and son bowed to me, and asked me to excuse them on account of urgent business! That is the story of our visit. Well, he has seen his daughter at any rate. How he can refuse to acknowledge her I cannot think, for they are as like as two peas."

The boarders dropped in one after another, interchanging greetings and the empty jokes that certain classes of Parisians regard as humorous and witty. Dullness is their prevailing ingredient, and the whole point consists in pronunciation or gesture. This kind of argot is always changing. The essence of the jest consists in some catchword suggested by a political event, an incident in the police courts, a street song, or a bit of burlesque at some theater, and forgotten in a month. Anything and everything serves to keep up a game of battledore and shuttlecock with words and ideas. The diorama, a recent invention, which carried an optical illusion a degree further than panoramas, had given rise to a mania among art students for ending every word with *rama*. The Maison Vauquer had caught the infection from a young artist among the boarders.

"Well, Monsieur-r-r Poiret," said the employee from the Museum, "how is your health-orama?" Then, without waiting for an answer, he turned to Mme Couture and Victorine with a "Ladies, you seem melancholy."

"Is dinner ready?" cried Horace Bianchon, a medical student, and a friend of Rastignac's; "my stomach is sinking *usque ad talones*."

"There is an uncommon *frozerama* outside!" said Vautrin. "Make room there, Father Goriot! Confound it! your foot covers the whole front of the stove."

"Illustrious Monsieur Vautrin," put in Bianchon, "why do you say *frozerama*? It is incorrect; it should be *frozenrama*."

"No, it shouldn't," said the official from the Museum; "*frozerama* is right by the same rule that you say 'My feet are *froze*.'"

"Ah! ah!"

"Here is his Excellency the Marquis de Rastignac, Doctor of the Law of Contraries," cried Bianchon, seizing Eugène by the throat, and almost throttling him.

"Hallo there! hallo!"

Mlle Michonneau came noiselessly in, bowed to the rest of the party, and took her place beside the three women without saying a word.

"That old bat always makes me shudder," said Bianchon in a low voice, indicating Mlle Michonneau to Vautrin. "I have studied Gall's system, and I am sure she has the bump of Judas."

"Then you have seen a case before?" said Vautrin.

"Who has not?" answered Bianchon. "Upon my word, that ghastly old maid looks just like one of the long worms that will gnaw a beam through, give them time enough."

"That is the way, young man," returned he of the forty years and the dyed whiskers:

> "The rose has lived the life of a rose—
> A morning's space."

"Aha! here is a magnificent *soupe-au-rama*," cried Poiret as Christophe came in bearing the soup with cautious heed.

"I beg your pardon, sir," said Mme Vauquer; "it is *soupe aux choux*."

All the young men roared with laughter.

"Had you there, Poiret!"

"Poir-r-r-rette! she had you there!"

"Score two points to Mamma Vauquer," said Vautrin.

"Did anyone notice the fog this morning?" asked the official.

"It was a frantic fog," said Bianchon, "a fog unparalleled, doleful, melancholy, sea-green, asthmatical—a Goriot of a fog!"

"A Goriama," said the art student, "because vou couldn't see a thing in it."

"Hey! Milord Gâôriotte, they air talking about yoo-o-ou!"

Old Goriot, seated at the lower end of the table, close to the door through which the servant entered, raised his face; he had smelt at the piece of bread that lay under his table napkin, an old habit acquired in sampling flour, to which he sometimes reverted unconsciously.

"Well," Mme Vauquer cried in sharp tones, that rang above the rattle of spoons and plates and the sound of other voices, "and is there anything the matter with the bread?"

"Nothing whatever, madame," he answered; "on the contrary, it is made of the best quality of flour from Étampes."

"How could you tell?" asked Eugène.

"By the color, by the flavor."

"You knew the flavor by the smell, I suppose," said Mme Vauquer. "You have grown so economical, you will find out how to live on the smell of cooking at last."

"Take out a patent for it then," cried the Museum employee; "you would make a handsome fortune."

"Never mind him," said the artist; "he does that sort of thing to delude us into thinking that he was a vermicelli-maker."

"Your nose is a corn-sampler, it appears?" inquired the official.

"Corn *what*?" asked Bianchon.

"Corn-el."

"Corn-et."

"Corn-elian."

"Corn-ice."

"Corn-ucopia."

"Corn-crake."

"Corn-cockle."

"Corn-orama."

The eight responses came like a volley of musketry from every part of the room, and the laughter that followed was the more uproarious because poor old Goriot stared at the others with a puzzled look, like a man trying to make out the meaning of words in a foreign language.

"Corn?" he said, turning to Vautrin, his next neighbor.

"Corn on your foot, old man!" said Vautrin, and he drove old Goriot's cap down over his eyes by a blow on the crown.

The poor old man thus suddenly attacked was for a moment too bewildered to do anything. Christophe carried off his plate, thinking that he had finished his soup, so that when Goriot had pushed back his cap from his eyes his spoon encountered the table. Everyone burst out laughing. "You are a disagreeable joker, sir," said the old man, "and if you take any futher liberties with me——"

"Well, what then, old boy?" Vautrin interrupted.

"Well, then, you shall pay dearly for it some day——"

"In the infernal regions, eh?" said the artist; "in the little dark corner where they put naughty boys."

"Well, mademoiselle," Vautrin said, turning to Victorine, "you are eating nothing. So papa was refractory, was he?"

"A monster!" said Mme Couture.

"Mademoiselle might make application for aliment pending her suit; she is not eating anything. Eh! eh! just see how old Goriot is staring at Mademoiselle Victorine!"

The old man had forgotten his dinner, he was so absorbed in gazing at the poor girl; the sorrow in her face was unmistakable —the slighted love of a child whose father would not recognize her.

"We are mistaken about old Goriot, my dear boy," said Eugène in a low voice. "He is not an idiot, nor wanting in energy. Try your phrenological system on him, and let me know what you think. I saw him crush a silver dish last night as if it had been made of wax. There seems to be something extraordinary going on in his mind just now, to judge by his face. His life is so mysterious that it might be worth studying. Oh! you may laugh, Bianchon; I am not joking."

"The man is a subject, is he?" said Bianchon. "All right! I will dissect him, if he will give me a chance."

"No; feel his bumps."

"Hm!—his stupidity might be contagious."

Chapter 6

THE NEXT day Rastignac dressed himself very elegantly, and about three o'clock in the afternoon went to call on Mme de Restaud. On the way he indulged in the wild intoxicating dreams which fill a young head so full of delicious excitement. Young men at his age take no account of obstacles or of dangers; they see success in every direction; imagination has free play, and turns their lives into a romance. They are saddened or discouraged by the collapse of one of the wild schemes that have no existence save in their heated fancy. If youth were not ignorant and timid, our social world would be impossible.

Eugène took great pains to keep his shoes spotless, but on his way through the streets he began to think about Mme de Restaud and what he should say to her. He equipped himself with wit, rehearsed repartee in the course of an imaginary conversation, and prepared certain neat speeches *à la* Talleyrand, conjuring up a series of small events which should prepare the way for the declaration on which he had based his future. During these musings, however, the law student was bespattered with mud, and by the time he reached the Palais Royal he was obliged to have his boots blacked and his trousers brushed.

"If I were rich," he said, as he changed the five-franc piece he had brought with him in case anything might happen, "I would take a cab, then I could think at my ease."

At last he reached the Rue du Helder, and asked for the Comtesse de Restaud. He bore the contemptuous glances of the servants, who had seen him cross the court on foot, with the cold fury of a man who knows that he will succeed some day. He understood the meaning of their glances at once, for he had felt his inferiority as soon as he entered the court, where a smart cab was waiting. All the delights of life in Paris seemed to be implied by this visible and manifest sign of luxury and extravagance. A fine horse, in magnificent harness, was pawing the ground, and all at once the law student felt out of humor with himself. Every compartment in his brain which he had thought to find so full of wit was bolted fast; he grew positively stupid. He sent up his name to the countess, and waited in the antechamber, standing on one foot before a window that looked out upon the court, mechanically leaning his elbow against the sash, and staring before him. The time seemed long; he would have left the house but for the southern tenacity of purpose which works wonders when it is single-minded.

"Madame is in her boudoir, and cannot see anyone at present, sir," said the servant. "She gave me no answer; but if you will go into the drawing-room, there is someone already there."

Rastignac was impressed with a sense of the formidable power of the lackey who can accuse or condemn his masters by a word. He coolly opened the door by which the man had just entered the antechamber, meaning, no doubt, to show these insolent flunkeys that he was familiar with the house, but he found that he had precipitated himself into a small room full of dressers, where lamps were standing, and hot-water pipes, on which towels were being dried; a dark passage and a back staircase lay beyond it. Stifled laughter from the antechamber added to his confusion.

"This way to the drawing-room, sir," said the servant, with the exaggerated respect which seemed to be one more jest at his expense.

Eugène turned so quickly that he stumbled against a bath. By good luck, he managed to keep his hat on his head, and saved it from immersion in the water; but just as he turned, a door opened at the further end of the dark passage, dimly lighted by a small lamp. Rastignac heard voices and the sound of a kiss. One of the speakers was Mme de Restaud, the other was old Goriot. Eugène followed the servant through the dining room into the drawing-room; he went to a window that looked out into the courtyard, and stood there for a while. He meant to know whether this Goriot was really the Goriot that he knew. His heart beat violently as he remembered Vautrin's hideous insinuations. A well-dressed young man suddenly emerged from the inner room almost as Eugène entered it, saying impatiently to the servant who stood at the door: "I am going, Maurice. Tell Madame la Comtesse that I waited more than half an hour for her."

Whereupon this insolent being, who, doubtless, had a right to be insolent, sang an Italian trill, and went towards the window where Eugène was standing, moved thereto quite as much by a desire to see the student's face as by a wish to look out into the courtyard.

"But Monsieur le Comte had better wait a moment longer, Madame is disengaged," said Maurice, as he returned to the antechamber.

Just at that moment old Goriot appeared close to the gate; he had emerged from a door at the foot of the back staircase. The worthy soul was preparing to open his umbrella regardless of the fact that the great gate had opened to admit a tilbury, in which a young man with a ribbon at his buttonhole was seated. Old Goriot had scarcely time to start back and save himself. The horse took fright at the umbrella, swerved, and dashed forward towards the flight of steps. The young man looked round in annoyance, saw old Goriot, and greeted him as he went out with constrained courtesy, such as people usually show to a money lender so long as they require his services, or the sort of respect they feel it necessary to show for someone whose reputation has been blown upon, so that they blush to acknowledge his acquaintance. Old Goriot gave him a little friendly nod and a good-natured smile. All this happened with lightning speed. Eugène was so deeply interested that he forgot

that he was not alone till he suddenly heard the voice of Mme
de Restaud.

"Oh, Maxime, were you going away?" she said reproachfully,
with a shade of pique in her manner. The countess had not seen
the incident or the entrance of the tilbury. Rastignac turned
abruptly and saw her standing before him, coquettishly dressed
in a loose white cashmere gown with knots of rose-colored
ribbon here and there; her hair was carelessly coiled about her
head, as is the wont of Parisian women in the morning; there
was a soft fragrance about her—doubtless she was fresh from a
bath; her graceful form seemed more flexible, her beauty more
luxuriant. Her eyes glistened. A young man can see everything
at a glance; he feels the radiant influence of woman as a plant
discerns and absorbs its nutriment from the air; he did not need
to touch her hands to feel their cool freshness. He saw faint
rose tints through the cashmere of the dressing-gown; it had
fallen slightly open, giving glimpses of a bare throat, on which
the student's eyes rested. The countess had no need of the ad-
ventitious aid of corsets; her belt defined the outlines of her
slender waist; her throat was a challenge to love; her feet, thrust
into slippers, were daintily small. As Maxime took her hand and
kissed it, Eugène became aware of Maxime's presence, and the
countess saw Eugène.

"Oh, is that you, Monsieur de Rastignac? I am very glad to see
you," she said, but there was something in her manner that a
shrewd observer would have taken as a hint to depart.

Maxime, as the Countess Anastasie had called the young man
with the haughty insolence of bearing, looked from Eugène to
the lady, and from the lady to Eugène; it was sufficiently evident that he wished to be rid of the latter. An exact and faithful
rendering of the glance might be given in the words: "Look
here, my dear; I hope you intend to send this little whippersnapper about his business."

The countess consulted the young man's face with an intent

submissiveness that betrays all the secrets of a woman's heart, and Rastignac all at once began to hate him violently. To begin with, the sight of the fair, carefully arranged curls on the other's comely head had convinced him that his own crop was hideous; Maxime's boots, moreover, were elegant and spotless, while his own, in spite of all his care, bore some traces of his recent walk; and, finally, Maxime's overcoat fitted the outline of his figure gracefully; he looked like a pretty woman, while Eugène was wearing a black coat at half-past two. The quick-witted son of the Charente felt the disadvantage at which he was placed beside this tall, slender dandy, with the clear gaze and the pale face, one of those men who would ruin orphans without scruple. Mme de Restaud fled into the next room without waiting for Eugène to speak, shaking out the skirts of her dressing-gown in her flight, so that she looked like a white butterfly. Maxime hurried after her. Eugène, in a fury, followed Maxime and the countess, and the three stood once more face to face by the hearth in the large drawing-room. The law student felt quite sure that the odious Maxime found him in the way, and even at the risk of displeasing Mme de Restaud, he meant to annoy the dandy. It had struck him all at once that he had seen the young man before at Mme de Beauséant's ball; he guessed the relation between Maxime and Mme de Restaud; and with the youthful audacity that commits prodigious blunders or scores great success, he said to himself, "This is my rival; I mean to cut him out."

Rash resolve! He did not know that M. le Comte Maxime de Trailles would wait till he was insulted, so as to fire first and kill his man. Eugène was a sportsman and a good shot, but he had not yet hit the bull's-eye twenty times out of twenty-two. The young count dropped into a low chair by the hearth, took up the tongs, and made up the fire so violently and so sulkily that Anastasie's fair face suddenly clouded over. She turned to Eugène with a cool, questioning glance that asked plainly, "Why do you not go?" a glance which well-bred people regard as a cue to make their exit.

Eugène assumed an amiable expression.

"Madame," he began, "I hastened to call upon you——"

He stopped short. The door opened, and the owner of the tilbury suddenly appeared. He had left his hat outside, and did not greet the countess; he looked meditatively at Rastignac, and held out his hand to Maxime with a cordial "Good morning," that astonished Eugène not a little. The young provincial did not understand the amenities of a triple alliance.

"Monsieur de Restaud," said the countess, introducing her husband to the law student.

Eugène bowed profoundly.

"This gentleman," she continued, presenting Eugène to her husband, "is Monsieur de Rastignac; he is related to Madame la Vicomtesse de Beauséant through the Marcillacs; I had the pleasure of meeting him at her last ball."

Related to Mme la Vicomtesse de Beauséant through the Marcillacs! These words, on which the countess threw ever so slight an emphasis, by reason of the pride that the mistress of a house takes in showing that she receives only people of distinction, produced a magical effect. The count's stiff manner relaxed at once as he returned the student's bow.

"Delighted to have an opportunity of making your acquaintance," he said.

Maxime de Trailles himself gave Eugène an uneasy glance, and suddenly dropped his insolent manner. The mighty name had all the power of a fairy's wand; those closed compartments in the southern brain flew open again; Rastignac's carefully drilled faculties returned. It was as if a sudden light had pierced the obscurity of this upper world of Paris, and he began to see, though everything was indistinct as yet. Mme Vauquer's lodginghouse and old Goriot were very far from his thoughts.

"I thought that the Marcillacs were extinct," the Comte de Restaud said, addressing Eugène.

"Yes, they are extinct," answered the law student. "My great-uncle, the Chevalier de Rastignac, married the heiress of the Marcillac family. They had only one daughter, who married the Maréchal de Clarimbault, Madame de Beauséant's grandfather on the mother's side. We are the younger branch of the family, and the younger branch is all the poorer because my great-uncle, the vice-admiral, lost all that he had in the king's service. The government during the Revolution refused to admit our claims when the Compagnie des Indes was liquidated."

"Was not your great-uncle in command of the *Vengeur* before 1789?"

"Yes."

"Then he would be acquainted with my grandfather, who commanded the *Warwick*."

Maxime looked at Mme de Restaud and shrugged his shoulders, as who should say, "If he is going to discuss naval affairs with that fellow, we shall not get a word together." Anastasie understood the glance that M. de Trailles gave her. With a woman's admirable tact, she began to smile, and said:

"Come with me, Maxime; I have something to say to you. We will leave you two gentlemen to sail in company on board the *Warwick* and the *Vengeur*."

She rose to her feet and signed to Maxime to follow her, mirth and mischief in her whole attitude, and the two went in the direction of the boudoir. The *morganatic* couple (to use a convenient German expression which has no exact equivalent) had reached the door, when the count interrupted himself in his talk with Eugène.

"Anastasie!" he cried pettishly, "just stay a moment, dear. You know very well that——"

"I am coming back in a minute," she interrupted; "I have a

commission for Maxime to execute, and I want to tell him about
it."

She came back almost immediately. She had noticed the in-
flection in her husband's voice, and knew that it would not be
safe to retire to the boudoir: like all women who are compelled
to study their husbands' characters in order to have their own
way, and whose business it is to know exactly how far they can
go without endangering a good understanding, she was very
careful to avoid petty collisions in domestic life. It was Eugène
who had brought about this untoward incident; so the countess
looked at Maxime and indicated the law student with an air of
exasperation. M. de Trailles addressed the count, the countess,
and Eugène with the pointed remark, "You are busy; I do not
want to interrupt you. Good day," and left the room.

"Just wait a moment, Maxime!" the count called after him.

"Come and dine with us," said the countess, leaving Eugène
and her husband together once more. She followed Maxime into
the little drawing-room, where they sat together sufficiently
long to feel sure that Rastignac had taken his leave.

The law student heard their laughter, and their voices, and
the pauses in their talk; he grew malicious, exerted his conversational powers for M. de Restaud, flattered him, and drew him
into discussions, to the end that he might see the countess again
and discover the nature of her relations with old Goriot. This
countess with a husband and a lover, for Maxime clearly was
her lover, was a mystery. What was the secret tie that bound
her to the old tradesman? This mystery he meant to penetrate,
hoping by its means to gain some power over this fair typical
Parisian.

"Anastasie!" the count called again to his wife.

"Poor Maxime!" she said, addressing the young man. "Come,
we must resign ourselves. This evening——"

"I hope, Nasie," he said in her ear, "that you will give orders
not to admit that youngster, whose eyes light up like live coals

when he looks at you. He will make you a declaration, and compromise you, and then you will compel me to kill him."

"Are you mad, Maxime?" she said. "A young lad of a student is, on the contrary, a capital lightning-conductor; isn't that so? Of course, I mean to make Restaud furiously jealous of him."

Maxime burst out laughing, and went out, followed by the countess, who stood at the window to watch him into his carriage; he shook his whip, and made his horse prance. She only returned when the great gate had been closed after him.

"What do you think, dear?" cried the count, her husband, "this gentleman's family estate is not far from Verteuil, on the Charente; his great-uncle and my grandfather were acquainted."

"Delighted to find that we have acquaintances in common," said the countess, with a preoccupied manner.

"More than you think," said Eugène, in a low voice.

"What do you mean?" she asked quickly.

"Why, only just now," said the student, "I saw a gentleman go out at the gate, old Goriot, my next-door neighbor in the house where I am lodging."

At the sound of this name, and the prefix that embellished it, the count, who was stirring the fire, let the tongs fall as though they had burned his fingers, and rose to his feet.

"Sir," he cried, "you might have called him 'Monsieur Goriot'!"

The countess turned pale at first at the sight of her husband's vexation, then she reddened; clearly she was embarrassed, her answer was made in a tone that she tried to make natural, and with an air of assumed carelessness:

"You could not know anyone who is dearer to us both . . ."

She broke off, glanced at the piano as if some fancy had crossed her mind, and asked, "Are you fond of music, Monsieur de Rastignac?"

"Exceedingly," answered Eugène, flushing, and disconcerted

by a dim suspicion that he had somehow been guilty of a clumsy piece of folly.

"Do you sing?" she cried, going to the piano, and, sitting down before it, she swept her fingers over the keyboard from end to end. R-r-r-r-ah!

"No, madame."

The Comte de Restaud walked to and fro.

"That is a pity; you are without one great means of success. *Ca-ro, ca-a-ro, ca-a-a-ro, non du-bi-ta-re*," sang the countess.

Eugène had a second time waved a magic wand when he uttered Goriot's name, but the effect seemed to be entirely opposite to that produced by the formula "related to Mme de Beauséant." His position was not unlike that of some visitor permitted as a favor to inspect a private collection of curiosities, when by inadvertence he comes into collision with a glass case full of sculptured figures, and three or four heads, imperfectly secured, fall at the shock. He wished the earth would open and swallow him. Mme de Restaud's expression was reserved and chilly, her eyes had grown indifferent, and sedulously avoided meeting those of the unlucky student of law.

"Madame," he said, "you wish to talk with Monsieur de Restaud; permit me to wish you good day——"

The countess interrupted him by a gesture, saying hastily, "Whenever you come to see us, both Monsieur de Restaud and I shall be delighted to see you."

Eugène made a profound bow and took his leave, followed by M. de Restaud, who insisted, in spite of his remonstrances, on accompanying him into the hall.

"Neither your mistress nor I will be at home to that gentleman when he calls," the count said to Maurice.

As Eugène set foot on the steps, he saw that it was raining.

"Well," said he to himself, "somehow I have just made a mess of it, I do not know how. And now I am going to spoil my hat and coat into the bargain. I ought to have stayed at home and grubbed away at law, and never tried to be anything but a boorish country magistrate. How can I go into society, when to manage properly you want a lot of cabs, varnished boots, gold watch-chains, and all sorts of things? In the morning you have to wear white doeskin gloves that cost six francs, and primrose kid gloves for evening. A fig for that old humbug of a Goriot!"

When he reached the street door, the driver of a hackney coach, who had probably just deposited a wedding party at their door, and asked nothing better than a chance of making a little money for himself without his employer's knowledge, saw that Eugène had no umbrella, remarked his black coat, white waistcoat, yellow gloves, and varnished boots, and stopped and looked at him inquiringly. Eugène, in the blind desperation that drives a young man to plunge deeper and deeper into an abyss, as if he might hope to find a fortunate issue in its lowest depths, nodded in reply to the driver's signal, and stepped into the cab; a few stray petals of orange blossom and scraps of wire bore witness to its recent occupation by a wedding party.

"Where am I to drive, sir?" demanded the man, who by this time had taken off his white gloves.

"Confound it!" Eugène said to himself, "I am in for it now, and at least I will not spend cab-hire for nothing! Drive to the Hôtel Beauséant," he said aloud.

"Which?" asked the man, a portentous word that reduced Eugène to confusion. This young man of fashion, *species incerta*, did not know that there were two Hôtels Beauséant; he was not aware how rich he was in relations who did not care about him.

"The Vicomte de Beauséant, Rue——"

"De Grenelle," interrupted the driver, with a jerk of his head. "You see, there are the hôtels of the Marquis and Comte de Beauséant in the Rue Saint-Dominique," he added, drawing up the step.

"I am aware of that," said Eugène, severely. "Everybody is

laughing at me today, it seems!" he thought, as he deposited his hat on the opposite seat. "This escapade will cost me a king's ransom, but, at any rate, I shall call on my so-called cousin in a thoroughly aristocratic fashion. Goriot has cost me ten francs already, the old scoundrel! My word! I'll tell Madame de Beauséant about my adventure; perhaps it may amuse her. Doubtless she will know the secret of the criminal relation between that handsome woman and the old rat without a tail. It would be better to find favor in my cousin's eyes than to come in contact with that shameless woman, who seems to me to have very expensive tastes. Surely the beautiful vicomtesse's personal interest would turn the scale for me, when the mere mention of her name produces such an effect. Aim high. If you set yourself to carry the heights of heaven, you must face God."

The innumerable thoughts that surged through his brain might be summed up in these phrases. He grew calmer, and recovered something of his assurance as he watched the falling rain. He told himself that though he was about to squander two of the precious five-franc pieces that remained to him, the money was well laid out in preserving his coat, boots, and hat; and his cabman's cry of "Gate, if you please," almost put him in spirits. A Swiss, in scarlet and gold, appeared, the great door groaned on its hinges, and Rastignac, with sweet satisfaction, beheld his equipage pass under the archway and stop before the flight of steps beneath the awning. The driver, in a blue-and-red greatcoat, dismounted and let down the step. As Eugène stepped out of the cab, he heard smothered laughter from the peristyle. Three or four lackeys were making merry over the festal appearance of the vehicle. In another moment the law student was enlightened as to the cause of their hilarity; he felt the full force of the contrast between his equipage and one of the smartest broughams in Paris. A coachman, with powdered hair, seemed to find it difficult to hold a pair of spirited horses, who stood chafing the bit. In Mme de Restaud's courtyard, in the Chaussée d'Antin, he had seen the neat turn-out of a young man of six-and-twenty; in the Faubourg Saint-Germain he found the luxurious equipage of a man of rank; thirty thousand francs would not have purchased it.

"Who can be here?" said Eugène to himself. He began to understand, though somewhat tardily, that he must not expect to find many women in Paris who were not already appropriated, and that the capture of one of these queens would be likely to cost more money than blood. "Confound it all! I expect my cousin also has her Maxime."

He went up the steps, feeling that he was a blighted being. The glass door was opened for him; the servants were as solemn as jackasses under the currycomb. So far, Eugène had only been in the ballroom on the ground floor of the Hôtel Beauséant. The fête had followed so closely on the invitation that he had not had time to call on his cousin, and had therefore never seen Mme de Beauséant's apartments. He was about to behold for the first time a great lady among the wonderful and elegant surroundings that reveal her character and reflect her daily life. He was the more curious, because Mme de Restaud's drawing-room had provided him with a standard of comparison.

At half-past four the Vicomtesse de Beauséant was visible. Five minutes earlier she would not have received her cousin, but Eugène knew nothing of the recognized routine of various houses in Paris. He was conducted up the wide, white-painted, crimson-carpeted staircase, between the gilded balusters and masses of flowering plants, to Mme de Beauséant's apartments. He did not know the rumor current about Mme de Beauséant, was not aware that her affairs were being discussed in whispers every evening in the salons of Paris.

Chapter 7

FOR THREE years past she had been on terms of intimate friendship with a wealthy and distinguished Portuguese noble, the Marquis d'Ajuda-Pinto. It was one of those innocent *liaisons* which possess so much charm for the two thus attached to each other that they find the presence of a third person intolerable. The Vicomte de Beauséant, therefore, had himself set an example to the rest of the world by respecting the alliance with as good a grace as might be. Anyone who came to call on the vicomtesse in the early days of this friendship was sure to find the Marquis d'Ajuda-Pinto there. As, under the circumstances, Mme de Beauséant could not very well shut her door against these visitors, she gave them such a cold reception, and showed so much interest in the study of the ceiling, that they could not fail to understand how much they bored her; and when it became known in Paris that Mme de Beauséant was bored by callers between two and four o'clock, she was left in perfect solitude during that interval. She went to the Bouffons or to the opera with M. de Beauséant and M. d'Ajuda-Pinto; and M. de Beauséant, like a well-bred man of the world, always left his wife and the Portuguese as soon as he had installed them. But M. d'Ajuda-Pinto must marry, and a Mlle de Rochefide was the young lady. In the whole fashionable world there was but one person who as yet knew nothing of the arrangement, and that was Mme de Beauséant. Some of her friends had hinted at the possibility, and she had laughed at them, believing that envy had prompted those ladies to try to make mischief. And now, though the banns were about to be published, and although the handsome Portuguese had come that day to break the news to the vicomtesse, he had not found courage as yet to say one word about his treachery. How was it? Nothing is more difficult than announcing a decision of this kind. There are men who feel more at their ease when they stand up before another man who threatens their lives with sword or pistol than in the presence of a woman who, after two hours of lamentations and reproaches, falls into a dead swoon and requires smelling salts. At this moment, therefore, M. d'Ajuda-Pinto was on thorns, and anxious to take his leave. He told himself that in some way or other the news would reach Mme de Beauséant; he would write, it would be much better to do it by letter, and not to utter the words that should stab her to the heart.

So when the servant announced M. Eugène de Rastignac, the Marquis d'Ajuda-Pinto trembled with joy. To be sure, a loving woman shows even more ingenuity in inventing doubts of her lover than in varying the monotony of his happiness; and when she is about to be forsaken, she instinctively interprets every gesture as rapidly as Vergil's courser detected the presence of his companion by sniffing the breeze. It was impossible, therefore, that Mme de Beauséant should not detect that involuntary thrill of satisfaction. Slight though it was, it was appalling in its artlessness.

Eugène had yet to learn that no one in Paris should present himself in any house without first making himself acquainted with the whole history of its owner, and of its owner's wife and family, so that he may avoid making any of the terrible blunders which in Poland draw forth the picturesque exclamation, "Harness five bullocks to your cart!"—probably because you will need them all to pull you out of the quagmire into which a false step has plunged you. If, up to now, our language has no name for these conversational disasters, it is probably because they are believed to be impossible, the publicity given in Paris to every scandal is so prodigious. After the awkward incident at Mme de Restaud's, no one but Eugène could have reappeared in his character of bullock-driver in Mme de Beauséant's drawing-room. But if Mme de Restaud and M. de Trailles had found him horribly in the way, M. d'Ajuda hailed his coming with relief.

"Good-bye," said the Portuguese, hurrying to the door, as Eugène made his entrance into a dainty little pink-and-gray drawing-room, where luxury seemed nothing more than good taste.

"Until this evening," said Mme de Beauséant, turning her head to give the Marquis a glance. "We are going to the Bouffons, are we not?"

"I cannot go," he said, with his fingers on the door handle.

Mme de Beauséant rose and beckoned to him to return. She did not pay the slightest attention to Eugène, who stood there dazzled by the sparkling marvels around him; he began to think that this was some story out of the *Arabian Nights* made real, and did not know where to hide himself, when the woman before him seemed to be unconscious of his existence. The vicomtesse had raised the forefinger of her right hand, and gracefully signed to the marquis to seat himself beside her. The marquis felt the imperious sway of passion in her gesture; he came back towards her. Eugène watched him, not without a feeling of envy.

"That is the owner of the brougham!" he said to himself. "But is it necessary to have a pair of spirited horses, servants in livery, and torrents of gold to draw a glance from a woman here in Paris?"

The demon of luxury gnawed at his heart, greed burned in his veins, his throat was parched with the thirst of gold. He had a hundred and thirty francs every quarter. His father, mother, brothers, sisters, and aunt did not spend two hundred francs a month among them. This swift comparison between his present condition and the aims he had in view helped to benumb his faculties.

"Why not?" the vicomtesse was saying, as she smiled at the Portuguese. "Why cannot you come to the Italiens?"

"Business! I am to dine with the English Ambassador."

"But you can leave early."

When a man once enters on a course of deception, he is compelled to add lie to lie. M. d'Ajuda therefore said, smiling, "Do you insist?"

"Yes, certainly."

"That was what I wanted to have you say to me," he answered, dissembling his feelings in a glance which would have reassured any other woman.

He took the vicomtesse's hand, kissed it, and went.

Eugène ran his fingers through his hair, and constrained himself to bow. He thought that now Mme de Beauséant would give him her attention; but suddenly she sprang forward, rushed to a window in the gallery, and watched M. d'Ajuda step into his carriage; she listened to the order that he gave, and heard the Swiss repeat it to the coachman:

"To Monsieur de Rochefide's house."

Those words, and the way in which M. d'Ajuda flung himself back in the carriage, were like a lightning flash and a thunderbolt for her; she walked back again with a deadly fear gnawing at her heart. The most terrible catastrophes only happen among the heights. The vicomtesse went to her own room, sat down at a table, and took up a sheet of dainty notepaper.

"When, instead of dining with the English Ambassador," she wrote, "you go to the Rochefides, you owe me an explanation, which I am waiting to hear."

She retraced several of the letters, for her hand was trembling so that they were indistinct; then she signed the note with an initial C for "Claire de Bourgogne," and rang the bell.

"Jacques," she said to the servant, who appeared immediately, "take this note to Monsieur de Rochefide's house at half-past seven, and ask for the Marquis d'Ajuda. If Monsieur d'Ajuda is there, leave the note without waiting for an answer; if he is not there, bring the note back to me."

"Madame la Vicomtesse, there is a visitor in the drawing-room."

"Ah! yes, of course," she said, opening the door.

Eugène was beginning to feel very uncomfortable, but at last the vicomtesse appeared; she spoke to him, and the tremulous tones of her voice vibrated through his heart.

"Pardon me, monsieur," she said; "I had a letter to write. Now I am quite at liberty."

She scarcely knew what she was saying, for even as she spoke she thought, "Ah! he must intend to marry Mademoiselle de Rochefide. But is he still free? This evening the marriage shall be broken off, or else . . . But before tomorrow I shall know."

"Cousin . . ." the student began.

"Eh?" said the countess, with an insolent glance that sent a cold shudder through Eugène. He understood what that "Eh?" meant. He had learned a great deal in three hours, and his wits were on the alert. He reddened.

"Madame . . ." He hesitated a moment, and then went on. "Pardon me; I am in such need of protection that the merest scrap of relationship would not be wasted on me."

Mme de Beauséant smiled, but there was sadness in her smile; even now she felt forebodings of the coming pain, the air she breathed was heavy with the storm that was about to burst.

"If you knew how my family are situated," he went on, "you would love to play the part of a beneficent fairy godmother who graciously clears the obstacles from the path of her protégé."

"Well, cousin," she said, laughing, "and how can I be of service to you?"

"How can I tell you? I am distantly related to you, and this obscure and remote relationship is even now a perfect godsend to me. You have confused my ideas; I cannot remember the things that I meant to say to you. I know no one else here in Paris.

. . . Ah! if I could only ask you to advise me, ask you to look upon me as a poor child who would cling to the hem of your dress, who would lay down his life for you."

"Would you kill a man for me?"

"Two," said Eugène.

"Foolish boy! Yes, you are a boy," she said, keeping back the tears that came to her eyes; "you would love sincerely."

"Oh!" he cried, flinging up his head.

The audacity of the student's answer interested the vicomtesse in him. The southern brain was beginning to scheme for the first time. Between Mme de Restaud's blue boudoir and Mme de Beauséant's rose-colored drawing-room he had made a three years' advance in a kind of law which is not a recognized study in Paris, although it is a sort of higher jurisprudence, and, when well understood, is a high road to success of every kind.

"Ah, this is what I meant to say!" said Eugène. "I met Madame de Restaud at your ball, and this morning I went to see her."

"You must have been very much in the way," said Mme de Beauséant, smiling as she spoke.

"Yes, indeed. I am a novice, and my blunders will set everyone against me, if you do not give me your counsel. I believe that in Paris it is very difficult to meet with a young, beautiful, and wealthy woman of fashion who would be willing to teach me what you women can explain so well—life. I shall find a Monsieur de Trailles everywhere. So I have come to you to ask you to give me a key to a puzzle, to entreat you to tell me what sort of blunder I made this morning. I mentioned an old man——"

"Madame la Duchesse de Langeais," Jacques cut the student short. Eugène gave expression to his intense annoyance by a gesture.

"If you mean to succeed," said the vicomtesse in a low voice, "in the first place, you must not be so demonstrative."

"Ah! good morning, dear," she continued, and rising and crossing the room, she grasped the duchess' hands as affectionately as if they had been sisters; the duchess responded in the prettiest and most gracious way.

"Two intimate friends!" said Rastignac to himself. "Henceforward I shall have two protectresses; those two women are great friends, no doubt, and this newcomer will doubtless interest herself in her friend's cousin."

"To what happy inspiration do I owe this piece of good fortune, dear Antoinette?" asked Mme de Beauséant.

"Well, I saw Monsieur d'Ajuda-Pinto at Monsieur de Rochefide's door, so I thought that if I came I should find you alone."

Mme de Beauséant's mouth did not tighten, her color did not rise, her expression did not alter; rather, her brow seemed to clear as the duchess uttered those deadly words.

"If I had known that you were engaged—" the speaker added, glancing at Eugène.

"This gentleman is Monsieur Eugène de Rastignac, one of my cousins," said the vicomtesse. "Have you any news of General de Montriveau?" she continued. "Sérizy told me yesterday that he never goes anywhere now; has he been to see you today?"

It was believed that the duchess was desperately in love with M. de Montriveau, and that he was a faithless lover; she felt the intended stab, and her face flushed as she answered:

"He was at the Élysée yesterday."

"In attendance?"

"Claire," returned the duchess, and hatred overflowed in the glances she threw at Mme de Beauséant, "of course you know that d'Ajuda-Pinto is going to marry Mademoiselle de Rochefide; the banns will be published tomorrow."

This thrust was too cruel. The vicomtesse's face grew white, but she answered, laughing, "One of those rumors that fools amuse themselves with. What should induce Monsieur d'Ajuda

to take one of the noblest names in Portugal to the Rochefides?
The Rochefides were only ennobled yesterday."

"But Berthe will have two hundred thousand livres a year,
they say."

"Monsieur d'Ajuda is too wealthy to marry for money."

"But, my dear, Mademoiselle de Rochefide is a charming girl."

"Indeed?"

"And, as a matter of fact, he is dining with them today; the
thing is settled. I am astonished that you don't know about it."

Mme de Beauséant turned to Rastignac. "What was the
blunder that you made, monsieur?" she asked. "The poor boy
is only just launched into the world, Antoinette, so that he
understands nothing of all this that we are speaking of. Be merci-
ful to him, and let us finish our talk tomorrow. Everything will
be announced tomorrow, you know, and your kind informal
communication can be accompanied by official confirmation."

The duchess gave Eugène one of those insolent glances that
measure a man from head to foot and leave him crushed and
annihilated.

"Madame, I have unwittingly plunged a dagger into Madame
de Restaud's heart; unwittingly—that is the offense," said the law
student, whose keen brain had served him sufficiently well, for
he had detected the biting epigrams that lurked beneath this
friendly talk. "You continue to receive, possibly you fear, those
who know the amount of pain that they deliberately inflict;
but a clumsy blunderer who has no idea how deeply he wounds
is looked upon as a fool who does not know how to make use
of his opportunities, and everyone despises him."

Mme de Beauséant gave the student a glance, one of those
glances in which a great soul can mingle dignity and gratitude.
It was like balm to the student, who was still smarting under
the duchess' insolent scrutiny; she had looked at him as an
auctioneer might look at some article to appraise its value.

"Imagine, too, that I had just made some progress with the

Comte de Restaud; for I should tell you, madame," he went on, turning to the duchess with a mixture of humility and malice in his manner, "that as yet I am only a poor devil of a student, very much alone in the world, and very poor——"

"You should not tell us that, Monsieur de Rastignac. We women never value anything that others do not value."

"Bah!" said Eugène. "I am only twenty-two, and I must make up my mind to the drawbacks of my time of life. Besides, I am confessing my sins, and it would be impossible to kneel in a more charming confessional; you commit your sins in one drawing-room, and receive absolution for them in another."

The duchess' expression grew colder; she did not like the flippant tone of these remarks, and showed that she considered them to be in bad taste by turning to the vicomtesse with: "This gentleman has only just come——"

Mme de Beauséant began to laugh outright, both at her cousin and at the duchess.

"He has only just come to Paris, dear, and is in search of someone who will give him lessons in good taste."

"Madame la duchesse," said Eugène, "is it not natural to wish to be initiated into the mysteries which charm us?" ("Come, now," he said to himself, "I'm talking just like a hair-dresser.")

"But Madame de Restaud is herself, I believe, Monsieur de Trailles' pupil," said the duchess.

"Of that I had no idea, madame," answered the law student, "so rashly I came between them. In fact, I got on very well with the lady's husband, and his wife tolerated me for a time until I took it into my head to tell them that I knew someone of whom I had just caught a glimpse as he went out by a back staircase, a man who had given the countess a kiss at the end of a passage."

"Who was it?" both women asked together.

"An old man who lives at the rate of two louis a month in the Faubourg Saint-Marceau. where I, a poor student, live myself. He is a miserable old fellow; everybody laughs at him—we all call him 'Father Goriot.' "

"Why, child that you are," cried the vicomtesse, "Madame de Restaud was a Mademoiselle Goriot!"

"The daughter of a vermicelli manufacturer," the duchess added; "and when the little creature went to court, the daughter of a pastry-cook was presented on the same day. Do you remember, Claire? The king began to laugh, and made some joke in Latin about flour. People—what was it?—people——"

"*Ejusdem farinae*," said Eugène.

"Yes, that was it," said the duchess.

"Oh, is that her father?" the law student continued, aghast.

"Yes, certainly. The old man had two daughters. He dotes on them, so to speak, though they have both cast him off."

"Didn't the second daughter marry a banker with a German name?" the vicomtesse asked, turning to Mme de Langeais, "a Baron de Nucingen? And her name is Delphine, is it not? Isn't she a fair-haired woman who has a side-box at the opera? She comes sometimes to the Bouffons, and laughs loudly to attract attention."

The duchess smiled, and said:

"I wonder at you, dear. Why do you take so much interest in people of that kind? One must have been as madly in love as Restaud was, to be infatuated with Mademoiselle Anastasie and her flour sacks. Oh, he will not find her a good bargain! She is in Monsieur de Trailles' hands, and he will ruin her."

"And they have cast off their father!" Eugène repeated.

"Oh! well, yes, their father, the father, a father," replied the vicomtesse, "a kind father who gave them each five or six hundred thousand francs, it is said, to secure their happiness by marrying them well; while he only kept eight or ten thousand francs a year for himself, thinking that his daughters would always be his daughters, thinking that in them he would live his life twice over again, that in their houses he should find two homes, where he would be loved and looked up to, and made much of. And in two years' time both his sons-in-law had turned him out of their houses as if he were one of the lowest outcasts."

Tears came into Eugène's eyes. He was still under the spell of youthful beliefs, he had but just left home, pure and sacred feelings had been stirred within him, and this was his first day on the battlefield of civilization in Paris. Genuine feeling is so infectious that for a moment the three looked at each other in silence.

"Good heavens!" said Mme de Langeais. "Yes, it seems horrible, and yet we see such things every day. Is there not a reason for it? Tell me, dear, have you ever really thought what a son-in-law is? A son-in-law is the man for whom we bring up, you and I, a dear little one, bound to us very closely in innumerable ways; for seventeen years she will be the joy of her family, its 'white soul,' as Lamartine says, and suddenly she may become its scourge. When *he* comes and takes her from us, his love from the very beginning is like an axe laid to the root of all the old affection in our darling's heart, and all the ties that bound her to her family are severed. Only yesterday our little daughter thought of no one but her mother and father, as we had no thought that was not for her; by tomorrow she will have become a hostile stranger. The tragedy is going on under our eyes all the time. On the one hand you see a father who has sacrificed himself to his son, and his daughter-in-law shows him the last degree of insolence. On the other hand, it is the son-in-law who turns his wife's mother out of the house. I sometimes hear it said that there is nothing dramatic about society in these days; but the Drama of the Son-in-law is appalling, to say nothing of our marriages, which have come to be very poor farces. I can explain how it all came about in the old vermicelli-maker's case. I think I recollect that Foriot——"

"Goriot, madame."

"Yes, that Moriot was once president of his section during the

Revolution. He was in the secret of the famous scarcity of grain, and laid the foundation of his fortune in those days by selling flour for ten times its cost. He had as much flour as he wanted. My grandmother's steward sold him immense quantities. No doubt Noriot shared the profits with the Committee of Public Safety, as that sort of person always did. I recollect the steward telling my grandmother that she might live at Grandvilliers in complete security, because her corn was as good as a certificate of citizenship. Well, then, this Loriot, who sold corn to those butchers, has never had but one passion, they say—he idolizes his daughters. He settled one of them under Restaud's roof, and grafted the other into the Nucingen family tree, the Baron de Nucingen being a rich banker who had turned royalist. You can quite understand that so long as Bonaparte was emperor, the two sons-in-law could manage to put up with the old Jacobin of Ninety-three; but after the restoration of the Bourbons, Restaud felt bored by the old man's society, and the banker was still more tired of it. His daughters were still fond of him; they wanted 'to keep the goat and the cabbage,' so they used to see the Joriot whenever there was no one there, under pretense of affection. 'Come today, papa, we shall have you all to ourselves, and that will be much nicer!' and all that sort of thing. As for me, my dear, I believe that love has second sight: poor Ninety-three, his heart must have bled! He saw that his daughters were ashamed of him, that if they loved their husbands his visits must make mischief. So he sacrificed himself. He made the sacrifice because he was a father; he went into voluntary exile. His daughters were satisfied, so he thought that he had done the best thing he could; but it was a family crime, and father and daughters were accomplices. You see this sort of thing everywhere. What could this old Doriot have been but a splash of mud in his daughters' drawing-rooms? He would only have been in the way, and bored other people, besides being bored himself. And this that happened between father and daughters may happen to the prettiest

woman in Paris and the man she loves the best; if her love grows
tiresome, he will go; he will descend to the basest trickery to
leave her. It is the same with all love and friendship. Our heart
is a treasury; if you pour out all its wealth at once, you are bank-
rupt. We think just as little of those who spend all their love as
we do of those prodigals who throw away every cent they have.
Their father had given them all he had. For twenty years he had
given his whole heart to them; then, one day, he gave them all
his fortune too. The lemon was squeezed; the girls left the rind
in the gutter."

"The world is very base," said the vicomtesse, plucking at the
threads of her shawl. She did not raise her eyes as she spoke; the
words that Mme de Langeais had meant for her in the course
of the story had cut her to the quick.

"Base? Oh, no," answered the duchess, "the world goes its
own way, that is all. If I speak in this way, it is only to show that
I am not duped by it. I think as you do," she said, pressing the
vicomtesse's hand. "The world is a slough; let us try to live on
the heights above it."

She rose to her feet and kissed Mme de Beauséant on the forehead as she said: "You look very charming today, dear. I have
never seen such a lovely color in your cheeks before."

Then she went out with a slight inclination of the head to
the student.

"Old Goriot is sublime!" said Eugène to himself, as he remembered how he had watched his neighbor work the silver vessel
into a shapeless mass during the night.

Mme de Beauséant did not hear him; she was absorbed in her
own thoughts. For several minutes the silence remained un-
broken till the youth became almost paralyzed with embarrassment, and was equally afraid to go or stay or speak a word.

"The world is basely ungrateful and ill-natured," said the vicomtesse at last. "No sooner does trouble befall you than a friend
is ready to bring the tidings and to probe your heart with the

point of a dagger while calling on you to admire the handle. Epigrams and sarcasms so soon! Ah! I will defend myself!"

She raised her head like the great lady that she was, and lightning flashed from her proud eyes.

"Ah!" she said, as she saw Eugène, "are you there?"

"Still here," he said humbly.

"Well, then, Monsieur de Rastignac, learn to deal with the world as it deserves. You are determined to succeed? I will help you. You shall sound the depths of corruption in woman; you shall measure the extent of man's pitiful vanity. Deeply as I am versed in such learning, there were pages in the book of life that I had not read. Now I know all. The more cold-blooded your calculations, the further you will go. Strike ruthlessly; you will be feared. Men and women for you must be nothing more than post-horses; take a fresh relay, and leave the last to drop by the roadside; in this way you will reach the goal of your ambition. You will be nothing here, you see, unless a woman interests herself in you; and she must be young and wealthy, and a woman of the world. Yet, if you have a heart, lock it carefully away like a treasure; do not let anyone suspect it, or you will be lost; you would cease to be the executioner, you would take the victim's place. And if ever you should love, never let your secret escape you! trust no one until you are very sure of the friend to whom you open your heart. Learn to mistrust everyone; take every precaution for the sake of the love which does not exist as yet. Listen, Miguel"—the name slipped from her so naturally that she did not notice her mistake—"there is something still more appalling than the ingratitude of those daughters who have cast off their old father and wish that he were dead, and that is a rivalry between the two sisters. Restaud comes of a good family. His wife has been received into their circle and has been presented at court; and her sister, her wealthy sister, Delphine de Nucingen, the wife of a great capitalist, is consumed with envy, and

ready to die of spleen. There is a gulf set between the sisters—
indeed, they are sisters no longer—the two women who refuse
to acknowledge their father do not acknowledge each other. So
Madame de Nucingen would lap all the mud that lies between
the Rue Saint-Lazare and the Rue de Grenelle to gain admittance
to my salon. She fancied that she should gain her end through
de Marsay; she has made herself de Marsay's slave, and she bores
him. De Marsay cares very little about her. If you will introduce
her to me, you will be her darling, her Benjamin; she will idolize
you. If, after that, you can love her, do so; if not, make her useful. I will ask her to come once or twice to one of my great
crushes, but I will never receive her here in the morning. I will
bow to her when I see her, and that will be quite sufficient. You
have shut the Comtesse de Restaud's door against you by mentioning old Goriot's name. Yes, my good friend, you may call
at her house twenty times, and every time out of the twenty you
will find that she is not at home. The servants have their orders,
and will not admit you. Very well, then, now let old Goriot gain
the right of entry into her sister's house for you. The beautiful
Madame de Nucingen will give the signal for a battle. As soon
as she singles you out, other women will begin to lose their heads
about you, and her enemies and rivals and intimate friends will
all try to take you from her. There are women who will fall in
love with a man because another woman has chosen him; like
the middle-class housewives, poor things, who copy our milli-
nery and hope thereby to acquire our manners. You will have a
success, and in Paris success is everything; it is the key of power.
If the women credit you with wit and talent, the men will follow
suit so long as you do not undeceive them yourself. There will
be nothing you may not aspire to; you will go everywhere, and
you will find out what the world is—an assemblage of fools and
knaves. But you must be neither the one nor the other. I am
giving you my name like Ariadne's clue of thread to take with
you into this labyrinth; make no unworthy use of it," she said,

with a queenly glance; "give it back to me unsullied. And now, go; leave me. We women also have our battles to fight."

"And if you should ever need someone who would gladly set a match to a mine for you——"

"Well?" she asked.

He tapped his heart, smiled in answer to his cousin's smile, and went out.

It was five o'clock, and Eugène was hungry. He was afraid he should not be in time for dinner, a misgiving which made him feel that it was pleasant to be borne so quickly across Paris. This sensation of physical comfort left his mind free to grapple with the thoughts that assailed him. A mortification usually sends a young man of his age into a furious rage; he shakes his fists at society, and vows vengeance when his belief in himself is shaken. Just then Rastignac was overwhelmed by the words, "You have shut the countess' door against you."

"I shall call!" he said to himself, "and if Mme de Beauséant is right, if I never find her at home—I . . . well, Mme de Restaud shall meet me in every salon in Paris. I shall learn to fence, and have some pistol practice, and kill that Maxime of hers!"

"And what about money?" cried an inward monitor. "Where is that to come from?" And all at once the wealth displayed in the Comtesse de Restaud's drawing-room rose before his eyes. That was the luxury which Goriot's daughter had loved too well; the gilding, the ostentatious splendor, the unintelligent luxury of the parvenu, the riotous extravagance of a courtesan. Then the attractive vision suddenly went under an eclipse as he remembered the stately grandeur of the Hôtel de Beauséant. As his fancy wandered among these lofty regions in the great world of Paris, innumerable dark thoughts gathered in his heart; his ideas widened, and his conscience grew more elastic. He saw the world as it is; saw how the rich lived beyond the jurisdiction of law and public opinion, and found in success the *ultima ratio mundi*.

"Vautrin is right, success is virtue!" he said to himself.

Arrived in the Rue Neuve-Sainte-Geneviève, he rushed up to his room for ten francs wherewith to satisfy the demands of the cabman, and went in to dinner. He glanced round the squalid room, saw the eighteen poverty-stricken creatures about to feed like cattle in their stalls, and the sight filled him with loathing. The transition was too sudden, and the contrast was so violent that it could not but act as a powerful stimulant; his ambition developed and grew beyond all bounds. On the one hand, he beheld a vision of social life in its most charming and refined forms, of quick-pulsed youth, of fair, impassioned faces invested with all the charm of poetry, framed in a marvelous setting of luxury or art; and, on the other hand, he saw a somber picture of degradation, in which passion was extinct and nothing was left but the cords and pulleys and bare mechanism. Mme de Beau-séant's counsels, the words uttered in anger by the forsaken lady, her petulant offer, came to his mind, and poverty was a ready expositor. Rastignac determined to open two parallel trenches, so as to ensure success; he would be a learned doctor of law and a man of fashion. Clearly he was still a child! Those two lines are asymptotes, and will never meet.

"You are very dull, my lord marquis," said Vautrin, with one of the shrewd glances that seem to read the innermost secrets of another mind.

"I am not in the humor to stand jokes from people who call me 'my lord marquis,'" answered Eugène. "A marquis here in Paris, if he is not the veriest sham, ought to have a hundred thousand livres a year at least; and a lodger in the Maison Vauquer is not exactly fortune's favorite."

Vautrin's glance at Rastignac was half-paternal, half-contemp-tuous. "Puppy!" it seemed to say; "I should make one mouthful of him!" Then he answered:

"You are in a bad humor; perhaps your visit to the beautiful Comtesse de Restaud was not a success."

"She has shut her door against me because I told her that her father dined at our table," cried Rastignac.

Glances were exchanged all round the room; old Goriot looked down, and turned aside to wipe his eye.

"You have sent some snuff into my eye," he said to his neighbor.

"Anyone who annoys Father Goriot will have to reckon with me," said Eugène, looking at the old man's neighbor. "He is worth all the rest of us put together. I am not speaking of the ladies," he added, turning in the direction of Mlle Taillefer.

Eugène's remarks produced a sensation, and his tone silenced the dinner table. Vautrin alone spoke. "If you are going to champion Father Goriot, and make yourself responsible for all he says and does into the bargain, you had need be a crack shot and know how to handle the foils," he said, banteringly.

"So I intend," said Eugène.

"Then you are taking the field today?"

"Perhaps," Rastignac answered. "But I owe no account of myself to anyone, especially as I do not try to find out what other people do of a night."

Vautrin looked askance at Rastignac.

"If you do not mean to be deceived by the puppets, my boy, you must go behind and see the whole show, and not peep through holes in the curtain. That is enough," he added, seeing that Eugène was about to fly into a passion. "We can have a little talk by ourselves whenever you like."

There was a general feeling of gloom and constraint. Old Goriot was so deeply dejected by the student's remark that he did not notice the change in the attitude of his fellow-lodgers, nor know that a champion capable of putting an end to his persecution had taken up his defense.

"Then Monsieur Goriot sitting there is the father of a countess," said Mme Vauquer in a low voice.

"And of a baroness," answered Rastignac.

"That is about all he is capable of," said Bianchon to Rastignac; "I have taken a look at his head; there is only one bump—the bump of Paternity; he must be an Eternal Father."

Eugène was too intent on his thoughts to laugh at Bianchon's joke. He determined to profit by Mme de Beauséant's counsels, and was asking himself how he could obtain the necessary money. He grew grave. The wide plains of the world stretched before his eyes; all things lay before him, nothing was his. Dinner came to an end, the others went, and he was left in the dining room.

"So you have seen my daughter?" Goriot spoke tremulously, and the sound of his voice broke in upon Eugène's dreams. The young man took the elder's hand, and looked at him almost tenderly.

"You are a good and noble man," he said. "We will have some talk about your daughters by and by."

He rose without waiting for Goriot's answer, and went to his room. There he wrote the following letter to his mother:

My DEAR MOTHER,—Can you nourish your child from your breast again? I am in a position to make a rapid fortune, but I want twelve hundred francs—I must have them at all costs. Say nothing about this to my father; perhaps he might make objections, and unless I have the money, I may be led to put an end to myself, and so escape the clutches of despair. I will tell you everything when I see you. I will not begin to try to describe my present situation; it would take volumes to put the whole story clearly and fully. I have not been gambling, my kind mother, I owe no one a penny; but if you would preserve the life that you gave me, you must send me the sum I mention. As a matter of fact, I go to see the Vicomtesse de Beauséant; she is using her influence for me; I am obliged to go into society, and I have not a penny to lay out on clean gloves. I can manage to exist on bread and water, or go without food, if need be, but I cannot do without the tools with which they cultivate the vineyards in this part of the country. I must firmly determine at once to make my way, or stick in the mire for the rest of my days. I know that all your hopes are set on me, and I want to realize them quickly. Sell some of your old jewelry, my dearest mother; I will give you other jewels very soon. I know enough of our affairs at home to know all that such a sacrifice means, and you must not think that I would lightly ask you to make it; I should be a monster if I could. You must think of my entreaty as a cry forced from me by imperative necessity. Our whole future lies in the subsidy with which I must begin my first campaign, for life in Paris is one continual battle. If you cannot otherwise procure the whole of the money, and are forced to sell our aunt's lace, tell her that I will send her some still handsomer,

and so forth.

He wrote to ask each of his sisters for their savings—would they despoil themselves for him, and keep the sacrifice a secret from the family? To his request he knew that they would not fail to respond gladly, and he added to it an appeal to their delicacy by touching the chord of honor that rings so true in young and highly strung natures.

Yet when he had written the letters, he could not help feeling misgivings in spite of his youthful ambition; his heart beat fast, and he trembled. He knew the pure nobleness of the lives buried away in the lonely manor house; he knew what trouble and what joy his request would cause his sisters, and how happy they would be as they talked at the bottom of the orchard of that dear brother of theirs in Paris. Visions rose before his eyes; a sudden strong light revealed his sisters secretly counting over their little store, devising some girlish stratagem by which the money could be sent to him *incognito*, essaying, for the first time in their lives, a piece of deceit that reached the sublime in its unselfishness.

"A sister's heart is a diamond for purity, a deep sea of tenderness!" he said to himself. He felt ashamed of those letters.

What power there must be in the petitions put up by such

hearts! How pure the fervor that bears their souls to Heaven in prayer! What exquisite joy they would find in self-sacrifice! What a pang for his mother's heart if she could not send him all that he asked for! And this noble affection, these sacrifices made at such terrible cost, were to serve as the ladder by which he was to climb to Delphine de Nucingen. A few tears, like the last grains of incense flung upon the sacred altar fire of the hearth, fell from his eyes. He walked up and down, and despair mingled with his emotion. Old Goriot saw him through the half-open door.

"What is the matter, sir?" he asked from the threshold.

"Ah, my good neighbor, I am as much a son and brother as you are a father. You do well to fear for the Countess Anastasie; there is one Monsieur Maxime de Trailles, who will be her ruin."

Old Goriot withdrew, stammering some words, but Eugène failed to catch their meaning.

The next morning Rastignac went out to post his letters. Up to the last moment he wavered and doubted, but he ended by flinging them into the box. "I shall succeed!" he said to himself. So says the gambler; so says the great captain; but the three words that have been the salvation of some few, have been the ruin of many more.

Chapter 8

A few days after this Eugène called at Mme de Restaud's house; she was not at home. Three times he tried the experiment, and three times he found her doors closed against him, though he was careful to choose an hour when M. de Trailles was not there. The vicomtesse was right.

The student studied no longer. He put in an appearance at lectures simply to answer at roll-call, and after thus attesting his presence, he departed. He had been through a reasoning process familiar to most students. He had seen the advisability of deferring his studies to the last moment before going up for his examinations; he made up his mind to cram his second and third year's work into the third year, when he meant to study hard, and to complete his studies in law with one great effort. In the meantime he had fifteen months in which to navigate the ocean of Paris, to spread the nets and set the lines that should bring him a protectress and a fortune. Twice during that week he called on Mme de Beauséant; he did not go to her house until he had seen the Marquis d'Ajuda drive away.

Victory for yet a few more days was with the great lady, the most poetic figure in the Faubourg Saint-Germain; and the marriage of the Marquis d'Ajuda-Pinto with Mlle de Rochefide was postponed. The dread of losing her happiness filled those days with a fever of joy unknown before, but the end was only so much nearer. The Marquis d'Ajuda and the Rochefides agreed that this quarrel and reconciliation was a very fortunate thing. Mme de Beauséant (so they hoped) would gradually become reconciled to the idea of the marriage, and in the end would be brought to sacrifice d'Ajuda's morning visits to the exigencies of a man's career, exigencies which she must have foreseen. In spite of the most solemn promises, daily renewed, M. d'Ajuda was playing a part, and the vicomtesse was eager to be deceived. "Instead of taking the leap heroically from the window, she is falling headlong down the staircase," said her most intimate friend, the Duchesse de Langeais. Yet this after-glow of happiness lasted long enough for the vicomtesse to be of service to her young cousin. She had a half-superstitious affection for him. Eugène had shown her sympathy and devotion at a crisis when a woman sees no pity, no real comfort in any eyes; when if a man is ready with soothing flatteries, it is because he has an interested motive.

Rastignac made up his mind that he must learn the whole of

Goriot's previous history; he would come to his bearings before attempting to board the Maison de Nucingen. The results of his inquiries may be given briefly as follows:

In the days before the Revolution, Jean-Joachim Goriot was simply a workman in the employ of a vermicelli-maker. He was a skillful, thrifty workman, sufficiently enterprising to buy his master's business when the latter fell a chance victim to the disturbances of 1789. Goriot established himself in the Rue de la Jussienne, close to the Grain Exchange. His plain good sense led him to accept the position of President of the Section, so as to secure for his business the protection of those in power at that dangerous epoch. This prudent step had led to success; the foundations of his fortune were laid in the time of the Scarcity (real or artificial), when the price of grain of all kinds rose enormously in Paris. People used to fight for bread at the bakers' doors; while others went to the grocers' shops and bought Italian paste foods without brawling over it. It was during this year that Goriot made the money which at a later time was to give him all the advantage of the great capitalist over the small buyer; he had, moreover, the usual luck of average ability; his mediocrity was his salvation. He excited no one's envy; it was not even suspected that he was rich till the peril of being rich was over, and all his intelligence was concentrated, not on political, but on commercial speculations. Goriot was an authority second to none on all questions relating to wheat, flour, and "middlings"; and the production, storage, and quality of grain. He could estimate the yield of the harvest, and foresee market prices; he bought his cereals in Sicily, and imported Russian wheat. Anyone who had heard him hold forth on the regulations that control the importation and exportation of grain, who had seen his grasp of the subject, his clear insight into the principles involved, his appreciation of weak points in the way that the system worked, would have thought that here was the stuff of which a minister is made. Patient, active, and persevering, energetic and prompt in action, he surveyed his business horizon with an eagle's eye. Nothing there took him by surprise; he foresaw all things, knew all that was happening, and kept his own counsel; he was a diplomatist in his quick comprehension of a situation, and in the routine of business he was as patient and plodding as a soldier on the march. But beyond this business horizon he could not see. He used to spend his hours of leisure on the threshold of his shop, leaning against the framework of the door. Take him from his dark little counting-house, and he became once more the rough, slow-witted workman, a man who cannot understand a piece of reasoning, who is indifferent to all intellectual pleasures, and falls asleep at the play, a Parisian Doliban in short, against whose stupidity other minds are powerless.

Natures of this kind are nearly all alike; in almost all of them you will find hidden some deep affection. Two all-absorbing affections filled the vermicelli-maker's heart to the exclusion of every other feeling; into them he seemed to put all the force of his nature, as he put the whole power of his brain into the grain trade. He had regarded his wife, the only daughter of a rich farmer of La Brie, with a devout admiration; his love for her had been boundless. Goriot had felt the charm of a lovely and sensitive nature, which, in its delicate strength, was the very opposite of his own. Is there any instinct more deeply implanted in the heart of man than the pride of protection, a protection which is constantly exerted for a fragile and defenseless creature? Join love to this, the warmth of gratitude that all generous souls feel for the source of their pleasures, and you have the explanation of many strange incongruities in human nature.

After seven years of unclouded happiness, Goriot, unfortunately for him, lost his wife. She was beginning to gain an ascendancy over him; possibly she might have brought that barren soil under cultivation, she might have widened his ideas and given other directions to his thoughts. But when she was dead, the instinct of fatherhood developed in him till it almost became a mania. All the emotion balked by death was now concentrated on his daughters, and he found full satisfaction for his heart in loving them. More or less brilliant proposals were made to him from time to time; wealthy merchants or farmers with daughters vied with each other in offering inducements to him to marry again, but he was determined to remain a widower. His father-in-law, the only man for whom he felt a decided friendship, gave out that Goriot had made a vow to be faithful to his wife's memory. The frequenters of the Grain Exchange, who could not comprehend this sublime piece of folly, joked about it among themselves, and found a ridiculous nickname for him. One of them ventured (after a glass over a bargain) to call him by it, and a blow from the vermicelli-maker's fist sent him headlong into a gutter in the Rue Oblin.

He could think of nothing else when his children were concerned; his love for them made him fidgety and anxious; and this was so well known, that one day a competitor, who wished to get rid of him to secure the field to himself, told Goriot that Delphine had just been knocked down by a cab. The vermicelli-maker turned pale, left the Exchange at once, and did not return for several days afterward; he was ill in consequence of the shock and the subsequent relief on discovering that it was a false alarm. This time, however, the offender did not escape with a bruised shoulder; at a critical moment in the man's affairs, Goriot drove him into bankruptcy, and forced him to disappear from the Grain Exchange.

As might have been expected, the two girls were spoiled. With an income of sixty thousand francs, Goriot scarcely spent twelve hundred on himself, and found all his happiness in satisfying the whims of the two girls. The best masters were engaged, that Anastasie and Delphine might be endowed with all the accomplishments which distinguish a good education. They had a chaperon—luckily for them, she was a woman who had sense and good taste; they learned to ride; they had a carriage for their use; they lived as the mistress of a rich old lord might live; they had only to express a wish, their father would hasten to give them their most extravagant desires, and asked nothing of them in return but a kiss. Goriot had raised the two girls to the level of the angels; and, quite naturally, he himself was left beneath them. Poor man! he loved them even for the pain that they gave him.

When the girls were old enough to be married, they were left free to choose for themselves. Each had half her father's fortune as her dowry; and when the Comte de Restaud came to woo Anastasie for her beauty, her social aspirations led her to leave her father's house for a more exalted sphere. Delphine wished for money; she married Nucingen, a banker of German extraction, who became a Baron of the Holy Roman Empire. Goriot remained a vermicelli-maker as before. His daughters and his sons-in-law began to demur; they did not like to see him still engaged in trade, though his whole life was bound up with his business. For five years he stood out against their entreaties, then he yielded, and consented to retire on the amount realized by the sale of his business and the savings of the last few years. It was this capital that Mme Vauquer, in the early days of his residence with her, had calculated would bring in eight or ten thousand livres in a year. He had taken refuge in her lodginghouse, driven there by despair when he knew that his daughters were compelled by their husbands not only to refuse to receive him as an inmate in their houses, but even to see him no more except in private.

This was all the information which Rastignac gained from a M. Muret who had purchased Goriot's business, information which confirmed the Duchesse de Langeais' suppositions, and herewith the preliminary explanation of this obscure but terrible Parisian tragedy comes to an end.

Towards the end of the first week in December Rastignac received two letters—one from his mother, and one from his eldest sister. His heart beat fast, half with happiness, half with fear, at the sight of the familiar handwriting. Those two little scraps of paper contained life or death for his hopes. But while he felt a shiver of dread as he remembered their dire poverty at home, he knew their love for him so well that he could not help fearing that he was draining their very life-blood. His mother's letter ran as follows:

My DEAR CHILD,—I am sending you the money that you asked for. Make a good use of it. Even to save your life I could not raise so large a sum a second time without your father's knowledge, and there would be trouble about it. We should be obliged to mortgage the land. It is impossible to judge of the merits of schemes of which I am ignorant; but what sort of schemes can they be, that you should fear to tell me about them? Volumes of explanation would not have been needed; we mothers can understand at a word, and that word would have spared me the anguish of uncertainty. I do not know how to hide the painful impression that your letter has made upon me, my dear son. What can you have felt when you were moved to send this chill of dread through my heart? It must have been very painful to you to write the letter that gave me so much pain as I read it. To what courses are you committed? You are going to appear to be something that you are not, and your whole life and success depends upon this? You are about to see a society into which you cannot enter without rushing into expense that you cannot afford, without losing precious time that is needed for your studies? Ah! my dear Eugène, believe your mother, crooked ways cannot lead to great ends. Patience and endurance are the two qualities most needed in your position. I am not scolding you; I do not want any tinge of bitterness to spoil our offering. I am only talking like a mother whose trust in you is as great as her foresight for you. You know the steps that you must take, and I, for my part, know your purity of heart, and how good your intentions are; so I can say to you without a doubt, "Go forward, beloved!" If I tremble, it is because I am a mother, but my prayers and blessings will be with you at every step. Be very careful, dear boy. You must have a man's prudence, for it lies with you to shape the destinies of five others who are dear to you, and must look to you. Yes, our fortunes depend upon you, and your success is ours. We all pray to God to be with you in all that you do. Your aunt Marcillac has been most generous beyond words in this matter; she saw at once how it was, even down to your gloves. "But I have a weakness for the eldest!" she said gaily. You must love your aunt very much, dear Eugène. I shall wait till you have succeeded before telling you all that she has done for you, or her money would burn your fingers. You, who are young, do not know what it is to part with something that is a piece of your past! But what would we not sacrifice for your sake? Your aunt says that I am to send you a kiss on the forehead from her, and that kiss is to bring you luck again and again, she says. She would have written to you herself, the dear kind-hearted woman, but she is troubled with the gout in her fingers just now. Your father is very well. The vintage of 1819 has turned out better than we expected. Good-bye, dear boy; I will say nothing about your sisters, because Laure is writing to you, and I must let her have the pleasure of giving you all the home news. Heaven send that you may succeed! Oh! yes, dear Eugène, you must succeed. I have come, through you, to a knowledge of a pain so sharp that I do not think I could endure it a second time. I have come to know what it is to be poor, and to long for money for my children's sake. There, good-bye! Do not leave us for long without news of you; and here, at the last, take a kiss from your mother.

By the time Eugène had finished the letter he was in tears. He thought of Father Goriot crushing his silver keepsake into a shapeless mass before he sold it to meet his daughter's bill of exchange.

"Your mother has broken up her jewels for you," he said to himself. "Your aunt shed tears over those relics of hers before she sold them for your sake. What right have you to heap execrations on Anastasie? You have followed her example; you have selfishly sacrificed others to your own future, and she sacrifices her father to her lover; and of you two, which is the worse?"

He was ready to renounce his attempts; he could not bear to take that money. The fires of remorse burned in his heart, and gave him intolerable pain, the generous secret remorse which men seldom take into account when they sit in judgment upon their fellow men; but perhaps the angels in heaven, beholding it, pardon the criminal whom our justice condemns. Rastignac opened his sister's letter; its simplicity and kindness revived his heart.

Your letter came just at the right time, dear brother. Agathe and I had thought of so many different ways of spending our money that we did not know what to buy with it; and now you have come in, and, like the servant who upset all the watches that belonged to the King of Spain, you have restored harmony; for, really and truly, we did not know which of all the things we wanted we wanted most, and we were always quarreling about it, never thinking, dear Eugène, of a way of spending our money which would satisfy us completely. Agathe jumped for joy. Indeed, we have been like two mad things all day, "to such a prodigious degree" (as aunt would say), that mother said, with her severe expression, "Whatever can be the matter with you, mesdemoiselles?" I think if we had been scolded a little, we should have been still better pleased. A woman ought to be very glad to suffer for one she loves! I, however, in my inmost soul, was doleful and cross in the midst of all my joy. I shall make a bad wife, I am afraid, I am too fond of spending. I had bought two sashes and a nice little stiletto for piercing eyelet-holes in my stays, trifles that I really did not want, so that I have less than that slow-coach Agathe, who is so economical, and hoards her money like a magpie. She had two hundred francs! And I have only one hundred and fifty! I am nicely punished! I could throw my sash down the well; it will be painful to me to wear it now. Poor dear. I have robbed you. And Agathe was so nice about it. She said, "Let us send the three hundred and fifty francs in our two names!" But I could not help telling you everything just as it happened.

Do you know how we managed to keep your commandments?
We took our glittering hoard, we went out for a walk, and when
once fairly on the highway we ran all the way to Ruffec, where
we handed over the coin, without more ado, to M. Grimbert
of the Messageries Royales. We came back again like swallows
on the wing. "Don't you think that happiness has made us
lighter?" Agathe said. We said all sorts of things, which I shall
not tell you, Monsieur le Parisien, because they were all about
you. Oh, we love you dearly, dear brother; it was all summed
up in those few words. As for keeping the secret, little mas-
queraders like us are capable of anything (according to our
aunt), even of holding our tongues. Mother has been on a mysterious journey to Angoulême, and the aunt went with her, not
without solemn councils, from which we were shut out, and
M. le Baron likewise. They are silent as to the weighty political
considerations that prompted their mission, and conjectures are
rife in the State of Rastignac. The Infantas are embroidering a
muslin robe with open-work sprigs for Her Majesty the Queen;
the work progresses in the most profound secrecy. There be but
two more breadths to finish. A decree has gone forth that no
wall shall be built on the side of Verteuil, but a hedge shall be
planted instead. Our subjects may sustain some disappointment
of fruit and espaliers, but strangers will enjoy a fair prospect.
Should the heir-presumptive lack pocket-handkerchiefs, be it
known unto him that the dowager Lady of Marcillac, exploring
the recesses of her drawers and boxes (known respectively as
Pompeii and Herculaneum), having brought to light a fair piece
of cambric whereof she wotted not, the Princesses Agathe and
Laure place at their brother's disposal their thread, their needles,
and hands somewhat too red. The two young Princes, Don Henri
and Don Gabriel, retain their fatal habits of stuffing themselves
with grape jelly, of teasing their sisters, of taking their pleasure
by going a-birdnesting, and of cutting switches for themselves
from the osier-beds, in defiance of the laws of the realm. Moreover, they list not to learn aught, wherefore the Papal Nuncio
(called of the commonalty, M. le Curé) threatened them with
excommunication, since that they neglect the sacred canons of

grammatical construction for the construction of other cannon, deadly engines made of the stems of elder.

Farewell, dear brother, never did letter carry so many wishes for your success, so much love fully satisfied. You will have a great deal to tell us when you come home! You will tell me everything, won't you? I am the oldest. From something the aunt let fall, we think you must have had some success.

Something was said of a lady, but nothing more was said ...

Of course not, in our family! Oh, by the by, Eugène, would you rather that we made that piece of cambric into shirts for you instead of pocket-handkerchiefs? If you want some really nice shirts at once, we ought to lose no time in beginning upon them; and if the fashion is different now in Paris, send us one for a pattern, particularly for the cuffs. Good-bye! good-bye! Take my kiss on the left side of your forehead, on the temple that belongs to me, and to no one else in the world. I am leaving the other side of the sheet for Agathe, who has solemnly promised not to read a word that I have written; but, all the same, I mean to sit by her while she writes, so as to be quite sure that she keeps her word.—Your loving sister,   LAURE DE RASTIGNAC.

"Yes!" said Eugène to himself. "Success at all costs now! Riches could not repay such devotion as this. I wish I could give them every sort of happiness! Fifteen hundred and fifty francs," he went on after a pause. "Every shot must go to the mark! Laure is right. Trust a woman! I have only calico shirts. Where someone else's welfare is concerned, a young girl becomes as ingenious as a thief. Guileless where she herself is in question, and full of foresight for me—she is like a heavenly angel forgiving earthly sins without understanding them."

The world lay before him. His tailor had been summoned and sounded, and had finally surrendered. When Rastignac met M. de Trailles, he had seen at once how great a part the tailor plays in a young man's career. A tailor is either a deadly enemy or a staunch friend, with an invoice for a bond of friendship; between these two extremes there is, alack! no middle term. Eugène discovered a man who understood that his was a sort of paternal function for young men at their entrance into life, who regarded himself as a stepping-stone between a young man's present and future. And Rastignac in gratitude made the man's fortune by an epigram of a kind in which he excelled at a later period of his life:

"I have twice known a pair of trousers turned out by him make a match of twenty thousand livres a year!"

Chapter 9

FIFTEEN HUNDRED francs, and as many suits of clothes as he chose to order! At that moment the poor child of the South felt no more doubts of any kind. The young man went down to breakfast with the indefinable air which the consciousness of the possession of money gives to youth. No sooner are the coins slipped into a student's pocket than his wealth, in imagination at least, is piled into a fantastic column, which affords him a moral support. He begins to hold up his head as he walks; he is conscious that he has a means of bringing his powers to bear on a given point; he looks you straight in the face; his gestures are quick and decided. Only yesterday he was diffident and shy, anyone might have pushed him aside; tomorrow, he will get the better of a prime minister. A miracle has been wrought in him. Nothing is beyond the reach of his ambition, and his ambition soars at random; he is light-hearted, generous, and enthusiastic. In short, the fledgling bird has discovered that he has wings. A poor student snatches at every chance pleasure much as a dog runs all sorts of risks to steal a bone, cracking it and sucking the marrow as he flies from pursuit, but a young man who can rattle a few runaway gold coins in his pocket can take his pleasure deliberately, can taste the whole of the sweets of secure possession; he soars far above earth; he has forgotten what the word *poverty* means; all Paris is his. Those are days when the whole world shines radiant with light, when everything glows and sparkles before the eyes of youth, days that bring joyous energy that is never brought into harness, days of debts and of painful fears that go hand in hand with every delight. Those who do not know the left bank of the Seine between the Rue Saint-Jacques and the Rue des Saints-Pères know nothing of life.

"Ah! if the women of Paris but knew," said Rastignac, as he devoured Mme Vauquer's stewed pears (at five for a penny), "they would come here in search of a lover."

Just then a porter from the Messageries Royales appeared at the door of the room. They had previously heard the bell ring as the wicket opened to admit him. The man asked for M. Eugène de Rastignac, holding out two bags for him to take, and a receipt for his signature. Vautrin's keen glance cut Eugène like a lash.

"Now you will be able to pay for those fencing lessons and go to the shooting gallery," he said.

"Your ship has come in," said Mme Vauquer, looking at the bags.

Mlle Michonneau did not dare to look at the money, for fear her eyes should betray her cupidity.

"You have a good mother," said Mme Couture.

"You have a good mother, sir," echoed Poiret.

"Yes, mamma has been drained dry," said Vautrin, "and now you can have your fling, go into society, and fish for heiresses, and dance with countesses who have peach blossoms in their hair. But take my advice, young man, and don't neglect your pistol practice."

Vautrin struck an attitude, as if he were facing an antagonist. Rastignac, meaning to give the porter a tip, felt in his pockets and found nothing. Vautrin flung down a franc piece on the table.

"Your credit is good," he remarked, eyeing the student, and Rastignac was forced to thank him, though, since the sharp encounter of wits at dinner that day, after Eugène came in from calling on Mme de Beauséant, he had made up his mind that Vautrin was insufferable. For a week, in fact, they had both kept silence in each other's presence, and watched each other. The student tried in vain to account to himself for this attitude.

An idea, of course, gains in force by the energy with which it is expressed; it strikes where the brain sends it, by a law as mathematically exact as the law that determines the course of a shell from a mortar. The amount of impression it makes is not to be determined so exactly. Sometimes, in a sensitive nature, the idea works havoc, but there are, no less, natures so robustly protected, that this sort of projectile falls flat and harmless on skulls of triple brass, as cannon-shot against solid masonry. Then there are flaccid and spongy-fibered natures into which ideas from without sink like spent bullets into the earthworks of a redoubt.

Rastignac's head was something of a powder-magazine; the least shock sufficed to bring about an explosion. He was too quick, too young, not to be readily accessible to ideas, and open to that subtle influence of thought and feeling in others which causes so many strange phenomena that make an impression upon us of which we are all unconscious at the time. Nothing escaped his mental vision; he was lynx-eyed; in him the mental powers of perception, which seem like duplicates of the senses, had the mysterious power of swift projection that astonishes us in intellects of a high order—slingers who are quick to detect the weak spot in any armor.

In the past month Eugène's good qualities and defects had rapidly developed with his character. Intercourse with the world and the endeavor to satisfy his growing desires had brought out his defects. But Rastignac came from the south side of the Loire, and had the good qualities of his countrymen. He had the impetuous courage of the South, that rushes to the attack of a difficulty, as well as the southern impatience of delay or suspense. These traits are held to be defects in the North; they made the fortune of Murat, but they likewise cut short his career. The moral would appear to be that when the dash and boldness of the south side of the Loire meets, in a southern temperament, with the guile of the North, the character is complete, and such a man may aspire to the crown of Sweden.

Rastignac, therefore, could not stand the fire from Vautrin's batteries for long without discovering whether this was a friend or a foe. He felt as if this strange being was reading his inmost soul and dissecting his feelings, while Vautrin himself was so close and secretive that he seemed to have something of the profound impassiveness of a sphinx, seeing and hearing all and saying nothing. Eugène, conscious of the money in his pocket, rebelled.

"Be so good as to wait a moment," he said to Vautrin, as the latter rose, after slowly emptying his coffee cup, sip by sip.

"What for?" inquired the older man, as he put on his large-brimmed hat and took up the sword-cane that he was wont to twirl with the air of one who will face three or four footpads without flinching.

"I will repay you in a minute," returned Eugène. He unsealed one of the bags as he spoke, counted out a hundred and forty francs, and pushed them towards Mme Vauquer. "Short reckonings make good friends," he added, turning to the widow; "that clears our accounts till the end of the year. Can you give me change for a five-franc piece?"

"Good friends make short reckonings," echoed Poiret, with a glance at Vautrin.

"Here is your franc," said Rastignac, holding out the coin to the sphinx in the black wig.

"Anyone might think that you were afraid to owe me a trifle," exclaimed Vautrin, with a searching glance that seemed to read the young man's inmost thoughts, and the satirical and cynical smile which Eugène had seen scores of times already, and which exasperated him almost beyond endurance.

"Well—so I am," he answered. He held both the bags in his hand, and had risen to go up to his room.

Vautrin made as if he were going out through the sitting room, and the student turned to go through the second door that opened into the square lobby at the foot of the staircase.

"Do you know, Monsieur le Marquis de Rastignacorama, that what you were saying just now was not exactly polite?" Vautrin remarked, as he rattled his sword-cane across the panels of the sitting-room door, and came up to the student.

Rastignac looked coolly at Vautrin, drew him to the foot of the staircase, and shut the dining-room door. They were standing in the little square lobby between the kitchen and the dining room; the place was lighted by an iron-barred fanlight above a door that gave access into the garden. Sylvie came out of her kitchen, and Eugène chose that moment to say:

"*Monsieur* Vautrin, I am not a marquis, and my name is not Rastignacorama."

"They will fight," said Mlle Michonneau, in a tone of indifference.

"Fight!" echoed Poiret.

"Not they," replied Mme Vauquer, lovingly fingering her pile of coins.

"But there they are under the lime-trees," cried Mlle Victorine, who had risen so that she might see out into the garden. "Poor young man! He was in the right, after all."

"We must go upstairs, my pet," said Mme Couture; "it is no business of ours."

At the door, however, Mme Couture and Victorine found their progress barred by the portly form of Sylvie.

"What ever can have happened?" she said. "Monsieur Vautrin said to Monsieur Eugène, 'Let us have an explanation!' Then he took him by the arm, and there they are, trampling down our artichokes."

Vautrin came in while she was speaking. "Mamma Vauquer," he said, smiling, "don't frighten yourself at all. I am only going to try my pistols under the lime-trees."

"Oh, monsieur," cried Victorine, clasping her hands as she spoke, "why do you want to kill Monsieur Eugène?"

Vautrin stepped back a pace or two, and gazed at Victorine.

"Oh, this is something new!" he exclaimed in a bantering tone, that brought the color into the poor girl's face. "That young fellow yonder is very nice, isn't he?" he went on. "You have given me a notion, my pretty child; I will make you both happy."

Mme Couture laid her hand on the arm of her ward and drew the girl away, saying in her ear:

"Why, Victorine, I cannot imagine what has come over you this morning."

"I don't want any shots fired in my garden," said Mme Vauquer. "You will frighten the neighborhood and bring the police up here all in a moment."

"Come, keep cool, Mamma Vauquer," answered Vautrin. "There, there; it's all right; we will go to the shooting-gallery."

He went back to Rastignac, laying his hand familiarly on the young man's arm.

"When I have given you ocular demonstration of the fact that I can put a bullet through the ace on a card five times running at thirty-five paces," he said, "that won't take away your courage, I suppose? You look to me like a man who would balk at nothing, who would get himself killed as soon as not—like a blockhead."

"Do you wish to back out?" asked Eugène.

"Don't try to raise my temperature," answered Vautrin; "it

is not cold this morning. Let us go and sit over there," he added, pointing to the green-painted garden seats; "no one can overhear us. I want a little talk with you. You are not a bad sort of youngster, and I have no quarrel with you. I like you, take Tromp—confound it!—take Vautrin's word for it. What makes me like you? I will tell you by and by. Meantime, I can tell you that I know you as well as if I had made you myself, as I will prove to you in a minute. Put down your bags," he continued, pointing to the round table.

Rastignac deposited his money on the table, and sat down. He was consumed with curiosity, excited by the sudden change in the manner of the man before him. Here was a strange being who, a moment ago, had talked of killing him, and now posed as his protector.

"You would like to know who I really am, what I was, and what I do now," Vautrin went on. "You want to know too much, youngster. Come! come! keep cool! You will hear more astonishing things than that. I have had my misfortunes. Just hear me out first, and you shall have your turn afterwards. Here is my past in three words. Who am I? Vautrin. What do I do? Just what I please. Let us change the subject. You want to know my character. I am good-natured to those who do me a good turn, or to those whose hearts speak to mine. These last may do anything they like with me; they may bruise my shins, and I shall not tell them to 'mind what they are about'; but, *nom d'une pipe*, the devil himself is not an uglier customer than I can be if people annoy me, or if I don't happen to take to them; and you may just as well know at once that I think no more of killing a man than of that," and he spat before him as he spoke. "Only when it is absolutely necessary to do so, I do my best to kill him properly. I am what you call an artist. I have read Benvenuto Cellini's *Memoirs* and, what is more, in Italian! A fine-spirited fellow he was! From him I learned to follow the example set us by Providence, who strikes us down at random, and to admire the beautiful whenever and wherever it is found. And, setting other questions aside, is it not a glorious part to play, when you pit yourself against mankind, and the luck is on your side?

"I have thought a good deal about the constitution of your present social Dis-order. A duel is downright childish, my boy, utter nonsense and folly! When one of two living men must be got out of the way, none but an idiot would leave chance to decide which it is to be; and in a duel it is a toss-up—heads or tails—and there you are! Now I, for instance, can hit the ace in the middle of a card five times running, send one bullet after another through the same hole, and at thirty-five paces, to boot! With that little accomplishment you might think yourself certain of killing your man, mightn't you? Well, I have fired, at twenty paces, and missed, and the rogue who had never handled a pistol in his life—look here!" he unbuttoned his waistcoat and exposed his chest, as shaggy as a bear's back; the student gave a startled shudder—"he was a raw lad, but he made his mark on me," the extraordinary man went on, drawing Rastignac's fingers over a deep scar on his breast. "But that happened when I myself was a mere boy; I was twenty-one then (your age), and I had some beliefs left—in a woman's love, and in a pack of rubbish that you will be over head and ears in directly. You and I were to have fought just now, weren't we? You might have killed me. Suppose that I were put under the earth, where would you be? You would have to clear out of this, go to Switzerland, draw on papa's money—only he hasn't got any. I mean to open your eyes to your real position, that is what I am going to do; but I shall do it from the point of view of a man who, after studying the world very closely, sees that there are but two alternatives—stupid obedience or revolt. I obey nobody; is that clear? Now, do you know how much you will want at the pace you are going? A million, and promptly, too, or that little head of yours will be swaying to and fro in the dragnets at Saint-

Cloud, while we are gone to find out whether or no there is a Supreme Being. I will put you in the way of that million."

He stopped for a moment and looked at Eugène.

"Aha! you do not look so sourly at Papa Vautrin now! At the mention of the million you look like a young girl when somebody has said, 'I will come tonight!' and she betakes herself to her toilette as a cat licks its whiskers over a saucer of milk. All right. Come, now, let us go into the question, young man; all between ourselves, you know. We have a papa and mamma down yonder, a great-aunt, two sisters (aged eighteen and seventeen), two young brothers (one fifteen, and the other ten). That's the whole crew. The aunt brings up the two sisters; the curé comes and teaches the boys Latin. Boiled chestnuts are oftener on the table than white bread. Papa makes a suit of clothes last a long while; if mamma has a different dress winter and summer, it is about as much as she has; the sisters manage as best they can. I know all about it; I have lived in the South.

"That is how things are at home. They send you twelve hundred francs a year, and the entire property only brings in three thousand francs all told. We have a cook and a manservant; papa is a baron, and we must keep up appearances. Then we have our ambitions; we are connected with the Beauséants, and we go afoot through the streets; we want to be rich, and we have not a penny; we eat Mme Vauquer's messes, and we like grand dinners in the Faubourg Saint-Germain; we sleep on a pallet, and dream of a mansion! I do not blame you for wanting these things. It is not given to everyone to have ambition, my little trump. What sort of men do the women run after? Men of ambition. Men of ambition have stronger frames, their blood is richer in iron, their hearts are warmer than those of ordinary men. Women feel that when their power is greatest they look their best, and that those are their happiest hours; they like power in men, and prefer the strongest even if it is a power that may be their own destruction. I am going to make an inventory of your desires in order to put the question at issue before you. Here it is:

"We are as hungry as a wolf, and those newly-cut teeth of ours are sharp. What are we to do to keep the pot boiling? In the first place, we have the Code to browse upon; it is not amusing, and we are none the wiser for it, but that cannot be helped. So far so good. We mean to make an advocate of ourselves with a prospect of one day being made President of a Court of Assize, when we shall send poor devils, our betters, to the galleys with a T F[1] on their shoulders, so that the rich may sleep in peace. There is no fun in that; and you are a long while coming to it; for, to begin with, there are two years of nauseous drudgery in Paris, while we see all the plums that we long for out of our reach. It is tiresome to want things and never to have them. If you were a pallid creature of the mollusc order, you would have nothing to fear, but it is different when you have the hot blood of a lion and are ready to get into a score of scrapes every day of your life. This is the ghastliest form of torture known in this inferno of God's making, and you will give in to it. Or suppose that you are a good boy, drink nothing stronger than milk, and bemoan your hard lot; you, with your generous nature, will endure hardships that would drive a dog mad, and make a start, after long waiting, as deputy to some rascal or other in a hole of a place where the Government will fling you a thousand francs a year like the scraps that are thrown to the butcher's dog. Bark at thieves, plead the cause of the rich, send men of heart to the guillotine, that is your work! Many thanks! If you have no influence, you may rot in your provincial tribunal. At thirty you will be a Justice with twelve hundred francs a year, if you have not flung off the gown for good before then. By the time you are forty you may look to marry a miller's daughter, an heiress with some six thousand livres a year. Much

[1] *Travaux forcés*, the term applied to convicts who had served time in the galleys.

obliged! If you have influence, you may possibly be Public Prosecutor by the time you are thirty; with a salary of a thousand crowns, you could look to marry the mayor's daughter. Some petty piece of political trickery, such as mistaking Villèle for Manuel in a bulletin (the names rhyme, and that quiets your conscience), and you will probably be Procureur Général by the time you are forty, with a chance of becoming a deputy. Please to observe, my dear boy, that our conscience will have been a little damaged in the process, and that we shall endure twenty years of drudgery and hidden poverty, and that our sisters are wearing Dian's livery. I have the honor to call your attention to another fact: to wit, that there are but twenty Procureurs Généraux at a time in all France, while there are some twenty thousand of you young men who aspire to that elevated position; that there are some mountebanks among you who would sell their family to screw their fortunes a peg higher.

"If this sort of thing sickens you, try another course. The Baron de Rastignac thinks of becoming an advocate, does he? There's a nice prospect for you! Ten years of drudgery straight away. You are obliged to live at the rate of a thousand francs a month; you must have a library of law books, live in chambers, go into society, go down on your knees to ask a solicitor for briefs, lick the dust off the floor of the Palais de Justice. If this kind of business led to anything, I should not say no; but just give me the names of five advocates here in Paris who by the time that they are fifty are making fifty thousand francs a year! Bah! I would sooner turn pirate on the high seas than have my soul shrivel up inside me like that. How will you make money then? There is but one way: marry a rich woman. There is no fun in it. You hang a stone round your neck. And if you marry for money, what becomes of our exalted notions of honor and so forth? You might as well fly in the face of social conventions at once. Is it nothing to crawl like a serpent before your wife, to lick her mother's shoes, to descend to dirty actions that would

sicken a pig—faugh!—never mind if you at least make your fortune. But you will be as doleful as a dripstone if you marry for
money. It is better to wrestle with men than to wrangle at home
with your wife. You are at the crossroads of life, my boy; choose
your way.

"But you have chosen already. You have gone to see your
cousin de Beauséant, and you have had a glimpse of luxury;
you have been to Mme de Restaud's house, and in Father
Goriot's daughter you have scented the Parisienne for the first
time. That day you came back with a word written upon your
forehead. I knew it, I could read it—'*Success!*' Yes, success at
any price. 'Bravo,' said I to myself, 'here is the sort of fellow
for me.' You wanted money. Where was it to come from? You
have drained your sisters' little hoards: all brothers sponge more
or less on their sisters. Those fifteen hundred francs of yours
(got together, God knows how! in a country where there are
more chestnuts than five-franc pieces) will slip away like soldiers after pillage. And, then, what will you do—begin to work?
Work, or what you understand by work at this moment, means,
for a man like Poiret, an old age in Mamma Vauquer's lodginghouse. There are fifty thousand young men in your position at
this moment, all bent as you are on solving one and the same
problem—how to acquire a fortune rapidly. You are but a unit
in that aggregate. You can guess, therefore, what efforts you
must make, how desperate the struggle is. There are not fifty
thousand good positions for you; you must fight and devour one
another like spiders in a pot.

"Do you know how a man makes his way here? By brilliant
genius or by skillful corruption. You must either cut your way
through these masses of men like a cannon-ball, or steal among
them like a plague. Honesty is nothing to the purpose. Men
bow before the power of genius; they hate it, and try to slander
it, because genius does not divide the spoil; but if genius persists, they bow before it. To sum it all up in a phrase, if they

fail to smother genius in the mud, they fall on their knees and worship it. Corruption is a great power in the world, and talent is scarce. So corruption becomes the weapon of mediocrity; you will be made to feel it everywhere. You will see women who spend more than ten thousand francs a year on dress, while their husband's salary (his whole income) is six thousand francs. You will see officials buying estates on twelve hundred francs a year. You will see women who sell themselves body and soul to drive in a carriage belonging to the son of a peer of France, who has a right to drive in the middle rank at Longchamp. You have seen that poor fool of a Goriot obliged to meet a bill with his daughter's name at the back of it, though her husband has fifty thousand francs a year. I defy you to walk a couple of yards anywhere in Paris without stumbling on some infernal complication. I'll bet my head to a head of that salad that you will stir up a hornets' nest the first time you fall in love with a young, rich, and pretty woman. They are all dodging the law, all at loggerheads with their husbands. If I were to begin to tell you all that vanity or necessity (virtue is not often mixed up in it, you may be sure), all that vanity and necessity drive them to do for lovers, finery, housekeeping, or children, I should never come to an end. So an honest man is the common enemy.

"But do you know what an honest man is? Here, in Paris, an honest man is the man who keeps his own counsel, and will not divide the plunder. I am not speaking now of those poor slaves who do the work of the world without a reward for their toil—God Almighty's outcasts, I call them. Among them, I grant you, is virtue in all the flower of its stupidity, but poverty is no less their portion. At this moment, I think I see the long faces those good folk would pull if God played a practical joke on them and stayed away at the Last Judgment.

"Well, then, if you mean to make a fortune quickly, you must either be rich to begin with, or make people believe that you are rich. It is no use playing here except for high stakes; once take to low play, it is all up with you. If in the scores of professions that are open to you, there are ten men who rise very rapidly, people are sure to call them thieves. You can draw your own conclusions. Such is life. It is no cleaner than a kitchen; it reeks like a kitchen; and if you have fish to fry, you must expect to soil your hands. The real art is in getting them clean again, and therein lies the whole morality of our epoch. If I take this tone in speaking of the world to you, I have the right to do so; I know it well. Do you think that I am blaming it? Far from it; the world has always been as it is now. Moralists' strictures will never change it. People are not perfect, but one age is more or less hypocritical than another, and then fools say that its morality is high or low. I do not think that the rich are any worse than the poor; man is much the same, high or low, or wherever he is. In a million of these human cattle there may be half a score of bold spirits who rise above the rest, above the law; I am one of them. And you, if you are cleverer than your fellows, make straight to your end, and hold your head high. But you will have to struggle against envy and slander and mediocrity—in short, the world. Napoleon met with a Minister of War, Aubry by name, who all but sent him to the colonies.

"Feel your pulse. Think whether you can get up morning after morning, strengthened in yesterday's purpose. In that case I will make you an offer that no one would decline. Listen attentively. You see, I have an idea of my own. My idea is to live a patriarchal life on a vast estate, say a hundred thousand acres, somewhere in the Southern States of America. I mean to be a planter, to have slaves, to make a few snug millions by selling my cattle, timber, and tobacco; I want to live an absolute monarch, and to do just as I please; to lead such a life as no one here in these squalid dens of lath and plaster ever imagines. I am a great poet; I do not write my poems, I feel them, and act them. At this moment I have fifty thousand francs, which might possibly buy forty Negroes. I want two hundred thousand francs, because I want to have two hundred Negroes to carry out my notions of the patriarchal life properly. Negroes, you see, are like a sort of family ready grown, and there are no inquisitive public prosecutors out there to interfere with you. That investment in ebony ought to mean three or four million francs in ten years' time. If I am successful, no one will ask me who I am. I shall be Mr. Four Millions, an American citizen. I shall be fifty years old by then, and sound and hearty still; I shall enjoy life after my own fashion. In two words, if I find you an heiress with a million, will you give me two hundred thousand francs? Twenty per cent commission, eh? Is that too much? Your little wife will be very much in love with you. Once married, you will show signs of uneasiness and remorse; for a couple of weeks you will be depressed. Then, some night between two kisses, comes the confession. 'Two hundred thousand francs of debts, my darling!' This sort of farce is played every day in Paris, and by young men of the highest fashion. When a young wife has given her heart, she will not refuse her purse. Perhaps you are thinking that you will lose the money for good? Not you. You will make two hundred thousand francs again by some stroke of business. With your capital and your brains you should be able to accumulate as large a fortune as you could wish. *Ergo*, in six months you will have made your own fortune, and your old friend Vautrin's, and made an amiable woman very happy, to say nothing of your people at home, who must blow on their fingers to warm them, in the winter, for lack of firewood. You need not be surprised at my proposal, nor at the demand I make. Forty-seven out of every sixty great matches here in Paris are made after just such a bargain as this. The Chamber of Notaries compels my gentleman to——"

"What must I do?" said Rastignac, eagerly interrupting Vautrin's speech.

"Next to nothing," returned the other, with a slight involuntary movement, the suppressed exultation of the angler when he feels a bite at the end of his line. "Follow me carefully! The heart of a girl whose life is wretched and unhappy is a sponge that will thirstily absorb love—a dry sponge that swells at the first drop of sentiment. If you pay court to a young girl whose existence is a compound of loneliness, despair, and poverty, and who has no suspicion that she will come into a fortune, good Lord! it is quint and quatorze at piquet; it is knowing the numbers of the lottery beforehand; it is speculating in the funds when you have news from a sure source; it is building up a marriage on an indestructible foundation. The girl may come in for millions, and she will fling them, as if they were so many pebbles, at your feet. 'Take it, my beloved! Take it, Alfred, Adolphe, Eugène!' or whoever it was that showed his sense by sacrificing himself for her. And as for sacrificing himself, this is how I understand it. You sell a coat that is getting shabby, so that you can take her to the *Cadran bleu*, treat her to mushrooms on toast, and then go to the Ambigu-Comique in the evening; you pawn your watch to buy her a shawl. I need not remind you of the fiddle-faddle sentimentality that goes down so well with all women; you spill a few drops of water on your stationery, for instance; those are the tears you shed while far away from her. You look to me as if you were perfectly acquainted with the argot of the heart. Paris, you see, is like a forest in the New World, where you have to deal with a score of varieties of savages—Illinois and Hurons, who live on the proceeds of their social hunting. You are a hunter of millions; you set your snares; you use lures and nets; there are many ways of hunting. Some hunt heiresses, others a legacy; some fish for souls, yet others sell their clients, bound hand and foot. Everyone who comes back from the chase with his game-bag well filled meets with a warm welcome in good society. In justice to this hospitable part of the world, it must be said that you have to do with the most indulgent of great cities. If the proud aristocracies of the rest of Europe refuse admittance among their ranks to a disreputable millionaire, Paris stretches out a hand to him, goes to his banquets, eats his dinners, and hobnobs with his infamy."

"But where is such a girl to be found?" asked Eugène.

"Under your eyes; she is yours already."

"Mlle Victorine?"

"Precisely."

"And what was that you said?"

"She is in love with you already, your little Baronne de Rastignac!"

"She has not a penny," Eugène continued, much mystified.

"Ah, now we are coming to it! Just another word or two, and it will all be clear enough. Her father, Taillefer, is an old scoundrel. It is said that he murdered one of his friends at the time of the Revolution. He is one of your comedians that sets up to have opinions of his own. He is a banker—senior partner in the house of Frédéric Taillefer and Company. He has one son, and means to leave all he has to the boy, to the prejudice of Victorine. For my part, I don't like to see injustice of this sort. I am like Don Quixote, I have a fancy for defending the weak against the strong. If it should please God to take that youth away from him, Taillefer would have only his daughter left. He would want to leave his money to someone or other—an absurd notion, but it is only human nature, and he is not likely to have any more children, as I know. Victorine is gentle and amiable; she will soon twist her father round her fingers, and set his head spinning like a German top by plying him with sentiment! She will be too much touched by your devotion to forget you; you will marry her. I mean to play Providence for you, and Providence is to do my will. I have a friend whom I have attached closely to myself, a colonel in the Army of the Loire, who has just been transferred into the *garde royale*. He has taken my advice and turned ultra-royalist; he is not one of those fools who never change their opinions. Of all pieces

of advice, my cherub, I would give you this—don't stick to
your opinions any more than to your words. If anyone asks
you for them, let him have them—at a price. A man who prides
himself on going in a straight line through life is an idiot who
believes in infallibility. There are no such things as principles;
there are only events, and there are no laws but those of ex-
pediency: a man of talent accepts events and the circumstances
in which he finds himself, and turns everything to his own ends.
If laws and principles were fixed and invariable, nations would
not change them as readily as we change our shirts. The individual is not obliged to be more particular than the nation.
A man whose services to France have been of the very slightest
is looked on with superstitious awe because he has always seen
everything in red; but he is good, at the most, to be put into
the Museum of Arts and Crafts, among the automatic machines,
and labeled La Fayette; while the prince at whom everybody
flings a stone, the man who despises humanity so much that he
spits as many oaths as he is asked for in the face of humanity,
saved France from being torn in pieces at the Congress of
Vienna; and they who should have given him laurels fling mud
at him. Oh! I know something of affairs, I can tell you. I have
the secrets of many men! Enough. When I find three minds
in agreement as to the application of a principle, I shall have a
fixed and immovable opinion—I shall have to wait a long while
first. In the Tribunals you will not find three judges of the same
opinion on a single point of law. To return to the man I was
telling you of. He would crucify Jesus Christ again, if I bade
him. At a word from his old chum Vautrin he will pick a quarrel
with a scamp that will not send so much as five francs to his
sister, poor girl, and"—here Vautrin rose to his feet and stood
like a fencing-master about to lunge—"turn him off into the
dark!" he added.

"How frightful!" said Eugène. "You do not really mean it?
Monsieur Vautrin, you are joking!"

"There, there! Keep cool!" said the other. "Don't behave like
a baby. But if you find any amusement in it, be indignant, flare
up! Say that I am a scoundrel, a rascal, a rogue, a bandit, but
do not call me a blackleg or a spy! There, out with it, fire away!
I forgive you—it is quite natural at your age. I was like that
myself once. Only remember this, you will do worse things
yourself some day. You will flirt with some pretty woman and
take her money. You have thought of that, of course," said
Vautrin, "for how are you to succeed unless love is laid under
contribution? There are no two ways about virtue, my dear
student; it either is, or it is not. Talk of doing penance for your
sins! It is a nice system, when you pay for your crime by an
act of contrition! You seduce a woman that you may set your
foot on such and such a rung of the social ladder; you sow dis-
sension among the children of a family. You descend, in short,
to every base action that can be committed at home or abroad,
to gain your own ends for your own pleasure or your profit,
and can you imagine that these are acts of faith, hope, or charity?
How is it that a dandy, who in a night has fleeced a boy of half
his fortune, gets only a couple of months in prison, while a
poor devil who steals a banknote for a thousand francs, with
aggravating circumstances, is condemned to penal servitude?
Those are your laws. Not a single provision but lands you in
some absurdity. That man with yellow gloves and a golden
tongue commits many a murder; he sheds no blood, but he
drains his victim's veins as surely; a desperado forces open a
door with a crowbar, dark deeds both of them! You yourself
will do every one of the things that I suggest to you today, bar
the bloodshed. Do you believe that there is any absolute standard
in this world? Despise mankind and find out the meshes that you
can slip through in the net of the Code. The secret of a great
success for which you are at a loss to account is a crime that
has never been found out, because it was properly executed."

"Silence, sir! I will not hear any more; you make me doubt myself. At this moment my sentiments are all my science."

"Just as you please, my fine fellow; I did not think you were so weak-minded," said Vautrin. "I shall say no more about it. One last word, however," and he looked hard at the student— "you have my secret," he said.

"A young man who refuses your offer knows that he must forget it."

"Quite right; I am glad to hear you say so. Somebody else might not be so scrupulous. Keep in mind what I want to do for you. I will give you a fortnight. The offer is still open."

"What a head of iron the man has!" said Eugène to himself as he watched Vautrin walk unconcernedly away with his cane under his arm. "Yet Madame de Beauséant said as much more gracefully; he has only stated the case in cruder language. He would tear my heart with claws of steel. What made me think of going to Madame de Nucingen? He guessed my motives before I knew them myself. To sum it up, that outlaw has told me more about virtue than all I have learned from men and books. If virtue admits of no compromises, I have certainly robbed my sisters," he said, throwing down the bags on the table.

He sat down again and fell, unconscious of his surroundings, into deep thought.

"To be faithful to an ideal of virtue! A heroic martyrdom! Pshaw! everyone believes in virtue, but who is virtuous? Nations have made an idol of Liberty, but what nation on the face of the earth is free? My youth is still like a blue and cloudless sky. If I set myself to obtain wealth or power, does it not mean that I must make up my mind to lie, and fawn, and cringe, and swagger, and flatter, and dissemble? To consent to be the servant of others who have likewise fawned and lied, and flattered? Must I cringe to them before I can hope to be their accomplice? Well, then, I decline. I mean to work nobly and with a single heart. I will work day and night; I will owe my fortune to nothing but my own exertions. It may be the slowest of all roads to success, but I shall lay my head on the pillow at night untroubled by evil thoughts. Is there a greater or a better thing than this—to look back over your life and know that it is stainless as a lily? I and my life are like a young man and his betrothed. Vautrin has put before me all that comes after ten years of marriage. The devil! my head is swimming. I do not want to think at all; the heart is a sure guide."

Chapter 10

EUGENE WAS roused from his musings by the voice of the stout Sylvie, who announced that the tailor had come, and Eugène therefore made his appearance before the man with the two money bags, and was not ill pleased that it should be so. When he had tried on his dress suit, he put on his new morning costume, which completely metamorphosed him.

"I am quite equal to Monsieur de Trailles," he said to himself. "In short, I look like a gentleman."

"You asked me, sir, if I knew the houses where Madame de Nucingen goes," old Goriot's voice spoke from the doorway of Eugène's room.

"Yes."

"Very well then, she is going to the Maréchal Carigliano's ball on Monday. If you can manage to be there, I shall hear from you whether my two girls enjoyed themselves, and how they were dressed, and all about it."

"How did you find that out, my good Goriot?" said Eugène, putting a chair by the fire for his visitor.

"Her maid told me. I hear all about their doings from Thérèse and Constance," he added happily.

The old man looked like a lover who is still young enough to be made joyful by the discovery of some little stratagem which brings him information of his lady-love without her knowledge.

"*You* will see them both!" he said, giving artless expression to a pang of jealousy.

"I do not know," answered Eugène. "I will go to Madame de Beauséant and ask her for an introduction to the Maréchale."

Eugène felt a thrill of pleasure at the thought of appearing before the vicomtesse, dressed as henceforward he always meant to be. The "abysses of the human heart," in the moralists' phrase, are only insidious thoughts, involuntary promptings of personal interest. The instinct of enjoyment turns the scale; those rapid changes of purpose which have furnished the text for so much rhetoric are calculations prompted by the hope of pleasure. Rastignac beholding himself well dressed and impeccable as to gloves and boots, forgot his virtuous resolutions. Youth, moreover, when bent upon wrong doing does not dare to behold itself in the mirror of consciousness; mature age has seen itself; and therein lies the whole difference between these two phases of life.

A friendship between Eugène and his neighbor, old Goriot, had been growing up for several days past. This secret friendship and the antipathy that the student had begun to entertain for Vautrin arose from the same psychological causes. The bold philosopher who shall investigate the effects of mental action upon the physical world will doubtless find more than one proof of the material nature of our sentiments in the relations which they create between human beings and other animals. What physiognomist is as quick to discern character as a dog is to discover from a stranger's face whether this is a friend or no? Those by-words—"atoms," "affinities"—are facts surviving in modern languages for the confusion of philosophic wiseacres who amuse themselves by winnowing the chaff of language to find its grammatical roots. We *feel* that we are loved. Our sentiments make themselves felt in everything, even at a great distance. A letter is a living soul, and so faithful an echo of the voice that speaks in it, that finer natures look upon a letter as one of love's most precious treasures. Old Goriot's affection was of the instinctive order, a canine affection raised to a sublime pitch; he had scented compassion in the air, and the kindly respect and youthful sympathy in the student's heart. This friendship had, however, scarcely reached the stage at which confidences are made. Though Eugène had spoken of his wish to meet Mme de Nucingen, it was not because he counted on the old man to introduce him to her house, for he hoped that his own audacity might stand him in good stead. All that old Goriot had said as yet about his daughters had referred to the remarks that the student had made so freely in public on that day of the two visits.

"How could you think that Madame de Restaud bore you a grudge for mentioning my name?" he had said on the day following that scene at dinner. "My daughters are very fond of me; I am a happy father; but my sons-in-law have behaved badly to me, and rather than make trouble between my darlings and their husbands, I choose to see my daughters secretly. Fathers who can see their daughters at any time have no idea of all the pleasure that this mystery gives me. I cannot always see mine when I wish, do you understand? So when it is fine I walk out in the Champs-Élysées, after finding out from their maids whether my daughters mean to go out. I wait near the entrance; my heart beats fast when the carriages begin to come; I admire them in their dresses, and as they pass they give me a little smile, and it seems as if everything was lighted up for me by a ray of bright sunlight. I wait, for they always go back the same way, and then I see them again; the fresh air has done them good and brought color into their cheeks. All about me people say, 'What a beautiful woman that is!' and it does my heart good to hear them.

"Are they not my own flesh and blood? I love the very horses that draw them; I envy the little lap-dog on their knees. Their happiness is my life. Everyone loves after his own fashion, and mine does no one any harm; why should people trouble their heads about me? I am happy in my own way. Is there any law against my going to see my girls in the evening when they are going out to a ball? And what a disappointment it is when I get there too late, and am told that 'Madame has gone out'! Once I waited till three o'clock in the morning for Nasie; I had not seen her for two whole days. I was so pleased, that it was almost too much for me! Please do not speak of me unless it is to say how good my daughters are to me. They are always wanting to heap presents upon me, but I will not have it. 'Just keep your money,' I tell them. 'What should I do with it? I want nothing.' And what am I, sir, after all? An old carcass, whose soul is always where my daughters are. When you have seen Madame de Nucingen, tell me which you like the most," said the old man after a moment's pause, while Eugène put the last touches to his toilette. The student was about to go out to walk in the Garden of the Tuileries until the hour when he could venture to appear in Mme de Beauséant's drawing-room.

That walk was a turning-point in Eugène's career. Several women noticed him; he looked so handsome, so young, and so well dressed. This almost admiring attention gave a new turn to his thoughts. He forgot his sisters and the aunt who had robbed herself for him; he no longer remembered his own virtuous scruples. He had seen hovering above his head the fiend so easy to mistake for an angel, the devil with rainbow wings, who scatters rubies, and aims his golden shafts at palace fronts, who invests women with purple, and thrones with a glory that dazzles the eyes of fools till they forget the simple origins of royal dominion; he had heard the rustle of that Vanity whose tinsel seems to us to be the symbol of power. However cynical Vautrin's words had been, they had made an impression on his mind, as the sordid features of the old crone who whispers, "A lover, and gold in torrents," remain engraven on a young girl's memory.

Eugène lounged about the walks till it was nearly five o'clock, then he went to Mme de Beauséant, and received one of the terrible blows against which young hearts are defenseless. Hitherto the vicomtesse had received him with the kindly urbanity, the bland grace of manner that is the result of fine breeding, but is only complete when it comes from the heart.

Today Mme de Beauséant bowed constrainedly, and spoke curtly:

"Monsieur de Rastignac, I cannot possibly see you, at least not at this moment. I am engaged . . ."

An observer, and Rastignac instantly became an observer, could read the whole history, the character and customs of caste, in the phrase, in the tones of her voice, in her glance and bearing. He caught a glimpse of the iron hand beneath the velvet glove—the personality, the egoism beneath the manner, the wood beneath the varnish. In short, he heard that unmistakable I THE KING that issues from the plumed canopy of the throne, and finds its last echo under the crest of the simplest gentleman.

Eugène had trusted too implicitly to the generosity of a woman; he could not believe in her haughtiness. Like all the unfortunate, he had signed, in all good faith, the generous compact which should bind the benefactor to the recipient, and the first article in that bond, between two large-hearted natures, is a perfect equality. The kindness which knits two souls together is as rare, as divine, and as little understood as the passion of love, for both love and kindness are the lavish generosity of noble natures. Rastignac was set upon going to the Duchesse de Carigliano's ball, so he swallowed down this rebuff.

"Madame," he faltered out, "I would not have come to trouble you about a trifling matter; be so kind as to permit me to see you later, I can wait."

"Very well, come and dine with me," she said, a little confused by the harsh way in which she had spoken, for this lady was as genuinely kind-hearted as she was high-born.

Eugène was touched by this sudden relenting, but none the less he said to himself as he went away, "Crawl in the dust, put up with every kind of treatment. What must the rest of the world be like when one of the kindest of women forgets all her promises of befriending me in a moment, and tosses me aside like an old shoe? So it is everyone for himself? It is true that her house is not a shop, and I have put myself in the wrong by needing her help. You should cut your way through the world like a cannon-ball, as Vautrin said."

But the student's bitter thoughts were soon dissipated by the pleasure which he promised himself in this dinner with the vicomtesse. Fate seemed to determine that the smallest accidents in his life should combine to urge him into a career, which the terrible sphinx of the Maison Vauquer had described as a field of battle where you must either slay or be slain, and cheat to avoid being cheated. You leave your conscience and your heart at the barriers, and wear a mask on entering into this game of grim earnest, where, as in ancient Sparta, you must snatch your prize without being detected if you would deserve the crown.

On his return he found the vicomtesse gracious and kindly, as she had always been to him. They went together to the dining room, where the vicomte was waiting for his wife. In the time of the Restoration the luxury of the table was carried, as is well known, to the highest degree, and M. de Beauséant, like many jaded men of the world, had few pleasures left but those of good cheer; in this matter, in fact, he was a gourmand of the schools of Louis XVIII, and of the Duc d'Escars, and luxury was supplemented by splendor. Eugène, dining for the first time in a house where the traditions of grandeur had descended through many generations, had never seen any spectacle like this that now met his eyes. In the time of the Empire, balls had always ended with a supper, because the officers who took part in them must be fortified for immediate service, and even in Paris might be called upon to leave the ballroom for the battle-field. This arrangement had gone out of fashion under the Monarchy, and Eugène had so far only been asked to dances. The self-possession which pre-eminently distinguished him in later life already stood him in good stead, and he did not betray his amazement. Yet as he saw for the first time the finely wrought silver-plate, the completeness of every detail, the sumptuous dinner, noiselessly served, it was natural for such an ardent imagination to prefer this life of studied and refined luxury to the hardships of the life which he had chosen only that morning.

His thoughts went back for a moment to the lodginghouse, and with a feeling of profound loathing, he vowed to himself that at New Year he would go; prompted at least as much by a desire to live among cleaner surroundings as by a wish to shake off Vautrin, whose huge hand he seemed to feel on his shoulder at that moment. When you consider the numberless forms, clamorous or mute, that corruption takes in Paris, common sense begins to wonder what mental aberration prompted the State to establish great colleges and schools there, and assemble young men in the capital; how it is that pretty women are respected, or that the gold coin displayed in the money-changer's wooden saucers does not take to itself wings in the twinkling of an eye; and when you come to think further, how comparatively few cases of crime there are, and to count up the misdemeanors committed by youth, is there not a certain amount of respect due to these patient Tantaluses who wrestle with themselves and nearly always come off victorious? The struggles of the poor student in Paris, if skillfully drawn, would furnish a most dramatic picture of modern civilization.

In vain Mme de Beauséant looked at Eugène as if asking him to speak; the student was tongue-tied in the vicomte's presence.

"Are you going to take me to the Italiens this evening?" the vicomtesse asked her husband.

"You cannot doubt that I should obey you with pleasure," he answered, and there was a sarcastic tinge in his politeness which Eugène did not detect, "but I ought to go to meet someone at the Variétés."

"His mistress," said she to herself.

"Then, is not d'Ajuda coming for you this evening?" inquired the vicomte.

"No," she answered, petulantly.

"Very well, then, if you really must have an arm, take that of Monsieur de Rastignac."

The vicomtesse turned to Eugène with a smile.

"That would be a very compromising step for you," she said.

" 'A Frenchman loves danger, because in danger there is glory,' to quote Monsieur de Chateaubriand," said Rastignac, with a bow.

A few moments later he was sitting beside Mme de Beauséant in a brougham that whirled them through the streets of Paris to a fashionable theater. It seemed to him that some fairy magic had suddenly transported him into a box facing the stage. All the lorgnettes of the house were pointed at him as he entered, and at the vicomtesse in her charming costume. He went from enchantment to enchantment.

"You must talk to me, you know," said Mme de Beauséant. "Ah, look! There is Madame de Nucingen in the third box from ours. Her sister and Monsieur de Trailles are on the other side."

The vicomtesse glanced as she spoke at the box where Mlle de Rochefide should have been; M. d'Ajuda was not there, and Mme de Beauséant's face lighted up in a marvelous way.

"She is charming," said Eugène, after looking at Mme de Nucingen.

"She has white eyelashes."

"Yes, but she has such a pretty slender figure!"

"Her hands are large."

"Such beautiful eyes!"

"Her face is long."

"Yes, but length gives distinction."

"It is lucky for her that she has some distinction in her face. Just see how she fidgets with her opera-glass! The Goriot blood shows itself in every movement," said the vicomtesse, much to Eugène's astonishment.

Indeed, Mme de Beauséant seemed to be engaged in making a survey of the house, and to be unconscious of Mme Nucingen's existence; but no movement made by the latter was lost upon the vicomtesse. The house was full of the loveliest women in Paris, so that Delphine de Nucingen was not a little flattered to receive the undivided attention of Mme de Beauséant's young, handsome, and well-dressed cousin, who seemed to have no eyes for anyone else.

"If you look at her so persistently, you will make people talk, Monsieur de Rastignac. You will never succeed if you fling yourself at anyone's head like that."

"My dear cousin," said Eugène, "you have protected me indeed so far, and now if you would complete your work, I only ask of you a favor which will cost you but little, and be of very great service to me. I have lost my heart."

"Already!"

"Yes."

"And to that woman!"

"How could I aspire to find anyone else to listen to me?" he asked, with a keen glance at his cousin. "Her Grace the Duchesse de Carigliano is a friend of the Duchesse de Berri," he went on, after a pause; "you are sure to see her. Will you be so kind as to present me to her, and to take me with you to her ball on Monday? I shall meet Madame de Nucingen there, and enter upon my first skirmish."

"Willingly," she said. "If you have a liking for her already, your affairs of the heart are like to prosper. That is de Marsay over there in the Princesse Galathionne's box. Madame de Nucingen is racked with jealousy. There is no better time for approaching a woman, especially if she happens to be a banker's wife. All those ladies of the Chaussée-d'Antin love revenge."

"Then, what would you do yourself in such a case?"

"I should suffer in silence."

At this point the Marquis d'Ajuda appeared in Mme de Beauséant's box.

"I have made a muddle of my affairs to come to you," he said, "and I am telling you about it, so that it may not be a sacrifice."

Eugène saw the glow of joy on the vicomtesse's face, and knew that this was love, and learned the difference between love and the affectations of Parisian coquetry. He admired his cousin, grew mute, and yielded his place to M. d'Ajuda with a sigh.

"How noble, how sublime a woman is when she loves like that!" he said to himself. "And *he* could forsake her for a doll! Oh! how could anyone forsake her?"

There was a boy's passionate indignation in his heart. He could have flung himself at Mme de Beauséant's feet; he longed for the power of the devil if he could snatch her away and hide her in his heart, as an eagle snatches up some white lamb from the plains and bears it to his eyrie. It was humiliating to him to think that in all this gallery of fair pictures he had not one picture of his own. "To have a mistress and an almost royal position is a sign of power," he said to himself. And he looked at Mme de Nucingen as a man measures another who has insulted him.

The vicomtesse turned to him, and the expression of her eyes thanked him a thousand times for his discretion. The first act came to an end just then.

"Do you know Madame de Nucingen well enough to present

Monsieur de Rastignac to her?" she asked of the Marquis
d'Ajuda.

"She will be delighted," said the marquis. The handsome Portuguese rose as he spoke and took the student's arm, and in another moment Eugène found himself in Mme de Nucingen's box.

"Madame," said the Marquis, "I have the honor of presenting
to you the Chevalier Eugène de Rastignac; he is a cousin of
Madame de Beauséant's. You have made so deep an impression
upon him, that I thought I would fill up the measure of his happiness by bringing him nearer to his divinity."

Words spoken half jestingly to cover their somewhat disre-
spectful import; but such an implication, if carefully disguised,
never gives offense to a woman. Mme de Nucingen smiled, and
offered Eugène the place which her husband had just left.

"I do not venture to suggest that you should stay with me,
monsieur," she said. "Those who are so fortunate as to be in
Madame de Beauséant's company do not desire to leave it."

"Madame," Eugène said, lowering his voice, "I think that to
please my cousin I should remain with you. Before my lord
marquis came we were speaking of you and of your exceedingly
distinguished appearance," he added aloud.

M. d'Ajuda turned and left them.

"Are you really going to stay with me, monsieur?" asked the
baroness. "Then we shall make each other's acquaintance.
Madame de Restaud told me about you, and has made me anxious
to meet you."

"She must be very insincere, then, for she has shut her door
on me."

"What?"

"Madame, I will tell you honestly the reason why; but I must
crave your indulgence before confiding such a secret to you. I
am your father's neighbor; I had no idea that Madame de Restaud
was his daughter. I was rash enough to mention his name; I meant
no harm, but I annoyed your sister and her husband very much.

You cannot think how severely the Duchesse de Langeais and my cousin blamed this apostasy on a daughter's part, as a piece of bad taste. I told them all about it, and they both burst out laughing. Then Madame de Beauséant made some comparison between you and your sister, speaking in high terms of you, and saying how very fond you were of my neighbor, Monsieur Goriot. And, indeed, how could you help loving him? He adores you so passionately that I am jealous already. We talked about you this morning for two hours. So this evening I was quite full of all that your father had told me, and while I was dining with my cousin I said that you could not be as beautiful as affectionate. Madame de Beauséant meant to gratify such warm admiration, I think, when she brought me here, telling me, in her gracious way, that I should see you."

"Then, even now, I owe you a debt of gratitude, monsieur," said the banker's wife. "We shall be quite old friends in a little while."

"Although a friendship with you could not be like an ordinary friendship," said Rastignac, "I should never wish to be your friend."

Such stereotyped phrases as these, in the mouths of beginners, possess an unfailing charm for women, and are insipid only when read in cold type; for a young man's tone, glance, and attitude give a surpassing eloquence to the banal phrases. Mme de Nucingen thought that Rastignac was adorable. Then, woman-like, being at a loss how to reply to the student's outspoken admiration, she answered a previous remark.

"Yes, it is very wrong of my sister to treat our poor father as she does," she said; "he has been a Providence to us. It was not until Monsieur de Nucingen positively ordered me only to receive him in the mornings that I yielded the point. But I have been unhappy about it for a long while; I have shed many tears over it. This violence to my feelings, with my husband's brutal treatment, have been the two causes of my unhappy married life.

There is certainly no woman in Paris whose lot seems more enviable than mine, and yet, in reality, there is not one so much to be pitied. You will think I must be out of my senses to talk to you like this; but you know my father, and I cannot regard you as a stranger."

"You will find no one," said Eugène, "who longs as eagerly as I do to do you service. What do all women seek? Happiness." He answered his own question in low, vibrating tones. "And if happiness for a woman means that she is to be loved and adored, to have a friend to whom she can pour out her wishes, her fancies, her sorrows and joys; to whom she can lay bare her heart and soul, and all her fair defects and her gracious virtues, without fear of a betrayal, believe me, the devotion and the warmth that never fails can only be found in the heart of a young man who, at a bare sign from you, would go to his death, who neither knows nor cares to know anything as yet of the world, because you will be all the world to him. You see, I myself—you will laugh at my simplicity—have just come from a remote country district; I am quite new to this world of Paris; I have only known true and loving hearts; and I made up my mind that here I should find no love. Then I chanced to meet my cousin, and to see my cousin's heart from very near. I have divined the inexhaustible treasures of passion, and, like Cherubino, I am the lover of all women, until the day comes when I find *the* woman to whom I may devote myself. As soon as I saw you, as soon as I came into the theater this evening, I felt myself borne towards you as if by the current of a stream. I had so often thought of you already, but I had never dreamed that you would be so beautiful! Madame de Beauséant told me that I must not look so much at you. She does not know the charm of your red lips, your fair face, nor see how soft your eyes are. I also am beginning to talk nonsense; but let me talk."

Nothing pleases women better than to listen to such whispered words as these. The most puritanical among them listens even when she ought not to reply to them, and Rastignac, having once begun, continued to pour out his story, dropping his voice, that she might lean and listen; and Mme de Nucingen, smiling, glanced from time to time at de Marsay, who still sat in the Princesse Galathionne's box.

Rastignac did not leave Mme de Nucingen till her husband came to take her home.

"Madame," Eugène said, "I shall have the pleasure of calling upon you before the Duchesse de Carigliano's ball."

"If Matame infites you to come," said the baron, a thick-set Alsatian, with indications of a sinister cunning in his full-moon countenance, "you are quide sure of being well receifed."

"My affairs seem to be in a promising way," said Eugène to himself. " 'Can you love me?' I asked her, and she did not resent it. The bit is in the horse's mouth, and I have only to mount and ride"; and with that he went to pay his respects to Mme de Beauséant, who was leaving the theater on d'Ajuda's arm.

The student did not know that the baroness' thoughts had been wandering; that she was even then expecting a letter from de Marsay, one of those letters that bring about a rupture that rends the soul; so, happy in his delusion, Eugène went with the vicomtesse to the peristyle, where people were waiting till their carriages were announced.

"That cousin of yours is hardly recognizable for the same man," said the Portuguese laughingly to the vicomtesse, when Eugène had taken leave of them. "He will break the bank. He is as supple as an eel; he will go a long way, of that I am sure. Who else could have picked out a woman for him, as you did, just when she needed consolation?"

"But it is not certain that she does not still love the faithless lover," said Mme de Beauséant.

The student meanwhile walked back from the Théâtre-Italien to the Rue Neuve-Sainte-Geneviève, making the most delightful plans as he went. He had noticed how closely Mme de Restaud had scrutinized him when he appeared in the vicomtesse's box, and again when he sat beside Mme de Nucingen, and inferred that the countess' doors would not be closed in future. Four important houses were now open to him—for he meant to stand well with the Maréchale; he had four supporters in the inmost circle of society in Paris. Even now it was clear to him that, once involved in this intricate social machinery, he must attach himself to a spoke of the wheel that was to turn and raise his fortunes; he would not examine himself too curiously as to the methods, but he was certain of the end, and conscious of the power to gain and keep his hold.

"If Madame de Nucingen takes an interest in me, I will teach her how to manage her husband. That husband of hers is a great speculator; he might put me in the way of making a fortune by a single stroke."

He did not say this bluntly in so many words; as yet, indeed, he was not sufficient of a diplomatist to sum up a situation, to see its possibilities at a glance, and calculate the chances in his favor. These were nothing but hazy ideas that floated over his mental horizon; they were less cynical than Vautrin's notions, but if they had been tried in the crucible of conscience, no very pure result would have issued from the test. It is by a succession of such transactions that men sink at last to the level of the relaxed morality of this epoch, when there have never been so few of those who square their courses with their theories, so few of those noble characters who do not yield to temptation, for whom the slightest deviation from the line of rectitude is a crime. To these magnificent types of uncompromising Right we owe two masterpieces—the Alceste of Molière, and, in our own day, the characters of Jeanie Deans and her father in Sir Walter Scott's novel. Perhaps a work which should chronicle the opposite course, which should trace out all the devious courses through which a man of the world, a man of ambitions, drags his conscience, just steering clear of crime that he may gain his end and yet save appearances, such a chronicle would be no less edifying and no less dramatic.

Rastignac went home. He was fascinated by Mme de Nucingen; he seemed to see her before him, slender and graceful as a swallow. He recalled the intoxicating sweetness of her eyes, her fair hair, the delicate silken tissue of the skin, beneath which it almost seemed to him that he could see the blood coursing; the tones of her voice still exerted a spell over him; he had forgotten nothing; his walk perhaps heated his imagination by sending a glow of warmth through his veins. He knocked unceremoniously at Goriot's door.

"I have seen Madame Delphine, neighbor," said he.

"Where?"

"At the Italiens."

"Did she enjoy it? . . . Just come inside," and the old man left his bed, unlocked the door, and promptly got in bed again.

It was the first time that Eugène had been in old Goriot's room, and he could not control his feeling of amazement at the contrast between the den in which the father lived and the costume of the daughter whom he had just beheld. The window was curtainless, the walls were damp, in places the varnished wallpaper had come away and gave glimpses of the grimy yellow plaster beneath. The wretched bed on which the old man lay boasted but one thin blanket and a quilt made out of large pieces of Mme Vauquer's old dresses. The floor was damp and gritty. Opposite the window stood a chest of drawers made of rosewood, one of the old-fashioned kind with a curving front and brass handles, shaped like rings of twisted vine-stems covered with flowers and leaves. On a venerable piece of furniture with a wooden shelf stood a ewer and basin and shaving apparatus. A pair of shoes stood in one corner; a night-table by the bed had neither a door nor marble slab. There was not a trace of a fire in the empty grate; the square walnut table with the cross-bar against which old Goriot had crushed and twisted his posset-dish stood near the hearth. The old man's hat was lying on a broken-down bureau. An armchair stuffed with straw and a couple of chairs completed the list of ramshackle furniture. From the tester of the bed, tied to the ceiling by a piece of rag, hung a strip of some cheap material in large red and black checks. No poor drudge in a garret could be worse lodged than old Goriot in Mme Vauquer's lodginghouse. The mere sight of the room sent a chill through you and a sense of oppression; it was like the worst cell in a prison. Luckily, Goriot could not see the effect that his surroundings produced on Eugène as the latter deposited his candle on the night-table. The old man turned round, keeping the bedclothes huddled up to his chin.

"Well," he said, "and which do you like the best: Madame de Restaud or Madame de Nucingen?"

"I like Madame Delphine the best," said the law student, "because she loves you the best."

At the words so heartily spoken the old man's hand slipped out from under the bedclothes and grasped Eugène's.

"Thank you, thank you," he said, gratefully. "Then what did she say about me?"

The student repeated the baroness' remarks with some embellishments of his own, the old man listening the while as though he heard a voice from heaven.

"Dear child!" he said. "Yes, yes, she is very fond of me. But you must not believe all that she tells you about Anastasie. The two sisters are jealous of each other, you see; another proof of their affection. Madame de Restaud is very fond of me too. I know she is. A father sees his children as God sees all of us; he looks into the very depths of their hearts; he knows their intentions; and both of them are so loving. Oh! if I only had good sons-in-law, I should be too happy, and I dare say there is no perfect happiness here below. If I might live with them—simply hear their voices, know that they are there, see them go and come

as I used to do at home when they were still with me; why, my
heart bounds at the thought. . . . Were they nicely dressed?"

"Yes," said Eugène. "But, Monsieur Goriot, how is it that
your daughters have such fine houses, while you live in such a
den as this?"

"Dear me, why should I want anything better?" he replied,
with seeming carelessness. "I can't quite explain to you how it is;
I am not used to stringing words together properly, but it all lies
there—" he said, tapping his heart. "My real life is in my two
girls, you see; and so long as they are happy and smartly dressed,
and have soft carpets under their feet, what does it matter what
clothes I wear or where I lie down of a night? I shall never feel
cold so long as they are warm; I shall never feel dull if they are
laughing. I have no troubles but theirs. When you are a father
and you hear your children's little voices, you will say to yourself, 'That has all come from me.' You will feel that those little
ones are akin to every drop in your veins, that they are the very
flower of your life—and what else are they? You will cleave so
closely to them that you seem to feel every movement that they
make. Everywhere I hear their voices sounding in my ears. If
they are sad, the look in their eyes freezes my blood. Some
day you will find out that there is far more happiness in another's
happiness than in your own. It is something that I cannot explain,
something within that sends a glow of warmth all through you.
In short, I live my life three times over. Shall I tell you something
funny? Well, then, since I have been a father, I have come to
understand God. He is everywhere in the world, because the
whole world comes from Him. And it is just the same with my
children, monsieur. Only, I love my daughters better than God
loves the world, for the world is not so beautiful as God Himself is, but my children are more beautiful than I am. Their lives
are so bound up with mine that I felt somehow that you would
see them this evening. Great Heaven! If any man would make
my little Delphine as happy as a wife is when she is loved, I

would black his boots and run on his errands. That miserable de Marsay is a cur; I know all about him from her maid. A longing to wring his neck comes over me now and then. He does not love her! does not love a pearl of a woman, with a voice like a nightingale and shaped like a model. Where can her eyes have been when she married that great lump of an Alsatian? They ought both of them to have married young men, good-looking and good-tempered—but, after all, they had their own way."

Father Goriot was sublime. Eugène had never yet seen his face light up as it did now with the passionate fervor of a father's love. It is worthy of remark that strong feeling has a very subtle and pervasive power; the roughest nature, in the endeavor to express a deep and sincere affection, communicates to others the influence that has put resonance into the voice, and eloquence into every gesture, wrought a change in the very features of the speaker; for under the inspiration of passion the stupidest human being attains to the highest eloquence of ideas, if not of language, and seems to move in some sphere of light. In the old man's tones and gesture there was something just then of the same spell that a great actor exerts over his audience. But does not the poet in us find expression in our affections?

"Well," said Eugène, "perhaps you will not be sorry to hear that she is pretty sure to break with de Marsay before long. That sprig of fashion has left her for the Princesse Galathionne. As for me, I fell in love with Madame Delphine this evening."

"Nonsense!" said old Goriot.

"I did indeed, and she did not regard me with aversion. For a whole hour we talked of love, and I am to go to call on her on Saturday, the day after tomorrow."

"Oh! how I should love you, if she should like you. You are kind-hearted; you would never make her miserable. If you were to forsake her, I would cut your throat at once. A woman does not love twice, you see! Good heavens! what nonsense I am talking, Monsieur Eugène! It is cold; you ought not to stay.

Mon Dieu, you heard her speak! What message did she give you for me?"

"None at all," said Eugène to himself; aloud he answered, "She told me to tell you that your daughter sends you a good kiss."

"Good night, neighbor! Sleep well, and pleasant dreams to you! I have mine already made for me by that message from her. May God grant you all your desires! You have come in like a good angel on me tonight, and brought with you the air that my daughter breathes."

"Poor old fellow!" said Eugène as he lay down. "It is enough to melt a heart of stone. His daughter no more thought of him than of the Grand Turk."

After this conversation Goriot looked upon his neighbor as a friend, a confidant such as he had never hoped to find; and there was established between the two the only relationship that could attach this old man to another man. The passions never miscalculate. Old Goriot felt that this friendship brought him closer to his daughter Delphine; he thought that he should find a warmer welcome for himself if the baroness should care for Eugène. Moreover, he had confided one of his troubles to the younger man. Mme de Nucingen, for whose happiness he prayed a thousand times daily, had never known the joys of love. Eugène was certainly (to make use of his own expression) one of the nicest young men that he had ever seen, and some prophetic instinct seemed to tell him that Eugène was to give her the happiness which had not been hers. These were the beginnings of a friendship that grew up between the old man and his neighbor; but for this friendship the climax of the drama must have remained a mystery.

Chapter II

THE AFFECTION with which old Goriot regarded Eugène, by whom he seated himself at breakfast, the change in Goriot's face, which, as a rule, looked as expressionless as a plaster cast, and a few words that passed between the two, surprised the other lodgers. Vautrin, who saw Eugène for the first time since their interview, seemed desirous of reading the student's very soul. During the night Eugène had had some time in which to scan the vast field which lay before him; and now, as he remembered yesterday's proposal, the thought of Mlle Taillefer's dowry came, of course, to his mind, and he could not help thinking of Victorine as the most exemplary youth may think of an heiress. It chanced that their eyes met. The poor girl did not fail to see that Eugène looked very handsome in his new clothes. So much was said in the glance thus exchanged, that Eugène could not doubt but that he was associated in her mind with the vague hopes that lie dormant in a girl's heart and gather round the first attractive newcomer. "Eight hundred thousand francs!" a voice cried in his ears, but suddenly he took refuge in the memories of yesterday evening, thinking that his extemporized passion for Mme de Nucingen was a talisman that would preserve him from this temptation.

"They gave Rossini's *Barber of Seville* at the Italiens yesterday evening," he remarked. "I never heard such delicious music. Good gracious, how lucky people are to have a box at the Italiens!"

Old Goriot drank in every word that Eugène let fall, and watched him as a dog watches his master's slightest movement.

"You men are like fighting cocks," said Mme Vauquer; "you do what you like."

"How did you get back?" inquired Vautrin.

"I walked," answered Eugène.

"For my own part," remarked the tempter, "I do not care about doing things by halves. If I want to enjoy myself that way, I should prefer to go in my carriage, sit in my own box, and do the thing comfortably. Everything or nothing—that's my motto."

"And a good one, too," commented Mme Vauquer.

"Perhaps you will see Madame de Nucingen today," said Eugène, addressing Goriot in an undertone. "She will welcome you with open arms, I am sure; she would want to ask you for all sorts of little details about me. I have found out that she would do anything in the world to be known by my cousin Madame de Beauséant. Don't forget to tell her that I love her too well not to think of trying to arrange this."

Rastignac went at once to the law school. He had no mind to stay a moment longer than was necessary in that odious building. He wasted his time that day; he had fallen a victim to that fever of the brain that accompanies the too vivid hopes of youth. Vautrin's arguments had set him meditating on social life, and he was deep in these reflections when he happened on his friend Bianchon in the Jardin du Luxembourg.

"What makes you look so solemn?" said the medical student, putting an arm through Eugène's as they went towards the Palais.

"I am tormented by temptations."

"What kind? There is a cure for temptation."

"What?"

"Yielding to it."

"You laugh, but you don't know what it is all about. Have you read Rousseau?"

"Yes."

"Do you remember that he asks the reader somewhere what he would do if he could make a fortune by killing an old mandarin somewhere in China by mere force of wishing it, and without stirring from Paris?"

"Yes."

"Well, then?"

"Pshaw! I am at my thirty-third mandarin."

"Seriously, though. Look here, suppose you were sure that you could do it, and had only to give a nod. Would you do it?"

"Is he well stricken in years, this mandarin of yours? Pshaw! after all, young or old, paralytic, or well and sound, my word for it. . . . Well, then. Hang it, no!"

"You are a good fellow, Bianchon. But suppose you loved a woman well enough to lose your soul in hell for her, and that she wanted money, lots of money for dresses and a carriage, and all her whims, in fact?"

"Why, here you are taking away my reason, and want me to reason!"

"Well, then, Bianchon, I am mad; bring me to my senses. I have two sisters as beautiful and innocent as angels, and I want them to be happy. How am I to find two hundred thousand francs apiece for them in the next five years? Now and then in life, you see, you must play for heavy stakes, and it is no use wasting your luck on low play."

"But you are only stating the problem that lies before everyone at the outset of his life, and you want to cut the Gordian knot with a sword. If that is the way of it, dear boy, you must be an Alexander, or to the galleys you go. For my own part, I am quite contented with the little lot I mean to make for myself somewhere in the country, when I mean to step into my father's shoes and plod along. A man's affections are just as fully satisfied by the smallest circle as they can be by a vast circumference. Napoleon himself could only dine once, and he could not have more mistresses than an intern at the Capucins. Happiness, old man, depends on what lies between the sole of your foot and the crown of your head; and whether it costs a million or a hundred louis, the actual amount of pleasure that you receive rests entirely with you, and is just exactly the same in any case. I am for letting that mandarin live."

"Thank you, Bianchon; you have done me good. We will always be friends."

"I say," remarked the medical student, as they came to the end of a broad walk in the Jardin des Plantes, "I saw the Michonneau and Poiret a few minutes ago on a bench chatting with a gentleman whom I used to see during last year's troubles hanging about the Chamber of Deputies. He looked to me like a detective dressed up as a decent retired tradesman. We must keep an eye on that couple; I will tell you why some time. Goodbye; it is nearly four o'clock, and I must be in to answer to my name."

When Eugène reached the lodginghouse, he found old Goriot waiting for him.

"Here!" cried the old man, "here is a letter from her. Pretty handwriting, eh?"

Eugène broke the seal and read:

Sir,—I have heard from my father that you are fond of Italian music. I shall be delighted if you will do me the pleasure of accepting a seat in my box. La Fodor and Pellegrini will sing on Saturday, so I am sure that you will not refuse me. M. de Nucingen and I shall be pleased if you will dine with us; we shall be quite by ourselves. If you will come and be my escort, my husband will be glad to be relieved from his conjugal duties. Do not answer, but simply come.—Yours sincerely,   D. DE N.

"Let me see it," said old Goriot, when Eugène had read the letter. "You are going, aren't you?" he added, when he had smelt the writing paper. "How nice it smells! Her fingers have touched it, that is certain."

"A woman does not fling herself at a man's head in this way," the student was thinking. "She wants to use me to bring back de Marsay; nothing but pique makes a woman do a thing like this."

"Well," said old Goriot, "what are you thinking about?"

Eugène did not know the fever of vanity that possessed some women in those days; how should he imagine that to open a door in the Faubourg Saint-Germain a banker's wife would go to almost any length. For the coterie of the Faubourg Saint-Germain was a charmed circle, and the women who moved in it were at that time the queens of society; and among the greatest of these *Dames du Petit-Château,* as they were called, were Mme de Beauséant and her friends the Duchesse de Langeais and the Duchesse de Maufrigneuse. Rastignac was alone in his ignorance of the frantic efforts made by women who lived in the Chaussée-d'Antin to enter this seventh heaven and shine among the brightest constellations of their sex. But his cautious disposition stood him in good stead, making him aloof and giving him the not altogether enviable power of doing instead of accepting a favor.

"Yes, I am going," he replied.

So it was curiosity that drew him to Mme de Nucingen; while, if she had treated him disdainfully, passion perhaps might have brought him to her feet. Still he waited almost impatiently for tomorrow, and the hour when he could go to her. There is almost as much charm for a young man in a first flirtation as there is in first love. The certainty of success is a source of happiness to which men do not confess, and all the charm of certain women lies in this. The desire of conquest springs no less from the easiness than from the difficulty of triumph, and every passion is excited or sustained by one or other of these two motives which divide the empire of love. Perhaps this division is one result of the great question of temperaments; which, after all, dominates social life. The melancholy temperament may stand in need of the tonic of coquetry, while those of nervous or sanguine complexion withdraw if they meet with a too stubborn resistance.

In other words, the lymphatic temperament is essentially despondent, and the rhapsodic is bilious.

Eugène lingered over his dressing with an enjoyment of all its little details that is grateful to a young man's self-love, though he will not own to it for fear of being laughed at. He thought, as he arrranged his hair, that a pretty woman's glances would wander through the dark curls. He indulged in childish tricks like any young girl dressing for a dance, and gazed complacently at his graceful figure while he smoothed out the creases of his coat.

"There are worse figures, that is certain," he said to himself.

Then he went downstairs, just as the rest of the household were sitting down to dinner, and took with good humor the boisterous applause excited by his elegant appearance. The amazement with which any attention to dress is regarded in a lodginghouse is a very characteristic trait. No one can put on a new coat but everyone else must say his say about it.

"Clk! clk! clk!" cried Bianchon, making the sound with his tongue against the roof of his mouth, like a driver urging on a horse.

"He holds himself like a duke and a peer of France," said Mme Vauquer.

"Are you going a-courting?" inquired Mlle Michonneau.

"Cock-a-doodle-doo!" cried the artist.

"My compliments to my lady your wife," from the employee at the Museum.

"Monsieur has a wife?" asked Poiret.

"Yes, in compartments, water-tight and floats, guaranteed fast color, all prices from twenty-five to forty sous, neat check patterns in the latest fashion and best taste, will wash, half-linen, half-cotton, half-wool; a certain cure for toothache and other complaints under the patronage of the Royal College of Physicians! children like it! a remedy for headache, indigestion, and all other diseases affecting the throat, eyes, and ears!" cried Vautrin, with a comical imitation of the volubility of a quack at a fair. "And how much shall we say for this marvel, gentlemen? Twopence? No. Nothing of the sort. All that is left in stock after supplying the Great Mogul. All the crowned heads of Europe, including the Gr-r-r-rand Duke of Baden, have been anxious to get a sight of it. Walk up! walk up! gentlemen! Pay at the desk as you go in! Strike up the music there! Brooum, la, la, trinn! la, la, boum! boum! Mister Clarinet, there, you are out of tune!" he added gruffly; "I will rap your knuckles for you!"

"Goodness, what an amusing man!" said Mme Vauquer to Mme Couture; "I should never feel dull with him in the house."

This burlesque of Vautrin's was the signal for an outburst of merriment, and under cover of jokes and laughter Eugène caught a glance from Mlle Taillefer; she had leaned over to say a few words in Mme Couture's ear.

"The cab is at the door," announced Sylvie.

"But where is he going to dine?" asked Bianchon.

"With Madame la Baronne de Nucingen."

"Monsieur Goriot's daughter," said the law student.

At this, all eyes turned to the old vermicelli-maker; he was gazing at Eugène with something like envy in his eyes.

Rastignac reached the house in the Rue Saint-Lazare, one of those many-windowed houses with a mean-looking portico and slender columns, which are considered the thing in Paris; a typical banker's house, decorated in the most ostentatious fashion, the walls covered with stucco, the landings of marble mosaic. Mme de Nucingen was sitting in a little drawing-room, which was painted in the Italian fashion like a restaurant. The baroness seemed depressed. The effort that she made to hide her feelings aroused Eugène's interest; it was plain that she was not playing a part. He had expected a little flutter of excitement at his coming, and he found her dispirited and sad. The disappointment piqued his vanity.

"My claim to your confidence is very small, madame," he said, after rallying her on her abstracted mood, "but if I am in the way, I count on your kindness to tell me so frankly."

"No, stay with me," she said; "I shall be all alone if you go. Nucingen is dining in town, and I do not want to be alone; I want to be taken out of myself."

"But what is the matter?"

"You are the very last person whom I should tell," she exclaimed.

"Then I am connected in some way with this secret. I wonder what it is."

"Perhaps. Yet, no," she went on; "it is a domestic quarrel, which ought to be buried in the depths of the heart. I am very unhappy; did I not tell you so the day before yesterday? Golden chains are the heaviest of all fetters."

When a woman tells a young man that she is very unhappy, and when the young man is clever, and well dressed, and has fifteen hundred francs lying idle in his pocket, he is sure to think he is the cause of it all, and he becomes fatuous.

"What can you have left to wish for?" he answered. "You are young, beautiful, beloved, and rich."

"Do not let us talk of my affairs," she said, shaking her head mournfully. "We will dine together *tête-à-tête*, and afterwards we will go to hear the most exquisite music. Do I please you?" she went on, rising and displaying her gown of white cashmere, covered with Persian designs in the most superb taste

"I wish that you were altogether mine," said Eugène. "You are charming."

"You would have a forlorn piece of property," she said, smiling bitterly. "There is nothing about me that betrays my wretchedness, and yet, in spite of appearances, I am in despair. I cannot sleep; my troubles have broken my night's rest; I shall grow ugly."

"Oh, that is impossible!" cried the law student. "But I am

curious to know what these troubles can be that a devoted love cannot efface."

"Ah! if I were to tell you about them, you would shun me," she said. "Your love for me as yet is only the conventional gallantry that men use to masquerade in; and, if you really loved me, you would be driven to despair. I must keep silence, you see. Let us talk of something else for pity's sake," she added. "Let me show you my rooms."

"No, let us stay here," answered Eugène. He sat down on the sofa before the fire, and boldly took Mme de Nucingen's hand in his. She surrendered it to him; he even felt the pressure of her fingers in one of the spasmodic clutches that betray terrible agitation.

"Listen," said Rastignac, "if you are in trouble, you ought to tell me about it. I want to prove to you that I love you for yourself alone. You must speak to me frankly about your troubles, so that I can put an end to them, even if I have to kill half a dozen men; or I shall go, never to return."

"Very well," she cried, putting her hand to her forehead in an agony of despair, "I will put you to the proof, and this very moment. Yes," she said to herself, "I have no other resource left."

She rang the bell.

"Are the horses put in for the master?" she asked of the servant.

"Yes, madame."

"I shall take his carriage myself. He can have mine and my horses. Serve dinner at seven o'clock."

"Now, come with me," she said to Eugène, who thought as he sat in the banker's carriage beside Mme de Nucingen that he must surely be dreaming.

"To the Palais-Royal," she said to the coachman; "stop near the Théâtre-Français."

She seemed to be too troubled and excited to answer the in-

numerable questions that Eugène put to her. He was at a loss
what to think of her mute resistance, her obstinate silence.

"Another moment and she will escape me," he said to himself.

When the carriage stopped at last, the baroness gave the law
student a glance that silenced his wild words, for he was almost
beside himself.

"Is it true that you love me?" she asked.

"Yes," he answered, and in his manner and tone there was no
trace of the uneasiness that he felt.

"You will not think ill of me, will you, whatever I may ask
of you?"

"No."

"Are you ready to do my bidding?"

"Blindly."

"Have you ever been to a gambling house?" she asked in a
tremulous voice.

"Never."

"Ah! now I can breathe. You will have luck. Here is my
purse," she said. "Take it! There are a hundred francs in it, all
that such a fortunate woman as I can call her own. Go up into
one of the gambling houses—I do not know where they are,
but there are some near the Palais-Royal. Try your luck with
the hundred francs at a game they call roulette; lose it all, or
bring me back six thousand francs. I will tell you about my
troubles when you come back."

"Devil take me, I'm sure, if I have a glimmer of a notion of
what I am about, but I will obey you," he said, with inward
exultation, as he thought, "She has gone too far to draw back—
she can refuse me nothing now!"

Eugène took the dainty little purse, inquired the way of a
secondhand clothes-dealer, and hurried to number 9, which
happened to be the nearest gambling-house. He mounted the
staircase, surrendered his hat, and asked the way to the roulette
table, whither the attendant took him, not a little to the astonish-

ment of the regular comers. All eyes were fixed on Eugène as he asked, without bashfulness, where he was to deposit his stakes.

"If you put a louis on one only of those thirty-six numbers, and it turns up, you will win thirty-six louis," said a respectable-looking, white-haired old man in answer to his inquiry.

Eugène staked the whole of his money on the number 21—his own age. There was a cry of surprise; before he knew what he had done, he had won.

"Take your money off, sir," said the old gentleman; "you don't often win twice running by that system."

Eugène took the rake that the old man handed to him, and drew in his three thousand six hundred francs, and, still perfectly ignorant of what he was about, staked again on the red. The bystanders watched him enviously as they saw him continue to play. The disc turned, and again he won; the banker threw him three thousand six hundred francs once more.

"You have seven thousand two hundred francs of your own," the old gentleman said in his ear. "Take my advice and go away with your winnings; red has turned up eight times already. If you are charitable, you will show your gratitude for sound counsel by giving a trifle to an old prefect of Napoleon's who is down on his luck."

Rastignac's head was swimming; he saw ten of his louis pass into the white-haired man's possession, and went downstairs with his seven thousand francs; he was still ignorant of the game, and stupefied by his luck.

"So that is over; and now where will you take me?" he asked, as soon as the door was closed, and he showed the seven thousand francs to Mme de Nucingen.

Delphine flung her arms about him and kissed him effusively, but there was no passion in that wild embrace.

"You have saved me!" she cried, and tears of joy flowed fast.

"I will tell you everything, my friend. For you are my friend, aren't you? I am rich, you think, very rich; I have everything I want, or I seem as if I had everything. Very well, you must know that Monsieur de Nucingen does not allow me the control of a single penny; he pays all the bills for the house expenses; he pays for my carriages and opera box; he does not give me enough to pay for my clothing, and he reduces me to poverty in secret on purpose. I am too proud to beg from him. I should be the vilest of women if I could take his money at the price at which he offers it. Do you ask how I, with seven hundred thousand francs of my own, could let myself be robbed? It is because I was proud, and scorned to speak. We are so young, so artless when our married life begins! I never could bring myself to ask my husband for money; the words would have made my lips bleed, I did not dare to ask. I spent my savings first, and then the money that my poor father gave me, then I ran into debt. Marriage for me is a hideous farce; I cannot talk about it; let it suffice to say that Nucingen and I have separate rooms, and that I would fling myself out of the window sooner than consent to any other arrangement.

"I suffered agonies when I had to confess to my girlish extravagance, my debts for jewelry and trifles (for our poor father had never refused us anything, and spoiled us), but at last I found courage to tell him about them. After all, I had a fortune of my own. Nucingen flew into a rage; he said that I should be the ruin of him, and used frightful language! I wished myself a hundred feet down in the earth. He had my dowry, so he paid my debts, but he stipulated at the same time that my expenses in future must not exceed a certain fixed sum, and I gave way for the sake of peace. And then," she went on, "I wanted to gratify the self-love of someone whom you know. He may have deceived me, but I should do him the justice to say that there was nothing petty in his character. But, after all, he threw me over disgracefully. If, at a woman's utmost need, *somebody* heaps gold upon her, he ought never to forsake her; that love should last forever!

But you, at one-and-twenty, you, the soul of honor, with the unsullied conscience of youth, will ask me how a woman can bring herself to accept money in such a way? *Mon Dieu!* is it not natural to share everything with the one to whom we owe our happiness? When all has been given, why should we pause and hesitate over a part? Money is of no importance until love vanishes. Were we not bound to each other for life? Who that believes in love foresees such an end of love? You swear to love us eternally; how, then, can our interests be separate?

"You do not know how I suffered today when Nucingen refused to give me six thousand francs; he spends as much as that every month on his mistress, an opera dancer! I thought of killing myself. The wildest thoughts came into my head. There have been moments in my life when I have envied my servants, and would have changed places with my maid. It was madness to think of going to our father, for Anastasie and I have bled him dry; our poor father would have sold himself if he could have raised six thousand francs that way. I should have driven him frantic to no purpose. You have saved me from shame and death; I was beside myself with anguish. Ah! monsieur, I owed you this explanation after my mad ravings. When you left me just now, as soon as you were out of sight, I longed to escape, to run away . . . where, I did not know. Half the women in Paris lead such lives as mine; they live in apparent luxury, and in their souls are tormented by anxiety. I know of poor creatures even more miserable than I; there are women who are driven to ask their tradespeople to make out false bills, women who rob their husbands. Some men believe that an Indian shawl worth a hundred louis only cost five hundred francs, others that a shawl costing five hundred francs is worth a hundred louis. There are women, too, with small incomes, who scrape and save and starve their children to pay for a dress. I am innocent of these meannesses. But this is the last extremity of my torture. Some women will sell themselves to their husbands, and so obtain their way, but I, at any rate, am free. If I chose, Nucingen would cover me with gold, but I would rather weep on the breast of a man whom I can respect. Ah! tonight, Monsieur de Marsay will no longer have a right to think of me as a woman whom he has paid." She tried to conceal her tears from him, hiding her face in her hands. Eugène drew them away and looked at her; she seemed to him sublime at that moment.

"It is hideous, is it not," she cried, "to mix up money and love? You cannot love me after this," she added.

The incongruity between the ideas of honor which make women so great, and the errors in conduct which are forced upon them by the constitution of society, had thrown Eugène's thoughts into confusion. He uttered soothing and consoling words, and wondered at the beautiful woman before him, and at the artless imprudence of her cry of pain.

"You will not remember this against me?" she asked. "Promise me that you will not."

"Ah, madame, I am incapable of doing so," he said. She took his hand and held it to her heart, a movement full of grace that expressed her deep gratitude.

"I am free and happy once more, thanks to you," she said. "I have felt lately as if I were in the grasp of an iron hand. But after this I mean to live simply and to spend nothing. You will think me just as pretty, will you not, my friend? Keep this," she went on, as she took only six of the bank-notes. "In conscience I owe you a thousand crowns, for I really ought to go halves with you."

Eugène's maiden conscience resisted, but when the baroness said, "I am bound to look on you as an accomplice or as an enemy," he took the money.

"It shall be a last stake in reserve," he said, "in case of misfortune."

"That was what I was dreading to hear," she cried, turning pale. "Oh, if you want me to be something to you, swear to me that you will never return to the gambling table. Great heaven, that I should corrupt you! I should die of sorrow!"

They had reached the Rue Saint-Lazare by this time. The contrast between the ostentation of wealth in the house, and the wretched condition of its mistress, dazed the student; and Vautrin's cynical words began to ring in his ears.

"Seat yourself there," said the baroness, pointing to a low chair beside the fire. "I have a difficult letter to write," she added. "Tell me what to say."

"Say nothing," Eugène answered her. "Put the bills in an envelope, direct it, and send it by your maid."

"Oh, you are a darling!" she said. "See what it is to have been well brought up. That is the Beauséant through and through," she went on, smiling at him.

"She is charming," thought Eugène, more and more in love. He looked round him at the room; there was an ostentatious character about the luxury, a meretricious taste in the splendor.

"Do you like it?" she asked, as she rang for her maid.

"Thérèse, take this to Monsieur de Marsay, and give it into his hands yourself. If he is not at home, bring the letter back to me."

Thérèse went, but not before she had given Eugène a spiteful glance.

Dinner was announced. Rastignac gave his arm to Mme de Nucingen, she led the way into a pretty dining room, and again he saw the luxury of the table which he had admired in his cousin's house.

"Come and dine with me on opera evenings, and escort me to the theater afterwards," she said.

"I should soon grow used to the pleasant life if it could last, but I am a poor student, and I have my way to make."

"Oh, you will succeed!" she said, laughing. "You will see. All that you wish will come to pass. *I* did not expect to be so happy."

It is the wont of women to prove the impossible by the possible, and to annihilate facts by presentiments. When Mme de Nucingen and Rastignac took their places in her box at the Bouffons, her face wore a look of happiness that made her so lovely that everyone indulged in those small slanders against which women are defenseless; for the scandal that is uttered lightly is often seriously believed. Those who know Paris believe nothing that is said, and say nothing of what is done there.

Eugène took the baroness' hand in his, and by some light pressure of the fingers, or a closer grasp of the hand, they found a language in which to express the sensations which the music gave them. It was an evening of intoxicating delight for both. When it ended, and they went out together, Mme de Nucingen insisted on taking Eugène with her as far as the Pont Neuf, he disputing with her the whole of the way for one of those ardent kisses she had bestowed on him at the Palais-Royal; Eugène reproached her with inconsistency.

"That was gratitude," she said, "for devotion that I did not dare to hope for, but now it would be a promise."

"And will you give me no promise, ingrate?"

He grew moody. Then, with one of those impatient gestures that fill a lover with ecstasy, she gave him her hand to kiss, and he took it with a discontented air that delighted her.

"I shall see you at the ball on Monday," she said.

As Eugène went home in the moonlight, he fell to serious reflections. He was satisfied, and yet dissatisfied. He was pleased with an adventure which would probably give him his desire: one of the prettiest and best-dressed women in Paris; but, as a set-off, he saw his hopes of fortune brought to nothing; and as soon as he realized this fact, the vague thoughts of yesterday evening began to take a more decided shape in his mind. A check is sure to reveal to us the strength of our hopes. The more Eugène learned of the pleasures of life in Paris, the more impatient he felt of poverty and obscurity. He crumpled the bank-

note in his pocket, and found any quantity of plausible excuses
for appropriating it.

He reached the Rue Neuve-Sainte-Geneviève at last, and from
the stairhead he saw a light in Goriot's room; the old man had
lighted a candle, and set the door ajar, so that the student should
not pass him by, and go to his room without "telling him about
his daughter," to use his own expression. Eugène told him everything without reserve.

"Then they think that I am ruined!" cried old Goriot, in an
agony of jealousy and desperation. "Why, I have still thirteen
hundred livres a year! *Mon Dieu!* Poor girl, why did she not
come to me? I would have sold my *rentes;* she should have had
some of the principal, and I would have bought a life-annuity
with the rest. My good neighbor, why did not *you* come to tell
me of her difficulty? How had you the heart to go and risk her
poor little hundred francs? It's heart-breaking. You see what it
is to have sons-in-law. Oh, if I had hold of them, I would wring
their necks! *Mon Dieu! Crying!* Did you say she was crying?"

"With her head on my waistcoat," said Eugène.

"Oh, give it to me," said old Goriot. "My daughter's tears have
fallen there—my darling Delphine, who never used to cry when
she was a little girl! By the terms of her marriage-contract, she
ought to have the use of her property. Tomorrow morning I
will go and see Derville, an attorney. I will demand that her
money should be invested in her own name. I know the law.
I am an old wolf; I will show my teeth."

"Here, father, this is a bank-note for a thousand francs that
she wanted me to keep out of our winnings. Keep it for her, in
the pocket of the waistcoat."

Goriot looked hard at Eugène, reached out and took his hand,
and Eugène felt a tear fall on it.

"You will succeed," the old man said. "God is just, you see.
I know an honest man when I see him, and I can tell you, there
are not many men like you. I am to have another dear child in

you, am I? There, go to sleep; you can sleep, you are not yet a
father. She was crying! and I have to be told about it!—and I
was quietly eating my dinner, like an idiot, all the time—I, who
would sell the Father, Son, and Holy Ghost to keep either of
them from shedding a tear."

"An honest man!" said Eugène to himself as he lay down.
"Upon my word, I think I will be an honest man all my life; it is
so pleasant to obey the voice of conscience." Perhaps none but
believers in God do good in secret; and Eugène believed in
a God.

The next day Rastignac went at the appointed time to Mme
de Beauséant, who took him with her to the Duchesse de Carigliano's ball. The maréchale received Eugène most graciously.
Mme de Nucingen was there. Delphine's dress seemed to suggest
that she wished for the admiration of others, so that she might
shine the more in Eugène's eyes; she was eagerly expecting a
glance from him, hiding, as she thought, this eagerness from all
beholders. This moment is full of charm for the one who can
guess all that passes in a woman's mind. Who has not refrained
from giving his opinion, to prolong her suspense, concealing his
pleasure from a desire to tantalize, seeking a confession of love
in her uneasiness, enjoying the fears that he can dissipate by a
smile? In the course of the evening the law student began to
perceive his position; he saw that, as the cousin of Mme de Beauséant, he was a personage in society. He was already credited
with the conquest of Mme de Nucingen, and for this reason was
a conspicuous figure; he caught the envious glances of other
young men, and experienced the earliest pleasures of vanity.
People wondered at his luck, and scraps of these conversations
came to his ears as he went from room to room. All the women
prophesied his success, and Delphine, in her dread of losing him,
promised that this evening she would not refuse the kiss that all
his entreaties could scarcely win yesterday.

Rastignac received several invitations. His cousin presented him to other women who were present; women who could claim to be of the highest fashion; whose houses were looked upon as pleasant; and this was the loftiest and most fashionable society in Paris into which he was launched. So this evening had all the charm of a brilliant *début*. It was an evening that he was to remember even in old age, as a woman looks back on her first ball and the memories of her girlish triumphs.

The next morning, at breakfast, he related the story of his success for the benefit of old Goriot and the lodgers. Vautrin began to smile in a diabolical fashion.

"And do you suppose," cried that cold-blooded logician, "that a young man of fashion can live here in the Rue Neuve-Sainte-Geneviève, in the Maison Vauquer—an exceedingly respectable boardinghouse in every way, I grant you, but an establishment that, none the less, falls short of being fashionable? The house is comfortable, it is lordly in its abundance; it is proud to be the temporary abode of a Rastignac; but, after all, it is in the Rue Neuve-Sainte-Geneviève, and luxury would be out of place here, where we only aim at the purely *patriarchalorama*. If you mean to cut a figure in Paris, my young friend," Vautrin continued, with half-paternal jocularity, "you must have three horses, a tilbury for the mornings, and a closed carriage for the evening; you should spend altogether about nine thousand francs on your stables. You would show yourself unworthy of your destiny if you spent no more than three thousand francs with your tailor, six hundred in perfumery, a hundred crowns to your shoemaker, and a hundred more to your hatter. As for your laundress, there goes another thousand francs; a young man of fashion must of necessity make a great point of his linen; if your linen comes up to the required standard, people often do not look any further. Love and the Church demand a fair altar-cloth. That is fourteen thousand francs. I am saying nothing of gambling losses, bets, and presents; it is impossible to allow less than two thousand francs for pocket-money. I have led that sort of

life, and I know all about these expenses. Add the cost of necessaries next; three hundred louis for provender, a thousand francs
for a place to roost in. Well, my boy, for all these little wants of
ours we had need to have twenty-five thousand francs every
year in our purse, or we shall find ourselves in the kennel, and
people laughing at us, and our career is cut short, good-bye to
success, and good-bye to your mistress! I am forgetting your
valet and your groom! Is Christophe going to carry your *billets-
doux* for you? And do you mean to employ the stationery you
use at present? Suicidal policy! Take the advice of a man of
experience," he went on, his bass voice growing louder at each
syllable. "Either take up your quarters in a garret, live virtuously, and wed your work, or set about the thing in a different
way."

Vautrin winked and leered in the direction of Mlle Taillefer
to enforce his remarks by a look which recalled the late tempting
proposals by which he had sought to corrupt the student's mind.

Chapter 12

DURING the days that followed, Rastignac lived in a whirl of
gaiety. He dined almost every day with Mme de Nucingen, and
went wherever she went, only returning to the Rue Neuve-
Sainte-Geneviève in the small hours. He rose at midday, and
dressed to go into the Bois with Delphine if the day was fine,
squandering in this way time that was worth far more than he
knew. He turned as eagerly to learn the lessons of luxury, and
was as quick to feel its fascination, as the flowers of the date palm
to receive the fertilizing pollen. He played high, lost and won
large sums of money, and at last became accustomed to the
extravagant life that young men lead in Paris. He sent fifteen
hundred francs out of his first winnings to his mother and sisters,

sending handsome presents as well as the money. He had given out that he meant to leave the Maison Vauquer; but January came and went, and he was still there, still unprepared to go.

One rule holds good of most young men—whether rich or poor. They never have money for the necessaries of life, but they have always money to spare for their caprices—an anomaly which finds its explanation in their youth and in the almost frantic eagerness with which youth grasps at pleasure. They are reckless with anything obtained on credit, while everything for which they must pay in ready money is made to last as long as possible. If they cannot have all that they want, they make up for it, it would seem, by squandering what they have. To state the matter simply—a student is far more careful of his hat than of his coat, because the latter being a comparatively costly article of dress, it is in the nature of things that a tailor should be a creditor; but it is otherwise with the hatter; the sums of money spent with him are so modest, that he is the most independent and unmanageable of his tribe, and it is almost impossible to bring him to terms. The young man in the balcony of a theater who displays a gorgeous waistcoat for the benefit of the fair owners of opera glasses, has very probably no socks in his wardrobe, for the hosier is another of the genus of weevils that nibble at the purse.

This was Rastignac's condition. His purse was always empty for Mme Vauquer, always full at the demand of vanity; there was a periodical ebb and flow in his fortunes, which was seldom favorable to the payment of just debts. If he was to leave that unsavory and mean abode, where from time to time his pretensions met with humiliation, the first step was to pay his hostess for a month's board and lodging, and the second to purchase furniture worthy of the new lodgings he must take in his quality of dandy, a course that remained impossible. Rastignac, out of his winnings at cards, would pay his jeweler exorbitant prices for gold watches and chains, and then, to get money to gamble with, would carry them to the pawnbroker, that discreet and forbidding-looking friend of youth; but when it was a question of paying for board or lodging, or for the necessary implements for the cultivation of his Elysian fields, both his imagination and pluck deserted him. There was no inspiration to be found in vulgar necessity, in debts contracted for past requirements. Like most of those who trust to luck, he put off till the last moment the payment of debts that among the bourgeoisie are regarded as sacred engagements, acting on the plan of Mirabeau, who never settled his baker's bill until it took the brutal form of a promissory note.

It was about this time when Rastignac was down on his luck and fell into debt, that it became clear to the law student's mind that he must have some more certain source of income if he meant to continue along this path. But while he groaned over the thorny problems of his precarious situation, he felt that he could not bring himself to renounce the pleasures of this extravagant life, and decided that he must keep on at all costs. His dreams of obtaining a fortune appeared more and more chimerical, and the real obstacles grew more formidable. His initiation into the secrets of the Nucingen household had revealed to him that if he were to attempt to use this love affair as a means of mending his fortunes, he must swallow down all sense of decency, and renounce all the generous ideas which redeem the sins of youth. He had chosen this life of apparent splendor, but secretly gnawed by the canker-worm of remorse, a life of fleeting pleasure was paid for by persistent pain. Like *Le Distrait* of La Bruyère, he had descended so far as to make his bed in a ditch, but (also like *Le Distrait*) he himself was uncontaminated as yet by the mire that stained his garments.

"So we have killed our mandarin, have we?" said Bianchon one day as they left the dinner table.

"Not yet," he answered, "but he is at the last gasp."

The medical student took this for a joke, but it was not a jest.

Eugène had dined in the house that night for the first time for a long while, and had looked thoughtful during the meal. He had taken his place beside Mlle Taillefer, and stayed through the dessert, giving his neighbor an expressive glance from time to time. A few of the boarders discussed the walnuts at the table, and others walked about the room, continuing the discussion which had begun among them. People usually went when they chose; the amount of time that they lingered being determined by their interest in the conversation, or by the difficulty of the process of digestion. In wintertime the room was seldom empty before eight o'clock, when the four women had it all to themselves, and made up for the silence previously imposed upon them by the preponderating masculine element. Vautrin had noticed Eugène's preoccupation, and stayed in the room, though he had seemed to be in a hurry to finish his dinner and go. Through the talk afterwards he had kept out of sight of the law student, who thought that Vautrin had left the room. He now shrewdly took up his position in the sitting room instead of going when the last boarders went. He had fathomed the young man's thoughts, and felt that a crisis was at hand. Rastignac was, in fact, in a dilemma, which many another young man must have faced.

Mme de Nucingen might love him, or might merely be playing with him, but in either case Rastignac had been made to experience all the alternations of hope and despair of genuine passion, by employing on him all the diplomatic arts of a Parisienne. After compromising herself by continually appearing in public with Mme de Beauséant's cousin she still hesitated, and would not give him the lover's privileges which he appeared to enjoy. For a whole month she had so wrought on his senses, that at last she had made an impression on his heart. If in the earliest days the student had fancied himself to be the master, Mme de Nucingen had since become the stronger of the two, for she had skillfully roused and played upon every instinct, good or bad, in the two or three men comprised in a young student in Paris. This was not the result of deep design on her part, nor was she playing a part, for women are in a manner true to themselves even through their grossest deceit, because their actions are prompted by natural impulse. It may have been that Delphine, who had allowed this young man to gain such an ascendancy over her, conscious that she had been too demonstrative, was prompted by a sense of dignity, and either repented of her concessions or was pleased to suspend them. It is so natural to a Parisienne, even when passion has almost mastered her, to hesitate and pause before taking the plunge; to probe the heart of him to whom she entrusts her future. And once already Mme de Nucingen's hopes had been betrayed, and her loyalty to a selfish young lover had been scorned. She had good reason to be suspicious. Or it may have been that something in Eugène's manner—for his rapid success was making him conceited—had warned her that the unusual nature of their position had lowered her somewhat in his eyes. She doubtless wished to assert her dignity; he was young, and she would be great in his eyes; for the lover who had forsaken her had held her of small account. She was determined that Eugène should not think her an easy conquest, precisely because he knew that de Marsay had been his predecessor. Finally, after the degradation of submission to the pleasure of a heartless young rake, it was so sweet to her to wander in the flower-strewn realms of love, that it was not wonderful that she should wish to dwell awhile on the prospect, to tremble with the vibrations of love, to feel the freshness of the breath of its dawn. The true lover was suffering for the sins of the false. This unfortunate inconsistency is only to be expected so long as men do not know how many flowers are mown down in a young woman's soul by the first stroke of treachery.

Whatever her reasons may have been, Delphine was playing with Rastignac, and took pleasure in playing with him, doubtless because she felt sure of his love, and confident that she could put an end to the torture as soon as it was her royal pleasure to do so. Eugène's self-love was involved; he could not suffer his first passage of love to end in a defeat, and persisted in his suit, like a sportsman determined to bring down at least one partridge to celebrate his first Feast of Saint Hubert. The pressure of anxiety, his wounded vanity, his despair, real or feigned, attached him closer and closer to this woman. All Paris credited him with this conquest, and yet he was conscious that he had made no progress since the day when he saw Mme de Nucingen for the first time. He did not know as yet that a woman's coquetry is sometimes more delightful than the pleasure of secure possession of her love, and was possessed with helpless rage. If, at this time, while she denied herself to love, Eugène gathered the springtide spoils of his life, the fruit, somewhat sharp and green, and dearly bought, was no less delicious to the taste. There were moments when he had not a sou in his pockets, and at such times he thought in spite of his conscience of Vautrin's offer and the possibility of fortune by a marriage with Mlle Taillefer. Poverty would clamor so loudly that more than once he was on the point of yielding to the cunning temptations of the terrible sphinx, whose glance had so often fascinated him.

Poiret and Mlle Michonneau went up to their rooms. Rastignac, thinking that he was alone with the women in the dining room, sat between Mme Vauquer and Mme Couture, who was nodding over the woolen cuffs that she was knitting by the stove, and looked at Mlle Taillefer so tenderly that she lowered her eyes.

"Can you be in trouble, Monsieur Eugène?" Victorine said after a pause.

"Who has not his troubles?" answered Rastignac. "If we men were sure of being loved, sure of a devotion which would be our reward for the sacrifices which we are always ready to make, then perhaps we should have no troubles."

For answer Mlle Taillefer only gave him a glance, but it was impossible to mistake its meaning.

"You, for instance, mademoiselle; you feel sure of your heart today, but are you sure that it will never change?"

A smile flitted over the poor girl's lips; it seemed as if a ray of light from her soul had lighted up her face. Eugène was dismayed at the sudden explosion of feeling caused by his words.

"Ah! but suppose," he said, "that you should be rich and happy tomorrow, suppose that a vast fortune dropped down from the clouds for you, would you still love the man whom you loved in your days of poverty?"

A charming movement of the head was her only answer.

"Even if he were very poor?"

Again the same mute answer.

"What nonsense are you talking, you two?" exclaimed Mme Vauquer.

"Never mind," answered Eugène; "we understand each other."

"So there is to be an engagement of marriage between Monsieur le Chevalier Eugène de Rastignac and Mademoiselle Victorine Taillefer, is there?" The words were uttered in Vautrin's deep voice, and Vautrin appeared at the door as he spoke.

"Oh, how you startled me!" Mme Couture and Mme Vauquer exclaimed together.

"I might make a worse choice," said Rastignac, laughing. Vautrin's voice had thrown him into the most painful agitation that he had yet known.

"No bad jokes, gentlemen!" said Mme Couture. "My dear, let us go upstairs."

Mme Vauquer followed the two ladies, meaning to pass the evening in their room, an arrangement that economized fire and candlelight. Eugène and Vautrin were left alone.

"I felt sure you would come round to it," said the elder man with the coolness that nothing seemed to shake. "But stay a moment! I have as much delicacy as anybody else. Don't make up your mind on the spur of the moment; you are a little thrown off your balance just now. You are in debt, and I want you to come over to my way of thinking after sober reflection, and not in a fit of passion or desperation. Perhaps you want a thousand crowns. Here, you can have them if you like."

The tempter took out a pocketbook, and drew thence three bank-notes, which he fluttered before the student's eyes. Eugène was in a most painful dilemma. He had debts, debts of honor. He owed a hundred louis to the Marquis d'Ajuda and to the Comte de Trailles; he had not the money, and for this reason had not dared to go to Mme de Restaud's house, where he was expected that evening. It was one of those informal gatherings where tea and little cakes are handed round, but where it is possible to lose six thousand francs at whist in the course of a night.

"You must see," said Eugène, struggling to hide a convulsive tremor, "that after what has passed between us, I cannot possibly lay myself under any obligation to you."

"Quite right; I should be sorry to hear you speak otherwise," answered the tempter. "You are a fine young fellow, honorable, brave as a lion, and as gentle as a young girl. You would be a fine haul for the devil! I like youngsters of your sort. Get rid of one or two more prejudices, and you will see the world as it is. Make a little scene now and then, and act a virtuous part in it, and a man with a head on his shoulders can do exactly as he likes amid deafening applause from the fools in the gallery. A few days more, and you will be with us; and if you would only be tutored by me, I would put you in the way of achieving all your ambitions. You should no sooner form a wish than it should be realized to the full; you should have all your desires—honors, wealth, or women. Civilization should flow with milk and honey for you. You should be our pet and favorite, our Benjamin. We would all work ourselves to death for you with pleasure; every obstacle should be removed from your path. If you are still scrupulous, you may take me for a scoundrel. Well, Monsieur de Trenne, quite as honorable a man as you take yourself to be, had some little private transactions with bandits, and did not feel that his honor was tarnished. You would rather not lie under any obligation to me, eh? You need not draw back on that account," Vautrin went on, and a smile stole over his lips. "Take those bits of paper and write across this," he added, producing a piece of stamped paper, *Accepted the sum of three thousand five hundred francs due this day twelvemonth,* and fill in the date. The rate of interest is stiff enough to silence any scruples on your part; it gives you the right to call me a Jew. You can call quits with me on the score of gratitude. I am quite willing that you should despise me today, because I am sure that you will have a kindlier feeling towards me later on. You will find out fathomless depths in my nature, enormous and concentrated forces that weaklings call vices, but you will never find me base or ungrateful. In short, I am neither a pawn nor a bishop, but a castle, a tower of strength, my boy."

"What kind of man are you?" cried Eugène. "Were you created to torment me?"

"Why, no; I am a good-natured fellow, who is willing to do a dirty piece of work to put you high and dry above the mire for the rest of your days. Do you ask the reason of this devotion? All right; I will tell you that one of these days. A word or two in your ear will explain it. I have begun by shocking you, by showing you the way to ring the changes, and giving you a sight of the mechanism of the social machine; but your first fright will go off like a conscript's terror on the battlefield. You will grow used to regarding men as common soldiers who have made up their minds to lose their lives for some self-constituted king. Times have altered strangely. Once you could say to a bravo, 'Here are a hundred crowns; go and kill Monsieur So-and-so for me,' and you could sup quietly after sending someone into the shadows for the least thing in the world. But nowadays I propose to put you in the way of a handsome fortune; you have only to nod your head, it won't compromise you in any way, and you hesitate. People are soft nowadays."

Eugène signed the draft, and received the bank-notes in exchange for it.

"Well, well. Come, now, let us talk rationally," Vautrin continued. "I mean to leave this country in a few months' time for America, and set about planting tobacco. I will send you the cigars of friendship. If I make money at it, I will help you in your career. If I have no children—which will probably be the case, for I am not interested in raising slips of myself here—you shall inherit my fortune. That is what you may call standing by a man; but I have a liking for you. I have a mania, too, for devoting myself to someone else. I have done it before. You see, my boy, I live in a loftier sphere than other men do; I look on all actions as means to an end, and the end is all that I look at. What is a man's life to me? Not *that*," he said, and he snapped his thumbnail against his teeth. "A man, in short, is everything to me, or just nothing at all. Less than nothing if his name happens to be Poiret: you can crush him like a bug, he is flat and he is offensive. But a man is a god when he is like you. He is not a mechanism covered with a skin, but a theater in which the greatest sentiments are displayed—great thoughts and feelings —and for these, and these only, I live. A sentiment—what is that but the whole world in a thought? Look at old Goriot. For him, his two girls are the whole universe; they are the clue by which he finds his way through creation. Well, for my own part, and I have fathomed the depths of life, there is only one real sentiment—comradeship between man and man. Pierre and Jaffier, that is my passion. I know *Venice Preserved* by heart. Have you met many men plucky enough when a comrade says, 'Let us bury a dead body!' to go and do it without a word or plaguing him by taking a high moral tone? I have done it myself. I should not talk like this to just everybody, but you are not like an ordinary man; one can talk to you, you can understand things. You will not dabble about much longer among the tadpoles in this swamp. Well, then, it is all settled. You will marry. Both of us carry our point. Mine is made of iron, and will never soften, he! he!"

Vautrin went out. He would not wait to hear the student's protests; he wished to put Eugène at his ease. He seemed to understand the secret springs of the faint resistance still made by the younger man; the struggles in which men seek to preserve their self-respect by justifying their blameworthy actions to themselves.

"He may do as he likes; I shall certainly never marry Mademoiselle Taillefer," said Eugène to himself.

He regarded this man with abhorrence, and yet the very cynicism of Vautrin's ideas, and the audacious way in which he used other men for his own ends, raised him in the student's eyes; but the thought of a compact threw Eugène into a fever of apprehension, and not until he had recovered somewhat did he dress, call for a cab, and go to Mme de Restaud's.

For some days the countess had paid more and more attention to a young man whose every step seemed to take him nearer the heart of the great world; it seemed to her that he might be a formidable power before long. He paid Messieurs de Trailles and d'Ajuda, played whist for part of the evening, and made good his losses. Most men who have their way to make are more or less fatalists, and Eugène was superstitious; he chose to consider that his luck was Heaven's reward for his perseverance in sticking to the path of honor. As soon as possible on the following morning he asked Vautrin whether the bill that he had given was still in the other's possession, and on receiving a reply in the affirmative, he repaid the three thousand francs with a not unnatural relief.

"Everything is going well," said Vautrin.

"But I am not your accomplice," said Eugène.

"I know, I know," Vautrin broke in. "You are still acting like a child. Once across the threshold, you'll be all right."

Two days later, Poiret and Mlle Michonneau were sitting together on a bench in the sun. They had chosen a little-frequented alley in the Jardin des Plantes and a gentleman was chatting with them, the same person, as a matter of fact, about whom the medical student had, not without good reason, his own suspicions.

"Mademoiselle," this M. Gondureau was saying, "I do not see any cause for your scruples. His Excellency Monseigneur the Minister of Police——"

"Ah!" echoed Poiret, "His Excellency Monseigneur the Minister of Police!"

"Yes, His Excellency is taking a personal interest in the matter," said Gondureau.

Who would think it probable that Poiret, a retired clerk, doubtless possessed of some notions of civic virtue, though there might be nothing else in his head—who would think it likely that such a man would continue to lend an ear to this supposed independent gentleman of the Rue de Buffon, when the latter dropped the mask of a decent citizen by that word "police," and gave a glimpse of the features of a detective from the Rue de Jérusalem? And yet nothing was more natural. Perhaps the following remarks from the hitherto unpublished records made by certain observers will throw a light on the particular species to which Poiret belonged in the great family of fools. There is a race of quill-drivers, confined in the columns of the budget between the first degree of latitude (a kind of administrative Greenland where the salaries begin at twelve hundred francs) and the third degree, a more temperate zone, where incomes grow from three to six thousand francs, a climate where the bonus flourishes like a half-hardy annual in spite of some difficulties of culture. A characteristic trait that best reveals

the feeble narrow-mindedness of these inhabitants of petty officialdom is a kind of involuntary, mechanical, and instinctive
reverence for the Grand Lama of every Ministry, known to
the rank and file only by his signature—an illegible scrawl—
and by his title, "His Excellency Monseigneur le Ministre," five
words which produce as much effect as the *il Bondo Cani* of
the *Calife de Bagdad,* five words which in the eyes of this low
order of intelligence represent a sacred power from which there
is no appeal. The Minister is administratively infallible for the
clerks in the employ of the Government, as the Pope is infallible
for good Catholics. Something of his peculiar radiance invests
everything he does or says, or that is said or done in his name;
the robe of office covers everything and legalizes everything
done by his orders. Does not his very title—His Excellency—
vouch for the purity of his intentions and the righteousness of
his will, and serve as a sort of passport and introduction to ideas
that otherwise would not be entertained for a moment? Pro-
nounce the words "His Excellency," and these poor folk will
forthwith proceed to do what they would not do for their own
interests. Passive obedience is as well known in a Government
department as in the army itself; and the administrative system
silences consciences, annihilates the individual, and ends—give
it time enough—by fashioning a man into a vice or a thumb-
screw, and he becomes part of the machinery of Government.
Wherefore, M. Gondureau, who seemed to know something
of human nature, recognized Poiret at once as one of these dupes
of officialdom, and brought out for his benefit, at the proper
moment, the *deus ex machinâ*, the magical words "His Excellency," so as to dazzle Poiret just as he himself unmasked his
batteries, for he took Poiret and the Michonneau for the male
and female of the same species.

"If His Excellency himself, His Excellency the Minister . . .
Ah! that is quite another thing," said Poiret.

"You seem to be guided by this gentleman's opinion, and

you hear what he says," said the man of independent means, addressing Mlle Michonneau. "Very well, His Excellency is at this moment absolutely certain that the so-called Vautrin, who lodges at the Maison Vauquer, is a convict who escaped from penal servitude at Toulon, where he is known by the nickname Trompe-la-Mort."

"Trompe-la-Mort?" said Poiret. "Dear me, he is very lucky if he deserves that nickname."

"Well, yes," said the detective. "They call him so because he has been so lucky as not to lose his life in the very risky enterprises that he has carried through. He is a dangerous man, you see! He has extraordinary qualities. The thing he is wanted for, in fact, was a matter which gained him no end of credit with his own set——"

"Then is he a man of honor?" asked Poiret.

"Yes, according to his notions. He agreed to take another man's crime upon himself—a forgery committed by a very handsome young fellow that he had taken a great fancy to, a young Italian, a bit of a gambler, who has since gone into the army, where his conduct has been perfect."

"But if His Excellency the Minister of Police is certain that Monsieur Vautrin is this Trompe-la-Mort, why should he want me?" asked Mlle Michonneau.

"Oh, yes," said Poiret, "if the Minister, as you have been so obliging as to tell us, really knows for a certainty——"

"Certainty is not the word; he only suspects. You will soon understand how things are. Jacques Collin, nicknamed Trompe-la-Mort, is in the confidence of every convict in the three prisons; he is their man of business and their banker. He makes a very good thing out of managing their affairs, which want a *man of mark* to see about them."

"Ha! ha! do you see the pun, mademoiselle?" asked Poiret. "This gentleman calls him a *man of mark* because he is a *marked man*—branded, you know."

"This so-called Vautrin," said the detective, "receives the money belonging to my lords the convicts, invests it for them, and holds it at the disposal of those who escape, or hands it over to their families if they leave a will, or to their mistresses when they draw upon him for their benefit."

"Their mistresses! You mean their wives," remarked Poiret.

"No, sir. A convict's wife is usually an illegitimate connection. We call them concubines."

"Then they all live in a state of concubinage."

"Naturally."

"Why, these are abominations that His Excellency ought not to allow. Since you have the honor of seeing His Excellency, you, who seem to have philanthropic ideas, ought really to enlighten him as to their immoral conduct—they are setting a shocking example to the rest of society."

"But the Government does not hold them up as models of all the virtues, my dear sir."

"Of course not, sir, but still——"

"Just let the gentleman say what he has to say, dearie," said Mlle Michonneau.

"You see how it is, mademoiselle," Gondureau continued. "The Government may have the strongest reasons for getting this illicit hoard into its hands; it mounts up to something considerable, by all that we can make out. Trompe-la-Mort not only holds very large sums for his friends the convicts, but he has other amounts which are paid over to him by the Society of the Ten Thousand——"

"Ten Thousand Thieves!" cried Poiret in alarm.

"No. The Society of the Ten Thousand is not an association of petty offenders, but of people who set about their work on a large scale—they won't touch a matter unless there are ten thousand francs in it. It is composed of the most distinguished of the men who are sent straight to the Assize Courts when they come up for trial. They know the Code too well to risk their necks when they are nabbed. Collin is their confidential agent and legal adviser. By means of the large sums of money at his disposal he has established a sort of detective system of his own; it is widespread, and mysterious in its workings. We have had spies all about him for a twelvemonth, and yet we could not manage to fathom his games. His capital and his cleverness are at the service of vice and crime; this money furnishes the necessary funds for a regular army of blackguards in his pay who wage incessant war against society. If we can catch Trompe-la-Mort, and take possession of his funds, we should strike at the root of this evil. So this job is a kind of State affair and likely to redound to the honor of those who bring the thing to a successful conclusion. You, sir, for instance, might very well be taken into a Government department again; they might make you secretary to a Commissary of Police; you could accept that post without prejudice to your retiring pension."

Mlle Michonneau interposed at this point with, "What is there to hinder Trompe-la-Mort from making off with the money?"

"Oh," said the detective, "a man is told off to follow him everywhere he goes, with orders to kill him if he were to rob the convicts. Then it is not quite as easy to make off with a lot of money as it is to run away with a young lady of family. Besides, Collin is not the sort of fellow to play such a trick; he would consider himself disgraced."

"You are quite right, sir," said Poiret, "utterly disgraced he would be."

"But none of all this explains why you do not come and take him without more ado," remarked Mlle Michonneau.

"Very well, mademoiselle, I will explain—but," he added in her ear, "keep your companion quiet, or I shall never have done. The old boy ought to pay people handsomely for listening to him.—Trompe-la-Mort, when he came back here," he went on aloud, "slipped into the skin of an honest man. He turned up disguised as a decent Parisian citizen, and took up his quarters in an unpretentious lodginghouse. He is cunning, I tell you. You won't catch him napping. Then the real Vautrin is a man of consequence, who transacts a good deal of business."

"Naturally," said Poiret to himself.

"And suppose that the Minister were to make a mistake and get hold of the real Vautrin, he would put everyone's back up among the business men in Paris, and public opinion would be against him. Monsieur le Préfet de Police is on slippery ground; he has enemies. They would take advantage of any mistake. There would be a fine outcry and fuss made by the Opposition, and he would be sent packing. We must set about this just as we did about the Cogniard affair, the sham Comte de Sainte-Hélène; if he had been the real Comte de Sainte-Hélène, we should have been in the wrong box. We want to be quite sure what we are about."

"Yes, but what you want is a pretty woman," said Mlle Michonneau briskly.

"Trompe-la-Mort would not let a woman come near him," said the detective. "I will tell you a secret—he does not like them."

"Still, I do not see what I can do, supposing that I did agree to identify him for two thousand francs."

"Nothing simpler," said the stranger. "I will send you a little bottle containing a dose that will send a rush of blood to the head; it will do him no harm whatever, but he will fall down as if he were in a fit. The drug can be put into wine or coffee; either will do equally well. You carry your man to bed at once, and undress him to see that he is not dying. As soon as you are alone, you give him a slap on the shoulder, and, *presto!* the letters will appear."

"Why, that is just nothing at all," said Poiret.

"Well, do you agree?" said Gondureau, addressing the old maid.

"But, my dear sir, suppose there are no letters at all," said Mlle Michonneau; "am I to have the two thousand francs all the same?"

"No."

"What will you give me, then?"

"Five hundred francs."

"It is such a thing to do for so little! It lies on your conscience just the same, and I must quiet my conscience, sir."

"I assure you," said Poiret, "that mademoiselle has a great deal of conscience, and not only so, she is a very amiable person, and very intelligent."

"Well, now," Mlle Michonneau went on, "make it three thousand francs if he is Trompe-la-Mort, and nothing at all if he is an ordinary man."

"Done!" said Gondureau, "but on condition that the thing is settled tomorrow."

"Not quite so soon, my dear sir; I must consult my confessor first."

"You are a sly one," said the detective as he rose to his feet. "Good-bye till tomorrow, then. And if you should want to see me in a hurry, go to the Petite Rue Sainte-Anne at the bottom of the Cour de la Sainte Chapelle. There is only one door under the archway. Ask there for Monsieur Gondureau."

Bianchon, on his way back from Cuvier's lecture, overheard the sufficiently striking nickname of Trompe-la-Mort, and caught the celebrated chief detective's "Done!"

"Why didn't you close with him? It would be three hundred francs a year," said Poiret to Mlle Michonneau.

"Why didn't I?" she asked. "Why, it wants thinking over. Suppose that Monsieur Vautrin is this Trompe-la-Mort: perhaps we might do better for ourselves with him. Still, on the other hand, if you ask him for money, it would put him on his guard, and he is just the man to clear out without paying, and that would be an abominable sell."

"And suppose you did warn him," Poiret went on, "didn't that gentleman say that he was closely watched? You would spoil everything."

"Anyhow," thought Mlle Michonneau, "I can't abide him. He says nothing but disagreeable things to me."

"But you can do better than that," Poiret resumed. "As that gentleman said—and he seemed to me to be a very good sort of man, besides being very well got up—it is an act of obedience to the laws to rid society of a criminal, however virtuous he may be. Once a thief, always a thief. Suppose he were to take it into his head to murder us all? The deuce! We should be guilty of manslaughter, and be the first to fall victims into the bargain!"

Mlle Michonneau's musings did not permit her to listen very closely to the remarks that fell one by one from Poiret's lips like water dripping from a leaky tap. When once this elderly babbler began to talk, he would go on like clockwork unless Mlle Michonneau stopped him. He started on some subject or other, and wandered on through parenthesis after parenthesis till he came to regions as remote as possible from his premises without coming to any conclusions by the way.

By the time they reached the Maison Vauquer he had tacked together a whole string of examples and quotations more or less irrelevant to the subject in hand, which led him to give a full account of his own deposition in the case of the Sieur Ragoulleau *versus* Dame Morin, when he had been summoned as a witness for the defense.

As they entered the dining room, Eugène de Rastignac was chatting intimately with Mlle Taillefer. The conversation appeared to be of such thrilling interest that the pair never noticed the two older lodgers as they passed through the room. None of this was thrown away on Mlle Michonneau.

"I knew how it would end," remarked that lady, addressing Poiret. "They have been making eyes at each other in a heart-rending way for a week past."

"Yes," he answered. "So she was found guilty."

"Who?"

"Madame Morin."

"I am talking about Mademoiselle Victorine," said Mlle Michonneau, as she entered Poiret's room with an absent air, "and you answer, 'Madame Morin.' Who may Madame Morin be?"

"What can Mademoiselle Victorine be guilty of?" demanded Poiret.

"Guilty of falling in love with Monsieur Eugène de Rastignac, and going further and further without knowing exactly where she is going, poor innocent!"

Chapter 13

THAT MORNING Mme de Nucingen had driven Eugène to despair. In his own mind he had completely surrendered himself to Vautrin, but deliberately refused to probe the motive for the friendship which that extraordinary man professed for him, or consider the consequences of such an alliance. Nothing short of miracle could extricate him now out of the gulf into which he had walked an hour ago, when he exchanged vows in the softest whispers with Mlle Taillefer. To Victorine it seemed as if she heard an angel's voice, that heaven was opening above her; the Maison Vauquer took strange and wonderful hues, like a stage fairy-palace. She loved and she was beloved; at any rate, she believed that she was loved; and what woman would not likewise have believed after seeing Rastignac's face and listening to the tones of his voice during that hour snatched under the Argus eyes of the Maison Vauquer? He had trampled on his conscience, he knew that he was doing wrong, and did it deliberately; he had said to himself that a woman's happiness should atone for this venial sin. The energy of desperation had lent new beauty to his face; the lurid fire that burned in his heart shone from his eyes. Luckily for him, the miracle took place. Vautrin came in in high spirits, and at once read the hearts of these two young creatures whom he had brought together by the combinations of his infernal genius, but his deep voice broke in upon their bliss.

> "A charming girl is my Fanchette
> In her simplicity,"

he sang mockingly.

Victorine fled. Her heart was more full than it had ever been, but it was full of joy, and not of sorrow. Poor child! A pressure of the hand, the light touch of Rastignac's hair against her cheek, a word whispered in her ear so closely that she felt the student's warm breath on her, the pressure of a trembling arm about her waist, a kiss upon her throat—such had been her betrothal. The near neighborhood of the stout Sylvie, who might invade that glorified room at any moment, only made these first tokens of love more ardent, more eloquent, more entrancing than the noblest deeds done for love's sake in the most famous romances. This *plain-song* of love, to use the pretty expression of our forefathers, seemed almost criminal to the devout young girl who went to confession every fortnight. In that one hour she had poured out more of the treasures of her soul than she could give in later days of wealth and happiness, when her whole self followed the gift.

"The thing is arranged," Vautrin said to Eugène, who remained. "Our two dandies have fallen out. Everything was done in proper form. It is a matter of opinion. Our pigeon has insulted my hawk. They will meet tomorrow in the redoubt at

Clignancourt. By half-past eight in the morning Mademoiselle Taillefer, calmly dipping her bread and butter in her coffee cup, will be sole heiress of her father's fortune and affections. A funny way of putting it, isn't it? Taillefer's youngster is an expert swordsman, and quite cocksure about it, but he will be bled; I have just invented a thrust for his benefit, a way of raising your sword-point and driving it at the forehead. I must show you that thrust; it is an uncommonly handy thing to know."

Rastignac heard him in dazed bewilderment, unable to find a word in reply. Just then Goriot came in, and Bianchon and a few of the boarders likewise appeared.

"It's all just as I planned," Vautrin said. "You know quite well what you are about. Good, my little eaglet! You are born to command, you are strong, you stand firm on your feet, you are game! I respect you."

He made as though he would take Eugène's hand, but Rastignac hastily withdrew it, sank into a chair, and turned ghastly pale. It seemed to him that there was a sea of blood before his eyes.

"Oh! So we have still a few tattered shreds of the swaddling clothes of virtue about us!" murmured Vautrin. "But Papa Doliban has three millions; I know the amount of his fortune. Once have her dowry in your hands, and your character will be as white as the bride's white dress, even in your own eyes."

Rastignac hesitated no longer. He made up his mind that he would go that evening to warn the Taillefers, father and son. But just as Vautrin left him, old Goriot came up and said in his ear, "You look melancholy, my boy; I will cheer you up. Come with me."

The old vermicelli-dealer lighted his dip at one of the lamps as he spoke. Eugène went with him, his curiosity aroused.

"Let us go up to your room," the worthy soul remarked, when he had asked Sylvie for the law student's key. "This morning," he resumed, "you thought that *she* did not care about you, did you not? Eh? She would have nothing to say to you, and you went away out of humor and out of heart. Stuff and rubbish! She wanted you to go because she was expecting *me*! Now do you understand? We were to complete the arrangements for taking some chambers for you, a jewel of a place; you are to move into it in three days' time. Don't let her know I told you. She wants it to be a surprise, but I couldn't bear to keep the secret from you. You will be in the Rue d'Artois, only a step or two from the Rue Saint-Lazare, and you are to be housed like a prince! Anyone might have thought we were furnishing the house for a bride. Oh, we have done a lot of things in the last month, and you knew nothing about it. My attorney has appeared on the scene, and my daughter is to have thirty-six thousand francs a year, the interest on her money, and I shall insist on having her eight hundred thousand francs invested in sound securities, real estate that won't run away."

Eugène was dumb. He folded his arms and paced up and down his cheerless, untidy room. Old Goriot waited till the student's back was turned, and seized the opportunity to go to the chimney-piece and set upon it a little red morocco case with Rastignac's arms stamped in gold on the leather.

"My dear boy," said the kind soul, "I have been up to the eyes in this business. You see, there was plenty of selfishness on my part; I have an interested motive in helping you to change lodgings. You will not refuse me if I ask you something; will you, eh?"

"What is it?"

"There is a room on the fifth floor, up above your rooms, that is to let along with them; that is where I am going to live, isn't that so? I am getting old; I am too far from my girls. I shall not be in the way, but I shall be there, that is all. You will come and talk to me about her every evening. It will not put you out, will it? I shall have gone to bed before you come in, but I shall hear you come up, and I shall say to myself, 'He has just seen my little Delphine. He has been to a dance with her, and she is happy, thanks to him.' If I were ill, it would do my heart good to hear you moving about below, to know when you leave the house and when you come in. It is only a step to the Champs-Élysées, where they go every day, so I shall be sure of seeing them, whereas now I am sometimes too late. And then—perhaps she may come to see you! I shall hear her, I shall see her in her soft quilted pelisse tripping about as daintily as a kitten. In this one month she has become my little girl again, so light-hearted and gay. Her soul is recovering, and her happiness is due to you. Oh, I would do the impossible for you! Only just now she said to me, 'I am very happy, papa!' When they say 'father' stiffly, it sends a chill through me, but when they call me 'papa,' it is as if they were little girls again, and it brings all the old memories back. I feel most their father then. They are mine once more." The good man wiped his eyes; he was crying.

"It is a long while since I have heard them talk like that, a long time since she took my arm as she did today. Yes, indeed, it must be quite ten years since I walked side by side with one of my girls. How pleasant it was to keep step with her, to feel the touch of her gown, the warmth of her arm! Well, I took Delphine everywhere this morning; I went shopping with her, and I brought her home again. Oh, you must let me live near you. You may want someone to do you a service some of these days, and I shall be on the spot to do it. If only that great dolt of an Alsatian would die, if his gout would have the sense to attack his stomach, how happy my poor child would be! You would be my son-in-law; you would be her husband in the eyes of the world. She has known no happiness, that excuses everything. Our Father in heaven is surely on the side of fathers on earth who love their children. How fond of you she is!" he said, raising his head after a pause. "All the time we were going about together she chatted away about you. 'He is nice-looking, papa, isn't he? He is kind-hearted! Does he talk to you about me?' Pshaw! she said enough about you to fill whole volumes; between the Rue d'Artois and the Passage des Panoramas she poured her heart out into mine. I did not feel old once during that delightful morning; I felt as light as a feather. I told her how you had given that thousand-franc note to me; it moved my darling to tears. But what can this be on your chimney-piece?" said old Goriot at last. Rastignac had showed no sign, and he was dying of impatience.

Eugène stared at his neighbor in dumb and dazed bewilderment. He thought of Vautrin, of that duel to be fought tomorrow morning, and of this realization of his dearest hopes, and the violent contrast between the two sets of ideas gave him all the sensations of nightmare. He went to the chimney-piece, saw the little square case, opened it, and found a watch of Bréguet's make wrapped in paper, on which these words were written:

I want you to think of me every hour, *because.* . . .
DELPHINE.

That last word doubtless contained an allusion to some scene that had taken place between them. Eugène felt touched. Inside the gold watchcase his arms had been wrought in enamel. The chain, the key, the workmanship, and design of the trinket were all such as he had imagined, for he had long coveted such a possession. Old Goriot was radiant. Of course he had promised to tell his daughter every little detail of the scene and of the effect produced upon Eugène by her present. He shared in the pleasure and excitement of the young people, and seemed to be not the least happy of the three. He loved Rastignac already for his own as well as for his daughter's sake.

"You must go and see her; she is expecting you this evening. That great lout of an Alsatian is going to have supper with his opera-dancer. He looked very foolish when my attorney let him know how he stood. He says he idolizes my daughter, does he? He had better let her alone, or I will kill him. To think that my Delphine is his"—he heaved a sigh—"it is enough to make me murder him, but it would not be manslaughter to kill that pig with a calf's brains. You will take me with you, will you not?"

"Yes, dear Father Goriot; you know very well how fond I am of you——"

"Yes, I do know very well. You are not ashamed of me, are you? Not you! Let me embrace you," and he flung his arms round the student's neck. "You will make her very happy; promise me that you will! You will go to her this evening, will you not?"

"Oh, yes! I must go out; I have some urgent business on hand."

"Can I be of any use?"

"My word, yes! Will you go to old Taillefer's while I go to Madame de Nucingen? Ask him to make an appointment with me some time this evening; it is a matter of life and death."

"Really, young man!" cried old Goriot, with a change of countenance. "Are you paying court to his daughter, as those simpletons were saying down below? . . . *Tonnerre de Dieu!* you have no notion what a tap *à la Goriot* is like, and if you are playing a double game, I shall put a stop to it by one blow of the fist— But it's not possible!"

"I swear to you that I love but one woman in the world," said the student. "I only knew it a moment ago."

"Oh, what happiness!" cried Goriot.

"But young Taillefer is to fight a duel tomorrow morning, and I have heard it said that he may be killed."

"But what business is it of yours?" said Goriot.

"Why, I ought to tell him so, that he may prevent his son from putting in an appearance——"

Just at that moment Vautrin's voice broke in upon them; he was standing at the threshold of his door and singing:

> "Oh! Richard, oh my king!
> All the world abandons thee!
> Broum! broum! broum! broum! broum!
>
> The same old story everywhere,
> A roving heart and a . . . tra la la."

"Gentlemen!" shouted Christophe, "the soup is ready, and everyone is waiting for you."

"Here," Vautrin called down to him, "come and take a bottle of my Bordeaux."

"Do you think your watch is pretty?" asked Goriot. "She has good taste, hasn't she? Eh?"

Vautrin, old Goriot, and Rastignac came downstairs together and, all three of them being late, were obliged to sit together.

Eugène was as distant as possible in his manner to Vautrin during dinner; but the other, so charming in Mme Vauquer's opinion, had never been so witty. His lively sallies and sparkling talk put the whole table in good humor. His assurance and coolness filled Eugène with consternation.

"Why, what has got in to you today?" inquired Mme Vauquer. "You are as merry as a skylark."

"I am always in spirits after I have made a good bargain."

"Bargain?" said Eugène.

"Well, yes. I have just delivered a lot of goods, and I shall be paid a handsome commission on them. Mademoiselle Michonneau," he went on, seeing that the elderly spinster was scrutinizing him intently, "have you any objection to some feature in my face, that you are making those lynx eyes at me? Just let me know, and I will have it changed to oblige you. . . . We shall not fall out about it, Poiret, I daresay?" he added, winking at the superannuated clerk.

"Bless my soul, you ought to stand as model for a burlesque Hercules," said the young painter.

"I will, upon my word, if Mademoiselle Michonneau will consent to sit as the Venus of Père-Lachaise," replied Vautrin.

"There's Poiret," suggested Bianchon.

"Oh! Poiret shall pose as Poiret. He can be a garden god!" cried Vautrin; "his name means a pear——"

"A soft one!" Bianchon put in. "You will come in between the pear and the cheese."

"What nonsense you are all talking!" said Mme Vauquer. "You would do better to treat us to your Bordeaux; I see a glimpse of a bottle there. It will keep up our spirits, and it is good for the stomach besides."

"Gentlemen," said Vautrin, "the Lady President calls us to order. Mme Couture and Mlle Victorine will take your jokes in good part, but respect the innocence of the aged Goriot. I propose a glass or two of Bordeauxrama, rendered twice illustrious by the name of Lafitte, no political allusions intended.— Come, you Turk!" he added, looking at Christophe, who did not offer to stir. "Christophe! Here! What, you don't answer to your own name? Bring us some liquor, Turk!"

"Here it is, sir," said Christophe, holding out the bottle.

Vautrin filled Eugène's glass and Goriot's likewise, then he deliberately poured out a few drops into his own glass, and sipped it while his two neighbors drank their wine. All at once he made a grimace.

"Corked!" he cried. "The devil! You can drink the rest of this, Christophe, and go and find another bottle; take from the right-hand side, you know. There are sixteen of us; take down eight bottles."

"If you are going to stand treat," said the painter, "I will pay for a hundred chestnuts."

"Oh! oh!"

"Booououh!"

"Prrrr!"

These exclamations came from all parts of the table like squibs from a set firework.

"Come now, Mamma Vauquer, a couple of bottles of champagne," called Vautrin.

"Listen to that! Why not ask for the whole house at once? A couple of bottles of champagne—that means twelve francs! I shall never see the money again, I know! But if Monsieur Eugène has a mind to pay for it, I have some currant cordial."

"That currant cordial of hers is as bad as a dose of physic," muttered the medical student.

"Shut up, Bianchon," exclaimed Rastignac; "the very mention of it makes me feel— Yes, champagne, by all means; I'll pay for it," he added.

"Sylvie," called Mme Vauquer, "bring in some biscuits, and the little cakes."

"Those little cakes are moldy graybeards," said Vautrin. "But trot out the biscuits."

The Bordeaux circulated; the dinner table became a livelier scene than ever, and the fun grew fast and furious. Imitations of the cries of various animals mingled with the loud laughter; the Museum employee having taken it into his head to mimic a cat-call rather like the caterwauling of the animal in question, eight voices simultaneously struck up a chorus of well-known Parisian street cries:

"Scissors to grind!"

"Chick-weed for singing bir-ds!"

"Brandy-snaps, ladies!"

"China to mend!"

"Boat ahoy!"

"Sticks to beat your wives or your clothes!"

"Old clo'!"

"Cherries all ripe!"

But the palm was awarded to Bianchon for the nasal accent with which he rendered the cry of "Umbrellas to me-end!"

A few seconds later, and there was a head-splitting racket in the room, a storm of tomfoolery, a sort of cats' concert, with Vautrin as conductor of the orchestra, the latter keeping an eye the while on Eugène and old Goriot. The wine seemed to have gone to their heads already. They leaned back in their chairs, looking at the general confusion with an air of gravity, and drank but little; both of them were absorbed in the thought of what lay before them to do that evening, and yet neither of them felt able to rise from his chair. Vautrin gave a side glance at them from time to time, and watched the change that came over their faces, choosing the moment when their eyes drooped and seemed about to close, to bend over Rastignac and to say in his ear:

"My little lad, you are not quite shrewd enough to outwit Papa Vautrin yet, and he is too fond of you to let you make a mess of your affairs. When I have made up my mind to do a thing, no one short of Providence can put me off. Aha! we were for going round to warn old Taillefer, telling tales out of school! The oven is hot, the dough is kneaded, the bread is ready for the oven; tomorrow we will eat it up and whisk away the crumbs; and we are not going to spoil the baking! . . . No, no, it is all as good as done. We may suffer from a few conscientious scruples, but they will be digested along with the bread. While we are having our forty winks, Colonel Count Franchessini will clear the way to Michel Taillefer's inheritance with the point of his sword. Victorine will come in for her brother's money, a snug fifteen thousand francs a year. I have made inquiries already, and I know that her late mother's property amounts to more than three hundred thousand——"

Eugène heard all this, but he had no power to answer. His tongue seemed to be glued to the roof of his mouth, an irresistible drowsiness was creeping over him. He still saw the table and the faces round it, but it was through a bright mist. Soon the noise began to subside, one by one the boarders went. At last, when their numbers had so dwindled that the party consisted of Mme Vauquer, Mme Couture, Mlle Victorine, Vautrin, and old Goriot, Rastignac watched as though in a dream how Mme Vauquer busied herself by collecting the bottles, and drained the remainder of the wine out of each to fill others.

"Oh, how uproarious they are! What a thing it is to be young!" said the widow.

These were the last words that Eugène heard and understood.

"There is no one like Monsieur Vautrin for a bit of fun like this," said Sylvie. "There, just listen to Christophe—snoring like a top."

"Good-bye, mamma," said Vautrin; "I am going to a theater on the boulevard to see Marty in *Le Mont Sauvage*, a fine play taken from *Le Solitaire*. . . . If you like, I will take you and these two ladies——"

"Thank you; I must decline," said Mme Couture.

"What! My good lady," cried Mme Vauquer, "decline to see a play founded on the *Le Solitaire*, a work by Atala de Chateaubriand! We were so fond of that book that we cried over it like Magdalens under the *line-trees* last summer; it's an improving work that might edify your young lady."

"We are forbidden to go to the play," answered Victorine.

"Just look, those two yonder have dropped off where they sit," said Vautrin, shaking the heads of the two sleepers in a comical way.

He altered the sleeping student's position, settled his head more comfortably on the back of his chair, kissed him warmly on the forehead, and began to sing;

> "Sleep, little darlings;
> I watch while you slumber."

"I am afraid he may be ill," said Victorine.

"Then stop and take care of him," returned Vautrin. " 'Tis your duty as a meek and obedient wife," he whispered in her ear. "The young fellow worships you, and you will be his little wife—there's your fortune for you. In short," he added aloud, " 'they lived happily ever afterwards, were much looked up to in all the country-side, and had a numerous family.' That is how all the romances end.—Now, mamma," he went on, as he turned to Mme Vauquer and put his arm round her waist, "put on your bonnet, your best flowered silk, and the countess' scarf, while I go out to call a cab—all my own self."

And he started out, singing as he went:

> "Oh! sun! divine sun!
> Ripening the pumpkins every one."

"My goodness! Do you know, Madame Couture, I could live happily in a garret with a man like that.—There, now!" she added, looking round for the old vermicelli-maker, "there is that old Goriot half-seas over. *He* never thought of taking me anywhere, the old skinflint. But he will measure his length somewhere. My word, it is disgraceful to lose his senses like that, at his age! You will be telling me that he couldn't lose what he hadn't got— Sylvie, just take him up to his room!"

Sylvie took him by the arm, supported him upstairs, and flung him just as he was, like a package, across the bed.

"Poor young fellow!" said Mme Couture, putting back Eugène's hair that had fallen over his eyes. "He is like a young girl; he didn't know the wine would be too much for him."

"Well, I can tell you this," said Mme Vauquer, "I have taken lodgers these thirty years, and a good many have passed through my hands, as the saying is, but I have never seen a nicer or a more aristocratic-looking young man than Monsieur Eugène. How handsome he looks sleeping! Just let his head rest on your shoulder, Madame Couture. Pshaw! he falls over towards Mademoiselle Victorine. There's a special providence for young

things. A little more, and he would have cracked his head against
the knob of the chair. They'd make a pretty pair, those two
would!"

"Hush, my good neighbor," cried Mme Couture, "you are
saying things which——"

"Pooh!" put in Mme Vauquer, "he does not hear.— Here,
Sylvie, come and help me to dress. I shall put on my best stays."

"What! Your best stays just after dinner, madame?" said
Sylvie. "No, you can get someone else to lace you. I am not
going to be your murderer. It's a rash thing to do, and might
cost you your life."

"I don't care, I must do honor to Monsieur Vautrin."

"Are you so fond of your heirs as all that?"

"Come, Sylvie, don't argue," said the widow, as she left the
room.

"At her age, too!" said the cook to Victorine, pointing to
her mistress as she spoke.

Mme Couture and her ward were left in the dining room,
and Eugène slept on on Victorine's shoulder. The sound of
Christophe's snoring echoed through the silent house; Eugène's
quiet breathing seemed all the quieter by force of contrast; he
was sleeping as peacefully as a child. Victorine was very happy
in performing one of those acts of charity which serve as an
innocent outlet for all the overflowing sentiments of a woman's
nature. He was so close to her that she could feel the throbbing
of his heart. A look of almost maternal protection and a conscious pride glowed in Victorine's face. Among the countless
thoughts that crowded up in her young innocent heart, there
was a wild flutter of joy at this close contact.

"Poor, dear child!" said Mme Couture, squeezing her hand.

The old lady looked at the girl. Victorine's innocent, pathetic
face, so radiant with the new happiness that had befallen her,
called to mind some naïve work of medieval art, when the
painter neglected the accessories, reserving all the magic of his

brush for the quiet, austere outlines and ivory tints of the face, which seems to have caught something of the golden glory of heaven.

"After all, he only took two glasses, mamma," said Victorine, passing her fingers through Eugène's hair.

"Indeed, if he had been a dissipated young man, child, he would have carried his wine like the rest of them. His drowsiness does him credit."

There was a sound of wheels outside in the street.

"There is Monsieur Vautrin, mamma," said the girl. "Just take Monsieur Eugène. I would rather not have that man see me like this; he has a way of looking at you that seems to sully your soul and makes you feel as though you had nothing on."

"Oh, no, you are wrong!" said Mme Couture. "Monsieur Vautrin is a worthy man; he reminds me a little of my late husband, rough but kindhearted; his bark is worse than his bite."

Vautrin came in while she was speaking; he did not make a sound, but looked for a while at the picture of the two young faces—the lamplight falling full upon them seemed to caress them.

"Well," he remarked, folding his arms, "here is a picture! It would have suggested some pleasing pages to Bernardin de Saint-Pierre, good soul, who wrote *Paul et Virginie*. Youth is very charming, Madame Couture!—Sleep on, poor boy," he added, looking at Eugène, "luck sometimes comes while we are sleeping. There is something touching and attractive to me about this young man, madame," he continued; "I know that his nature is in harmony with his face. Just look, the head of a cherub on an angel's shoulder! He deserves to be loved. If I were a woman, I would die—no, not such a fool—I would live for him." He bent lower and spoke in the widow's ear. "When I see those two together, madame, I cannot help thinking that Providence meant them for each other; He works by secret ways, and tries the reins and the heart," he said in a loud voice. "And when I see you, my children, thus united by a like purity and by all human affections, I say to myself that it is quite impossible that the future should separate you. God is just." He turned to Victorine. "It seems to me," he said, "that I have seen the line of success in your hand. Let me look at it, Mademoiselle Victorine. I am well up in palmistry, and I have told fortunes many a time. Come, now, don't be frightened. Ah, what do I see? Upon my word, you will be one of the richest heiresses in Paris before very long. You will heap wealth on the man who loves you. Your father will want you to go and live with him. You will marry a young and handsome man with a title, and he will idolize you."

The heavy footsteps of the coquettish widow, who was coming down the stairs, interrupted Vautrin's fortunetelling. "Here is Mamma Vauquerre, fair as a star-r-r, dressed within an inch of her life. Aren't we a trifle pinched for room?" he inquired, with his arm round the lady. "We are screwed up very tightly about the bust, mamma! If we are much agitated, there may be an explosion; but I will pick up the fragments with all the care of an antiquary."

"There is a man who can talk the language of French gallantry!" said the widow, bending to speak in Mme Couture's ear.

"Good-bye, little ones!" said Vautrin, turning to Eugène and Victorine. "Bless you both!" and he laid a hand on either head. "Take my word for it, young lady, an honest man's prayers are worth something; they should bring you happiness, for God hears them."

"Good-bye, dear," said Mme Vauquer to her lodger. "Do you think that Monsieur Vautrin means to run away with me?" she added, lowering her voice.

"Lack-a-day!" said the widow.

"Oh, mamma dear, suppose it should really happen as that

kind Monsieur Vautrın said!" said Victorine with a sigh, as she looked at her hands. The two women were alone together.

"Why, it wouldn't take much to bring it to pass," said the elder lady; "just a fall from his horse, and your monster of a brother——"

"Oh, mamma!'

"Good Lord! Well, perhaps it is a sin to wish bad luck to an enemy," the widow remarked. "I will do penance for it. Still, I would strew flowers on his grave with the greatest pleasure, and that is the truth. Black-hearted, that he is! The coward couldn't speak up for his own mother, and cheats you out of your share by trickery. My cousin had a pretty fortune of her own, but, unluckily for you, nothing was said in the marriage contract about anything that she might come in for."

"It would be hard to bear if my good fortune is to cost someone else his life," said Victorine. "If I cannot be happy unless my brother is to be taken out of the world, I would rather stay here all my life."

"*Mon Dieu!* it is just as that good Monsieur Vautrin says, and he is full of piety, you see," Mme Couture remarked. "I am very glad to find that he is not an unbeliever like the rest of them that talk of the Almighty with less respect than they do of the Devil. Well, as he was saying, who can know the ways by which it may please Providence to lead us?"

With Sylvie's help the two women at last succeeded in getting Eugène up to his room; they placed him on the bed, and the cook unfastened his clothes to make him more comfortable. Before they left the room, Victorine snatched an opportunity when her guardian's back was turned, and pressed a kiss on Eugène's forehead, feeling all the joy that this stolen pleasure could give her. Then she looked round the room, and gathering up, as it were, into one single thought all the untold bliss of that day, she made a picture of her memories, and dwelt upon it until she fell asleep, the happiest creature in Paris.

That evening's merrymaking, in the course of which Vautrin had given the drugged wine to Eugène and old Goriot, was his own ruin. Bianchon, flustered with wine, forgot to open the subject of Trompe-la-Mort with Mlle Michonneau. The mere mention of the name would have set Vautrin on his guard; for Vautrin, or, to give him his real name, Jacques Collin, was in fact the notorious escaped convict.

But it was the joke about the Venus of Père-Lachaise that finally decided his fate. Mlle Michonneau had very nearly made up her mind to warn the convict and to throw herself on his generosity, with the idea of making a better bargain for herself by helping him to escape that night; but as it was, she went out escorted by Poiret in search of the famous chief of detectives in the Petite Rue Saint-Anne, still thinking that it was the district superintendent—one Gondureau—with whom she had to do. The head of the department received his visitors courteously. There was a little talk, and the details were definitely arranged. Mlle Michonneau asked for the draught that she was to administer in order to set about her investigation. But the great man's evident satisfaction set Mlle Michonneau thinking; and she began to see that this business involved something more than the mere capture of a runaway convict. She racked her brains while he looked in a drawer in his desk for the little phial, and it dawned upon her that in consequence of treacherous revelations made by the prisoners the police were hoping to lay their hands on a considerable sum of money. But on hinting her suspicions to the old fox of the Petite Rue Saint-Anne, that officer began to smile, and tried to put her off the scent.

"A delusion," he said. "Collin's *sorbonne* is the most dangerous that has yet been found among the dangerous classes. That is all, and the rascals are quite aware of it. They rally round him; he is the backbone of the federation, its Bonaparte, in short; he is very popular with them all. The rogue will never leave his *tronche* in the Place de Grève."

As Mlle Michonneau seemed mystified, Gondureau explained the two slang words for her benefit. *Sorbonne* and *tronche* are two forcible expressions borrowed from thieves' Latin, thieves, of all people, being compelled to consider the human head in its two aspects. A *sorbonne* is the head of a living man, his faculty of thinking—his council; a *tronche* is a contemptuous epithet that implies the worthlessness of the head after the axe has done its work.

"Collin is playing us off," he continued. "When we come across a man like a bar of steel tempered in the English fashion, there is always one resource left—we can kill him if he takes it into his head to make the least resistance. We are reckoning on several methods of killing Collin tomorrow morning. It saves a trial, and society is rid of him without all the expense of guarding and feeding him. What with getting up the case, summoning witnesses, paying their expenses, and carrying out the sentence, it costs a lot to go through all the proper formalities before you can get quit of one of these good-for-nothings, over and above the three thousand francs that you are going to have. There is a saving in time as well. One good thrust of the bayonet into Trompe-la-Mort's paunch will prevent scores of crimes, and save fifty scoundrels from following his example; they will be very careful to keep themselves out of the police courts. That is doing the work of the police thoroughly, and any philanthropist will tell you that it is better to prevent crime than to punish it."

"And you do a service to our country," said Poiret.

"Really, you are talking sense tonight, that you are," said the head of the department. "We serve our country, but people are unfair toward us. We do society very great services that are not recognized. In fact, a superior man must rise above vulgar prejudices, and a Christian must resign himself to the mishaps that doing right entails, when right is done in an out-of-the-way style. Paris is Paris, you see! That is the explanation of my life

I have the honor to wish you a good evening, mademoiselle. I shall bring my men to the Jardin du Roi in the morning. Send Christophe to the Rue du Buffon, tell him to ask for Monsieur Gondureau in the house where you saw me before.—Your servant, sir. If you should ever have anything stolen from you, come to me, and I will do my best to get it back for you."

"Well, now," Poiret remarked to Mlle Michonneau, "there are idiots who are scared out of their wits by the word police. That was a very pleasant-spoken gentleman, and what he wants you to do is as easy as saying 'Good day.'"

Chapter 14

THE NEXT day was destined to be one of the most extraordinary in the annals of the Maison Vauquer. Hitherto the most startling occurrence in its tranquil existence had been the portentous, meteor-like apparition of the sham Comtesse de l'Ambermesnil. But the catastrophes of this great day were to cast all previous events into the shade, and supply an inexhaustible topic of conversation for Mme Vauquer for the rest of her life.

In the first place, Goriot and Eugène de Rastignac both slept till close upon eleven o'clock. Mme Vauquer, who came home about midnight from the Gaîté, lay a-bed till half-past ten. Christophe, after a prolonged slumber (he had finished Vautrin's first bottle of wine), was behindhand with his work, but Poiret and Mlle Michonneau uttered no complaint, though breakfast was delayed. As for Victorine and Mme Couture, they also slept late. Vautrin went out before eight o'clock, and only came back just as breakfast was ready. Nobody protested, therefore, when Sylvie and Christophe went up at a quarter-past eleven, knocked at all the doors, and announced that breakfast was waiting. While Sylvie and the man were upstairs, Mlle Michonneau, who came down first, poured the contents of the phial into the silver cup belonging to Vautrin, in which the cream for the morning coffee was being kept warm in the bain-marie. The spinster had reckoned on this custom of the house to do her stroke of business. The seven lodgers were at last collected together, not without some difficulty. Just as Eugène came downstairs, stretching himself and yawning, a commissionaire handed him a letter from Mme de Nucingen. It ran as follows:

I feel neither false vanity nor anger where you are concerned, my friend. Till two o'clock this morning I waited for you. Oh, that waiting for one whom you love! No one that had passed through that torture could inflict it on another. I know now that you have never loved before. What can have happened? Anxiety has taken hold of me. I would have come myself to find out what had happened, if I had not feared to betray the secrets of my heart. How can I walk out or drive out at this time of day? Would it not be ruin? I have felt to the full how wretched it is to be a woman. Send a word to reassure me, and explain how it is that you have not come after what my father told you. I shall be angry, but I will forgive you. One word, for pity's sake. You will come to me very soon, will you not? If you are busy, a word will be enough. Say, "I will hasten to you," or else, "I am ill." But if you were ill my father would have come to tell me so. What can have happened? . . .

"Yes, indeed, what has happened?" exclaimed Eugène, and, hurrying down to the dining room, he crumpled up the letter without reading any more. "What time is it?"

"Half-past eleven," said Vautrin, dropping a lump of sugar into his coffee.

The escaped convict cast a glance of cold fascination at Eugène; men gifted with this magnetic power can subdue maniacs in a madhouse by such a glance, it is said. Eugène shook in every limb. There was the sound of wheels in the street, and in another moment a man with a scared face rushed into the

room. It was one of M. Taillefer's servants; Mme Couture recognized the livery at once.

"Mademoiselle," he cried, "your father is asking for you—
something terrible has happened! Monsieur Frédéric has had a
sword-thrust in the forehead in a duel, and the doctors have
given him up. You will scarcely be in time to say good-bye to
him! He is unconscious."

"Poor young fellow!" exclaimed Vautrin. "How can people
brawl when they have a certain income of thirty thousand
livres? Young people don't know how to behave, and that's
a fact."

"Sir!" cried Eugène.

"Well, what then, you big baby!" said Vautrin, swallowing
down his coffee imperturbably, an operation which Mlle
Michonneau watched with such close attention that she had no
emotion to spare for the amazing news that had struck the
others dumb with amazement. "Are there not duels every morning in Paris?" added Vautrin.

"I will go with you, Victorine," said Mme Couture, and the
two women hurried away at once without either hats or shawls.
But before she went, Victorine, with her eyes full of tears, gave
Eugène a glance that said: "How little I thought that our happiness should cost me tears!"

"Dear me, you are a prophet, Monsieur Vautrin," said Mme
Vauquer.

"I am all things," said Vautrin.

"Queer, isn't it?" said Mme Vauquer, stringing together a
succession of commonplaces suited to the occasion. "Death
takes us off without asking us about it. The young often go
before the old. It is a lucky thing for us women, that we are not
liable to fight duels, but we have other complaints that men
don't suffer from. We bear children, and it takes a long time
to get over it. What a windfall for Victorine! Her father will
have to acknowledge her now!"

"There!" said Vautrin, looking at Eugène, "yesterday she had not a penny; this morning she is worth several millions."

"I say, Monsieur Eugène!" cried Mme Vauquer, "you have landed on your feet!"

At this exclamation, old Goriot looked at the student, and saw the crumpled letter still in his hand.

"You have not read it through! What does this mean? Are you going to be like the rest of them?" he asked.

"Madame, I shall never marry Mademoiselle Victorine," said Eugène, turning to Mme Vauquer with an expression of terror and loathing that surprised the onlookers at this scene.

Old Goriot caught the student's hand and grasped it warmly. He could have kissed it.

"Oh, ho!" said Vautrin, "the Italians have a good proverb— *Col tempo.*"

"Is there any answer?" said Mme de Nucingen's messenger, addressing Eugène.

"Say I am coming."

The man went away. Eugène was in a state of such violent excitement that he could not be prudent.

"What is to be done?" he exclaimed aloud. "There are no proofs!"

Vautrin began to smile. Though the drug he had taken was doing its work, the convict was so vigorous that he rose to his feet, gave Rastignac a look, and said in hollow tones, "Luck comes to us while we sleep, young man," and fell stiff and stark, as if he were struck dead.

"The justice of God!" said Eugène.

"Why, what has happened to that poor dear Monsieur Vautrin?"

"A stroke!" cried Mlle Michonneau.

"Here, Sylvie, my girl, run for the doctor!" called the widow. "Oh, Monsieur Rastignac, just go for Monsieur Bianchon, and be as quick as you can; Sylvie might not be in time to catch our doctor, Monsieur Grimprel."

Rastignac, glad of an excuse to leave that den of horrors, rushed away at top speed.

"Here, Christophe, go round to the chemist's and ask for something that's good for apoplexy."

Christophe likewise went.

"Father Goriot, just help us to get him upstairs."

Vautrin was taken up among them, carried carefully up the narrow staircase, and laid upon his bed.

"I can do no good here, so I shall go to see my daughter," said M. Goriot.

"Selfish old thing!" cried Mme Vauquer. "Yes, go; I hope you die like a dog."

"Just go and see if you can find some ether," said Mlle Michonneau to Mme Vauquer; the former, with some help from Poiret, had unfastened the sick man's clothes.

Mme Vauquer went down to her room, and left Mlle Michonneau mistress of the situation.

"Now! just pull down his shirt and turn him over, quick! You might be of some use in sparing my modesty," she said to Poiret, "instead of standing there like a stock."

Vautrin was turned over; Mlle Michonneau gave his shoulder a sharp slap, and the two portentous letters appeared, white against the red.

"There, you have earned your three thousand francs very easily," exclaimed Poiret, supporting Vautrin while Mlle Michonneau slipped on the shirt again. "Ouf! how heavy he is," he added, as he laid the convict down.

"Hush! Suppose there is a strong box here!" said the old maid briskly. Her glance seemed to pierce the walls; she scrutinized every article of the furniture with greedy eyes. "Could we find some excuse for opening that desk?"

"It mightn't be quite right," responded Poiret to this.

"Where is the harm? It is money stolen from all sorts of people, so it doesn't belong to anyone now. But we haven't time—there is the Vauquer."

"Here is the ether," said that lady. "I must say that this is an eventful day. Lord! that man can't have had a stroke; he is as white as a chicken."

"White as a chicken," echoed Poiret.

"And his pulse is steady," said the widow, laying her hand on his breast.

"Steady?" said the astonished Poiret.

"He is all right."

"Do you think so?" asked Poiret.

"Lord, yes, he looks as if he were sleeping. Sylvie has gone for a doctor. I say, Mademoiselle Michonneau, he is sniffing the ether. Pooh! it is only a spasm. His pulse is good. He is as strong as a Turk. Just look, mademoiselle, what a fur tippet he has on his chest. He will live to be a hundred. His wig holds on tightly. Dear me! it is glued on, and his own hair is red; that is why he wears a wig. They always say that red-haired people are either the worst or the best. Is he one of the good ones, I wonder?"

"Good to hang," said Poiret.

"Round a pretty woman's neck, you mean," said Mlle Michonneau, hastily. "Just go away, Monsieur Poiret. It is a woman's duty to nurse you men when you are ill. Besides, for all the good you are doing, you may as well take yourself off," she added. "Mme Vauquer and I will take great care of dear Monsieur Vautrin."

Poiret went out on tiptoe without a murmur, like a dog kicked out of the room by his master.

Rastignac had gone out for the sake of physical exertion; he wanted to breathe the air, for he felt stifled. Yesterday evening he had meant to prevent the murder arranged for half-past eight that morning. What had happened? What ought he to do now? He trembled to think that he himself might be implicated. Vautrin's coolness still further dismayed him.

"Yet, what if Vautrin should die without saying a word?" Rastignac asked himself.

He hurried along the alleys of the Luxembourg Gardens as if the hounds of justice were after him, and he already heard the baying of the pack.

Bianchon shouted to him, "Have you seen the *Pilote*?"

The *Pilote* was a Radical sheet, edited by M. Tissot. It came out several hours later than the morning papers, and was meant for the benefit of country subscribers, for it brought the morning's news into provincial districts twenty-four hours sooner than the ordinary local journals.

"There is a wonderful story in it," said the intern of the Hôpital Cochin. "Young Taillefer called out Count Franchessini, of the Old Guard, and the count put a couple of inches of steel into his forehead. And here is little Victorine one of the richest heiresses in Paris! If we had known that, eh? What a game of chance death is! They said Victorine was sweet on you; was there any truth in it?"

"Shut up, Bianchon; I shall never marry her. I am in love with a charming woman, and she is in love with me, so——"

"You said that as if you were screwing yourself up to be faithful to her. I should like to see the woman worth the sacrifice of Taillefer's money!"

"Are all the devils of hell at my heels?" cried Rastignac.

"What is the matter with you? Are you mad? Give us your hand," said Bianchon, "and let me feel your pulse. You are feverish."

"Just go to Mother Vauquer's," said Rastignac; "that scoundrel Vautrin has dropped down like a dead man."

"Aha!" said Bianchon, leaving Rastignac to his reflections, "you confirm my suspicions, and now I mean to make sure for myself."

The law student's long walk was a memorable one for him. He made a thorough survey of his conscience. After a close scrutiny, after hesitation and self-examination, his honor at any rate came out scatheless from this sharp and terrible ordeal, like a bar of iron tested in the English fashion. He remembered old Goriot's confidences of the evening before, the rooms taken for him in the Rue d'Artois, so that he might be near Delphine; and then he thought of his letter, and read it again and kissed it.

"Such a love is my anchor of safety," he said to himself. "How the old man's heart must have been wrung! He says nothing about all that he has been through; but who could not guess? Well, then, I will be like a son to him; he shall be made happy. If she cares for me, she will often come to spend the day with him. That grand Comtesse de Restaud is a heartless thing; she would make her father into her hall porter. Dear Delphine! She is kinder to the old man—she is worthy to be loved. Ah! this evening I shall be so happy!"

He took out his watch and admired it.

"I have had nothing but success! If two people mean to love each other forever, they may help each other, and I can take this. Besides, I shall succeed, and I will repay her a hundred-fold. There is nothing criminal in this *liaison;* nothing that could cause the most austere moralist to frown. How many respectable people contract similar unions! We deceive nobody; it is deception that makes a position humiliating. If you lie, you lower yourself at once. She and her husband have lived apart for a long while. I'll just tell that big Alsatian he should give up a wife whom he cannot make happy."

Rastignac's battle with himself went on for a long while; and though the scruples of youth inevitably gained the day, an irresistible curiosity led him, about half-past four, to return to the Maison Vauquer through the gathering dusk. Although he swore to leave the place forever, he must find out if Vautrin had died.

Bianchon had given Vautrin an emetic, reserving the contents of the stomach for chemical analysis at the hospital. Mlle Michonneau's officious alacrity had still further strengthened his suspicions of her. Vautrin, moreover, had recovered so quickly, that it was impossible not to suspect some plot against the leader of all frolics at the lodginghouse. Vautrin was standing in front of the stove in the dining room when Rastignac came in. All the lodgers were assembled sooner than usual by the news of young Taillefer's duel. They were anxious to hear any detail about the affair, and to talk over the probable change in Victorine's prospects. Old Goriot alone was absent, but the rest were chatting. No sooner did Eugène come into the room, than his eyes met the inscrutable gaze of Vautrin. It was the same look that had read his thoughts before—the look that had such power to waken evil thoughts in his heart. He shuddered.

"Well, dear boy," said the escaped convict, "I am likely to cheat death for a good while yet. According to these ladies, I have had a stroke that would have felled an ox, and come off with flying colors."

"A bull, you might say," cried the widow.

"You really might be sorry to see me still alive," said Vautrin in Rastignac's ear, thinking that he guessed the student's thoughts. "You must be mighty sure of yourself."

"Mademoiselle Michonneau was talking the day before yesterday about a gentleman nicknamed Trompe-la-Mort," said Bianchon; "and, upon my word, that name would do very well for you."

Vautrin seemed thunderstruck. He turned pale, and staggered back. He turned his magnetic glance, like a ray of vivid light, on Mlle Michonneau. The old maid shrank and trembled under the influence of that strong will, and collapsed into a chair. The mask of good-nature had dropped from the convict's face; from the unmistakable ferocity of that sinister look, Poiret felt that the old maid was in danger, and hastily stepped between them.

None of the lodgers understood this scene in the least; they looked on in mute amazement. There was a pause. Just then a sound of tramping feet was heard; there were soldiers outside, it seemed, for there was a rattle of muskets on the pavement. Collin was mechanically looking round the walls for a way of escape, when four men entered by way of the sitting room. The first was the chief of the detective police, and the three others were members of his force.

"In the name of the King and the law!" said an officer, but the words were almost lost in a murmur of astonishment.

Silence fell on the room. The lodgers made way for three of the men, each of whom had his hand on a cocked pistol in a side pocket. Two policemen, who followed the detectives, kept the entrance to the sitting room, and two more appeared in the doorway that gave access to the staircase. A sound of footsteps came from the garden, and again the rifles of several soldiers rang on the cobblestones under the window. All chance of flight was cut off for Trompe-la-Mort, to whom all eyes instinctively turned. The chief walked straight up to him, and commenced operations by giving him a sharp blow on the head, so that the wig fell off, and Collin's face was revealed in all its ugliness. There was a terrible suggestion of strength mingled with cunning in the short, brick-red crop of hair; the whole head was in harmony with his powerful frame, and at that moment the fires of hell seemed to gleam from his eyes. In that flash the real Vautrin shone forth, revealed at once before them all; they understood his past, his present, and future, his pitiless doctrines, his actions, the religion of his own good pleasure, the power with which his cynicism and contempt for mankind invested him, the physical strength of an organism proof against all trials. The blood flew to his face, and his eyes glared like the eyes of a wildcat. He started back with savage energy and a fierce growl that drew exclamations of alarm from the lodgers. At that leonine start the police caught at their pistols under cover of the general clamor. Collin saw the gleaming muzzles of the weapons, saw his danger, and instantly gave proof of a power of the highest order. There was something horrible and majestic in the spectacle of the sudden transformation in his face; he could only be compared to a boiler full of the steam that can blast mountains, a terrific force which is dispelled in a moment by a drop of cold water. The drop of water that cooled his wrathful fury was a reflection that flashed across his brain like lightning. He began to smile, and looked down at his wig.

"You are not in the politest of humors today," he remarked to the chief, and he held out his hands to the policemen with a jerk of his head.

"Gentlemen," he said, "put on the bracelets or the handcuffs. I call on those present to witness that I do not resist."

A murmur of admiration ran through the room at the sudden outpouring like fire and lava flood from this human volcano, and its equally sudden cessation.

"That puts an end to your fun, Mr. House-breaker," the convict added, looking at the famous director of police.

"Come, strip!" said he of the Petite Rue Saint-Anne, contemptuously.

"Why?" asked Collin. "There are ladies present. I deny nothing, and give myself up."

He paused, and looked round the room like an orator who is about to overwhelm his audience.

"Take this down, Daddy Lachapelle," he went on, addressing a little, white-haired old man who had seated himself at the end of the table; and after drawing a printed form from a portfolio, was proceeding to draw up a document. "I acknowledge myself to be Jacques Collin, otherwise known as Trompe-la-Mort, condemned to twenty years' penal servitude, and I have just proved that I have come fairly by my nickname. If I had as much as raised my hand," he went on, addressing the other lodgers, "those three sneaking wretches yonder would have drawn claret on Mamma Vauquer's domestic hearth. The rascals have plotted to set a trap for me."

Mme Vauquer felt sick and faint at these words.

"Good Lord!" she cried, "this does give one a turn; and me at the Gaîté with him only last night!" she said to Sylvie.

"Summon your philosophy, mamma," Collin resumed. "Is it a misfortune to have sat in my box at the Gaîté yesterday evening? After all, are you better than we are? The brand upon our shoulders is less shameful than the brand set on your hearts, you flabby members of a society rotten to the core. Not the best man among you could stand up to me." His eyes rested upon Rastignac, to whom he spoke with a pleasant smile that seemed strangely at variance with the savage expression in his eyes.— "Our little bargain still holds good, dear boy; you can accept any time you like! Do you understand?" and he sang:

> "A charming girl is my Fanchette
> In her simplicity.

"Don't you trouble yourself," he went on; "I can get in my money. They are too much afraid of me to swindle me."

The language and customs of the prison, its sudden sharp transitions from the humorous to the horrible, its appalling grandeur, its triviality and dark depths, were all revealed in turn by the speaker's discourse. He seemed to be no longer a man, but the type and mouthpiece of a degenerate race, a brutal, supple, clear-headed race of savages. In one moment Collin became the poet of an inferno, where in all thoughts and passions that move human nature (save repentance) find a place. He looked about him like a fallen archangel who is for war to the end. Rastignac lowered his eyes, and acknowledged this kinship claimed by crime in expiation of his own evil thoughts.

"Who betrayed me?" said Collin, and his terrible eyes traveled round the room. Suddenly they rested on Mlle Michonneau.

"It was you, old cat!" he said. "That sham stroke of apoplexy was your doing, lynx eyes! . . . Two words from me, and your throat would be cut in less than a week, but I forgive you. I'm a Christian. It was not you who sold me out. But who did?— Aha! you may rummage upstairs," he shouted, hearing the police officers opening his cupboards and taking possession of his effects. "The nest is empty, the birds flew away yesterday, and you will be none the wiser. My ledgers are here," he said, tapping his forehead. "Now I know who sold me! It could only be that blackguard Fil-de-Soie. Isn't that so, old catchpoll?" he said, turning to the chief. "It was timed so neatly to get the bank-notes up above there. There is nothing left for you—spies! As for Fil-de-Soie, he will be under the daisies in less than a fortnight, even if you were to tell off the whole force to protect him. How much did you give the Michonnette?" he asked of the police officers. "A thousand crowns? Oh, you decayed Ninon, Pompadour in tatters, Venus of the graveyard, I was worth more than that! If you had given me warning, you should have had six thousand francs. Ha! You had no suspicion of that, old trafficker in flesh and blood, or I should have had the preference. Yes, I would have given six thousand francs to save myself an inconvenient journey and some loss of money," he said, as they fastened the handcuffs on his wrists. "These folks will amuse themselves by dragging out this business till the end of time to keep me idle! If they were to send me straight to jail, I should soon be back at my old tricks in spite of the duffers at the Quai des Orfèvres. Down there they would all turn themselves inside out to help their general—good Trompe-la-Mort— to get clear away. Is there a single one among you that can say, as I can, that he has ten thousand brothers ready to do anything for him?" he asked proudly. "There is some good there," he said, tapping his heart; "I have never betrayed anyone!—Look here, you slut," he said to the old maid, "they are all afraid of me, you see? but the sight of you makes them sick. Rake in your gains."

He was silent for a moment, and looked round at the lodgers' faces.

"What dolts you are, all of you! Have you never seen a convict before? A convict of Collin's stamp, here before you, is a man less weak-kneed than others; he lifts up his voice against the colossal fraud of the Social Contract, as Jean-Jacques did, whose pupil he is proud to declare himself. In short, I stand here single-handed against a Government and a whole subsidized machinery of courts and police, and I am a match for them all."

"The devil!" cried the painter. "What a magnificent sketch I could make of him now!"

"Look here, you gentlemen-in-waiting to his highness the gibbet, master of ceremonies to the Widow"—a nickname full of somber poetry, given by prisoners to the guillotine,—"be a good fellow, and tell me if it really was Fil-de-Soie who sold me. I don't want him to pay the price for someone else—that would not be fair."

But before the chief had time to answer, the rest of the party returned from making their investigations upstairs. Everything had been opened and inventoried. A few words passed between them and the chief, and the official preliminaries were complete.

"Gentlemen," said Collin, addressing the lodgers, "they will take me away directly. You have all made my stay among you very agreeable, and I shall look back upon it with gratitude. Receive my adieux, and permit me to send you figs from Provence."

He advanced a step or two, and then turned to look once more at Rastignac.

"Good-bye, Eugène," he said, in a sad and gentle tone, a strange transition from his previous rough and stern manner. "If you should be hard up, I have left you a devoted friend," and, in spite of his shackles, he managed to assume a posture of defense, called, "One! two!" like a fencing master, and lunged. "If anything goes wrong, apply in that quarter. Man and money, all at your service."

This strange being put so much drollery into his last words that no one but Rastignac knew there was a serious meaning underlying the pantomime.

As soon as the police, soldiers, and detectives had left the house, Sylvie, who was rubbing her mistress' temples with vinegar, looked round at the bewildered lodgers.

"Well," said she, "he was a good man, all the same."

Her words broke the spell. Everyone had been too much excited, too much moved by various feelings to speak. But now the lodgers began to look at each other, and then all eyes were turned at once on Mlle Michonneau, a thin, shriveled, dead-alive, mummy-like figure crouching by the stove. Her eyes were downcast, as if she feared that the green eye-shade could not shut out the expression of those faces from her. This figure and the feeling of repulsion she had so long excited were explained all at once. A smothered murmur filled the room; it was so unanimous, that it seemed as if the same feeling of loathing had pitched all the voices in one key. Mlle Michonneau heard it, and did not stir. It was Bianchon who was the first to move. He bent over his neighbor, and said in a low voice, "If that creature if going to stop here and have dinner with us, I shall clear out."

In a flash it was clear that everyone in the room, save Poiret, was of the medical student's opinion, so that the latter, strong in the support of the majority, went up to that elderly person.

"You are more intimate with Mlle Michonneau than the rest of us," he said; "speak to her, make her understand that she must go, and go at once."

"At once!" echoed Poiret in amazement.

Then he went across to the crouching figure, and spoke a few words in her ear.

"I have paid in advance for the quarter, and I have as much right to be here as anyone else," she said, with a viperous look at the boarders.

"Never mind that! We will club together and pay you the money back," said Rastignac.

"Monsieur is taking Collin's part," she said, with a questioning, malignant glance at the law student. "It is not difficult to guess why."

Eugène started forward at the words, as if he meant to spring upon her and strangle her. That glance, and the depths of treachery that it revealed, had been a hideous enlightenment.

"Let her alone!" cried the boarders.

Rastignac folded his arms, and was silent.

"Let us have no more of Mademoiselle Judas," said the painter, turning to Mme Vauquer. "If you don't show the Michonneau the door, madame, we shall all leave your barracks, and wherever we go we shall say that there are only convicts and spies left here. If you do the other thing, we will hold our tongues about the business; for when all is said and done, it might happen in the best society until they brand galley-slaves on the forehead. They ought not to let convicts go about Paris disguised like decent citizens, so they can play their tricks like the rascals they are."

At this Mme Vauquer recovered miraculously. She sat up and folded her arms; her eyes were wide open now, and there was no sign of tears in them.

"Why, do you really mean to be the ruin of my establishment, my dear sir? There is Monsieur Vautrin— Goodness," she cried, interrupting herself, "I can't help calling him by the honest name he passed himself off by! There is one room to let already, and you want me to turn out two more lodgers in the middle of the season, when no one is moving——"

"Gentlemen, let us take our hats and go and dine at Flicoteaux's in the Place Sorbonne," cried Bianchon.

Mme Vauquer glanced round, and saw in a moment on which side her interest lay. She waddled across to Mlle Michonneau.

"Come, now," she said; "you would not be the ruin of my establishment, would you, eh? There's a dear, kind soul. You see what a pass these gentlemen have brought me to; just go up to your room for this evening."

"Not a bit of it!" cried the boarders. "She must go, and go this minute!"

"But the poor lady has had no dinner," said Poiret, with piteous entreaty.

"She can go and dine where she likes!" shouted several voices.

"Turn her out, the spy!"

"Turn them both out! Spies!"

"Gentlemen," cried Poiret, his heart swelling with the courage that love gives to an old ram, "respect the weaker sex!"

"Spies are of no sex!" said the painter.

"A precious sexorama!"

"Turn her into the streetorama!"

"Gentlemen, this is indecent! If you turn people out of the house, it ought not to be done so unceremoniously and with no notice at all. We have paid our money, and we are not going," said Poiret, putting on his cap, and taking a chair beside Mlle Michonneau, with whom Mme Vauquer was remonstrating.

"Naughty boy!" said the painter, with a comical look; "run away, naughty little boy!"

"Look here," said Bianchon; "if you do not go, all the rest of us will," and the boarders, to a man, made for the sitting room door.

"Oh, mademoiselle, what is to be done?" cried Mme Vauquer. "I am a ruined woman. You can't stay here; they will go further, do something violent."

Mlle Michonneau rose to her feet.

"She is going!—She is not going!—She is going!—No, she isn't."

These alternate exclamations, and a suggestion of hostile intent, borne out by the behavior of the insurgents, compelled Mlle Michonneau to take her departure. She made some stipulations, speaking in a low voice in her hostess' ear, and then—"I shall go to Madame Buneaud's," she said, with a threatening look.

"Go where you please, mademoiselle," said Mme Vauquer, who regarded this choice of an opposition establishment as an atrocious insult. "Go and lodge with the Buneaud; the wine would give a cat the colic, and the food is cheap and nasty."

The boarders stood aside in two rows to let her pass; not a word was spoken. Poiret looked so wistfully after Mlle Michonneau, and so artlessly revealed that he was in two minds whether to go or stay, that the boarders, in their joy at being quit of Mlle Michonneau, burst out laughing at the sight of him.

"Hist!—st!—st! Poiret," shouted the painter. "Hallo! I say, Poiret, hallo!" The employee from the Museum began to sing a well-known ballad:

> "Partant pour la Syrie,
> Le jeune et beau Dunois . . ."

"Get along with you; you must be dying to follow—*trahit sua quemque voluptas!*" cried Bianchon.

"Everyone to his taste—free rendering from Vergil," said the tutor.

Mlle Michonneau made a movement as if to take Poiret's arm, with an appealing glance that he could not resist. The two went out together, the old maid leaning upon him, and there was a burst of applause, followed by peals of laughter.

"Bravo, Poiret!"

"Who would have thought it of old Poiret!"

"Apollo Poiret!"

"Mars Poiret!"

"Intrepid Poiret!"

A messenger came in at that moment with a letter for Mme Vauquer, who read it through, and collapsed in her chair.

"The house might as well be burned down at once," cried she, "if there are to be any more of these thunderbolts! Young Taillefer died at three o'clock this afternoon. It serves me right for wishing well to those ladies at that poor young man's expense. Mme Couture and Victorine want me to send their things, because they are going to live with her father. Monsieur Taillefer allows his daughter to keep old Madame Couture with her as lady companion. Four rooms to let! And five lodgers gone!"

She sat up, and seemed about to burst into tears. "Bad luck has come to lodge here, I think," she cried.

Once more there came a sound of wheels from the street outside.

"What! Another windfall for somebody!" was Sylvie's comment.

But it was Goriot who came in, looking so radiant, so flushed with happiness, that he seemed to have grown young again.

"Goriot in a cab!" cried the boarders. "The world is coming to an end."

The good soul made straight for Eugène, who was standing rapt in thought in a corner, and laid a hand on the young man's arm.

"Come," he said, in a happy tone.

"Then you haven't heard the news?" said Eugène. "Vautrin was an escaped convict; they have just arrested him. And young Taillefer is dead."

"Very well, but what business is it of ours?" replied old Goriot. "I am going to dine with my daughter *in your house*, do you understand? She is expecting you. Come!"

He took Rastignac by the arm, and carried him off as if he were a lover.

"Now, let us have dinner," cried the painter, and everyone drew his chair to the table.

"Well, I never!" said the portly Sylvie. "Nothing goes right today! The haricot mutton is stuck to the pan! Bah! you will have to eat it, burnt as it is, more's the pity!"

Mme Vauquer was so dispirited that she could not say a word as she looked round the table and saw only ten people where eighteen should be; but everyone tried to comfort and cheer her. At first the dinner contingent, as was natural, talked about Vautrin and the day's events; but the conversation wound round to such topics of interest as duels, jails, justice, prison life, and changes that ought to be made in the laws. They soon wandered miles away from Jacques Collin and Victorine and her brother. There might be only ten of them, but they made noise enough for twenty; indeed, there seemed to be more of them than usual; that was the only difference between yesterday and today. Indifference to the fate of others is a matter of course in this selfish world, which, the day after a tragedy, seeks among the events of Paris for a fresh sensation for its daily renewed appetite, and this indifference soon gained the upper hand. Mme Vauquer herself grew calmer under the soothing influence of hope, and the mouthpiece of hope was the portly Sylvie.

Chapter 15

THAT DAY had gone by like a dream for Eugène, and the sense of unreality lasted into the evening; so that, in spite of his strength of character and clear-headedness, his ideas were chaotic as he sat beside Goriot in the cab. The old man's voice was full of unwonted happiness, but Eugène had been shaken by so many emotions that the words sounded in his ears like words spoken in a dream.

"It was finished this morning! All three of us are going to dine there together, together! Do you understand? I have not dined with my Delphine, my little Delphine, these four years, and I shall have her for a whole evening! We have been at your lodging the whole time since morning. I have been working like a porter in my shirt-sleeves, helping to carry in the furniture. Aha! you don't know what pretty ways she has; at table she will look after me, 'Here, papa, just try this, it is nice.' And I shall not be able to eat. Oh, it is a long while since I have been with her in quiet everyday life as we shall have her."

"It really seems as if the world had been turned upside down."

"Upside down?" repeated old Goriot. "Why, the world has never been so right-side up. I see none but smiling faces in the streets, people who shake hands cordially and embrace each other, people who all look as happy as if they were going to dine with their daughter, and gobble down a nice little dinner that she went with me to order of the chef at the Café des Anglais. But, pshaw! with her beside you gall and wormwood would taste as sweet as honey."

"I feel as if I were coming back to life again," said Eugène.

"Hurry up there!" cried old Goriot, letting down the window in front. "Get on faster; I will give you five francs if you get to the place I told you of in ten minutes."

With this prospect before him the cabman dashed across Paris with lightning speed.

"How that fellow crawls!" said old Goriot.

"But where are you taking me?" Eugène asked him.

"To your own apartment," said Goriot.

The cab stopped in the Rue d'Artois. Old Goriot stepped out first and flung ten francs to the man with the recklessness of a widower returning to bachelor ways.

"Come along upstairs," he said to Rastignac. They crossed a courtyard, and climbed up to the third floor of a new and handsome house. There was no need to ring; the door was opened by

Thérèse, Mme de Nucingen's maid. Eugène found himself in a charming bachelor establishment; an ante-room, a little drawing-room, a bedroom, and a study, looking out upon a garden. The furniture and the decoration of the little drawing-room were of the most daintily charming description, the room was full of soft light, and Delphine rose from a low chair by the fire and stood before him. She set her fire-screen down on the chimney-piece, and spoke with tenderness.

"So we had to go in search of you, sir, you who are so slow to understand!"

Thérèse left the room. The student took Delphine in his arms and held her in a tight clasp, his eyes filled with tears of joy. This last contrast between his present surroundings and the scenes he had just witnessed was too much for Rastignac's overwrought nerves, after the day's strain and excitement that had wearied heart and brain; he was almost overcome by it.

"I felt sure myself that he loved you," murmured old Goriot, while Eugène lay back bewildered on the sofa, utterly unable to speak a word or to reason out how and why the magic wand had been waved to bring about this final transformation scene.

"But you must see your rooms," said Mme de Nucingen. She took his hand and led him into a room carpeted and furnished like her own. Indeed, down to the smallest details, it was a reproduction in miniature of Delphine's apartment.

"There is no bed," said Rastignac.

"No, monsieur," she answered, reddening, and pressing his hand. Eugène, looking at her, understood, young though he yet was, how deeply modesty is implanted in the heart of a woman who loves.

"You are one of those beings whom we cannot choose but to adore forever," he said in her ear. "Yes, the deeper and truer love is, the more mysterious and closely veiled it should be; I can dare to say so, since we understand each other so well. No one shall learn our secret."

"Oh! so I am nobody, I suppose," growled the father.

"You know quite well that 'we' means you."

"Ah, that is what I wanted. You will not mind me, will you? I shall go and come like a good fairy who makes himself felt everywhere without being seen, shall I not? Eh, Delphinette, Ninette, Dedel—was I not right to tell you, 'There are some nice rooms to let in the Rue d'Artois; let us furnish them for him'? And she would not hear of it! I am the author of your happiness and of your existence. Fathers must always be giving if they would be happy themselves; always giving—they would not be fathers otherwise."

"Was that how it happened?" asked Eugène.

"Yes. She would not listen to me. She was afraid that people would talk, as if what they say about you were to be compared with happiness! Why, all women dream of doing what she has done——"

Father Goriot found himself without an audience, for Mme de Nucingen had led Rastignac into the study; he heard a kiss given and taken, low though the sound was. This room was furnished as elegantly as the others, complete to the last detail.

"Have we guessed your wishes rightly?" she asked, as they returned to the drawing-room for dinner.

"Yes," he said, "only too well, alas! For all this luxury so well carried out, this realization of pleasant dreams, the elegance that satisfies all the romantic fancies of youth, appeals to me so strongly that I cannot but feel that it is my rightful possession, but I cannot accept it from you, and I am too poor as yet to——"

"Ah! You dare to resist me already!" she said with arch imperiousness, and a charming little pout, a woman's way of laughing away scruples.

But Eugène had submitted so lately to that solemn self-questioning, and Vautrin's arrest had so plainly shown him the depths of the pit that lay at his feet, that the instincts of generosity and honor had been strengthened in him, and he could not allow himself to be coaxed into abandoning his high-minded determination. A profound sadness came over him.

"Do you really mean to refuse?" said Mme de Nucingen. "And do you know what such a refusal means? That you are not sure of yourself, that you do not dare to bind yourself to me. Are you really afraid of betraying my affection? If you love me, if I—love you, why should you shrink back from such a slight obligation? If you but knew what a pleasure it has been to see after all the arrangements of these rooms, you would not hesitate, you would ask me to forgive you for your hesitation. I had some money that belonged to you, and I have made good use of it, that is all. You think you are grown-up, and you are not. You are asking me for far more than this . . . "Ah!" she cried, as Eugène's passionate glance was turned on her, "and you are making difficulties about the merest trifles. Oh, if you feel no love whatever for me, refuse, by all means. My fate hangs on a word from you. Speak!—Father," she said after a pause, "make him listen to reason. Can he imagine that I am less fastidious than he is on the point of honor?"

Old Goriot was looking on and listening to this pretty quarrel with a placid smile, as if he had found some balm for all the sorrows of life.

"Child that you are!" she cried again, catching Eugène's hand. "You are just beginning life; you find barriers at the outset that many a man finds insurmountable; a woman's hand opens the way, and you shrink back! Why, you are sure to succeed! You will have a brilliant future. Success is written on that broad forehead of yours. Can you not then repay me my loan of today? Did not a lady in olden times arm her knight with sword and helmet and coat of mail, and find him a charger, so that he might fight for her in the tournament? Well, then, Eugène, these things that I offer you are the weapons of this age. Anyone who means to be something must have such tools as these. A pretty place your garret must be if it is like papa's room! See, dinner is waiting all this time. Do you want to make me unhappy?—Why don't you answer?" she said, shaking his hand. "*Mon Dieu!* papa, make up his mind for him, or I'll go away and never see him any more."

"I can settle it," said Goriot, coming down from the clouds. "Now, my dear Monsieur Eugène, you were going to borrow money of the Jews, weren't you?"

"I'll have to do it," said Eugène.

"All right, I will give you credit," said the other, drawing out a cheap leather pocketbook, much the worse for wear. "I'll be a Jew myself; I paid for everything; here are the invoices. You do not owe a penny for anything here. It did not come to very much—five thousand francs at most, and I am going to lend you the money myself. I am not a woman—you cannot refuse me. You shall give me a receipt on a scrap of paper, and you can return it some time or other."

Delphine and Eugène looked at each other in amazement, tears sprang to their eyes. Rastignac held out his hand and grasped Goriot's warmly.

"Well, what of it? Are you not my children?"

"Oh, my poor father," said Mme de Nucingen, "how did you do it?"

"Ah! now you ask me. When I made up my mind to move him nearer to you, and saw you buying things as if they were wedding presents, I said to myself, 'She will never be able to pay for them.' The attorney says that those law proceedings will last six months before your husband can be made to disgorge your fortune. Well and good. I sold out my property in the funds that brought in thirteen hundred and fifty livres a year, and bought a safe annuity of twelve hundred francs a year for fifteen thousand francs. Then I paid your tradesmen out of the rest of the capital. As for me, children, I have a room upstairs for which I pay fifty crowns a year; I can live like a prince on two francs a day, and still have something left over. I shall not have to spend anything much on clothes, for I never wear anything out. This fortnight past I have been laughing in my sleeve, thinking to myself, 'How happy they are going to be!' and—well, now, are you not happy?"

"Oh, papa, papa!" cried Mme de Nucingen, springing to her father, who took her on his knee. She covered him with kisses, her fair hair brushed his cheek, her tears fell on the withered face that had grown so bright and radiant. "Dear father, what a father you are! No, there is not another father like you under the sun. If Eugène loved you before, what must he feel for you now?"

"Why, children! Why, Delphinette!" cried Goriot, who had not felt his daughter's heart beat against his breast for ten years, "do you want me to die of joy? My poor heart will break! Come, Monsieur Eugène, we are quits already." And the old man strained her to his breast with such fierce and passionate force that she cried out.

"Oh, you are hurting me!" she said.

"I am hurting you!" He grew pale at the words. The pain expressed in his face seemed greater than it is given to humanity to know. The agony of this Christ of paternity can only be compared with the masterpieces of those princes of the palette who have left for us the record of their visions of an agony suffered for a whole world by the Saviour of men. Old Goriot pressed his lips very gently against the waist that his fingers had grasped too roughly.

"Oh, no, no!" he cried. "I have not hurt you, have I?" and his smile seemed to repeat the question. "*You* have hurt me with that cry just now. The things cost rather more than that," he said in her ear, with another gentle kiss, "but I had to deceive him about it, or he would have been angry."

Eugène sat dumb with amazement in the presence of this inexhaustible love; he gazed at Goriot, and his face betrayed the artless admiration which shapes the beliefs of youth.

"I will be worthy of all this," he cried.

"Oh! my Eugène, that is nobly said," and Mme de Nucingen kissed the law student on the forehead.

"He gave up Mlle Taillefer and her millions for you," said old Goriot. "Yes, the little thing was in love with you, and now that her brother is dead she is as rich as Croesus."

"Oh! why did you tell her?" cried Rastignac.

"Eugène," Delphine said in his ear, "I have one regret now to mar this evening. Ah, how I will love you! and forever!"

"This is the happiest day I have had since you girls were married!" cried Goriot. "God may send me any suffering, so long as I do not suffer through you, and I can still say, 'In this short month of February I had more happiness than other men have in their whole lives.'—Look at me, Fifine!" he said to his daughter. "She is very beautiful, is she not? Tell me, now, have you seen many women with that pretty soft color—that little dimple of hers? No, I thought not. Well, but for me this lovely woman would never have been. And very soon happiness will make her a thousand times lovelier, happiness through you. I could give up my place in heaven to you, neighbor, if needs be, and go down to hell instead. Come, let us have dinner," he added, scarcely knowing what he said, "everything is ours."

"Poor dear father!"

He rose and went over to her, and took her face in his hands, and set a kiss on the plaits of hair. "If you only knew, little one, how happy you can make me—how little it takes to make me happy! Will you come and see me sometimes? I shall be just above, so it is only a step. Promise me, say that you will!"

"Yes, dear father."

"Say it again."

"Yes, I will, my kind father."

"Hush, hush! I should make you say it a hundred times over if I followed my own wishes. Let us have dinner."

They behaved like children that evening, old Goriot as childish as the others. He sat at his daughter's feet, gazed into her eyes, laid his head against her dress. No young lover could have been more extravagant or more tender.

"You see!" Delphine said with a look at Eugène, "so long as my father is with us, he monopolizes me. He will be rather in the way sometimes."

Eugène had himself already felt certain twinges of jealousy, and could not censure this speech, although it contained the germ of all ingratitude.

"And when will the rooms be ready?" asked Eugène, looking round. "We must all leave them this evening, I suppose."

"Yes, but tomorrow you must come and dine with me," she answered, with an eloquent glance. "It is our night at the Italiens."

"I shall go to the pit," said her father.

It was midnight. Mme de Nucingen's carriage was waiting for her, and old Goriot and the student walked back to the Maison Vauquer, talking of Delphine, and warming over their talk till there grew up a curious rivalry between the two violent passions. Eugène could not help seeing that the father's selfless love was deeper and more steadfast than his own. For this worshiper Delphine was always pure and fair, and her father's adoration drew its fervor from the past as well as the future.

They found Mme Vauquer by the stove, with Sylvie and Christophe keeping her company. The old landlady, sitting like Marius among the ruins of Carthage, was waiting for the two lodgers that yet remained to her, and bemoaning her lot with the sympathetic Sylvie. Tasso's lamentations as recorded in Byron's poem are undoubtedly eloquent, but for sheer force of truth they fall far short of Mme Vauquer's cry from the depths.

"Only three cups of coffee in the morning, Sylvie! Oh dear! To have your house emptied in this way is enough to break your heart. What is life, now my lodgers are gone? Nothing at all. Just think of it! It is just as if all the furniture had been taken out of the house, and your furniture is your life. How have I offended Heaven to draw down all this trouble upon me? And haricot beans and potatoes laid in for twenty people! The police in my house, too! We shall have to live on potatoes now, and Christophe will have to go!"

The Savoyard, who was fast asleep, suddenly woke up at this, and said, "Madame?" questioningly.

"Poor fellow," said Sylvie, "he is like a dog."

"In the dull season, too! Nobody is moving now. I would like to know where the lodgers are to drop down from. It drives me distracted. And that old witch of a Michonneau goes and takes Poiret with her! What can she have done to him to make him so fond of her? He runs about after her like a puppy."

"Lord!" said Sylvie, flinging up her head, "those old maids are up to all sorts of tricks."

"There's that poor Monsieur Vautrin that they made out to be a convict," the widow went on. "Well, you know that is too much for me, Sylvie; I can't bring myself to believe it. Such a lively man as he was, and paid fifteen francs a month for his coffee of an evening, paid you every penny on the nail, too."

"And open-handed he was!" said Christophe.

"There is some mistake," said Sylvie.

"Why, no there isn't! He admitted it himself!" said Mme Vauquer. "And to think that all these things have happened in my house, and in a quarter where you never see a cat go by. On my word as an honest woman, it's like a dream. For, look here, we saw Louis XVI meet with his mishap; we saw the fall of the Emperor; and we saw him come back and fall again; there was nothing out of the way in all that, but lodginghouses are not liable to revolutions. You can do without a king, but you must eat all the same; and so long as a decent woman, a de Conflans born and bred, will give you all sorts of good things for dinner, nothing short of the end of the world ought to—but there, it is the end of the world, that is just what it is!"

"And to think that Mademoiselle Michonneau who made all this mischief is to have a thousand crowns a year for it, so I hear," cried Sylvie.

"Don't speak of her, she is a wicked woman!" said Mme Vauquer. "She is going to the Buneaud, who charges less than cost. But the Buneaud is capable of anything; she must have done frightful things, robbed and murdered people in her time. *She ought to be put in jail for life instead of that poor dear——*"

Eugène and Goriot rang the doorbell at that moment.

"Ah, here are my two faithful lodgers," said the widow, sighing.

But the two faithful lodgers, who retained but shadowy recollections of the misfortunes of their lodginghouse, announced to their hostess without more ado that they were about to remove to the Chaussée d'Antin.

"Sylvie," cried the widow, "this is the last straw! Gentlemen, this will be the death of me! It has quite upset me! There's a weight on my chest! I am ten years older for this day! Upon my word, I shall go out of my senses! And what is to be done with the haricots? Oh, well, if I am to be left here all by myself, you shall go tomorrow, Christophe.—Good night, gentlemen," and she went.

"What is the matter now?" Eugène inquired of Sylvie.

"Lord! Everybody is leaving because of that business this morning, and it has addled her wits. There! She is crying upstairs. It will do her good to snivel a bit. It's the first time she has cried since I've been with her."

By morning Mme Vauquer, to use her own expression, had "made up her mind to it." True, she still wore a doleful countenance, as might be expected of a woman who had lost all her lodgers, and whose manner of life had been suddenly revolutionized, but she had all her wits about her. Her grief was genuine and profound; it was real pain of mind, for her purse had suffered, the routine of her existence had been broken. A lover's farewell glance at his lady-love's window is not more mournful than Mme Vauquer's survey of the empty places round her table. Eugène administered comfort, telling the widow that Bianchon, whose term of residence at the hospital was about to expire, would doubtless take his (Rastignac's) place; that the official from the Museum had often expressed a desire to have Mme Couture's rooms; and that in a very few days her household would be on the old footing.

"God send it may, my dear sir! But bad luck has come to lodge here. There'll be a death in the house before ten days are out, you'll see," and she gave a lugubrious look round the dining room. "Whose turn will it be, I wonder?"

"It is just as well that we are moving out," said Eugène to old Goriot in a low voice.

"Madame," said Sylvie, running in with a scared face, "I have not seen Mistigris these three days."

"Ah, well, if my cat is dead, if *he* has gone and left us, I——"

The poor woman could not finish her sentence; she clasped her hands and hid her face on the back of her armchair, quite overcome by this dreadful portent.

At twelve o'clock, when the postman reaches that quarter, Eugène received a letter. The dainty envelope bore the Beauséant arms on the seal, and contained an invitation addressed to M. and Mme de Nucingen for the great ball, which had been talked of in Paris for a month. A little note for Eugène was slipped in with the card.

I think, monsieur, that you will undertake with pleasure to interpret my sentiments to Mme de Nucingen, so I am sending the card for which you asked me to you. I shall be delighted to make the acquaintance of Mme de Restaud's sister. Pray introduce that charming lady to me, and do not let her monopolize all your affection, for you owe me not a little in return for mine.

VICOMTESSE DE BEAUSÉANT.

"Well," said Eugène to himself, as he read the note a second time, "Madame de Beauséant says pretty plainly that she does not want the Baron de Nucingen."

He went to Delphine at once. He had procured this pleasure for her, and doubtless he would receive payment for it. Mme de Nucingen was dressing. Rastignac waited in her boudoir, enduring as best he might the natural impatience of an eager temperament for the reward desired and withheld for so long. Such sensations are only known once in a life. The first woman to whom a man is drawn, if she is really a woman—that is to say, if she appears to him amid the splendid accessories that form a necessary background in the world of Paris—will never have a rival.

Love in Paris is a thing apart; for in Paris neither men nor women are the dupes of the common-places by which people seek to throw a veil over their motives, or to parade a fine affectation of disinterestedness in their sentiments. In this country within a country, it is not merely required of a woman that she should satisfy the senses and the soul; she knows perfectly well that she has still greater obligations to discharge, that she must fulfill the countless demands of a vanity that enters into every fiber of that living organism called society. Love, for her, is above all things, and by its very nature, a vainglorious, brazen-fronted, ostentatious, thriftless charlatan. If at the Court of Louis XIV there was not a woman but envied Mlle de la Vallière the reckless devotion that led the grand monarch to tear the priceless ruffles at his wrists in order to assist the entry of a Duc de Vermandois into the world—what can you expect of the rest of society? You must have youth and wealth and rank; nay, you must, if possible, have more than these, for the more incense you bring with you to burn at the shrine of the god, the more favorably will he regard the worshiper. Love is a religion, and his cult must in the nature of things be more costly than those of all other deities; Love stays for a moment and then passes on; like the urchin of the streets, his course may be traced by the damage he has done. The wealth of feeling and imagination is the poetry of the garret; without it, how could love exist there?

If there are exceptions to these Draconian laws of the Parisian code, they are solitary examples. Such souls live so far out of the main current that they are not borne away by the doctrines of society. They dwell beside some clear spring of everflowing water, without seeking to leave the green shade, happy to listen to the echoes of the infinite in everything around them and in their own souls, waiting in patience to take their flight for heaven, while they look with pity upon those of earth.

Rastignac, like most young men who have been early impressed by power and grandeur, meant to enter the contest fully armed; the burning ambition of conquest possessed him already; perhaps he was conscious of his powers, but as yet he knew neither the end to which his ambition was to be directed, nor the means of attaining it. In default of the pure and sacred love that fills a life, ambition may become something very noble, subduing to itself every thought of personal interest, and setting as the end—the greatness, not of one man, but of a whole nation.

But the student had not yet reached the time of life when a man surveys the whole course of life and judges it soberly. Hitherto he had scarcely so much as shaken off the spell of the fresh and gracious influences that envelop a childhood in the country as with leafy foliage. He had hesitated on the brink of the Parisian Rubicon, and in spite of the prickings of ambition, he still clung to an old ideal—the peaceful life of the noble in his château. But yesterday evening, at the sight of his rooms, those scruples had vanished. He had learned what it was to enjoy the material advantages of fortune, as he had already enjoyed the social advantages of birth; he ceased to be a provincial from that moment, and slipped naturally and easily into a position which opened up a prospect of a brilliant future.

So, as he waited for Delphine in the pretty boudoir, where he felt that he had a certain right to be, he felt so far away from the Rastignac who came back to Paris a year ago, that he asked himself whether that past self bore any resemblance to the Rastignac of that moment.

"Madame is in her room," Thérèse came to tell him. The woman's voice made him start.

He found Delphine lying back in her low chair by the fireside, looking fresh and bright. The sight of her among the flowing draperies of filmy muslin suggested some beautiful tropical flower, where the fruit is set amid the blossom.

"Well," she said, with a tremor in her voice, "here you are."

"Guess what I have brought you," said Eugène, sitting down beside her. He took possession of her arm to kiss her hand.

Mme de Nucingen gave a joyful start as she saw the card. She turned to Eugène; there were tears in her eyes as she flung her arms about his neck, and drew him towards her in a frenzy of gratified vanity.

"And I owe this happiness to you—to *thee*" (she whispered the more intimate word in his ear); "but Thérèse is in my dressing-room, let us be prudent. This happiness—yes, for I may call it so, when it comes to me through *you*—is surely more than a triumph of vanity? No one has been willing to introduce me into that set. Perhaps just now I may seem to you to be frivolous, petty, shallow, like a Parisienne, but remember, my friend, that I am ready to give up all for you; and that if I long more than ever for an entrance into the Faubourg Saint-Germain, it is because that society is yours."

"Madame de Beauséant's note seems to say very plainly that she does not expect to see the *Baron* de Nucingen at her ball; don't you think so?" said Eugène.

"Why, yes," said the baroness as she returned the letter. "Those women have a talent for insolence. But it doesn't matter. I shall go. My sister is sure to be there, and sure to be very beautifully dressed. Eugène," she went on, lowering her voice, "she will go to dispel ugly suspicions. You do not know the things that people are saying about her! Only this morning Nucingen came to tell me that they had been discussing her at the club. Great heavens! on what does a woman's character and the honor of a whole family depend! I feel that I am involved in these attacks on my poor sister. According to some people, Monsieur de Trailles must have put his name to bills for a hundred thousand francs, nearly all of them are overdue, and proceedings are threatened. In this predicament, it seems that my sister sold her diamonds to a Jew—the beautiful diamonds that belonged to her husband's mother, Madame de Restaud the elder—you have seen her wearing them. In fact, nothing else has been talked about for the last two days. So I can see that Anastasie is sure to come to Madame de Beauséant's ball in tissue of gold, and ablaze with diamonds, to draw all eyes upon her; and I will not be outshone. She has tried to eclipse me all her life; she has never been kind to me, and I have helped her so often, and always had money for her when she had none. But never mind other people now. Today I mean to be perfectly happy."

At one o'clock that morning Eugène was still with Mme de Nucingen. In the midst of their lover's farewell, a farewell full of hope of joys to come, she said in a troubled voice, "I am very fearful, superstitious. Give what name you like to my presentiments, but I am afraid that my happiness will be paid for by some horrible catastrophe."

"Child!" said Eugène.

"Ah, have we changed places, and am I the child tonight?" she asked laughingly.

Eugène went back to the Maison Vauquer, never doubting but that he should leave it for good on the morrow; and on the way he fell to dreaming the bright dreams of youth, when the taste of happiness is still sweet on the lips.

"Well?" cried Goriot, as Rastignac passed his door.

"Yes," said Eugène, "I will tell you everything tomorrow."

"Everything, will you not?" cried the old man. "Go to bed. Tomorrow our happy life will begin."

Chapter 16

NEXT DAY, Goriot and Rastignac were ready to leave the lodginghouse, and only awaited the good pleasure of a porter to move out of it; but towards noon there was a sound of wheels in the Rue Neuve-Sainte-Geneviève, and a carriage stopped before the door of the Maison Vauquer. Mme de Nucingen alighted, and asked if her father was still in the house, and, receiving an affirmative reply from Sylvie, ran lightly upstairs.

It so happened that Eugène was at home all unknown to his neighbor. At breakfast time he had asked Goriot to superintend the removal of his goods, saying that he would meet him in the Rue d'Artois at four o'clock; but Rastignac's name had been called early on the list at the law school, and he had gone back at once to the Rue Neuve-Sainte-Geneviève. No one had seen him come in, for Goriot had gone to find a porter, and the mistress of the house was likewise out. Eugène had thought to pay her himself, not wishing to leave the bill with Goriot, who in his zeal would probably pay for him. As it was, Eugène went up to his room to see that nothing had been forgotten, and blessed his foresight when he saw the blank bill bearing Vautrin's signature lying in the drawer where he had carelessly thrown it on the day when he had repaid the amount. There was no fire in the grate, so he was about to tear it into little pieces, when he heard a voice in Goriot's room, which he recognized as that of Delphine. He made no more noise, and stood still to listen, thinking that she should have no secrets from him;

but after the first few words, the conversation between the father and daughter was so strange and interesting that it absorbed all his attention.

"Ah! thank heaven that you thought of asking him to give an account of the money settled on me before I was utterly ruined, father. Is it safe to talk?" she added.

"Yes, there is no one in the house," said her father in a strange tone.

"What is the matter with you?" asked Mme de Nucingen.

"God forgive you! You have just dealt me a staggering blow, child!" said the old man. "You cannot know how much I love you, or you would not have burst in upon me like this, with such news, especially if all is not lost. Has something so important happened that you must come here about it? In a few minutes we should have been in the Rue d'Artois."

"Does one think what one is doing after a catastrophe? It has turned my head. Your lawyer has found out the state of things now, but it was bound to come out sooner or later. We shall need your long business experience; and I came to you like a drowning man who catches at a branch. When Derville found that Nucingen was throwing all sorts of difficulties in his way, he threatened him with proceedings, and told him plainly that he would soon obtain an order from the President of the Tribunal. So Nucingen came to my room this morning, and asked if I meant to ruin us both. I told him that I knew nothing whatever about it, that I had a fortune, and ought to be put into possession of my fortune, and that my lawyer was acting for me in the matter. I said again that I knew absolutely nothing about it, and could not possibly go into the subject with him. Wasn't that what you told me to tell him?"

"Yes, quite right," answered Goriot.

"Well, then," Delphine continued, "he told me all about his affairs. He had just invested all his capital and mine in business speculations; they have only just been started, and very large sums of money are locked up. If I were to compel him to refund my dowry now, he would be forced to file his petition; but if I will wait a year, he undertakes, on his honor, to double or treble my fortune, by investing it in building land, and I shall be mistress at last of the whole of my property. He was speaking the truth, father dear; he frightened me! He asked my pardon for his conduct and he has given me my liberty. I am free to act as I please on condition that I leave him to carry on business in my name. To prove his sincerity, he promised that Derville might inspect the accounts as often as I pleased, so that I might be assured that everything was being conducted properly. In short, he put himself into my power, bound hand and foot. He wishes the present arrangements as to the expenses of house-keeping to continue for two more years, and entreated me not to exceed my allowance. He showed me plainly that it was all that he could do to keep up appearances; he has broken with his opera-dancer; he will be compelled to practice the most rigid though secret economy if he is to bide his time with un-shaken credit. I scolded, I did all I could to drive him to despera-tion, so as to find out more. He showed me his ledgers—he broke down and cried at last. I never saw a man in such a state. He lost his head completely, talked of killing himself, and raved till I felt quite sorry for him."

"Do you really believe that silly rubbish?" cried her father. "It was all got up for your benefit! I have had business dealings with Germans; honest and straightforward they are pretty sure to be, but when with their simplicity and frankness they are sharpers and humbugs as well, they are the worst rogues of all. Your husband is taking advantage of you. As soon as pressure is brought to bear on him he shams dead; he means to be more the master under your name than in his own. He will take advantage of the position to secure himself against the risks of business. He is as sharp as he is treacherous; he is a bad lot! No, no; I am not going to leave my girls behind me without a penny when I go to

Père-Lachaise. I know something about business still. He has sunk his money in speculation, he says; very well then, there is something to show for it—bills, receipts, papers of some sort. Let him produce them, and come to an arrangement with you. We will choose the most promising of his speculations, take them over at our own risk, and have the securities transferred into your name; they shall represent the separate estate of Delphine Goriot, wife of the Baron de Nucingen. Does that fellow really take us for idiots? Does he imagine that I could stand the idea of your being without fortune, without bread, for forty-eight hours? I would not stand it a day—no, not a night, not a couple of hours! If there had been any foundation for the idea, I should never get over it. What! I have worked hard for forty years, carried sacks on my back, and sweated and pinched and saved all my life for you, my darlings, for you who made the toil and every burden borne for you seem light, and now, my fortune, my whole life, is to vanish in smoke! I should die raving mad if I believed a word of it. By all that's holiest in heaven and earth, we will have this cleared up at once; go through the books, have the whole business looked thoroughly into! I will not sleep, nor rest, nor eat until I have satisfied myself that your fortune is intact. Your money is settled upon you, God be thanked! and, luckily, your lawyer, Maître Derville, is an honest man. Good Lord! You shall have your snug little million, your fifty thousand francs a year, as long as you live, or I will raise a racket in Paris! If the Tribunals put upon us, I will appeal to the Chambers. If I knew that you were well and comfortably off as far as money is concerned, that thought would keep me easy in spite of bad health and troubles. Money? Why, it is life! Money does everything. That great dolt of an Alsatian shall sing another tune! Look here, Delphine, don't give way, don't make a concession of half a quarter of a farthing to that fathead, who has ground you down and made you miserable. If he can't do without you, we will give him a good cudgeling, and keep him in order. Great heavens! My brain is on fire; it is as if there were something red-hot inside my head. My Delphine lying on straw! You, my Fifine! Good gracious! Where are my gloves? Come, let us go at once; I mean to see everything with my own eyes— books, cash and correspondence—the whole business. I shall have no peace until I know for certain that your fortune is secure "

"Oh, dear father, be careful how you set about it! If there is the least hint of vengeance in the business, if you show yourself openly hostile, it will be all over with me. He knows whom he has to deal with; he thinks it quite natural that if you put the idea into my head, I should be uneasy about my money; but I swear to you that he has it in his own hands, and that he had meant to keep it. He is just the man to abscond with all the money and leave us, the scoundrel! He knows quite well that I will not dishonor the name I bear by bringing him into a court of law. His position is strong and weak at the same time. If we drive him to despair, I am lost."

"Why, then, the man is a rogue?"

"Yes, father," she said, flinging herself into a chair. "I wanted to keep it from you to spare your feelings," and she burst into tears. "I did not want you to know that you had married me to such a man. He is just the same in private life—body and soul and conscience—the same through and through—hideous! I hate him, I despise him! Yes, after all that that despicable Nucingen has told me, I cannot respect him any longer. A man capable of mixing himself up in such affairs, and of talking about them to me as he did, without the slightest scruple—it is because I have read him through and through that I am afraid of him. He, my husband, frankly proposed to give me my liberty, and do you know what that means? It means that if things turn out badly for him, I am to play into his hands, and be his stalking-horse."

"But there is law to be had! There is a Place de Grève for men like that," cried her father; "why, I would guillotine him myself if there was no headsman to do it."

"No, father, the law cannot touch him. Listen, this is what he says, stripped of all his circumlocutions: 'Take your choice, you and no one else can be my accomplice; either everything is lost, you are ruined and have not a farthing, or you will let me carry this business through myself.' Is that plain speaking? He *must* have my assistance. He is assured that his wife will deal fairly by him; he knows that I shall leave his money to him and be content with my own. It is an unholy and dishonest compact, and he holds out threats of ruin to compel me to consent to it. He is buying my conscience, and the price is liberty to be Eugène's wife in all but name. 'I connive at your errors, and you allow me to commit crimes and ruin poor families!' Is that clear? Do you know what he means by speculations? He buys up land in his own name, then he finds men of straw to run up houses upon it. These men make a bargain with a contractor to build the houses, paying them by bills at long dates; then in consideration of a small sum they leave my husband in possession of the houses, and finally slip through the fingers of the deluded contractors by going into bankruptcy. The name of the firm of Nucingen has been used to dazzle the poor contractors. I saw that. I noticed, too, that Nucingen had sent bills for large amounts to Amsterdam, London, Naples, and Vienna, in order to prove if necessary that large sums had been paid away by the firm. How could we get possession of those bills?"

Eugène heard a dull thud on the tiled floor; old Goriot must have fallen on his knees.

"Great heavens! What have I done to you? Bound my daughter to this scoundrel who does as he likes with her! Oh! my child, my child! forgive me!" cried the old man.

"Yes, I am in the depths of despair, and perhaps you are to blame," said Delphine. "We have so little sense when we marry! What do we know of the world, of business, of men, or life? Our fathers should think for us! Dear father, I am not reproaching you in the least; forgive me for what I said. This is all my own fault. Don't cry, papa," she said, kissing him.

"Don't you cry either, my little Delphine. Look up and let me kiss away the tears. There! I shall find my wits and unravel this tangle your husband has made of your affairs."

"No, let me manage him. He is fond of me, well and good; I shall use my influence to make him invest my money as soon as possible in landed property in my own name. Very likely I could get him to buy back Nucingen in Alsace in my name; that has always been a pet idea of his. Still, come tomorrow and go through the books, and look into the business. Monsieur Derville knows little of mercantile matters. No, not tomorrow though. I do not want to be upset. Madame de Beauséant's ball will be the day after tomorrow, and I must keep quiet, so as to look my best and freshest, and do honor to my dear Eugène! Come, let us see his room."

But as she spoke a carriage stopped in the Rue Neuve-Sainte-Geneviève, and the sound of Mme de Restaud's voice came from the staircase. "Is my father in?" she asked of Sylvie.

This accident was luckily timed for Eugène, whose one idea had been to throw himself down on the bed and pretend to be asleep.

"Oh, father, have you heard about Anastasie?" said Delphine, when she heard her sister speak. "It looks as though some strange things had been happening in her household."

"What sort of things?" asked Goriot. "This is going to be the death of me. My poor head will not stand a double misfortune."

"Good morning, father," said the countess from the threshold. "Oh, Delphine, are you here?"

Mme de Restaud seemed taken aback by her sister's presence.

"Good morning, Nasie," said the baroness. "What is there so extraordinary in my being here? *I* see our father every day."

"Since when?"

"If you came yourself you would know."

"Don't tease, Delphine," said the countess fretfully. "I am very miserable, I am lost. Oh, my poor father, it is hopeless this time!"

"What is it, Nasie?" cried Goriot. "Tell us all about it, child! How white she is! Quick, do something, Delphine; be kind to her, and I will love you even better, if that were possible."

"Poor Nasie!" said Mme de Nucingen, drawing her sister to a chair. "We are the only two people in the world whose love is always sufficient to forgive you everything. Family affection is the surest, you see." She gave her sister smelling salts to inhale, and the countess revived.

"This will kill me!" said their father. "There," he went on, stirring the smoldering fire, "come nearer, both of you. It is cold. What is it, Nasie? Be quick and tell me. This is enough to——"

"Well, then, my husband knows everything," said the countess. "Just imagine it. Do you remember, father, that bill of Maxime's some time ago? Well, that was not the first. I had paid ever so many before that. About the beginning of January Monsieur de Trailles seemed very much troubled. He said nothing to me, but it is so easy to read the hearts of those you love, a mere trifle is enough; and then you feel things instinctively. Indeed, he was more tender and affectionate than ever, and I was happier than I had ever been before. Poor Maxime! He was really saying good-bye to me, so he has told me since; he meant to blow his brains out! At last I worried him so, and begged and implored so hard; for two hours I knelt at his knees and prayed and entreated, and at last he told me—that he owed a hundred thousand francs. Oh, papa, a hundred thousand francs! I was beside myself! You had not the money, I knew. I had eaten up all that you had——"

"No," said Goriot; "I could not have got it for you unless I had stolen it. But I would have done that for you, Nasie! I will do it yet."

The words came from him like a sob, a hoarse sound like the death-rattle of a dying man; it seemed indeed like the agony of death when the father's love was powerless. There was a pause, and neither of the sisters spoke. It must have been selfishness indeed that could hear unmoved that cry of anguish that, like a pebble thrown over a precipice, revealed the depths of his despair.

"I found the money, father, by selling what was not mine to sell," and the countess burst into tears.

Delphine was touched; she laid her head on her sister's shoulder, and cried too.

"Then it is all true," she said.

Anastasie bowed her head, Mme de Nucingen flung her arms about her, kissed her tenderly, and held her sister to her heart.

"I shall always love you and never judge you, Nasie," she said.

"My angels!" murmured Goriot faintly. "Oh, why should it be trouble that draws you together?"

This warm and palpitating affection seemed to give the countess courage.

"To save Maxime's life," she said, "to save all my own happiness, I went to the money-lender you know of, that man from hell; nothing can melt him; I took all the family diamonds that Monsieur de Restaud is so proud of—his and mine too—and sold them to that Monsieur Gobseck. *Sold them!* Do you understand? I saved Maxime, but I am lost. Restaud found it all out."

"How? Who told him? I will kill him," cried Goriot.

"Yesterday he sent to tell me to come to his room. I went. 'Anastasie,' he said in a voice—oh! such a voice; that was enough, it told me everything—'where are your diamonds?' 'In my room.' 'No,' he said, looking straight at me, 'there they are on that chest of drawers—' and he lifted his handkerchief and showed me the casket. 'Do you know where they come from?' he said. I fell at his feet. I cried; I asked him what death he wished me to die."

"You said that!" cried Goriot. "By God in heaven, whoever lays a hand on either of you so long as I am alive may reckon on being roasted by slow fires! Yes, I will cut him in pieces like—" Goriot stopped; the words died away in his throat.

"And then, dear, he asked something worse than death of me. Oh! heaven preserve all other women from hearing such words as I heard then!"

"I will murder that man," said Goriot quietly. "But he has only one life, and he deserves to die twice. And then, what next?" he added, looking at Anastasie.

"Then," the countess resumed, "there was a pause, and he looked at me. 'Anastasie,' he said, 'I will bury this in silence; there shall be no separation; there are the children. I will not kill de Trailles. I might miss him if we fought, and as for other ways of getting rid of him, I should come into collision with the law. If I killed him in your arms, it would bring dishonor on *those* children. But if you do not want to see your children perish, nor their father nor me, you must first of all submit to two conditions. Answer me. Have I a child of my own?' I answered, 'Yes.' 'Which?' 'Ernest, our eldest boy.' 'Very well,' he said, 'and now swear to obey me in this particular from this time forward.' I swore. 'You will make over your property to me when I require you to do so.' "

"Do nothing of the kind!" cried Goriot. "Aha! Monsieur de Restaud, you could not make your wife happy; she has looked for happiness and found it elsewhere, and you make her suffer for your own incapacity? He will have to reckon with me. Make yourself easy, Nasie. Aha! he cares about his heir! Good, very good. I will get hold of the boy. Isn't he my grandson? Good heavens! I can surely go to see the brat! I will stow him away somewhere. I will take care of him, you may be quite easy. I will bring Restaud to terms, the monster! I will say to him, 'A word or two with you! If you want your son back again, give my daughter her property, and leave her to do as she pleases.' "

"Father!"

"Yes. I am your father, Nasie, a father indeed! That rogue of a great lord had better not ill-treat my daughter. *Tonnerre!* What is it in my veins? There is the blood of a tiger in me; I could tear those two men to pieces! Oh! children, children! so this is what your lives are! Why, it is death! What will become of you when I shall no longer be here? Fathers ought to live as long as their children. Ah! God in heaven! how ill Thy world is ordered! Thou hast a Son, if what they tell us is true, and yet Thou leavest us to suffer so through our children. My darlings, my darlings, to think that trouble only should bring you to me, that I should only see you with tears on your faces! Ah! yes, yes, you love me, I see that you love me. Come to me and pour out your griefs to me; my heart is large enough to hold them all. Oh! you might rend my heart in pieces, and every fragment would make a father's heart. If only I could bear all your sorrows for you! Ah, you were so happy when you were little and still with me."

"We have never been happy since," said Delphine. "Where are the old days when we slid down the sacks in the great granary?"

"That is not all, father," said Anastasie in Goriot's ear. The old man gave a startled shudder. "The diamonds only sold for a hundred thousand francs. Maxime is hard pressed. There are twelve thousand francs still to pay. He has given me his word that he will be steady and give up gambling. His love is all that I have left in the world. I have paid such a fearful price for it that I shall die if I lose him now. I have sacrificed my fortune, my honor, my peace of mind, and my children for him. Oh, do something, so that at the least Maxime may be at large and live undisgraced in the world! He will yet make a career for himself. Something more than my happiness is at stake; the children have nothing, and if he is sent to Sainte-Pélagie all will be lost."

"I haven't the money, Nasie. I have *nothing*—nothing left. This is the end of everything. Yes, the world is crumbling into ruin, I am sure. Fly! Save yourselves! Ah!—I have still my silver buckles left, and half a dozen silver spoons and forks, the first I ever had in my life. But I have nothing else except my life annuity, twelve hundred francs——"

"Then what has become of your money in the funds?"

"I sold out, and only kept a trifle for my wants. I wanted twelve thousand francs to furnish some rooms for Delphine."

"In your own house?" asked Mme de Restaud, looking at her sister.

"What does it matter where they were?" asked Goriot. "The money is spent now."

"I can guess," said the countess. "Rooms for Monsieur de Rastignac. Poor Delphine, look at me and take warning!"

"Monsieur de Rastignac is incapable of ruining the woman he loves, dear."

"Thanks! Delphine, I thought you would have been kinder to me in my troubles, but you never did love me."

"Yes, yes, she loves you, Nasie!" cried Goriot. "She was say-ing so only just now. We were talking about you, and she insisted that you were beautiful, and that she herself was only pretty!"

"Pretty!" said the countess. "She is as hard as a marble statue."

"And if I am?" cried Delphine, flushing up. "How have you treated me? You would not recognize me; you closed the doors of every house against me; you have never let an opportunity of mortifying me slip by. And when did I come, as you were always doing, to drain our poor father, a thousand francs at a time, till he is left as you see him now? That is all your doing, sister! I myself have seen my father as often as I could. I have not turned him out of the house, and then come and fawned upon him when I wanted money. I did not so much as know that he had spent those twelve thousand francs on me. I am economical, as you know; and when papa has made me presents, it has never been because I came and begged for them."

"You were better off than I. Monsieur de Marsay was rich, as you have reason to know. You always were as slippery as gold. Good-bye; I have neither sister nor——"

"Oh, hush, hush, Nasie!" cried her father.

"Nobody else would repeat what everybody has ceased to believe. You are an unnatural sister!" cried Delphine.

"Oh, children, children! Hush! or I will kill myself before your eyes."

"There, Nasie, I forgive you," said Mme de Nucingen; "you are very unhappy. But I am kinder than you are. How could you say *that* just when I was ready to do anything in the world to help you, even to be reconciled with my husband, which for my own sake I—— Oh! it is just like you; you have behaved cruelly to me all through these nine years."

"Children, children, kiss each other!" cried the father. "You are angels, both of you."

"No. Let me alone," cried the countess, shaking off the hand that her father had laid on her arm. "She is more merciless than my husband. A model of all the virtues indeed!"

"I would rather have people think that I owed money to Monsieur de Marsay than own that Monsieur de Trailles had cost me more than two hundred thousand francs," retorted Mme de Nucingen.

"*Delphine!*" cried the countess, stepping towards her sister.

"I shall tell you the truth about yourself if you begin to slander me," said the baroness coldly.

"Delphine! You are a——"

Old Goriot sprang between them, grasped the countess' hand, and laid his own over her mouth.

"Good heavens, father! What have you been handling this morning?" said Anastasie.

"Ah, I ought not to have touched you," said the poor father, wiping his hands on his trousers, "but I have been packing up my things. I did not know that you were coming to see me."

He was glad that he had drawn down her wrath upon himself. "Ah," he sighed, as he sat down, "you children have broken my heart between you. This is killing me. My head feels as if it were on fire. Be good to each other and love each other! This will be the death of me! Delphine! Nasie! Come, be sensible; you are both in the wrong. Come, Dedel," he added, looking through his tears at the baroness, "she must have twelve thousand francs, you see. Let us see if we can find them for her. Oh, my girls, do not look at each other like that!" and he sank on his knees beside Delphine. "Ask her to forgive you—just to please me," he said in her ear. "She is more miserable than you are. Come now, Dedel."

"Poor Nasie!" said Delphine, alarmed at the wild extravagant grief in her father's face, "I was in the wrong, kiss me——"

"That is like balm to my heart," cried Father Goriot. "But how are we to find twelve thousand francs? I might offer myself as a substitute in the army——"

"Oh, father!" they both exclaimed, flinging their arms about him. "No, no!"

"God reward you for the thought. We are not worth it, are we, Nasie?" asked Delphine.

"And besides, father dear, it would only be a drop in the bucket," observed the countess.

"But is flesh and blood worth nothing?" cried the old man in his despair. "I would give body and soul to save you, Nasie. I would do a murder for the man who would rescue you. I would do, as Vautrin did, go to the hulks, go—" he stopped as if struck by a thunderbolt, and put both hands to his head. "Nothing left!" he cried, tearing his hair. "If I only knew of a way to steal money, but it is so hard, and then you can't set to work by yourself; it takes time to rob a bank. Yes, it is time I was dead. There is nothing left me to do but to die. I am no good in the world. I am no longer a father! No. She has come to me in her extremity, and, wretch that I am, I have nothing to give her. Ah, you put your money into a life annuity, old scoundrel! Had you not daughters? You did not love them. Die, die in a ditch, like the dog that you are! Yes, I am worse than a dog—a beast would not have done as I have done! Oh, my head—it throbs as if it would burst!"

"Papa," cried both the young women at once, "do be reasonable!" and they clung to him to prevent him from dashing his head against the wall. There was a sound of sobbing.

Eugène, greatly alarmed, took the bill that bore Vautrin's signature, saw that the stamp would suffice for a larger sum, altered the figures, made it into a regular bill for twelve thousand francs, payable to Goriot's order, and went to his neighbor's room.

"Here is the money, madame," he said, handing the piece of paper to Madame de Restaud. "I was asleep; your conversation awoke me, and by this means I learned all that I owed to Monsieur Goriot. This bill can be discounted, and I shall meet it punctually at the due date."

The countess stood motionless and speechless, but she held the bill in her fingers.

"Delphine," she said, with a white face, and her whole frame quivering with indignation, anger, and rage, "I forgave you everything. God is my witness that I forgave you, but I cannot forgive this! So this gentleman was there all the time, and you knew it! Your petty spite has led you to wreak your vengeance on me by betraying my secrets, my life, my children's lives, my shame, my honor! There, you are nothing to me any longer. I hate you. I will do all that I can to injure you. I . . ."

Anger paralyzed her; the words died in her dry parched throat.

"Why, he is my son, my child; he is your brother, your preserver!" cried Goriot. "Kiss his hand, Nasie! Stay, I will embrace him myself," he said, straining Eugène to him in a frenzied clasp. "Oh, my boy! I will be more than a father to you. I would be everything in the world to you. If I had God's power, I would fling worlds at your feet. Why don't you kiss him, Nasie? He is not a man, but an angel, an angel from heaven."

"Never mind her, father; she is mad just now."

"Mad, am I? And what are you?" cried Mme de Restaud.

"Children, children, I shall die if you go on like this," cried the old man, and he staggered and fell on the bed as if a bullet had struck him. "They are killing me between them," he said to himself.

The countess fixed her eyes on Eugène, who stood stock-still; all his faculties were numbed by this violent scene.

"Sir?" she said, doubt and inquiry in her face, tone and bearing; she took no notice now of her father or of Delphine, who was hastily unfastening his waistcoat.

"Madame," said Eugène, answering the question before it was asked, "I will meet the bill, and keep silence about it."

"You have killed our father, Nasie!" said Delphine, pointing to Goriot, who lay unconscious on the bed. The countess fled.

"I freely forgive her," said the old man, opening his eyes. "Her position is horrible; it would turn an older head than hers. Comfort Nasie, and be nice to her, Delphine. Promise it to your poor father before he dies," he asked, holding Delphine's hand in a convulsive clasp.

"Oh, what ails you, father?" she cried in real alarm.

"Nothing, nothing," said Goriot; "it will go off. There is something heavy pressing on my forehead, a little headache. Ah! poor Nasie, what a life lies before her!"

Just as he spoke, the countess came back again and flung herself on her knees before him. "Forgive me!" she cried.

"Come," said her father, "you are hurting me still more."

"Monsieur," the countess said, turning to Rastignac, "misery made me unjust to you. You will be a brother to me, will you not?" and she held out her hand. Her eyes were full of tears as she spoke.

"Nasie," cried Delphine, flinging her arms round her sister, "my little Nasie, let us forget and forgive."

"No, no," cried Nasie; "I shall never forget!"

"Dear angels," cried Goriot, "it is as if a dark curtain over my eyes had been raised; your voices have called me back to life. Kiss each other once more. Well, now, Nasie, that bill will save you, won't it?"

"I hope so. I say, papa, will you write your name on it?"

"Why, how stupid of me to forget that! But I am not feeling at all well, Nasie, so you must not remember it against me. Send and let me know as soon as you are out of your troubles. No, I will go to you. No, after all, I will not go! I might meet your husband, and I should kill him on the spot. And as for signing away your property, I shall have a word to say about that. Quick, my child, and keep Maxime in order in future."

Eugène was too bewildered to speak.

"Poor Anastasie, she always had a violent temper," said Mme de Nucingen, "but she has a good heart."

"She came back for the endorsement," said Eugène in Delphine's ear.

"Do you think so?"

"I only wish I could think otherwise. Do not trust her," he answered, raising his eyes as if he confided to God the thoughts that he did not venture to express.

"Yes. She is always acting a part to some extent."

"How do you feel now, dear Father Goriot?" asked Rastignac.

"I should like to go to sleep," he replied.

Eugène helped him to bed, and Delphine sat by the bedside, holding his hand until he fell asleep. Then she went.

"This evening at the Italiens," she said to Eugène, "and you can let me know how he is. Tomorrow you will leave this place, monsieur. Let us go into your room. Oh! how frightful!" she cried on the threshold. "Why, you are even worse lodged than our father. Eugène, you have behaved well. I would love you more if that were possible; but, dear boy, if you are to succeed in life, you must not begin by flinging twelve thousand francs out of the window like that. The Comte de Trailles is a confirmed gambler. My sister shuts her eyes to it. He would have made the twelve thousand francs in the same way that he wins and loses heaps of gold."

A groan from the next room brought them back to Goriot's bedside. To all appearance he was asleep, but the two lovers caught the words, "They are not happy!" Whether he was awake or sleeping, the tone in which they were spoken went to his daughter's heart. She stole up to the pallet-bed on which her father lay, and kissed his forehead. He opened his eyes.

"Ah, Delphine!" he said.

"How are you now?" she asked.

"Quite comfortable. Do not worry about me; I shall get up presently. Don't stay with me, children. Go, go and be happy."

Eugène went back with Delphine as far as her door; but he was not easy about Goriot, and would not stay to dinner, as she proposed. He wanted to be back at the Maison Vauquer. Old Goriot had left his room, and was just sitting down to dinner as he came in. Bianchon had placed himself where he could watch the old man carefully; and when the old vermicelli-maker took up his square of bread and smelt it to find out the quality of the flour, the medical student, studying him closely, saw that the action was purely mechanical, and shook his head.

"Just come and sit over here, you Cochin intern," said Eugène.

Bianchon went the more willingly because his change of place brought him nearer to the old lodger.

"What is wrong with him?" asked Rastignac.

"He's done for, or I am much mistaken. Something very extraordinary must have taken place; he looks to me as if he were in imminent danger of apoplexy. The lower part of his

face is composed enough, but the upper part is drawn and distorted. Then there is that peculiar look about the eyes that
indicates an effusion of serum in the brain; they look as though
they were covered with a film of fine dust, do you notice? I
shall know more about it by tomorrow morning."

"Is there any cure for it?"

"None. It might be possible to stave death off for a time if
a way could be found of setting up a reaction in the lower
extremities, but if the symptoms continue until tomorrow evening, it will be all over with him, poor old fellow! Do you know
what has happened to bring this on? There must have been some
violent shock, and his mind has given way."

"Yes, there was," said Rastignac, remembering how the two
daughters had struck blow on blow at their father's heart.

"But Delphine at any rate loves her father," he said to himself.

Chapter 17

THAT EVENING at the opera Rastignac chose his words carefully,
lest he should give Mme de Nucingen needless alarm.

"Do not be anxious about him," she said, as soon as Eugène
began; "our father has really a strong constitution, but this
morning we gave him a shock. Our whole fortunes were in peril,
so the thing was serious, you see. I could not live if your affection did not make me insensible to troubles that I should once
have thought too hard to bear. At this moment I have but one
fear left, but one misery to dread—to lose the love that has made
me feel so glad to live. Everything else is as nothing to me compared with your love; I care for nothing else, for you are all the
world to me. If I feel glad to be rich, it is for your sake. To my
shame be it said, I think of my lover before my father. Do you
ask why? I cannot tell you, but all my life is in you. My father

gave me a heart, but you have taught it to beat. The whole world may condemn me; what does it matter if I stand acquitted in your eyes, for you have no right to think ill of me for the faults which a tyrannous love has forced me to commit for you! Do you think me an unnatural daughter? Oh, no; no one could help loving such a dear kind father as ours. But how could I hide the inevitable consequences of our miserable marriages from him? Why did he allow us to marry when we did? Was it not his duty to think and judge for us? Today I know he suffers as much as we do, but how can it be helped? And as for comforting him, we could not comfort him in the least. Our resignation would give him more pain and hurt him far more than complaints and upbraidings. There are times in life when everything turns to bitterness."

Eugène was silent; the simple and sincere outpouring touched him.

Parisian women are often false, intoxicated with vanity, selfish and self-absorbed, frivolous and shallow; yet when they love, they sacrifice all trivial sentiments to their passion; they rise so much the higher for all the pettiness overcome, and become sublime. Eugène was struck by the profound insight displayed by this woman in judging of natural affection, when a privileged affection had separated and set her at a distance apart. Mme de Nucingen was piqued by the silence.

"What are you thinking about?" she asked.

"I am thinking about what you said just now. Hitherto I have always felt sure that I cared far more for you than you did for me."

She smiled, and would not give way to the happiness she felt, lest their talk should exceed the conventional limits of propriety. She had never heard the vibrating tones of a sincere and youthful love; a few more words, and she feared for her self-control.

"Eugène," she said, changing the conversation, "I wonder whether you know what has been happening? All Paris will go to Mme de Beauséant's tomorrow. The Rochefides and the Marquis d'Ajuda have agreed to keep the matter a profound secret, but tomorrow the king will sign the marriage-contract, and your poor cousin the vicomtesse knows nothing of it as yet. She cannot put off her ball, and the marquis will not be there. People are wondering what will happen."

"The world laughs at baseness and connives at it. But this will kill Madame de Beauséant."

"Oh, no," said Delphine, smiling, "you do not know that kind of woman. Why, all Paris will be there, and so shall I. I ought to go there for your sake."

"Perhaps, after all, it is one of those absurd reports that people set in circulation here."

"We shall know the truth tomorrow."

Eugène did not return to the Maison Vauquer. He could not forgo the pleasure of occupying his new rooms in the Rue d'Artois. Yesterday evening he had been obliged to leave Delphine soon after midnight, but that night it was Delphine who stayed with him until two o'clock in the morning. He rose late, and waited for Mme de Nucingen, who came about noon to breakfast with him. Youth snatches eagerly at these moments of happiness, and Eugène had almost forgotten Goriot's existence. The pretty things that surrounded him were growing familiar; this domestication in itself was one long festival for him, and Mme de Nucingen was there to glorify it all by her presence. It was four o'clock before they thought of Goriot, and of how he had looked forward to the new life in that house. Eugène said that the old man ought to be moved at once, lest he should grow too ill to move. He left Delphine, and hurried back to the lodginghouse. Neither old Goriot nor young Bianchon was in the dining room with the others.

"Aha!" said the painter as Eugène came in, "Father Goriot has broken down at last. Bianchon is upstairs with him. One of his daughters—the Comtesse de Restaurama—came to see the

old gentleman, and he would get up and go out, and made himself worse. Society is about to lose one of its brightest ornaments."

Rastignac sprang to the staircase.

"Hey! Monsieur Eugène!"

"Monsieur Eugène, the mistress is calling you," shouted Sylvie.

"Monsieur," said the widow, "you and Father Goriot should
by rights have moved out on the fifteenth of February. That was
three days ago; today is the eighteenth: I ought really to be paid
a month in advance, but if you will engage to pay for both, I
shall be quite satisfied."

"Why can't you trust him?"

"Trust him, indeed! If the old gentleman went off his head
and died, those daughters of his would not pay me a sou, and
his things won't fetch ten francs. This morning he went out
with all the spoons and forks he has left; I don't know why. He
had got himself up to look quite young, and—Lord, forgive me
—I thought he had rouge on his cheeks. He looked quite young
again."

"I will be responsible," said Eugène, shuddering with horror,
for he foresaw the end.

He climbed the stairs and reached old Goriot's room. The
old man was tossing on his bed. Bianchon was with him.

"Good evening, father," said Eugène.

The old man turned his glassy eyes on him, smiled gently,
and said:

"How is *she*?"

"She is quite well. But how are you?"

"There is nothing much the matter."

"Don't tire him," said Bianchon, drawing Eugène into a corner of the room.

"Well?" asked Rastignac.

"Nothing but a miracle can save him now. Serous congestion

has set in. I have put on mustard plasters, and luckily he can feel them; they are acting."

"Is it possible to move him?"

"Quite out of the question. He must stay where he is, and be kept as quiet as possible——"

"Dear Bianchon," said Eugène, "we will nurse him between us."

"I have had the head physician round from my hospital to see him."

"And what did he say?"

"He will give no opinion till tomorrow evening. He promised to look in again at the end of the day. Unluckily, the preposterous creature had to go and do something foolish this morning; he will not say what it was. He is as obstinate as a mule. As soon as I begin to talk to him he pretends not to hear, and lies as if he were asleep instead of answering, or if he opens his eyes he begins to groan. Some time this morning he went out on foot in the streets Nobody knows where. He took everything that he had of any value with him. He has been driving some confounded bargain, and it has been too much for his strength. One of his daughters has been here."

"Was it the countess?" asked Eugène. "A tall, dark-haired woman, with large bright eyes, slender figure, and little feet?"

"Yes."

"Leave him to me for a bit," said Rastignac. "I will make him confess; he will tell me all about it."

"And meanwhile I will get my dinner. But try not to excite him; there is still some hope left."

"All right."

"How they will enjoy themselves tomorrow," said old Goriot when they were alone. "They are going to a grand ball."

"What were you doing this morning, papa, to make yourself so poorly this evening that you have to stay in bed?"

"Nothing."

"Did not Anastasie come to see you?" demanded Rastignac.

"Yes," said old Goriot.

"Well, then, don't keep anything from me. What more did she want of you?"

"Oh, she was very miserable," he answered, gathering up all his strength to speak. "It was this way, my boy. Since that affair of the diamonds, Nasie has not had a penny of her own. For this ball she had ordered a golden gown like a setting for a jewel. Her dressmaker, a woman without a conscience, would not give her credit, so Nasie's maid advanced a thousand francs on account. Poor Nasie! reduced to such shifts! It cut me to the heart to think of it! But when Nasie's maid saw how things were between her master and mistress, she was afraid of losing her money, and came to an understanding with the dressmaker, and the woman refuses to send the ball-dress until the money is paid. The gown is ready, and the ball is tomorrow night; Nasie was in despair. She wanted to borrow my forks and spoons to pawn them. Her husband is determined that she shall go and wear the diamonds, so as to contradict the stories that are told all over Paris. How can she go to that heartless scoundrel and say, 'I owe a thousand francs to my dressmaker; pay her for me'? She cannot. I saw that myself. Delphine will be there too in a superb toilette, and Anastasie ought not to be outshone by her younger sister. And then—she was drowned in tears, poor girl! I felt so humbled yesterday when I had not the twelve thousand francs, that I would have given the rest of my miserable life to wipe out that wrong. You see, I could have borne anything once, but latterly this want of money has broken my heart. Oh! I did not do it by halves; I titivated myself up a bit, and went out and sold my spoons and forks and buckles for six hundred francs; then I went to old Daddy Gobseck, and sold a year's interest in my annuity for four hundred francs down. Pshaw! I can live on dry bread, as I did when I was a young man. If I have done it before, I can do it again. My Nasie shall have one happy evening, at any rate. She shall be smart. The bank-note for a thousand francs is here under my pillow; it warms me to have it lying there under my head, for it is going to make my poor Nasie happy. She can turn that bad girl Victoire out of the house. A servant that cannot trust her mistress, did any-one ever hear the like! I shall be quite well tomorrow. Nasie is coming at ten o'clock. They must not think that I am ill, or they will not go to the ball; they will stop and take care of me. To-morrow Nasie will come and hold me in her arms as if I were one of her children; her kisses will make me well again. After all, I might have spent the thousand francs on medicine; I would far rather give them to my little Nasie, who can charm all the pain away. At any rate, I am some comfort to her in her misery; and that makes up for my unkindness in buying an annuity. She is in the depths, and I cannot draw her out of them now. Oh, I will go into business again, I will buy wheat in Odessa. Out there, wheat fetches a quarter of the price it sells for here. There is a law against the importation of grain, but the good folk who made the law forgot to prohibit the introduction of wheat products and foodstuffs made from corn. Hey! hey! . . . That struck me this morning. There is a fine trade to be done in starch."

Eugène, watching the old man's face, thought that his friend was delirious. "Come," he said, "don't talk any more, you must rest." Just then Bianchon came up, and Eugéne went down to dinner.

The two students sat up with him that night, relieving each other in turn. Bianchon brought up his medical books and studied; Eugène wrote letters home to his mother and sisters. Next morning Bianchon thought the symptoms more hopeful, but the patient's condition demanded continual attention, which the two students alone were willing to give—a task impossible to describe in the squeamish phraseology of the epoch. Leeches must be applied to the wasted body, with poultices and hot footbaths, and other details of the treatment required the physical strength and devotion of the two young men. Mme de Restaud did not come, but she sent a messenger for the money.

"I expected she would come herself; still, it's just as well; she would have been anxious about me," said the father, apparently well content.

At seven o'clock that evening Thérèse came with a letter from Delphine:

What are you doing, dear friend? Barely loved, am I already neglected? In the confidences of heart and heart, I have learned to know your soul—you are too noble not to be faithful forever, for you know that love with all its infinite subtle changes of feeling is never the same. Once you said, as we were listening to the Prayer in *Moses in Egypt*, "For some it is the monotony of a single note; for others, it is the infinite of sound." Remember that I am expecting you this evening to take me to Mme de Beauséant's ball. Everyone knows now that the king signed M. d'Ajuda's marriage-contract this morning, and the poor vicomtesse knew nothing of it until two o'clock this afternoon. All Paris will flock to her house, of course, just as a crowd fills the Place de Grève to see an execution. It is horrible, is it not, to go out of curiosity to see if she will hide her anguish, and whether she will die courageously? I certainly should not go, my friend, if I had been at her house before; but, of course, she will not receive society any more after this, and all my efforts would be in vain. My position is a very unusual one, and besides, I am going there partly on your account. I am waiting for you. If you are not beside me in less than two hours, I do not know whether I could pardon you for the crime.

Rastignac took up a pen and wrote:

I am waiting till the doctor comes to know if there is any hope of your father's life. He is dying. I will come and bring you the news, but I am afraid it may be a sentence of death. When I come you will decide whether you can go to the ball.—Yours a thousand times.

At half-past eight the doctor arrived. He did not take a very hopeful view of the case, but thought that there was no immediate danger of death. Improvements and relapses might be expected, and the good man's life and reason hung in the balance.

"It would be better for him to die at once," the doctor said, as he took leave.

Eugène left Goriot to Bianchon's care, and went to carry the sad news to Mme de Nucingen. Family feeling lingered in her, and would put an end for the present to her plans of amusement.

"Tell her to enjoy her evening as if nothing had happened," said Goriot. He had been lying in a sort of stupor, but he suddenly sat upright as Eugène went out.

Eugène, half heartbroken, entered Delphine's room. Her hair had been dressed; she wore her dancing slippers; she had only to put on her ball-dress; but when the artist is giving the finishing stroke to his creation, the last touches require more time than the whole groundwork of the picture.

"Why, you are not dressed!" she cried.

"Madame, your father——"

"My father again!" she exclaimed, breaking in upon him. "You need not teach me what is due to my father, I have known my father this long while. Not a word, Eugène. I will hear what you have to say when you are dressed. My carriage is waiting, take it, go round to your rooms and dress. Thérèse has put out everything in readiness for you. Come back as soon as you can. We will talk about my father on the way to Madame de Beauséant's. We must go early, for if we have to wait our turn in a row of carriages, we shall be lucky if we get there by eleven o'clock."

"Madame——"

"Quick! Not a word!" she cried, darting into her dressing-room for a necklace.

"Do go, Monsieur Eugène, or you will vex Madame," said

Thérèse, hurrying him away; and Eugène was too horror-stricken by this elegant parricide to resist.

He went to his rooms and dressed, filled with melancholy reflections. The world of Paris was like an ocean of mud for him just then, and it seemed that whoever set foot in that black mire must needs sink into it up to the chin.

"Their crimes are paltry," said Eugène to himself. "Vautrin was greater."

He had seen society in its three great phases—Obedience, Struggle, and Revolt; the Family, the World, and Vautrin; and he hesitated in his choice. Obedience was dull, Revolt impossible, Struggle hazardous. His thoughts wandered back to the home circle. He thought of the quiet uneventful life, the pure happiness of the days spent among those who loved him there. Those loving and beloved beings passed their lives in obedience to the natural laws of the hearth, and in that obedience found a deep and constant serenity, unvexed by torments such as these. Yet, for all his good impulses, he could not bring himself to make profession of the religion of pure souls to Delphine, or to prescribe the duties of piety to her in the guise of love. His education had begun to bear its fruits; he loved selfishly already. Besides, his tact had discovered to him the real nature of Delphine; he divined instinctively that she was capable of stepping over her father's corpse to go to the ball, and within himself he felt that he had neither the strength of mind to play the part of mentor, nor the strength of character to vex her, nor the courage to leave her to go alone.

"She would never forgive me for putting her in the wrong over it," he said to himself. Then he turned the doctor's dictum over in his mind. He tried to believe that Goriot was not so dangerously ill as he had imagined, and ended by collecting together a sufficient quantity of traitorous excuses for Delphine's conduct. She did not know how ill her father was; the kind old man himself would have made her go to the ball if she had gone to see him. So often it happens that this one or that stands condemned by the social laws that govern family relations; and yet there are peculiar circumstances in the case, differences of temperament, divergent interests, innumerable complications of family life that excuse the apparent offense.

Eugène did not wish to see too clearly; he was ready to sacrifice his conscience to his mistress. Within the last few days his whole life had undergone a change. Woman had entered into his world and thrown it into chaos, family claims dwindled; she had appropriated all his being to her uses. Rastignac and Delphine found each other at a point in their lives when their union gave them the most poignant bliss. Their passion, so long tested, had only gained in strength by the gratified desire that often extinguishes it. In possessing this woman, Eugène realized that until then he had only desired her. He loved her from the moment of his happiness; perhaps love is only gratitude for pleasure. This woman, vile or sublime, he adored for the pleasures she had brought as her dower; and Delphine loved Rastignac as Tantalus would have loved some angel who had satisfied his hunger and quenched the burning thirst in his parched throat.

"Well," said Mme de Nucingen, when he came back in evening dress, "how is my father?"

"Very dangerously ill," he answered; "if you will grant me a proof of your affection, we will just go in to see him on the way."

"Very well," she said. "Yes, but afterwards. Dear Eugène, do be nice, and don't preach to me. Come."

They set out. Eugène said nothing for a while.

"What is it now?" she asked.

"I can hear the death-rattle in your father's throat," he said, almost angrily. And with the hot indignation of youth, he told the story of Mme de Restaud's vanity and cruelty, of her father's final act of self-sacrifice, that had brought about this struggle between life and death, of the price that had been paid for Anastasie's golden embroideries. Delphine cried.

"I shall look frightful," she thought. She dried her tears.

"I will nurse my father; I will not leave his bedside," she said aloud.

"Ah, now you are as I would have you!" exclaimed Rastignac.

The lamps of five hundred carriages lit up the darkness about the Hôtel de Beauséant. A gendarme in all the glory of his uniform stood on either side of the brightly lighted gateway. The great world was flocking there that night in its eager curiosity to see the great lady at the moment of her fall, and the rooms on the ground floor were already full to overflowing, when Mme de Nucingen and Rastignac appeared. Never since Louis XIV tore her lover away from La Grande Mademoiselle, and the whole court hastened to visit that unfortunate princess, had a disastrous love affair made such a sensation in Paris. But the youngest daughter of the almost royal house of Burgundy had risen proudly above her pain, and moved till the last moment like a queen in this world—its vanities had always been valueless for her, save in so far as they contributed to the triumph of her passion. The salons were filled with the most beautiful women in Paris, resplendent in their costumes, and radiant with smiles. Ministers and ambassadors, the most distinguished men at court, men bedizened with decorations, stars, and ribbons, men who bore the most illustrious names in France, had gathered about the vicomtesse.

The music of the orchestra vibrated in wave after wave of sound from the golden ceiling of the palace, now made desolate for its queen.

Mme de Beauséant stood at the door of the first salon to receive the guests who were styled her friends. She was dressed in white, and wore no ornament in the plaits of hair braided about her head; her face was calm; there was no sign of pride, or of pain, or of joy that she did not feel. No one saw into her heart. She stood there like some Niobe carved in marble. For a few intimate friends there was a tinge of satire in her smile; but no scrutiny saw any change in her—she looked the same as in the days of her happiness. The most callous of her guests admired her as young Romans applauded some gladiator who could die smiling. It seemed as if society had adorned itself for a last audience of one of its sovereigns.

"I was afraid that you would not come," she said to Rastignac.

"Madame," he said, in an unsteady voice, taking her speech as a reproach, "I shall be the last to go, that is why I am here."

"Good," she said, and she took his hand. "You are perhaps the only one that I can trust here among all these. Oh, my friend, when you love, love a woman whom you are sure that you can love always. Never forsake a woman."

She took Rastignac's arm, and went towards a sofa in the card-room.

"I want you to go to the marquis," she said. "Jacques, my footman, will go with you; he has a letter that you will take. I am asking the marquis to give my letters back to me. He will give them all up, I like to think that. When you have my letters, go up to my room with them. Someone will bring me word."

She rose to go to meet the Duchesse de Langeais, her most intimate friend, who had come like the rest of the world.

Rastignac went. He asked for the Marquis d'Ajuda at the Hôtel Rochefide, feeling certain that the latter would be spending his evening there, and so it proved. The marquis went to his own house with Rastignac, and gave a casket to the student, saying as he did so, "They are all there."

He seemed as if he was about to say something to Eugène, to ask about the ball, or the vicomtesse. Perhaps he was on the brink of the confession that, even then, he was in despair, and knew that his marriage had been a fatal mistake; but a proud gleam shone in his eyes, and with a warped kind of courage he kept his noblest feelings a secret.

"Do not even mention my name to her, my dear Eugène." He grasped Rastignac's hand sadly and affectionately, and turned away from him. Eugène went back to the Hôtel Beauséant, and the servant took him to the vicomtesse's room. There were signs there of preparations for a journey. He sat down by the fire, fixed his eyes on the cedarwood casket, and fell into deep mournful musings. Mme de Beauséant loomed large in these imaginings, like a goddess in the Iliad.

"Ah! my friend!" said the vicomtesse; she crossed the room and laid her hand on Rastignac's shoulder. He saw the tears in his cousin's uplifted eyes, saw that one hand was raised to take the casket, and that the fingers of the other trembled. Suddenly she took the casket, put it in the fire, and watched it burn.

"They are dancing," she said. "They arrived punctually, but death will be long in coming. Hush, my friend," and she laid a finger on Rastignac's lips, seeing that he was about to speak. "I shall never see Paris again. I am taking my leave of this world. At five o'clock this morning I shall set out on my journey. I mean to bury myself in the remotest part of Normandy. I have had very little time to make my arrangements. Since three o'clock this afternoon I have been busy signing documents, setting my affairs in order; there was no one whom I could send to—" She broke off.

"He was sure to be—" Again she broke off; the weight of her sorrow was more than she could bear. In such agonizing moments as these, some words it is impossible to utter.

"And so I counted upon you to do me this last piece of service this evening," she said. "I should like to give you some pledge of friendship. I shall often think of you. You have seemed to me to be kind and noble, fresh-hearted and true, in this world where such qualities are seldom found. I should like you to think sometimes of me. Stay," she said, glancing about her, "there is this box that has held my gloves. Every time I opened it before going to a ball or to the theater, I used to feel that I must be beautiful, because I was so happy; and I never touched it except to lay some gracious memory in it: there is so much of my old self in it, of a Madame de Beauséant who now lives no longer. Will you take it? I will leave directions that it is to be sent to you in the Rue d'Artois. Madame de Nucingen looked very charming this evening. Eugène, you must love her. Perhaps we may never see each other again, my friend, but be sure of this, that I shall pray for you who have been kind to me. Now let us go downstairs. People shall not think that I am weeping. I have all time and eternity before me, and where I am going I shall be alone, and no one will ask me the reason of my tears. One last look round first."

She stood for a moment. Then she covered her eyes with her hands for an instant, dashed away the tears, bathed her face with cold water, and took the student's arm.

"Let us go!" she said.

This suffering, endured with such noble fortitude, shook Eugène with a more violent emotion than he had felt before. They went back to the ballroom, and Mme de Beauséant went through the rooms on Eugène's arm—the last delicately gracious act of a gracious woman. On entering the ballroom Rastignac at once observed one of those couples whose possession of great beauty makes them glorious to watch. Never had he beheld such perfection. The man was a god-like creature, and his good manners only enhanced the effect which his fine appearance created. The woman, slight as a fairy, attracted the eyes, aroused the senses, and, in short, drew to her even the most indifferent. Everyone regarded the couple with pleasure, and envied the happiness which shone in their eyes and which was revealed in the harmony of their movements.

"Heavens! Who is that woman?" asked Rastignac.

"Oh, that most beautiful of women is Lady Brandon," answered the vicomtesse. "She is as celebrated for her happiness as for her beauty. She has sacrificed everything for that young man. They have children, people say. But misfortune is catching up with them. They say Lord Brandon has sworn vengeance against his wife and her lover. They are happy, but live in a state of constant dread."

"And the man?"

"Oh, do you not know Colonel Franchessini?"

"The one who fought a duel?"

"Yes, three days ago; he was insulted by some banker's son. He didn't mean to hurt him, but unfortunately he killed him."

"Oh!"

"What is the matter? You are shivering," said the vicomtesse.

"It's nothing," murmured Rastignac. A cold sweat broke out on his back. Vautrin's face of bronze appeared before him—and the thought of the great man of the underworld in contact with this idol of ballrooms changed for him the whole aspect of society. In another moment he saw the sisters, Mme de Restaud and Mme de Nucingen. The countess shone in all the glory of her magnificent diamonds. Every stone must have scorched like fire. She was never to wear them again. Strong as love and pride might be in her, she found it difficult to meet her husband's eyes. The sight of her was scarcely calculated to lighten Rastignac's sad thoughts; through the blaze of those diamonds he seemed to see the wretched pallet-bed on which old Goriot was lying. The vicomtesse misread his melancholy; she withdrew her hand from his arm.

"Come," she said, "I must not deprive you of a pleasure."

Eugène was soon claimed by Delphine. She was delighted with the impression that she had made, and eager to lay at her lover's feet the homage she had received in this new world in which she hoped to live and move henceforth.

"What do you think of Nasie?" she asked him.

"She has discounted everything, even her own father's death," said Rastignac.

Towards four o'clock in the morning the rooms began to

empty. A little later the music ceased, and the Duchesse de Langeais and Rastignac were left in the great ballroom. The vicomtesse, who thought to find the student there alone, came back
there at the last. She had taken leave of M. de Beauséant, who
had gone off to bed, saying again as he went, "You're making
a mistake, my dear, to shut yourself up at your age! Better stay
among us."

Mme de Beauséant saw the duchess, and, in spite of herself,
an exclamation broke from her.

"I saw how it was, Clara," said Mme de Langeais. "You are
going from among us, and you will never come back. But you
must not go until you have heard me, until we have understood
each other."

She took her friend's arm, and they went together into the
next room. There the duchess looked at her with tears in her
eyes; she held her friend in a close embrace, and kissed her cheek.

"I could not let you go without a word, dearest. The remorse
would have been too hard to bear. You can count upon me as
surely as upon yourself. You have shown yourself great this
evening. I feel that I am worthy of our friendship, and I mean
to prove myself worthy of it. I have not always been kind; I was
in the wrong: forgive me, dearest. I wish I could unsay anything
that may have hurt you. One common sorrow has brought us
together again, for I do not know which of us is the more miserable. Monsieur de Montriveau was not here tonight; do you
understand what that means? None of those who saw you tonight, Clara, will ever forget you. I mean to make one last effort.
If I fail, I shall go into a convent. Clara, where are you going?"

"Into Normandy, to Courcelles. I shall love and pray there
until the day when God shall take me from this world.—Monsieur de Rastignac!" called the vicomtesse, in a tremulous voice,
remembering that the young man was waiting there.

The student knelt to kiss his cousin's hand.

"Good-bye, Antoinette!" said Mme de Beauséant. "May you

be happy." She turned to the student. "You are young," she said; "you have some beliefs still left. I have been privileged, like some dying people, to find sincere and reverent feeling in those about me as I take my leave of this world."

It was nearly five o'clock that morning when Rastignac came away. He had put Mme de Beauséant into her traveling carriage, and received her last farewells, spoken amid fast-falling tears; for no greatness is so great that it can rise above the laws of human affection, or live beyond the jurisdiction of pain, as certain demagogues would have us believe. Eugène returned on foot to the Maison Vauquer through the cold and darkness. His education was nearly complete.

"There is no hope for poor old Goriot," said Bianchon, as Rastignac came into the room. Eugène looked for a while at the sleeping man, then he turned to his friend. "Dear fellow, you are content with the modest career you have marked out for yourself; keep to it. I am in hell, and I must stay there. Believe everything that you hear said of the world, nothing is too impossibly bad. No Juvenal could paint the horrors hidden away under the covering of gems and gold."

At two o'clock in the afternoon Bianchon came to wake Rastignac, and begged him to take charge of Goriot, who had grown worse as the day wore on. The medical student was obliged to go out.

"Poor old man, he has not two days to live, maybe not many hours," he said, "but we must do our utmost, all the same, to fight the disease. It will be a very troublesome case, and we shall want money. We can nurse him between us, of course, but, as for me, I have not a penny. I have turned out his pockets, and rummaged through his drawers—result, *nix*. I asked him about it while his mind was clear, and he told me he had not a sou of his own. What have you?"

"I have twenty francs left," said Rastignac; "but I will take them to the roulette table. I shall be sure to win."

"And if you lose?"

"Then I shall go to his sons-in-law and his daughters and ask them for money."

"And suppose they refuse?" Bianchon retorted. "The most pressing thing just now is not really money; we must put mustard poultices, as hot as they can be made, on his feet and legs. If he calls out, there is still some hope for him. You know how to set about doing it, and besides, Christophe will help you. I am going round to the dispensary to persuade them to let us have the things we want on credit. It is a pity that we could not move him to the hospital. Poor fellow, he would be better off there. Well, come along, I leave you in charge. You must stay with him till I come back."

The two young men went back to the room where the old man was lying. Eugène was startled at the change in Goriot's face, so livid and distorted.

"How are you, papa?" he said, bending over the pallet-bed. Goriot turned his dull eyes upon Eugène, looked at him attentively, and did not recognize him. It was more than the student could bear; the tears came into his eyes.

"Bianchon, ought we to have curtains put up in the windows?"

"No, the temperature and the light do not affect him now. It would be a good thing for him if he felt heat or cold; but we must have a fire in any case to make tisanes and heat the other things. I will send round a few sticks; they will last till we can have in some firewood. I burned all the bark fuel you had left, as well as his, poor man, yesterday and during the night. The place was so damp that the water stood in drops on the walls; I could hardly get the room dry. Christophe came in and swept the floor, but the place is like a stable; I had to burn juniper—the smell was something horrible."

"Good God!" said Rastignac. "Think of those daughters of his!"

"If he asks for something to drink, give him this," said the student, pointing to a large white jar. "If he begins to groan, and the belly feels hot and hard to the touch, you know what to do; get Christophe to help you. If he should happen to grow much excited, and begin to talk a good deal, and even to ramble in his talk, do not be alarmed. It would not be a bad symptom. But send Christophe to the Hospice Cochin. Our doctor, my chum, or I will come and apply moxas. We had a great consultation this morning while you were asleep. A surgeon, a pupil of Gall's, came, and our house surgeon, and the head physician from the Hôtel-Dieu. Those gentlemen considered that the symptoms were very unusual and interesting. The case must be carefully watched, for it throws a light on several obscure and rather important scientific problems. One of the authorities says that if there is more pressure of serum on one or other portion of the brain, it should affect his mental capacities in such and such directions. So if he should talk, notice very carefully what kind of ideas his mind seems to run on; whether memory, or penetration, or the reasoning faculties are exercised; whether sentiments or practical questions fill his thoughts; whether he makes forecasts or dwells on the past; in fact, you must be prepared to give an accurate report of him. It is quite likely that the extravasation fills the whole brain, in which case he will die in the imbecile state in which he is lying now. You cannot tell anything about these mysterious nervous diseases. Suppose the crash came here," said Bianchon, touching the back of the head; "very strange things have been known to happen; the brain sometimes partially recovers, and death is delayed. Or the congested matter may pass out of the brain altogether through channels which can only be determined by a post-mortem examination. There is an old man at the Hospital for Incurables, an imbecile patient; in his case the effusion has followed the direction of the spinal cord. He suffers horrid agonies, but he lives."

"Did they enjoy themselves?" It was old Goriot who spoke. He had recognized Eugène.

"Oh, he thinks of nothing but his daughters!" said Bianchon. "Scores of times last night he said to me, 'They are dancing now! She has her dress.' He called them by their names. He made me cry, the devil take it, calling with that tone in his voice, for 'Delphine, my little Delphine! and Nasie!' Upon my word," said the medical student, "it was enough to make anyone burst out crying."

"Delphine," said the old man, "she is there, isn't she? I knew she was there," and his eyes sought the door.

"I am going down now to tell Sylvie to get the poultices ready," said Bianchon. "They ought to go on at once."

Chapter 18

RASTIGNAC WAS left alone with the old man. He sat at the foot of the bed, and gazed at the face before him, so horribly changed that it was shocking to see.

"Noble natures cannot dwell in this world," he said; "Madame de Beauséant has fled from it, and there he lies dying. What place indeed is there in the shallow petty frivolous thing called society for noble thoughts and feelings?"

Pictures of yesterday's ball rose up in his memory, in strange contrast to the deathbed before him. Bianchon suddenly appeared.

"I say, Eugène, I have just seen our head surgeon at the hospital, and I ran all the way back here. If the old man shows any signs of reason, if he begins to talk, cover him with a mustard poultice from the neck to the base of the spine, and send round for us."

"Dear Bianchon!" exclaimed Eugène.

"Oh, it's an interesting case from a scientific point of view," said the medical student, with all the enthusiasm of a neophyte.

"So!" said Eugène. "Am I really the only one who cares for the poor old man for his own sake?"

"You would not have said so if you had seen me this morning," returned Bianchon, who did not take offense at this speech. "Doctors who have seen a good deal of practice never see anything but the disease, but, my dear fellow, I can see the patient still."

He went. Eugène was left alone with the old man, and with an apprehension of a crisis that set in, in fact, before very long.

"Ah, dear boy, is that you?" said old Goriot, recognizing Eugène.

"Do you feel better?" asked the law student, taking his hand.

"Yes. My head felt as if it were being screwed in a vice, but now it is set free again. Did you see my girls? They will be here soon; as soon as they know that I am ill they will hurry here. They used to take such care of me in the Rue de la Jussienne! Great Heavens, if only my room was fit for them to come into! There has been a young man here, who has burned up all my bark fuel."

"I can hear Christophe coming upstairs," Eugène answered. "He is bringing up some firewood that that young man has sent you."

"Good, but how am I to pay for the wood? I have not a penny left, dear boy. I have given away everything, everything. I am a pauper now. Well, at least the golden gown was grand, was it not? Ah! what pain this is! Thanks, Christophe! God will reward you, my boy; I have nothing left now."

Eugène went over to Christophe and whispered in the man's ear, "I will pay you well, and Sylvie too, for your trouble."

"My daughters told you that they were coming, didn't they, Christophe? Go again to them, and I will give you five francs. Tell them that I am not feeling well, that I should like to kiss them both and see them once again before I die. Tell them that, but don't alarm them more than you can help."

Rastignac signed to Christophe to go, and the man went.

"They will come before long," the old man went on. "I know them so well. My tender-hearted Delphine! If I am going to die, she will feel it so much! And so will Nasie. I do not want to die; they will cry if I die; and if I die, dear Eugène, I shall not see them any more. It will be very dreary there where I am going. For a father it is hell to be without his children; I have served my apprenticeship since they married. My heaven was in the Rue de la Jussienne. Eugène, do you think that if I go to heaven I could come back to earth, and be near them in spirit? I have heard some such things said. Is it true? It is as if I could see them at this moment as they used to be when we all lived in the Rue de la Jussienne. They used to come downstairs of a morning. 'Good morning, papa!' they would say, and I would take them on my knees. We had all sorts of little games, and they had such pretty coaxing ways. We always had breakfast together, too, every morning, and they had dinner with me— in fact, I was a father then. I enjoyed my children. They did not think for themselves so long as they lived in the Rue de la Jussienne; they knew nothing of the world; they loved me with all their hearts. My God! why could they not always be little girls? Oh! my head! this racking pain in my head! Ah! ah! forgive me, children; this pain is fearful; it must be agony indeed, for you have used me to endure pain. If only I held their hands in mine, I should not feel it at all. Do you think that they are on the way? Christophe is so stupid; I ought to have gone myself. *He* will see them. But you went to the ball yesterday; just tell me how they looked. They did not know that I was ill, did they, or they would not have been dancing, poor little things? Oh! I must not be ill any longer. They stand too much in need of me; their fortunes are in danger. And such husbands as they are bound to! I must get well! Oh! what pain this is!

what pain this is! . . . Ah! I must get well, you see, for they *must* have money, and I know how to set about making some. I will go to Odessa and manufacture starch there. I am an old hand, I will make millions. Oh! this is agony!"

Goriot was silent for a moment; it seemed to require his whole strength to endure the pain.

"If they were here, I should not complain," he said. "So why should I complain now?"

He seemed to grow drowsy with exhaustion, and lay quietly for a long time. Christophe came back, and Rastignac, thinking that Goriot was asleep, allowed the man to tell his story aloud.

"First of all, sir, I went to Madame la Comtesse," he said; "but she and her husband were so busy that I couldn't get to speak to her. When I insisted that I must see her, Monsieur de Restaud came out to me, himself, and went on like this: 'Monsieur Goriot is dying, is he? Very well, it is the best thing he can do. I want Madame de Restaud to transact some important business, when it is all finished she can go.' The gentleman looked angry, I thought. I was just going away when Madame de Restaud came out into an antechamber through a door that I did not notice, and said, 'Christophe, tell my father that my husband wants me to discuss some matters with him, and I cannot leave the house, the life or death of my children is at stake; but as soon as it is over, I will come.' As for Madame la Baronne, that is another story! I could not speak to her either, and I did not even see her. Her maid said, 'Ah, yes, but Madame only came back from the ball at a quarter to five this morning; she is asleep now, and if I wake her before midday she will be cross. As soon as she rings, I will go and tell her that her father is worse. It will be time enough then to tell her bad news!' I begged and prayed, but, there! it was no good. Then I asked for Monsieur le Baron, but he was out."

"So neither of his daughters will come!" exclaimed Rastignac. "I will write to them both."

"Neither of them!" cried the old man, sitting upright in bed. "They are busy, they are asleep, they will not come! I knew that they would not. Not until you are dying do you know your children. . . . Oh! my friend, do not marry; do not have children! You give them life; they give you your deathblow. You bring them into the world, and they send you out of it. No, they will not come. I have known that these ten years. Sometimes I have told myself so, but I did not dare to believe it."

The tears gathered and stood without overflowing the red sockets.

"Ah! if I were rich still, if I had kept my money, if I had not given all to them, they would be with me now; they would fawn on me and cover my cheeks with their kisses! I should be living in a great mansion; I should have grand apartments and servants and a fire in my room; and *they* would be about me all in tears and their husbands and their children. I should have had all that; now—I have nothing. Money brings everything to you, even your daughters. My money. Oh! where is my money? If I had plenty of money to leave behind me, they would nurse me and tend me; I should hear their voices, I should see their faces. Ah, God! who knows? They both of them have hearts of stone. I loved them too much; it was not likely that they should love me. A father ought always to be rich; he ought to keep his children well in hand, like unruly horses. I have gone down on my knees to them. Wretches! This is the crowning act that brings the last ten years to a proper close. If you but knew how much they made of me just after they were married. Oh! this is cruel torture! I had just given them each eight hundred thousand francs; they were bound to be civil to me after that, and their husbands too were civil. I used to go to their houses: it was, 'My kind father' here, 'My dear father' there. A place was always laid for me at their tables. I used to dine with their husbands now and then, and they were very respectful to me. I was still worth something, they thought. How should they know? I had not said anything about my affairs. It is worth while to be civil to a man who has given his daughters eight hundred thousand francs apiece; and they showed me every attention then—but it was all for my money. Grand people are not great. I found that out by experience! I went to the theater with them in their carriage; I might stay as long as I cared to stay at their evening parties. In fact, they acknowledged me their father; publicly they owned that they were my daughters. But I was always a shrewd one, you see, and nothing was lost upon me. Everything went straight to the mark and pierced my heart. I saw quite well that it was all sham and pretense, but there is no help for such things as these. I felt less at my ease at their dinner-table than I did downstairs here. I had nothing to say for myself. So these grand folks would ask in my son-in-law's ear, 'Who may that gentleman be?' 'The father-in-law with the dollars; he is very rich.' 'The devil, he is!' they would say, and look again at me with the respect due to my money. Well, if I was in the way sometimes, I paid dearly for my mistakes. And besides, who is perfect? My head is one sore! Dear Monsieur Eugène, I am suffering so now, that a man might die of the pain, but it is nothing, nothing to be compared with the pain I endured when Anastasie made me feel, for the first time, that I had said something stupid. She looked at me, and that glance of hers opened all my veins. I used to want to know everything, to be learned; and one thing I did learn thoroughly—I knew that I was not wanted here on earth.

"The next day I went to Delphine for comfort, and what should I do there but make some stupid blunder that angered her. I was like one driven out of his senses. For a week I did not know what to do; I did not dare to go to see them for fear they should reproach me. And that was how they both turned me out of the house.

"Oh, God! Thou knowest all the misery and anguish that I have endured; Thou hast counted all the wounds that have been dealt to me in these years that have aged and changed me and whitened my hair and drained my life; why dost Thou make me suffer so today? Have I not more than expiated the sin of loving them too much? They themselves have been the instruments of vengeance; they have tortured me for my sin of affection.

"Ah, well! fathers know no better; I loved them so; I went back to them as a gambler goes to the gambling table. This love was my vice, you see, my mistress—they were everything in the world to me. They were always wanting something or other, dresses and ornaments, and what not; their maids used to tell me what they wanted, and I used to give them the things for the sake of the welcome that they bought for me. But, at the same time, they used to give me little lectures on my behavior in society; they began about it at once. Then they began to feel ashamed of me. That is what comes of having your children well brought up. I could not go to school again at my time of life. This pain is fearful! Oh, God! These doctors, these doctors! If they would open my head, it would give me some relief! Oh, my daughters, my daughters! Anastasie! Delphine! If I could only see them! Send for the police, and make them come to me! Justice is on my side, the whole world is on my side, I have natural rights, and the law with me. I protest! The country will go to ruin if a father's rights are trampled underfoot. That is easy to see. The whole world turns on fatherly love; fatherly love is the foundation of society; it will crumble into ruin when children do not love their fathers. Oh, if I could only see them, and hear them, no matter what they said! If I could simply hear their voices, it would soothe the pain. Delphine! Delphine most of all. But tell them when they come not to look so coldly at me as they do. Oh, my friend, my good Monsieur Eugène, you do not know what it is when all the golden light in a glance suddenly turns to a leaden gray. It has been one long winter here since the light in their eyes shone no more for me. I have had nothing but disappointments to devour. Disappointment has been my daily bread; I have lived on humiliation and insults. I have swallowed down all the affronts for which they sold me my poor stealthy little moments of joy; for I love them so! Think of it—a father hiding himself to get a glimpse of his children! I have given all my life to them, and today they will not give me one hour! I am hungering and thirsting for them, my heart is burning in me, but they will not come to bring relief in the agony, for I am dying now, I feel that this is death. Do they not know what it means to trample on a father's corpse? There is a God in heaven who avenges us fathers whether we will or no.

"Oh, they will come! Come to me, darlings, and give me one more kiss; one last kiss, the Viaticum for your father, who will pray God for you in heaven. I will tell Him that you have been good children to your father, and plead your cause with God! It is not their fault. I tell you they are innocent, my friend. Tell everyone that it is not their fault, and no one need be distressed on my account. It is all my own fault, I taught them to trample upon me. I loved to have it so. It is no one's affair but mine; man's justice and God's justice have nothing to do in it. God would be unjust if He condemned them for anything they may have done to me. I did not behave to them properly; I was a fool to resign my rights. I would have humbled myself in the dust for them. What could you expect? The most beautiful nature, the noblest soul, would have been spoiled by such indulgence. I am a wretch, I am justly punished. I, and I only, am to blame for all their sins; I spoiled them. Today they are as eager for pleasure as they used to be for sugar-plums. When they were little girls I indulged them in every whim. They had a carriage of their own when they were fifteen. They have never been crossed. I am guilty, and not they—but I sinned through love.

"My heart would open at the sound of their voices. I can hear them—they are coming. Yes, yes, they are coming! The law demands that they should be present at their father's deathbed; the law is on my side. It would only cost them the hire of a cab. I would pay that. Write to them, tell them that I have millions to leave to them! On my word of honor, yes. I am going to manufacture Italian paste foods at Odessa. I understand the trade. There are millions to be made in it. Nobody has thought of the scheme as yet. You see, there will be no waste, no damage in transit, as there always is with wheat and flour. Hey! hey! and starch too. There are millions to be made in the starch trade! You will not be telling a lie. Millions, tell them; and even if they really come because they covet the money, I would rather let them deceive me; I shall see them in any case. I want my children! I gave them life; they are mine, mine!" and he sat upright. The head thus raised, with its scanty white hair, seemed to Eugène like a dire threat.

"There, there, dear father," said Eugène, "lie down again; I will write to them at once. As soon as Bianchon comes back I will go for them myself, if they do not come before."

"If they do not come?" repeated the old man, sobbing. "Why, I shall be dead before then; I shall die in a fit of rage, of rage! Anger is getting the better of me. I can see my whole life at this minute. I have been cheated! They do not love me—they have never loved me all their lives! It is all clear to me. They have not come, and they will not come. The longer they put off their coming, the less they are likely to give me this joy. I know them. They have never cared to guess my disappointments, my sorrows, my wants; they never cared to know my life; they will have no presentiment of my death; they do not even know the secret of my tenderness for them. Yes, I see it all now. I have laid my heart open so often, that they take everything I do for them as a matter of course. They might have asked me for the very eyes out of my head, and I would have bidden them to pluck them out. They think that all fathers are like theirs. You should always make your value felt. Their own children will avenge me. Why, for their own sakes they should come to me! Make them understand that they are laying up retribution for their own deathbeds. All crimes are summed up in this one. Go to them; just tell them that if they stay away it will be parricide! There is enough laid to their charge already without adding that to the list. Cry aloud as I do now, 'Nasie! Delphine! Come to your father, the father who has been so kind to you is lying ill!'—Not a sound; no one comes! Then am I to die like a dog? This is to be my reward—I am forsaken at the last. They are wicked, heartless women. Curses on them, I loathe them. I shall rise at night from my grave to curse them again; for, after all, my friends, have I done wrong? They are behaving very badly to me, eh? What am I saying? Did you not tell me just now that Delphine was in the room? She is more tender-hearted than her sister. Eugène, you are my son, you know. You will love her; be a father to her! Her sister is very unhappy. And there are their fortunes! Ah, God! I am dying, this anguish is almost more than I can bear! Cut off my head; leave me nothing but my heart."

"Christophe!" shouted Eugène, alarmed by the way in which the old man moaned, and by his cries, "go for Bianchon, and send a cab here for me.—I am going to fetch them, dear father. I will bring them back to you."

"Make them come! Compel them to come! Call out the Guard, the military, anything and everything, but make them come!" He looked at Eugène, and a last gleam of intelligence shone in his eyes. "Go to the authorities, to the Public Prosecutor, let them bring them here! Come they shall!"

"But you have cursed them."

"Who said that!" said the old man in dull amazement. "You know quite well that I love them, I adore them! I shall be quite well again if I can see them. . . . Go for them, my good neighbor, my dear boy, you are kind-hearted; I wish I could repay you for your kindness, but I have nothing to give you now, save the blessing of a dying man. Ah! if I could only see Delphine, to tell her to pay my debt to you. If the other cannot come, bring Delphine to me at any rate. Tell her that unless she comes, you will not love her any more. She is so fond of you that she will come to me then. Give me something to drink! There is a fire in my bowels. Press something against my forehead! If my daughters would lay their hands there, I think I should get better. . . . Oh, God! Who will recover their money for them when I am gone? . . . I will manufacture vermicelli in Odessa; I will go to Odessa for their sakes."

"Here is something to drink," said Eugène, supporting the dying man on his left arm, while he held a cup of tisane to Goriot's lips.

"How you must love your own father and mother!" said the old man, and grasped the student's hand in both of his. It was a feeble, trembling grasp. "I am going to die; I shall die without seeing my daughters. Do you understand? To be always thirsting, and never to drink—that has been my life for the last ten years. . . . I have no daughters, my sons-in-law killed them. No, since their marriages they have been dead to me. Fathers should petition the Chambers to pass a law against marriage. If you love your daughters, do not let them marry. A son-in-law is a rascal who poisons a girl's mind and contaminates her whole nature. Let us have no more marriages! It robs us of our daughters; we are left alone upon our deathbeds, and they are not with us then. They ought to pass a law for dying fathers. This is awful! It cries for vengeance! They cannot come, because my sons-in-law forbid them! Kill them! Restaud and the Alsatian, kill them both! They have murdered me between them! . . . Death or my daughters! . . . Ah! it is too late, I am dying, and they are not here! . . . Dying without them! . . . Nasie! Fifine! Why do you not come to me? Your papa is going——"

"Dear Father Goriot, calm yourself. There, there, lie quietly and rest; don't worry yourself, don't think."

"I shall not see them. Oh! the agony of it!"

"You *shall* see them."

"Really?" cried the old man, still wandering. "Oh, shall I see them—see them and hear their voices? I shall die happy. Ah! well, after all, I do not wish to live. I cannot stand this much longer—this pain that grows worse and worse. But, oh! to see them, to touch their dresses—ah! nothing but their dresses, that is very little; still, to feel something that belongs to them. Let me touch their hair with my fingers——"

His head fell back on the pillow, as if a sudden heavy blow had struck him down, but his hands groped feebly over the quilt, as if to find his daughters' hair.

"My blessing on them . . ." he said, making an effort, "my blessing . . ." His voice died away. Just at that moment Bianchon came into the room.

"I met Christophe," he said; "he is gone for your cab."

Then he looked at the patient, and raised the closed eyelids with his fingers. The two students saw how dead and lusterless the eyes beneath had grown.

"He will not get over this, I am sure," said Bianchon. He felt the old man's pulse, and laid a hand over his heart.

"The machinery works still, more's the pity. In his state it would be better for him to die."

"Ah, my word, it would!"

"What is the matter with you? You are as pale as death."

"Dear fellow, the moans and cries that I have just heard! There is a God! Ah! yes, yes, there is a God, and He has made a better world for us, or this world of ours would be a nightmare. I could have cried like a child; but this is too tragic, and I am sick at heart."

"We need a lot of things, you know. Where is the money to come from?"

Rastignac took out his watch.

"There, be quick and pawn it. I do not want to stop on the

way to the Rue du Helder; there is not a moment to lose, I am afraid, and I must wait here till Christophe comes back. I have not a farthing; I shall have to pay the cabman when I get home again."

Chapter 19

RASTIGNAC rushed down the stairs, and drove off to the Rue du Helder. The awful scene through which he had just passed quickened his imagination, and he grew fiercely indignant. He reached Mme de Restaud's house only to be told by the servant that his mistress could see no one.

"But I have brought a message from her father, who is dying," Rastignac told the man.

"The count has given us the strictest orders, sir——"

"If it is Monsieur de Restaud who has given the orders, tell him that his father-in-law is dying, and that I am here, and must speak with him at once."

The man went.

Eugène waited for a long while. "Perhaps her father is dying at this moment," he thought.

Then the man came back, and Eugène followed him to the little drawing-room. M. de Restaud was standing before the fireless grate, and did not ask his visitor to seat himself.

"Monsieur le Comte," said Rastignac, "Monsieur Goriot, your father-in-law, is lying at the point of death in a squalid den in the Latin Quarter. He has not a penny to pay for firewood; he is expected to die at any moment, and keeps calling for his daughter——"

"I feel very little affection for Monsieur Goriot, sir, as you probably are aware," the count answered coolly. "His character has been compromised in connection with Madame de Restaud;

he is the author of the misfortunes that have embittered my life and troubled my peace of mind. It is a matter of perfect indifference to me if he lives or dies. Now you know my feelings with regard to him. Public opinion may blame me, but I care nothing for public opinion. Just now I have other and much more important matters to think about than the things that fools and chatterers may say about me. As for Madame de Restaud, she cannot leave the house; she is in no condition to do so. And, besides, I shall not allow her to leave it. Tell her father that as soon as she has done her duty by her husband and child she shall go to see him. If she has any love for her father, she can be free to go to him shortly, if she chooses."

"Monsieur le Comte, it is no business of mine to criticize your conduct. You can do as you please with your wife, but may I count upon your keeping your word with me? Well, then, promise me to tell her that her father has not twenty-four hours to live; that he looks in vain for her, and has cursed her already as he lies on his deathbed—that is all I ask."

"Tell her yourself," the count answered, impressed by the tone of indignation in Eugène's voice.

The count led the way to the room where his wife usually sat. She was drowned in tears, and lay huddled in the depths of an armchair, as if she were tired of life and longed to die. It was piteous to see her. Before venturing to look at Rastignac, she glanced at her husband in evident and abject terror that spoke of complete prostration of body and mind; she seemed crushed by a tyranny both mental and physical. The count jerked his head towards her; she construed this as a permission to speak.

"I heard all that you said, monsieur. Tell my father that if he knew all he would forgive me. I did not think there was such torture in the world as this: it is more than I can endure, monsieur! But I will not give way as long as I live," she said, turning to her husband. "I am a mother. Tell my father that I have never sinned against him in spite of appearances!" she cried aloud in her despair.

Eugène bowed to the husband and wife; he guessed the meaning of the scene, and that this was a terrible crisis in the countess' life. M. de Restaud's manner had told him that his errand was a fruitless one; he saw that Anastasie had no longer any liberty of action. He came away amazed and bewildered, and hurried to Mme de Nucingen. Delphine was in bed.

"Poor dear Eugène, I am ill," she said. "I caught cold after the ball, and I am afraid of pneumonia. I am waiting for the doctor to come."

"If you were at death's door," Eugène broke in, "you must be carried somehow to your father. He is calling for you. If you could hear the faintest of those cries, you would not fancy yourself ill."

"Eugène, I dare say my father is not quite so ill as you say, but I cannot bear to do anything that you do not approve, so I will do as you wish. As for *him*, he would die of grief, I know, if I went out to see him and brought on a dangerous illness. Well, I will go as soon as I have seen the doctor. Ah," she cried out, "you are not wearing your watch! How is that?"

Eugène reddened.

"Eugène, Eugène! if you have sold it already or lost it . . . Oh, it would be very wrong of you!"

The student bent over Delphine and said in her ear, "Do you want to know? Very well, then, you shall know. Your father has nothing left to pay for the shroud that they will lay him in this evening. Your watch has been pawned, for I had nothing either."

Delphine sprang out of bed, ran to her desk, and took out her purse. She gave it to Eugène, and rang the bell, crying:

"I will go, I will go at once, Eugène. Leave me, I will dress. Why, I should be a monster! Go back; I will be there before you.—Thérèse," she called to her maid, "ask Monsieur de Nucingen to come upstairs at once and speak to me."

Eugène was almost happy when he reached the Rue Neuve-Sainte-Geneviève; he was so glad to bring the news to the dying man that one of his daughters was coming. He fumbled in Delphine's purse for money, so as to dismiss the cab at once; and discovered that the young, beautiful, and wealthy woman of fashion had only seventy francs in her private purse. He climbed the stairs and found Bianchon supporting Goriot, while the house surgeon from the hospital was applying moxas to the patient's back, under the direction of the physician—it was the last expedient of science, and it was tried in vain.

"Can you feel them?" asked the physician. But Goriot had caught sight of Rastignac, and answered, "They are coming, are they not?"

"There is hope yet," said the surgeon; "he can speak."

"Yes," said Eugène, "Delphine is coming."

"Oh, that is nothing!" said Bianchon; "he has been talking about his daughters all the time. He calls for them as a man impaled calls for water, they say——"

"We may as well give up," said the physician, addressing the surgeon. "Nothing more can be done now; the case is hopeless."

Bianchon and the house surgeon stretched the dying man out again on his loathsome bed.

"But the sheets ought to be changed," added the physician. "Even if there is no hope left, something is due to human nature. I shall come back again, Bianchon," he said, turning to the medical student. "If he complains again, rub some laudanum over the diaphragm."

He went, and the house surgeon went with him.

"Come, Eugène, pluck up heart, my boy," said Bianchon, as soon as they were alone; "we must set about changing his sheets, and put him into a clean shirt. Go and tell Sylvie to bring up some sheets and come and help us to make the bed."

Eugène went downstairs, and found Mme Vauquer engaged in setting the table; Sylvie was helping her. Eugène had scarcely opened his mouth before the widow walked up to him with the acidulous sweet smile of a cautious shopkeeper who is anxious neither to lose money nor to offend a customer.

"My dear Monsieur Eugène," she said, when he had spoken, "you know quite as well as I do that old Goriot has not a brass farthing left. If you give out clean linen for a man who is just going to turn up his eyes, you are not likely to see your sheets again, for one is sure to be wanted to wrap him in. Now, you owe me a hundred and forty-four francs as it is, add forty francs to that for the pair of sheets, and then there are several little things, besides the candle that Sylvie will give you. Altogether, it will all mount up to at least two hundred francs, which is more than a poor widow like me can afford to lose. Lord! now, Monsieur Eugène, look at it fairly. I have lost quite enough in these five days since this run of ill-luck set in for me. I would rather than ten crowns that the old gentleman had moved out as you said. It sets the other lodgers against the house. It would not take much to make me send him to the workhouse. In short, just put yourself in my place. I have to think of my establishment first, for I have my own living to make."

Eugène hurried up to Goriot's room.

"Bianchon," he cried, "where is the money for the watch?"

"There it is on the table, or the three hundred and sixty odd francs that are left of it. I paid up all the old scores out of it before they let me have the things. The pawn ticket lies there under the money."

Rastignac hurried downstairs.

"Here, madame," he said in disgust, "let us square accounts. Monsieur Goriot will not stay much longer in your house, nor shall I——"

"Yes, he will go out feet foremost, poor old gentleman," she said, counting the francs with a half-facetious, half-lugubrious expression.

"Let us get this over," said Rastignac.

"Sylvie, get some sheets, and go upstairs to help the gentleman."

"You won't forget Sylvie," said Mme Vauquer in Eugène's ear; "she has been sitting up these two nights."

As soon as Eugène's back was turned, the old woman hurried after her handmaid.

"Take the sheets that have had the sides turned into the middle, No. 7. Lord! they are plenty good enough for a corpse," she said in Sylvie's ear.

Eugène, by this time part of the way upstairs, did not hear these words.

"Quick," said Bianchon, "let us change his shirt. Hold him upright."

Eugène went to the head of the bed and supported the dying man, while Bianchon drew off his shirt; and then Goriot made a movement as if he tried to clutch something to his breast, uttering a low inarticulate moaning the while, like some dumb animal in mortal pain.

"Ah, yes!" cried Bianchon. "It is the little locket and the chain made of hair that he wants; we took it off a while ago when we put the blisters on him. Poor fellow! he must have it again. There it lies on the chimney-piece."

Eugène went to the chimney-piece and found a little plait of faded golden hair—Mme Goriot's hair, no doubt. He read the name on the little round locket, ANASTASIE on the one side, DELPHINE on the other. It was the symbol of his own heart that the father always wore on his breast. The curls of hair inside the locket were so fine and soft that it was plain they had been taken from two childish heads. When the old man felt the locket once more, his chest heaved with a long deep sigh of satisfaction, like a groan. It was something terrible to see, for it seemed as if the last quiver of the nerves were laid bare to their eyes, the last communication of ·sense to the mysterious point within whence our sympathies come and whither they go. A delirious joy lighted up the distorted face. The terrific and vivid force of the feeling that had survived the power of thought made such an impression on the students, that the dying man·felt their hot tears falling on him, and gave a shrill cry of delight.

"Nasie! Fifine!"

"There is life in him yet," said Bianchon.

"What does he go on living for?" said Sylvie.

"To suffer," answered Rastignac.

Bianchon made a sign to his friend to follow his example, knelt down and passed his arms under the sick man, and Rastignac on the other side did the same, so that Sylvie, standing in readiness, might draw the sheet from beneath and replace it with the one that she had brought. Those tears, no doubt, had misled Goriot; for he gathered up all his remaining strength in a last effort, stretched out his hands, groped for the students' heads, and as his fingers caught convulsively at their hair, they heard a faint whisper:

"Ah, my angels!"

Two words, two inarticulate murmurs, shaped into words by the soul which fled forth as they left his lips.

"Poor dear!" cried Sylvie, melted by that exclamation; the expression of the great love raised for the last time to a sublime height by that most ghastly and involuntary of lies.

The father's last breath must have been a sigh of joy, and in that sigh his whole life was summed up; he was cheated even at the last. They laid Father Goriot upon his wretched bed with reverent hands. Thenceforward there was no expression on his face, only the painful traces of the struggle between life and death that was going on in the machine; for consciousness that distinguishes between pleasure and pain was extinguished. The end would come soon.

"He will lie like this for several hours, and die so quietly at last, that we shall not know when he goes; there will be no rattle in the throat. The brain must be completely suffused."

As he spoke there was a footstep on the staircase, and a young woman hastened up, panting for breath.

"She has come too late," said Rastignac.

But it was not Delphine; it was Thérèse, her maid, who stood in the doorway.

"Monsieur Eugène," she said, "Monsieur and Madame have had a terrible scene about some money that Madame, poor thing, wanted for her father. She fainted, and the doctor came, and she had to be bled, calling out all the while, 'My father is dying! I want to see papa!' It was heartbreaking to hear her——"

"That will do, Thérèse. If she came now, it would be trouble thrown away. Monsieur Goriot cannot recognize anyone now."

"Poor, dear gentleman, is he as bad as that?" said Thérèse.

"You don't need me now; I'll go and look after my dinner; it is half-past four," remarked Sylvie. The next instant she all but collided with Mme de Restaud on the landing outside.

There was something awful and appalling in the sudden apparition of the countess. She saw the bed of death by the dim light of the single candle, and her tears flowed at the sight of her father's passive features, from which the life had almost ebbed. Bianchon tactfully left the room.

"I could not escape soon enough," she said to Rastignac.

The student bowed sadly in reply. Mme de Restaud took her father's hand and kissed it.

"Forgive me, father! You used to say that my voice would call you back from the grave; ah! come back for one moment to bless your penitent daughter. Do you hear me? Oh, this is fearful! No one on earth will ever bless me now! Everyone hates me; no one loves me but you in all the world. My own children will hate me. Take me with you, father; I will love you, I will take care of you. He does not hear me . . . I am mad . . . "

She fell on her knees, and gazed wildly at the human wreck before her.

"My cup of misery is full," she said, turning her eyes upon Eugène. "Monsieur de Trailles has fled, leaving enormous debts behind him, and I have found out that he was deceiving me. My husband will never forgive me, and I have left my fortune in his hands. I have lost all my illusions. Alas! I have forsaken the one heart that loved me"—she pointed to her father as she spoke—"and for whom? I have held his kindness cheap, and slighted his affection; many and many a time I have given him pain, ungrateful wretch that I am!"

"He knew it," said Rastignac.

Just then Goriot's eyelids unclosed. It was only a muscular contraction, but the countess' sudden start of reviving hope was no less dreadful than the dying eyes.

"Is it possible that he can hear me?" cried the countess. "No," she answered herself, and sat down beside the bed. As Mme de Restaud seemed to wish to sit by her father, Eugène went down to take a little food. The boarders were already assembled.

"Well," remarked the painter, as he joined them, "it seems that there is to be a death-orama upstairs."

"Charles, I think you might find something less painful to joke about," said Eugène.

"So we may not laugh here?" returned the painter. "What harm does it do? Bianchon said that the old man was quite insensible."

"Well, then," said the employee from the Museum, "he will die as he has lived.

"My father is dead!" shrieked the countess.

The terrible cry brought Sylvie, Rastignac, and Bianchon. Mme de Restaud had fainted away. When she recovered they carried her downstairs, and put her into the cab that stood waiting at the door. Eugène sent Thérèse with her, and bade the maid take the countess to Mme de Nucingen.

Bianchon came down to them.

"Yes, he is dead," he said.

"Come, sit down to dinner, gentlemen," said Mme Vauquer, "or the soup will be cold."

The two students sat down together.

"What is the next thing to be done?" Eugène asked of Bianchon.

"I have closed his eyes and composed his limbs," said Bianchon. "When the certificate has been officially registered at the Mayor's office, we will sew him in his winding sheet and bury him somewhere. What do you think we ought to do?"

"He will never sniff his bread any more," said the painter, mimicking the old man's little trick.

"Oh, hang it all!" cried the tutor, "let old Goriot drop. We've had enough of him. He's been served with every kind of sauce this hour or more. It is one of the privileges of the good city of Paris that anybody may be born, or live, or die there without attracting any attention whatsoever. Let us profit by the advantages of civilization. There are fifty or sixty deaths every day. If you have a mind to do it, you can sit down at any time and wail over whole hecatombs of dead in Paris. Old Goriot has gone off the hooks, has he? So much the better for him. If you venerate his memory, keep it to yourselves, and let the rest of us feed in peace."

"Oh, to be sure," said the widow, "it is all the better for him that he is dead. It looks as though he had had trouble enough, poor soul, while he was alive."

And this was the only funeral oration delivered over him who had been for Eugène the very incarnation of Fatherhood.

The fifteen lodgers began to talk as usual. When Bianchon and Eugène had satisfied their hunger, the rattle of spoons and forks, the boisterous conversation, the expressions on the faces that bespoke various degrees of want of feeling, gluttony, or indifference, everything about them made them shiver with loathing. They went out to find a priest to watch that night with the dead. It was necessary to measure their last pious cares by the scanty sum of money that remained. Before nine o'clock that evening the body was laid out on the bare sacking of the bedstead in the desolate room; a lighted candle stood on either side, and the priest watched at the foot. Rastignac made inquiries of this latter as to the expenses of the funeral, and wrote to the Baron de Nucingen and the Comte de Restaud, entreating both gentlemen to authorize their man of business to defray the charges of laying their father-in-law in the grave. He sent Christophe with the letters; then he went to bed, tired out, and slept.

Next day Bianchon and Rastignac were obliged to take the certificate to the registrar themselves, and by twelve o'clock the formalities were completed. Two hours went by; no word came from the count or from the baron; nobody appeared to act for them, and Rastignac had already been obliged to pay the priest. Sylvie asked ten francs for sewing the old man in his winding-sheet and making him ready for the grave, and Eugène and Bianchon calculated that they had scarcely sufficient to pay for the funeral, if nothing was forthcoming from the dead man's family. So it was the medical student who laid him in a pauper's coffin, despatched from Bianchon's hospital, whence he obtained it at a cheaper rate.

"Let us play those wretches a trick," said he. "Go to the cemetery, buy a grave for five years at Père-Lachaise, and arrange with the Church and the undertaker to have a third-class funeral. If the daughters and their husbands decline to repay you, you can carve this on the headstone—*"Here lies Monsieur Goriot, father of the Comtesse de Restaud and the Baronne de Nucingen, interred at the expense of two students."*

Eugène took part of his friend's advice, but only after he had gone in person first to M. and Mme de Nucingen, and then to M. and Mme de Restaud—a fruitless errand. He went no farther than the doorstep in either house. The servants had received strict orders to admit no one.

"Monsieur and Madame can see no visitors. They have just lost their father, and are in deep grief over their loss."

Eugène's Parisian experience told him that it was useless to press the point. Something clutched strangely at his heart when he saw that it was impossible to reach Delphine.

"Sell some of your ornaments," he wrote hastily in the porter's room, "so that your father may be decently laid in his last resting-place."

He sealed the note, and begged the porter to give it to Thérèse for her mistress; but the man took it to the Baron de Nucingen, who flung the note into the fire. Eugène, having finished his errands, returned to the lodginghouse about three o'clock. In spite of himself, the tears came into his eyes. The coffin, in its scanty covering of black cloth, was standing there on the pavement before the gate, on two chairs. A withered sprig of hyssop was soaking in the holy water bowl of silver-plated copper; there was not a soul in the street, not a passer-by had stopped to sprinkle the coffin; there was not even an attempt at a black drapery over the wicket. It was a pauper who lay there; no one made a pretense of mourning for him; he had neither friends nor kindred—there was no one to follow him to the grave.

Bianchon's duties compelled him to be at the hospital, but he had left a few lines for Eugène, telling his friend about the arrangements he had made for the burial service. The house student's note told Rastignac that a mass was beyond their means, that the ordinary office for the dead was cheaper, and must suffice, and that he had sent word to the undertaker by Christophe. Eugène had scarcely finished reading Bianchon's scrawl, when he looked up and saw the little circular gold locket that contained the hair of Goriot's two daughters in Mme Vauquer's hands.

"How dared you take it?" he asked.

"Good Lord! is that to be buried along with him?" retorted Sylvie. "It is gold."

"Of course it shall!" Eugène answered indignantly; "he shall at any rate take the one thing that represents his daughters into the grave with him."

When the hearse came, Eugène had the coffin carried into the house again, unscrewed the lid, and reverently laid on the old man's breast the token that recalled the days when Delphine and Anastasie were innocent little girls, before they began "to think for themselves," as he had moaned out in his agony.

Rastignac and Christophe and the two undertaker's men were the only followers of the funeral. The Church of Saint-Étienne du Mont was only a little distance from the Rue Neuve-Sainte-Geneviève. When the coffin had been deposited in a low, dark, little chapel, the law student looked round in vain for Goriot's two daughters or their husbands. Christophe was his only fellow-mourner—Christophe, who appeared to think it was his duty to attend the funeral of the man who had put him in the way of such handsome tips. As they waited there in the chapel for the two priests, the chorister, and the beadle, Rastignac grasped Christophe's hand. He could not utter a word just then.

"Yes, Monsieur Eugène," said Christophe, "he was a good and worthy man, who never said one word louder than another; he never did anyone any harm, and gave nobody any trouble."

The two priests, the chorister, and the beadle came, and said and did as much as could be expected for seventy francs in an age when religion cannot afford to say prayers for nothing.

The ecclesiastics chanted a psalm, the *Libera nos* and the *De profundis*. The whole service lasted about twenty minutes. There was but one mourning coach, which the priest and chorister agreed to share with Eugène and Christophe.

"There is no one else to follow us," remarked the priest, "so we may as well go quickly, and so save time; it is half-past five."

But just as the coffin was put in the hearse, two empty carriages, with the armorial bearings of the Comte de Restaud and the Baron de Nucingen, arrived and followed in the procession to Père-Lachaise. At six o'clock Goriot's coffin was lowered into the grave, his daughters' servants standing round the while. The ecclesiastic recited the short prayer that the students could afford to pay for, and then both priest and lackeys disappeared at once. The two gravediggers flung in several spadefuls of earth, and then stopped and asked Rastignac for their fee. Eugène felt in vain in his pockets, and was obliged to borrow five francs of Christophe. This thing, so trifling in itself, gave Rastignac a pang of intense sadness. It was growing dusk, the twilight fretted his nerves; he gazed down into the grave, and the tears he shed were drawn from him by the emotions of a pure heart. When such tears fall on earth, their exhalation reaches heaven. And with these tears Eugène Rastignac's youth ended. He folded his arms and gazed at the clouded sky. Christophe, after a glance at him, turned and went. Rastignac was alone.

He went a few paces further, to the highest point of the cemetery, and looked out over Paris and the windings of the Seine. The lamps were beginning to shine on either side of the river. His eyes turned almost eagerly to the space between the column of the Place Vendôme and the cupola of the Invalides. There lay the shining world that he had wished to enter. He glanced over that humming hive, as if already tasting its honey, and said defiantly:

"Henceforth there is war between us!"

As the first act of this challenge to society, Rastignac went to dine with Mme de Nucingen.

THE END